THE
BLEEDING SUN

Stephanie Bedwell-Grime

Paranormal Romance

New Concepts

Georgia

Be sure to check out our website for the very best in fiction at fantastic prices!

When you visit our webpage, you can:
* Read excerpts of currently available books
* View cover art of upcoming books and current releases
* Find out more about the talented artists who capture the magic of the writer's imagination on the covers
* Order books from our backlist
* Find out the latest NCP and author news--including any upcoming book signings by your favorite NCP author
* Read author bios and reviews of our books
* Get NCP submission guidelines
* And so much more!

We offer a 20% discount on all new Trade Paperback releases ordered from our website!

Be sure to visit our webpage to find the best deals in e-books and paperbacks! To find out about our new releases as soon as they are available, please be sure to sign up for our newsletter (http://www.newconceptspublishing.com/newsletter.htm) or join our reader group (http://groups.yahoo.com/group/new_concepts_pub/join)!

The newsletter is available by double opt in only and our customer information is *never* shared!

Visit our webpage at:
www.newconceptspublishing.com

New Concepts Publishing
5202 Humphreys Rd.
Lake Park, GA 31636

ISBN 1-58608-733-9
© Stephanie Bedwell-Grime
Cover art (c) copyright 2005 Eliza Black

NCP books are available at special quantity discounts for bulk purchases for sales promotions, premiums, fund raising, or educational use. For details, write, email, or phone New Concepts Publishing, 5202 Humphreys Rd., Lake Park, GA 31636; Ph. 229-257-0367, Fax 229-219-1097; orders@newconceptspublishing.com.

First NCP Trade Paperback Printing: November 2005

For my husband Derek, who is my first editor, my cheering section and my soulmate.

ACKNOWLEDGEMENTS:

My thanks to the members of The Lunatic Fringe: Aaron, Al, Anne, Doug, Jeff, Ian & Rebecca, for reading the manuscript in its many incarnations, and to Pen Pushers: Harley, Lisa, Lorena & Vera for their good humor with all my strange ideas; to my parents Jim & Jeanne Lynch, parents-in-law Diane & Brian Grime, brothers Jamie, David Peter, siblings-in-law Barry, Linn & Tracey and nephews Matthew & Brandon for all their love and encouragement, to long-time friends Evelyn, Helena, Marilyn and Pauline who were my very first readers; to Madris and Andrea at NCP for their enthusiasm for this project; to Eliza for the wonderful cover; and to the members of The Vampire's Kitchen for performing The Bleeding Sun when it was just a song and a dream.

CHAPTER ONE

The chandelier was crying, long tears of palest amber that streamed across her line of sight. Her mind was like shattered glass, jagged pieces that no longer fit together into a coherent whole. She lay, moored to the side of the large bed, that even now seemed to be pitching and heaving beneath her, and rummaged through her mind for thoughts that made sense....

Foremost in Melinda's mind was the paralyzing pain that ran down the right side of her body, emanating in dizzying waves from the welt on her neck. She probed gently at her throat, wincing as she touched the bruised and tender skin. Dried blood crumbled beneath her fingertips, as she ran her hands down her chest and arms to find the stinging traces of claw marks. She moaned and tried to turn over, but she was too stiff. She felt as if she'd been dissected and pieced back together.

Her memory yielded images unwillingly in self-defense, as she fought her way back to consciousness. She remembered fighting with her boyfriend, waiting alone on the deserted subway platform, and the bright lights of the approaching subway. She recalled boarding the train and staring at the drunken occupant who had passed out in the seat across the aisle. The train crossed a junction in the tracks, veering off to the right and downhill. The lights went out.

Something hunted her in the disorienting darkness, as she thrashed about the empty subway car trying to escape. Taloned hands tore through clothing and skin alike. She could still feel the hot breath upon her face, the odd pressure at her neck, followed by blinding pain, and the thick, black darkness that sucked her down into nothingness....

* * * *

"You're awake," said a soft voice from the end of the bed. He turned into the candlelight, and Melinda looked into the face of her nightmare.

With a hoarse cry, she scrambled away from him, crouching in the corner of the four-poster bed. The sudden effort sent points of light searing through her vision. She fought for breath, for the tenuous hold on consciousness.

"Shh," he whispered, coming to sit on the bed beside her. Melinda tried to move away from him, but succeeded only in falling forward. He caught her in his arms and placed a finger against her lips to quiet her. Helplessly, she looked up into eyes that were a deep brown, bordering on black. He didn't look like the horror her fragmented memory insisted he was. Rather, he resembled a dark angel with his handsome face and head of unruly curls. But the powerful hands that held her with much restrained strength ended in ten, long, talons. He let her down against the bed and propped the pillows up beneath her head. His hands lingered against her neck.

"Stiff?" he asked with genuine concern. His voice was deep and melodic. She nodded dumbly.

With strong, warm hands he tenderly massaged the feeling back into her neck. "It'll pass," he said. And, for the first time he looked human, almost.

Solemnly, he surveyed the damage, running a finger over the red welts on her throat and arms. "You're hurt," he said, more as a statement than a question.

"Yes," she croaked, her voice a rasping remnant of its former tone.

"I'm sorry, you must believe that."

Melinda choked back a sob and stared at him in mute terror.

"The first time is always a shock. But you're safe now."

"Safe?" she whispered in absolute horror, "I don't think so."

"You'll see," he said, almost sadly. For a moment he looked as if his mind was far away, dwelling on some old and familiar sorrow. He looked back at her suddenly, making her jump. "Besides Melinda," he said. "You really don't have any other choice."

"How do you know my name?" she asked, trying to keep the tremors that resonated out from her knees from working their way up into her voice.

"I looked at your driver's license, of course," he said, as if she was incredibly naive. Then he remembered his manners and said almost apologetically, "Well, you've been asleep for a day and a half, it wasn't as if I could ask you."

She stared at him, waiting. "I don't suppose I'll need my license when I'm dead," she said finally.

"Dead? Whatever gave you the idea I was going to kill you?"

"Look what you did to me!" She wanted to scream. "You were trying to kill me!"

"I am trying to save your life," he said and looked away.

An icy shiver snaked down her spine. She hugged her wounded arms and shuddered.

"Really," he said gently. "I have no more choice in this than you."

"I don't believe you."

"As you wish." He grasped her head in his taloned hands and turned her face so she was forced to look into his eyes. "But I want you to understand something. You are in a situation in which you have very few options. In a few short hours you will be thinking very differently about all of this. I will await your call."

He left the room, pulling the heavy metal door to with a loud resounding boom that had an ominous note of finality to it. As if in emphasis, she heard the jingle of keys as he locked the door.

The room was spinning, clockwise, then counterclockwise. Melinda looked about slowly, trying not to turn her head too fast and send the dizziness flooding back upon her.

The mammoth bed on which she lay was the only piece of furniture in the cavernous room. It was an imposing creation with its heavy curtains and towering columns. Judging from the tiled walls and floor and the persistent rumbling above, she suspected she was still underground. An abandoned subway station perhaps. She'd read once that there were a couple in the Toronto Subway System. The place had a haphazard look to it, as if he made do in surroundings less opulent than he was accustomed. Tapestries, embellished with gold and silver thread covered the walls, and Persian rugs warmed the utilitarian tiled floors. The foyer was flanked on either side by what looked to be a small study and a large closet.

Gingerly, Melinda placed one foot on the floor, then stood, holding on to the bedpost for support. She willed herself to remain upright. Awareness was her only defense. She had to find a way out.

Slowly, she walked about the perimeter of the room, lifting up the corners of the heavy tapestries, examining the wall underneath. She pounded on the tile, bruising her hand on the hard cement it covered. Not even an echo. The place was as solid as a tomb. It was doubtful anyone would even hear her screams.

There were no windows, and the door was locked as securely as it sounded. She threw herself against it, gaining only an aching shoulder for her efforts.

Desperate for clues, she lurched toward a desk in an alcove off the main bedroom and almost fell into the fragile antique chair.

She flipped through a stack of parchment papers on the side of the desk, searching for a means to defend herself.

Something silver slid from the paper, falling to the desk with a loud clink. Melinda turned the slender object over in her hands. Faded runes ran along the silver blade that was worn smooth by years of use. A blood-red jewel was set in the hilt. It could have been a dagger, but she guessed by its presence on the desk, he used it as a letter opener. She folded it tightly in her fist. As a last resort, it could be used as a weapon against him.

Melinda turned her attention to the row of leather-bound books on the back of the desk. A similar volume lay open before her, as if he had tossed it there expecting to return shortly.

She reached for the book, feeling its soft leather cover. The passages inside were scripted in a strong hand, a form of calligraphy so ancient and decorative it was difficult to read. The open page was dated the twenty-sixth of April. A few days ago then. Scrolls of red and black ink revealed the beginning of a poem, lovingly bordered with much care. Melinda read the words aloud, wondering at the odd imagery,

The blood of sunset stains the sky
lips, of ruby wine
darkness like a feather falls
into the depths of midnight
bless the glow of candlelight ...

Was he the author of the poem? She replaced the book carefully, and selected another from the row behind it.

A huge plume of dust burst from the book, as she opened it, making her cough. The pages were brittle and yellowed with age. Some leaves were loose, their corners ragged. She gasped aloud as she read the date, The First Day of May in the Year 1795. Identical handwriting stared back at her, disguised only the by antiquated patterns of speech. It had the look of a journal to it, an account of preparations for a trip to the country, including much annoyance over the hiring of a carriage.

The next entry was a sketch drawn in thick black strokes of ink. It was a portrait of two people, a man and a woman in historical dress. The inscription underneath read 'Kirsten and Me in the country'. The drawing was signed with a blood-red 'M'. She forced herself to breathe. The man in the picture was her captor, and he looked exactly the same.

Hastily, she replaced the book, not wanting to think about what her eyes were trying to tell her. Could these entries, nearly two hundred years apart, actually be written by the same person? Who was this creature that lived below the city in a forgotten rat-hole in royal splendor? More accurately, *what* was he?

She wanted to scream. For the first time in her adult life, she wanted her mother. But her parents lived in Unionville, too far away to be of assistance. Hysteria would accomplish nothing.

Research, she reminded herself. *That's what good detectives do before anything else.* She decided to tackle the closet on the other side of the room.

The contents were a lesson in fashion history. *The Textile Department at the Museum would love this!* Medieval cloaks, jeweled, brocaded jackets, frilly lace shirts were neatly arranged among blue jeans and black leather jackets. Melinda reached out a hand to feel the rich textures, pitching forward suddenly, her vision going black. She came to staring at her knees, and huddled there a moment, shivering and sweating while her head cleared.

A flash of brass caught her attention. Hidden away behind rows of old-fashioned clothing was a small trunk. It was fashioned of dark wood and decoratively hinged in brass. Melinda tried the lid. It wasn't locked. She cast a backward glance over her shoulder. The room was quiet. She lifted the lid and peered inside.

The box revealed a medieval woman's gown. It was a beautiful piece of work, fragile with age, hand sewn and lovingly decorated. It seemed curiously out of place among such male accouterments.

Who does it belong to? A past victim, a lost lover, someone dear to him ... the person who made him what he is? Strange, to keep an article of clothing instead of a portrait or a piece of jewelry ... Perhaps she left suddenly....

Steadying herself on the closet door, Melinda clawed her way to her feet. Except for the letter opener, her search had not turned up anything else that could be used as a weapon. Each hopeful discovery seemed to quash another plan of escape. She felt like a child who'd just been told that monsters did exist, that all her nightmares were real. If he really was what she suspected him to be, how could she reason with a being whose motives were nothing close to human? It was too much to think about, none of it having anything to do with logic or reason. She looked around at her absurd surroundings, the letter opener that was her only means of defense, and uttered a sob of hopelessness. She staggered back toward the bed, falling into the pillows, into darkness.

* * * *

Melinda awoke to the sounds of her own tortured screams. Searing pain radiated from the center of her stomach. Her veins throbbed with an agony that rendered her limbs useless. Every nerve, every cell in her body cried out in misery. Each rasping breath was an exhausting undertaking. She prayed and begged the empty air for anything that would end her suffering. Finally, he appeared beside her.

She looked up at him, desperately hoping against all reason that he would help her.

"You seem a little happier to see me this time," he said, gazing down at her.

"Make it stop," she whimpered.

Desire burned in those black eyes that flickered from her throat to her face. Desire and something else ... reluctance? "Only one thing will make it better," he said sadly.

"No," she gasped trying to sit up, but her weakened body would not obey. Too much effort was required to hold the letter opener in her fist. It fell from her hand, a silver flash in the golden candlelight.

"And what were you going to do with this?" he asked with the faintest hint of amusement. "Slit my throat perhaps?"

Melinda offered only a groan in reply. He walked to the desk and tossed it back on the pile of paper. He returned and stood looking down at her thoughtfully. She felt the bed give as he sat down to wait, as if he'd been through all this before, while she valiantly tried to resist the crushing anguish.

"Why do you make this so difficult?" he asked softly, when this had gone on for some time. "It won't get any better. You're half changed already. Either we continue, or you die."

She shuddered. "You're lying."

"Why would I do that?"

"So you can have it your way."

"I will have it my way."

"I'd rather die," she moaned, as a fresh wave of nausea washed over her.

"If I wanted you to die," he said quietly. "I would have killed you already."

Silence filled the room, punctuated only by her labored gasps.

"Why me?" she demanded through clenched teeth.

Whatever the reason, he didn't want to share it with her. "You were in the wrong place at the wrong time," he said at last. "Let me help you, Melinda. I hate to see you suffer so."

Her mind was a gray expanse of pain. The yearning within her urged to surrender to him, to let him do whatever unthinkable things would satisfying this intense longing. But logic reminded her how he'd pounced upon her in the empty subway car, torn at her neck with his piercing teeth and ripped through her flesh with his razor sharp claws. She whimpered and tried to slither away from him, but he stretched out beside her on the bed and gathered her into his arms.

"I promise it will only hurt for a second this time. A little pressure, a little pain, then you'll just feel very drowsy."

She wanted to tell him to go back to whatever hell he crawled out of, to leave her to die, but he was kissing her gently, wiping the tears from her eyes. And with every feather-soft touch, a little of the pain disappeared.

"Please don't suffer anymore," he whispered, "it's breaking my heart."

The last of her will crumbled. "Just do it."

He ran a taloned hand over her eyes, shutting them, and grasped her tightly. His lips traced a line of fire from her mouth to her neck. He lingered there for a moment, then she felt his lips draw back, baring his fangs. She heard him suck in his breath, and she held hers. His teeth pierced her neck.

She screamed in the first shock of pain and flailed against him. But he held her still, and soon she found she didn't have the strength to move at all.

Blood rushed from her neck under the gentle pull of his lips against her throat. Her body seemed to flow into his like melting wax. He shuddered in ecstasy, relaxing his grip a little, freeing a hand to caress her tenderly. She was feeling light-headed, it was difficult to hold on to consciousness. As he promised, the pain drifted away, dissolving into a total absence of feeling.

With great effort, he lifted his head from her neck and lay back onto the pillows, pulling her with him. He looked down at her, black eyes glazed with pleasure and lazily licked the last of her blood from his lips.

Moving was out of the question. Her body was unresponsive, her limbs as heavy as lead. She hovered somewhere on the brink of consciousness and tried not to think.

Pain jarred her back to wakefulness. She had the vague impression time had passed. But how much time. Hours? A day?

Something shifted in her jaw. With a wet sound, her gums tore.

She probed with the tip of her tongue and gasped as she cut herself on the razor-sharp points of her new teeth. She swallowed a mouthful of her own blood and looked at him in agonized bewilderment.

Gently, he drew back her upper lip. What he saw seemed to satisfy him. "It's almost over," he said, stroking her swollen lips.

To Melinda, the torment seemed endless. Cracked and flaking remnants of her nails lay in bloody pools about her cuticles. Beneath she could see a new set of coarse, white nails sprouting. They looked like claws.

Deep within her a desire was awakening, a sinister, compelling lust. It was a longing beyond sensual, a thirst that could only be quenched by something warm, red and salty. She stiffened in his arms, dismayed to discover it was blood she craved.

"Ah," he said. "Now you're beginning to understand."

"Oh, God. No!" Melinda pleaded, realization dawning on her with frightening clarity. She sat up, trying to free herself from his embrace, but he rose with her, preventing her escape.

He didn't seem perturbed at all, rather, he was patient, eager to have her participate in this carnal act. He held out his wrist in offering. "You might want to try the wrist. The neck takes a bit more skill."

She gagged and shivered. "I can't."

"You must."

"No--" She started to protest, but he raised his wrist to her lips.

"Come," he said softly, pointing out a thick, blue vein. "This one right here."

The desire was stronger than her will. Tentatively, she placed her teeth on his wrist. She was going to be sick.

"You'll have to apply a lot more pressure than that." He placed one strong hand behind her head to guide her.

He kissed her on the forehead in reassurance, then fixed her with that black stare of his. She looked helplessly into his eyes. "It's all right," he said. "You can't hurt me. This is a beautiful experience, the sharing of another's lifeblood."

She was falling, tumbling into the depths of those ebony eyes. She lowered her head and bit deeply into his wrist.

He winced at her clumsiness, drawing in a sharp breath. "Careful," he warned. He let the breath out slowly, going limp against her.

His blood was warm and thick like sherry. With each mouthful the pain and exhaustion receded, until she felt well and whole.

"Enough," he said abruptly. His hand gripped the back of her neck like a vice and gently disengaged his wrist from her mouth.

She swallowed blood and retched, letting her head fall to his shoulder. He held her quietly.

"Aren't you even going to ask my name?" he asked some time later.

"Your name," she repeated. It was hard to think of him as having something as simple as a name.

He held her away from him, facing her gravely. "I am called Valdemar."

"Valdemar," she repeated, trying out the unfamiliar syllables.

He smiled and pushed a sodden lock of hair from her face. "You're a mess."

She reached for his wrist, to assess the damage she'd done.

The wound was already beginning to heal itself.

* * * *

He took her hand and led her down to his bathing chamber, a level below the bedroom. Standing on the marble staircase, she looked in awe at the tiled pool that resembled a Roman bath.

"What is this place?"

"Lower Queen Subway Station."

"What?"

Valdemar smiled. Her interest seemed to please him. "From what I can gather, it was supposed to be a junction point for a proposed subway line. Apparently, the transit company decided not to build it. They locked it up and forgot about it."

"You built all of this?" In spite of her fear, she was fascinated.

He shrugged as if everyone constructed Roman Baths in their spare time. "Time is the one thing I have a lot of."

"No one ever found you here?"

"Not yet." Valdemar held out his hand. "Come, let's get you cleaned up."

* * * *

"You'll need a shirt," he said, standing in the doorway to his huge closet. He tossed the torn and blood-stained blouse aside. "Your jeans might be okay once they've been washed."

Melinda sat before the gilded mirror in his dressing chamber and tried on the borrowed shirt of soft suede.

"That's better," he said, turning and startling her by casting a reflection in the mirror.

"Surprised I have a reflection?"

"Now that you mention it, I'm surprised I can see myself."

"Well," he said, gesturing toward the mirror. "There you are. And you look beautiful."

She looked again at the creature in the mirror, seeing familiar features that now glowed with a beauty that was somehow cruel in its intensity. Her skin was the color of palest alabaster, her lips the color of deep red wine. She drew back her lips, revealing two sharply chiseled eyeteeth. They were only fractionally longer than her original teeth, barely noticeable, yet deadly sharp. Violet eyes stared calmly back at her. It was an illusion. She certainly didn't feel calm inside.

Tentatively, she touched her face. The sight of her long, white claws made her freeze mid-gesture. They were easily as thick as a dime. She suspected that even filed down, they would still be deadly. She ran a tentative claw over the tender skin on the back of her hand and watched in horror as it left a streak that soon turned an angry red. Such talons were fashioned for dismemberment, Melinda thought with a shudder. They'd caught on her clothing as she dressed and snagged in the cloud of thick sable hair that before had been straight and fine.

"But I shouldn't have a reflection," she protested. "I mean, in all the books I've read--"

"You shouldn't believe the superstitious nonsense you read in books."

She turned and really looked at him for the first time. He seemed so ordinary, standing there in his black jeans and ebony shirt. It was easy to think of him that way, until she looked into that face that seemed carved from whitest ivory, and knew that she was privy to a beauty too flawless to be entirely human. That striking face was framed by unruly black curls that spilled onto his forehead and over the collar of his shirt. He had the kind of innocent wide-eyed stare that beseeched her sympathy on one hand and looked right into her soul on the other. Melinda didn't want to look into those raven eyes that compelled her to do things against her better judgment. But, when he smiled, as he did now, he was blindingly handsome.

"Come to my parlor," he offered. "I'll explain it all to you."

CHAPTER TWO

Valdemar's living room was as impressive as his bathroom.

Priceless antiques adorned the cozy alcove that might have been a storeroom for the station's equipment. He poured her a glass of crimson wine from a crystal decanter and motioned her to the brocade couch. She took a sip of wine and choked.

"I drank your blood," she whispered in horror.

"But you're feeling better, aren't you?"

She couldn't deny it, even to herself. Physically, she was repaired. Emotionally, she was a tangle of conflicting feelings, each vying for dominance. Sharing blood was an intensely intimate act. She was at once repulsed, fearful, and yet strangely attracted to him. "What have you done to me?"

He sat on the couch beside her. "Melinda, I saved your life."

"Saved me?" Her voice rose in hysteria. "I'm a monster!"

He gripped her by the arms. "You are not a monster."

"What am I then? A vampire?"

"There are all kinds of words to describe what we are: vampire, vampir, sugnwr gwaed, incubi, succubi. Choose whatever word you like."

"I don't want to be a vampire," she said, trying to stay calm. "I just want to be the way I was."

"I'm afraid that's impossible."

"No, it can't be," she said, swallowing hard. Her mind fought to submerge the memory of relentless hunger. "The craving is...."

"Overwhelming?" he supplied.

"I can't bear the thought of drinking ... blood."

He sighed, and for the first time, looked truly weary. "You drank my blood willingly enough."

She looked at him, wanting only to cry.

"Blood," he said, more gently, "is a very versatile food. It's the only sustenance we need."

Melinda looked questioningly at the decanter of wine.

"Wine is something I've come to enjoy. It's a harmless vice. Alcohol has no effect on our metabolism."

"There has to be a way to reverse the process," she said, refusing to believe otherwise."

"I'm afraid not," Valdemar said quietly. "Contrary to the many legends, we are very difficult to kill. So please don't drive any wooden stakes through my heart." He looked long and hard at her. "You can also forget about silver bullets, we heal ourselves too quickly for them to be effective. They are, however, prettier than lead. Crosses are particularly useless. I have a rather nice collection, I'll show you sometime."

She drew in her breath and tried not to think of the taste of his blood. There was one question she had to ask. "What do you really look like?"

"I don't know what you mean. I look as you see me."

"I mean, in the movies, the vampire is usually a dried up husk of a corpse--"

"Movies! Books!" he sneered. "And I suppose you also believe I sleep in a coffin and I can turn myself into a bat."

"Well?" she asked. "Can't you?"

"I sleep in a bed," he spat the words at her, "just as you do. The very bed you've been sleeping in. You insult me with your primitive beliefs. As for bats and rotting corpses, we seem to embody everything you loathe and despise."

"Death frightens us."

"I'm not dead," he enunciated the words so she would make no mistake, "nor *undead*." He paused, waiting for her to disagree. When she said nothing, he continued. "We are an old race, perhaps even older than humans. But we are strong, immune to all your diseases."

"You're parasites," Melinda interjected with distaste. "You have no life of your own, except what you steal from others."

"I choose to believe we have a different respect for life." Valdemar ignored her venom. "We never fight among ourselves, we have no weapons of war, and we take only what we need, nothing more."

"Murder is something we abhor," she said icily, defending her kind.

"Nonsense," he countered. "Humans murder each other every day, not to mention what you do to other mammals, and nature as a whole."

They brooded on their separate thoughts.

"Were you always this way?" she asked hesitantly. "I mean, how long have you been...."

"A *vampire*?" he said the word with scornful humor. "A very long time."

"How long is a long time?"

"Eleven of your centuries." He let that thought sink in. "And no, I wasn't always this way, I was once human like you. Although," he admitted. "I can't really remember what that was like."

"The dress in your closet," Melinda said, deciding to test her theory. "Who did it belong to?"

Startled, he turned on her with a look of pure malice. "You're just full of surprises, aren't you Melinda? I suppose you read my journal too?"

She nodded. "Parts of it. Are you going to tell me about her?"

"No." he said. "You wouldn't understand."

Melinda plunged ahead. "She was the one who made you a vampire," she ventured, curiosity pushing her beyond the bounds of good sense.

"Yes," he bristled at her, his anger tangible.

"And she broke your heart."

To this he had no answer, he got up and poured himself a glass of wine, setting the decanter down with force a fraction less than was required to smash it.

The room was deathly quiet. He glowered at her coldly.

"What are you going to do with me, Valdemar?" Melinda asked, tossing caution to the icy wind that seemed to be blowing through the room. "Am I your dinner, your lover--what?"

For a moment he looked dumfounded, then he tipped his head back and laughed heartily. "Were you my dinner, you'd be long gone." He shook his head. "You are going to be nothing but trouble, aren't you? And you looked so innocent at the time."

"I'm sorry to disappoint you."

"Oh you haven't," he assured her. "I'm sure you'll make a most interesting companion."

"I have no intention of being your companion." she said.

He donned his most charming smile. "It's a little late for all of that. You have mated with a vampire. You and I are irrevocably bound. And for all your condescending talk, you are now no better than I."

"And I have no choice in the matter?" she asked.

"You have all the choice in the world, my dear. You are free to leave at any time. However, I would advise against it. Even young vampires have a few things to learn from the lessons of their elders. You could suffer a great deal before you learn the facts of life."

"Life?" she demanded. "I had a perfectly good life. I have responsibilities: a job, family and friends who care for me. I have a cat who's going to starve to death before someone realizes I'm missing and comes to investigate. Doesn't any of this suffering matter to you?"

"It is unfortunate," he conceded.

"Unfortunate," she screamed at him. "You've destroyed my life!"

"Destroyed your life? I am offering you eternity."

"I don't want eternity!" she sobbed. "I want my life back."

Valdemar sighed and rolled his eyes. "This is hard for me to understand, Melinda."

"I don't think I can forgive you," she said.

"Fine," he said quietly and left the room.

CHAPTER THREE

At another time, Valdemar had lived in a castle in the European countryside, hence the tapestries, the crystal, and the heavy antique furniture. That much he revealed to her, but he would not talk about the rest of his life, all eleven hundred years of it.

He was entirely at home in the cavernous rooms that comprised his underground dwelling. He filled his household with artifacts from his past and filched what little water and electricity he required from above. Yet he continued to illuminate his home with candlelight, saying he preferred it that way.

In the late fifties, he'd come to live in the underworld beneath the city. On careful reflection, urban living suited him perfectly. The city boasted a rich food supply, an abundance of anonymous souls who would never be missed. Valdemar presided over the underworld like a dark king, close to yet hidden away from the life he was never truly part of.

When it came to hunting, Valdemar was as cunning as he was resourceful. He had a talent for tinkering, for solving the mysteries of how things worked. The subway system's miles of deserted tunnels and abandoned stations intrigued him. In Lower Queen he'd found the old subway car and brought it back to life. As a hunter, it was his favorite trap, a mobile method of luring his prey. He roamed the tracks in the sleepy hours of early morning, cruising the rails after the last subway had left Union Station on its final route. Lingering drunks and petty criminals were his preferred delicacy. Most of them, intent on other mischief, would stagger into his trap, unaware of the deception until they were well on their way to being the main course.

He left her to grieve in private. Perhaps he knew that in her heart, Melinda still clung to the belief that given a little distance and a little time, she could go back to her old life. Desperately, she nurtured this hope, until the hunger struck.

Bloodlust, as Melinda discovered, was an ache beyond famine, a yearning that reached into the core of one's being, distorting all conscience, destroying all reason. Regardless of how thoroughly repulsed she had been by the taste of blood, once she had drunk from that well she would be forever thirsty.

Sitting alone in his bedroom, Melinda came to a painful decision. She would prove stronger than him. She would stop herself, even if it meant the end of her life. All she needed was the means to prevent herself from acting on that compelling lust. Melinda rummaged through his closet, finding a thick leather belt.

She roped herself to the bedpost, wrenching the belt as tight about her waist as she could. She twisted the belt so that the buckle was behind her back out of her reach. She waited for the onslaught of agony, but it came on quietly this time.

Like a gentle snowfall gradually gathering on the ground, it rose in intensity until she was gasping and moaning in spite of herself. Minutes crawled by, each second stretching into eternity. Her body shuddered so violently it felt as if the earth was quaking. Icy sweat rolled down between her shoulder blades. Every hair on her head, every eyelash cried out in its own individual agony. She felt nothing, saw nothing but the red haze of her pain.

Abruptly, the door slammed open, banging against the wall. Valdemar strode into the room, a storm brewing in his eyes. He clenched his talons into tight fists in an attempt to restrain his temper.

"You provoke me," he snarled. He brought his face up close against hers. "Do not be a fool," he said, his breath hot upon her face. "There is no way out of this."

He seized the belt where it met the bedpost, and with an effortless tug, sent the buckle clattering to the floor. He grasped her by the wrist, letting his claws dig cruelly into her flesh.

"There is only one way to appease the hunger, and that is to feed it," he said. "And if you are at all wise, you will believe me when I tell you this." He gave her a hard, measuring look. "Come on," he growled. "It's time you learned to hunt."

He hauled her unceremoniously through the antique-clustered living room and downstairs through the cavernous marble bathing chamber that was aglow with a multitude of candles.

Melinda's heels scraped across the tiled platform as he dragged her down the final staircase toward the waiting train. She tugged on her wrist, trying to free herself from his grasp, but he only tightened his grip and whirled on her in fury.

"You," he instructed, "will do as I say. I have come to the end of my patience."

Still tethered by the wrist, he dragged her after him into the train. If she had further objections, Melinda kept silent. His every look, every movement bristled with a dangerous energy that filled the air like static.

He threw her into the empty seat fixing her with a look of unbridled malice. "Stay there," he cautioned her. "Until I tell you to move.

"I won't do it," she told him rebelliously. "I won't kill!"

"You misunderstand," he said roughly. "You are the bait."

Valdemar cruised through the first few empty stations in silence, until he spied a couple of drunken men waiting alone on the platform up ahead. He glided slowly through the station, scrutinizing them carefully. They had a worn and haunted look, as if years of heavy drinking had finally caught up with them. Drunk on both alcohol and anger, they were itching for any opportunity to start a fight.

Valdemar coasted the car into the station. Melinda waited mutely, half of her hoping they would see through the trap and run. The other half salivated, anxiously anticipating the sweet taste of their blood.

They staggered through the open doors, hanging on to each other.

"Hi sweetheart," one of them slurred. He was thin and wiry, not much taller than Melinda. He wore his long, greasy hair parted in the middle and the bare arms that sprouted from his denim vest were covered in tattoos that showed women in a variety of lewd poses. His companion was attired in a black motorcycle jacket from which a belly swollen with beer proudly protruded.

To Melinda's complete repulsion, they tumbled into the seat beside her. The doors closed. Valdemar opened the throttle.

The drunk with the tattoos clamped his hand on Melinda's knee. She looked down at the collection of silver skull-shaped rings on the hand that gripped her leg. The smell of stale beer pulled her head upward to the pasty face that peered at her over a scruffy blond mustache.

Melinda offered him her most disapproving scowl. "Get your hand off my knee."

His companion sniggered at her discomfort. "Where else would you like him to put it love?"

They were goading her, waiting for any excuse to torment her further, to justify their assault. Were she still mortal, she would have been deathly afraid. They were like a time bomb, set to explode at any second. Melinda gasped as his hand slid up over her leg and torso and fastened on her breast.

They looked up briefly as the train slowed. The lights went out. The train cruised a few more feet into the tunnel and jerked to a standstill. She could feel Valdemar moving toward them in the darkness.

Melinda heard a hoarse scream, quickly silenced. Her tormentor raised his head, understanding nothing, except that he was suddenly in dire danger. He vaulted to his feet, fists raised to defend himself.

The smell of blood lay heavily in the air. Her body answered, pitching her forward to the source of nourishment, like a magnet. She felt nothing but the bitter hunger inside. She pounced on the hapless fool, heedless of his blind punches, and pinned him adroitly to the seat behind him.

"Get on with it," Valdemar hissed, raising his head from the still body he clutched in his claws. Blood dripped from his fangs. He caught a few drops with his tongue, then wiped his mouth on the back of his hand before lowering his head to drink again.

Melinda stifled her victim's screams with her hand. Her quarry bit her in return. She felt the pain, then nothing but fevered rage. She smacked the drunk across the side of the head, hearing the jaw break with a dull crack. Her prey subdued, Melinda sunk her teeth deeply into his neck. She missed the vein on the first couple of tries and chewed through cartilage and muscle before she tasted the saltiness of his blood.

Melinda drank as if she'd been thirsty for a million years, oblivious to all else but the all consuming pleasure.

Sometime later, Valdemar pulled her from the still body. They were home. He held her up by the scruff of the neck until her senses cleared. She let the body fall to the floor. The full reality of what she had done, what she was, came crashing down like a sledgehammer.

"We have work to do," Valdemar said impatiently.

They dug graves in a plot of soil beyond the station where the tracks trailed off into the dirt. Melinda labored like a woman possessed, trying to keep her mind from the dreaded realization that she had taken a life and snuffed it out as easily as blowing out a candle.

* * * *

She found him in the bedroom, lying across the bed, thoroughly sated. He looked up at her appraisingly, taking in her soiled and bloody clothes, the despondent look on her face.

"Don't look so depressed," he said trying to cheer her. "You did well."

"I murdered a person," she whispered, "with my own hands."

Valdemar shut his eyes, as if praying for strength. He reached for her hand, gently this time. "Hush, Melinda, you mustn't think of it so. It was self defense really. Those two certainly had no honorable intentions toward you."

"No," she said, "they would have likely raped me."

"I'm sure that is exactly what they intended, thinking you were easy prey."

"But, I was the *predator*," she objected, trembling with the realization it was true.

"And who would you have chosen as a victim instead?" When she offered no reply, he said, "It's really no different than any of the other animals you used to eat, cows, chickens...."

"Cows and chickens," she shrieked at him. "This was a human being--like me."

"You *were* human," Valdemar corrected. Then he sighed. "You really aren't adjusting to this at all well."

Melinda looked at him in amazement, as if he were speaking a language she didn't understand. He tried to explain.

"It can be a wonderful experience, you will come to see it as such."

"This isn't going to work," she said. "I loathe myself. I wish I were dead."

"It's a little late for all that," Valdemar counseled.

Melinda looked him squarely in the face. "How can you live with yourself?"

"I am what I am," he said simply. "Besides, what choice do I have?"

"Suicide," she suggested, then wished she hadn't said it.

"Really?" he asked menacingly. "And how does a vampire go about killing himself, Miss Melinda who knows so much?" This time she kept her mouth shut. "Well, trust me," he snarled, "it isn't possible."

Melinda set her jaw. "You said I was free to go."

"You are."

She stepped away from him. "Then I'm going," she said, and ran from the room.

He made an abortive attempt to catch her, snatching at the empty air as she fled from him. "Melinda!" she heard him call after her as she ran down the tracks. His cry echoed through the deserted tunnels. She raced on, desperate to escape his madness. She hated him. She hated herself.

CHAPTER FOUR

Melinda looked in disbelief at the daylight up ahead. How long she'd staggered through the deserted tunnels, she didn't know. Hours, days, all seemed the same in the gray underworld. She'd been walking in endless circles so long, she had almost forgotten what sunlight looked like.

Yet just as she was about to sink into despair, she glimpsed the gentle pink dawn. She limped to the mouth of the tunnel and looked about. Subway tracks veered off into the distance, as the route became surface transport. The rails were silent, the morning transit service had not yet commenced.

It was many blocks to the apartment she had left just a few nights ago. She kept to the shadows, not wanting to be seen scraped and bruised and still covered with the blood of her victim.

The apartment was much as she had left it, the extra key where she kept it hidden above the threshold. Melinda all but fell through the doorway, sending her unsuspecting cat scurrying for cover. She secured the entrance with its multitude of locks and placed her back against it for extra security. Little good that would do, she told herself. Valdemar could likely scale a building with little effort, were he motivated to do so.

Melinda had half expected to find him there since he still had her identification. She waited, crouched against the door, her arms about her battered and trembling body.

"Bandit," she called the Siamese cat who came to sit by her, waiting expectantly for the greeting scratch on the head and the customary offering of food. He looked remarkably well fed for an animal that had been locked up without sustenance for four days. Melinda craned her head for a look into the kitchen to where *Bandit* had made himself at home in a box of cat food under the counter. The evidence spilled out from under the sink, leaving a trail of kitty treats across the kitchen floor.

"Dumb cat," she said aloud to the contented feline. "Bet you didn't even miss me."

Surrounded by her own cherished possessions, she slowly began to relax. Terror was quickly being replaced by sheer exhaustion.

The sun was rising, casting a bright ray of light through the open window. Melinda watched it arc across the floor, with scant interest, until the sun rose above the building across the street and shone unhindered into her sanctuary.

Lightning exploded in her skull. Her eyes were useless, against the blinding glare. Tears poured from her face in an attempt to soothe the fierce burning.

Whimpering, she dove for the bedroom, with its dark blinds and heavy drapes. She huddled there on the bed, trapped between the door and the bright living room. So the legend about sensitivity to light was true, Valdemar had neglected to tell her that.

There was only one thing to do. She burrowed into the soothing darkness of the heavy blankets and slept.

Melinda awoke in the velvet shadows of early evening. She rose in the darkness, purposely leaving the lights off. A quick search of the kitchen yielded some emergency candles that provided a gentle illumination. She found a thick blanket to cover the living room windows. Her refuge secured once again, she wandered back into the kitchen, stopping by the fridge out of habit.

The freezer contained an assortment of leftover take out dinners. Pizza looked appetizing. She tossed it absently into the microwave to reheat, and considered the feline asleep on the forbidden kitchen table.

"Get off there!" she said sternly, shooing him from his place of rest. "I'm home now and the table is off limits."

The microwave beeped loudly, demanding her attention. She retrieved the pizza, grabbing a cola from the refrigerator en route.

Out of habit she stood at the counter, wolfing down a few quick bites with cola chasers. The food hit her stomach, she bit into the pizza for another mouthful, then froze. The pizza was on its way back up.

Melinda ran for the bathroom, skidding across the floor that seemed to be twisting and heaving. She crashed into the toilet, hitting her head against the porcelain before vomiting up the few morsels of food that had made it down. She slumped between the tub and the toilet, resting her forehead on the cool tile.

Eventually the world stopped spinning and the inferno in her gut quieted to a manageable smolder. She drew a bath and crawled in, somehow hoping it would wash away the evil exterior and leave her with her formerly human self.

When she emerged, the cat had devoured the last of the pizza. She dumped the cola down the drain.

Melinda wandered into the living room, looking for something to take the burning hunger from her mind. Out of habit, she hit the play button on her answering machine. It beeped, four hang-ups and a furious message from her boss.

"Barnes, if you're there you better be dying! You got some nerve not showing up two days in a row. You could at least give me the courtesy of a phone call since I've been doing your damned job!"

It was Tuesday then, 11:30 p.m. She'd been gone four days. She thought back to Saturday night and the vicious fight with her boyfriend that had set the whole thing in motion. No message from him.

"You could have called to say you were sorry, Jason." In frustration, she slammed her hand down on the offending answering machine, cringing when it shattered into pieces. "And now I'm going to get fired, too," she said, miserably.

She pictured the chaos at the station when she hadn't shown up for either prime-time shift, and winced. The hosts would be screaming, the product line-up wouldn't have been scheduled, the head of production would be calling for her resignation. As producer, she was the tenuous thread that held it all together. If she lived through this she'd be unemployed for sure.

"You think you've got problems," she told her cat wryly. She dialed the television station and left a message of profuse apologies and feigned illness for her boss. What she needed was a good stiff drink.

Her liquor cabinet amounted to a dusty bottle of scotch, a Christmas gift from the production crew. She dragged it to the couch with her, foregoing the glass. She choked down the first burning mouthful, the second didn't seem like such a good idea after all. She tossed the bottle aside.

The memory of Valdemar with fury in his eyes, was burned in her brain. She could still hear his snarled warning: "There is no way out of this." She had the demoralizing feeling that statement had been spoken from his own painful experience. "There's got to be, Valdemar," she whispered. "There just has to be, that's all."

But who could she tell? Who could she ask for advice, who wouldn't think she was completely crazy? Maybe that was the answer. Perhaps she should just go out and get herself institutionalized, locked up in some rubber room where she couldn't hurt anybody. Melinda cringed, thinking of all the defenseless patients who would be completely at her mercy, until they realized what they were dealing with. Then what? According to Valdemar, silver bullets were a waste of time.

Already, she could feel the first tinges of hunger gently seducing her mind. Soon she would need to feed. It was not the kind of need you could deny.

Thoughts of human contact scared her. She remembered a diagram of a cow she had seen at the butchers when she was a child. The figure of the cow was divided up into cuts of meat. Was this how she was doomed to think of human beings, as walking collections of flesh, veins, and blood? Even as a child the diagram had upset her. She had hated even to think of a cow that way. She'd burst into tears at the butcher shop and her mother had taken her home, never knowing why.

Her mother. Oh, God. She was due to visit next week!

Desperate for any plan of action, Melinda sat on the couch and looked around at the familiar comforts of home. Every nerve bristled with the desire for open air, for dark streets crowded with people. She could harm no one, she reasoned, if she remained securely bolted inside her apartment.

The desire was increasing in intensity, demanding release. She tried to occupy her mind with other thoughts. She tried praying, counting to one thousand, but her concentration was stolen by the obsessive demand that occupied both mind and body.

It was hard to think beyond the torment. Even breathing was a major accomplishment. She was feeling faint, losing connection with her tortured body. *Sleep*, she thought gratefully as awareness slipped away from her....

* * * *

There was blood. Everywhere.

Melinda let the cat's mangled body fall to the floor, awareness seeping slowly into her consciousness. Horrified, she jumped back against the wall, choking on blood clotted fur.

The living room was a mess. Mapped out in blood, she could see evidence of the dismal chase. Wounded, it had obviously escaped her, trailing blood across the sofa, the floor and the window sill, where in a bloody smudge against the glass she could see where she had cornered it for the final time.

Melinda surveyed the carnage, desperately trying to remember those last few seconds before the blank void in her memory. She recalled sitting on the couch, then nothing more.

Was that what the hunger did when will intervened? Did it commandeer both mind and body and appease itself regardless of the consequences?

Melinda looked at the scattered remains of her beloved pet who'd been her companion and confessor for most of her life. They had moved out of her parents' home together.

Devoid of all feeling, she wandered back into the kitchen, realizing even as she stepped onto the cold tile floor that suicide was her intention. She rummaged through the drawers, until her search turned up a large carving knife.

Leaning over the sink, she yanked up her sleeve, exposing her wrist. The knife was dull, and she had to saw at it, but eventually she cut into the vein.

Time seemed to slow then, as she watched the crimson pearls of blood gather along the knife blade, then splash to the sink. She forced the blade deeper, feeling a sickening sense of satisfaction as the blood gushed from her wrist in a hot wave. She stared at the blood with detached fascination as the flow diminished to a trickle and then quickly ceased.

Something moved on the periphery of her vision, something black, man sized. Valdemar!

He stood between her and the kitchen doorway, blocking her escape. With an almost imperceptible move, his eyes shifted toward the living room, taking in the carnage in a single glance. An odd expression crossed his face, as if he felt her pain and was both angered and agonized by it.

He advanced on her, looking every bit as dangerous as the night she'd met him. With his iron grip he seized the knife and pried it from her fingers. It fell to the sink with a loud clatter.

"This is useless," he said, restraining her with his boiling stare.

He reached for her hand turning it upward, so she was forced to look at the rapidly healing laceration.

A sob worked its way up her body. She choked it back, uttering a strangled cry. That pitiful little sound, so full of grief seemed to shatter his anger.

He drew her into his arms and pressed her head into the crook of his shoulder. He rocked her gently, shifting his weight from side to side. "Melinda," he whispered. "Why do you put yourself through this?"

"Kill me Valdemar," she said. "Finish what you started."

"No," he said. "I can't do that."

"You could if you wanted to," she argued.

Valdemar dropped his arms, freeing her. He wandered into the blood-stained living room, forcing himself to look at what she had done there. Then he sat on the bloody couch and rested his head in his hands. "Even if I knew of a way to end your life, Melinda, I don't think I could do it."

Hesitantly, she came to sit on the sofa beside him.

"Does it ever stop hurting?"

"It happens by itself, if you let it," he reassured her. "Every day you grow just a little less human, until one night you wake up, and you are truly a vampire and can't remember being anything else."

"Is that how it was for you?"

"No," he said, then nothing further.

"Meaning you aren't going to tell me."

"Maybe I will," he said, "But not now."

"So what am I supposed to do?" she demanded. "Thanks to you, my home is a shambles, and my life is a complete mess."

"It isn't safe for you to stay here," he observed matter-of-factly, as if he were talking of something other than the demise of everything she cared for.

"Obviously not," she admitted reluctantly. "How did you get in?"

"Your bedroom window."

"I thought I locked it."

"You did," he said with a sad smile. "Come with me Melinda. Stay with me long enough to learn what you need to know, long enough to straighten out your feelings. Then you can decide."

"I can't," she said desperately. "I want to trust you, but I can't shake that vision of--"

He held up a hand, silencing her. "Please don't--" he begged. "I wish I had the power to undo this, but I don't. So, please come with me. I don't want you to get hurt anymore than you've already been."

Melinda looked around desperately at the blood stained living room. Was this the fate of everything and everyone she loved? She was dangerous, not only to herself but to everyone who cared for her.

"It's nearly dawn," he said. "We don't have much time."

"All right," she said finally. "Just let me grab a few things."

The tiny apartment became a gallery of treasured possessions: old photographs, the antique ring that had been her grandmother's, the overstuffed chair that she loved to curl up in on cold nights and read. Leaving it was like cutting off a part of herself, erasing a crucial part of her identity. It was unthinkable that she could just leave in a pivotal second and never return.

And what would happen to her family and the friends who would come looking for her? How many years would they wonder what had become of her? They would agonize over the details: was she still alive somewhere? And then they would die, leaving her alone to preserve them in her memory. But, knowing the truth would bring them greater pain.

Melinda walked about the room aimlessly, picking up items, then putting them down. No, she decided, she couldn't take anything too obvious. Best to leave the apartment as it was and avoid as much suspicion as possible.

Valdemar watched her silently. He was anxious to leave, but he said nothing, abandoning her to her private agony.

In the end, she stuffed a duffel bag full of clothing, took her grandmother's ring and her scrapbook of old photographs, and followed Valdemar into the fading night.

Valdemar became the shadows, dark as he was, and dressed in black. He was agile and quick on his feet. Not only did his speed amaze her, she was shocked at how easily she matched his stride.

It was a soul-shattering experience to inhabit a body for twenty-six years and then awake to find it completely changed. Her entire identity was crumbling. All her life she'd believed that she was basically a good person. Discovering that she was capable of murder came as a horrible shock. And she was doomed to continue committing that sin for eternity. Guilt beyond measurement. Every ounce of remorse she had ever felt was grossly inadequate to the oppressive weight she now carried in her soul. Melinda had no skills, no frame of reference for embarking on this new life. She had only the guidance Valdemar could offer her, and he was hardly the kind of savior she needed.

Melinda followed his lead through the twisting maze of the underworld. He had the subway parked in an abandoned tunnel and he hustled her into it with urgency. Dawn was creeping up on them and the upper world was awakening.

Dazed and heartbroken, she let him drive her back to the hell she'd so recently escaped from. She moved when he said, she followed him when he asked until they were back in his lair, where he had wanted her all along. Melinda looked around at this place so full of the past. She was suddenly aware that she was more exhausted than she'd ever felt in her life.

"You better get some rest," Valdemar said when he looked at her. It was as good a suggestion as any. She imagined she must look quite ghastly by now.

Not knowing what else to do, she staggered off in the direction of his bedroom. She tumbled into his bed and willed her eyes to close.

* * * *

Warm hands caressed her. She sighed at the gentle touch, seeking more. And he seemed happy to oblige. His fingers trailed over the peaks of her breasts, dipping lower to explore the swell of her hips, inching closer to the center of her desire. She pushed impatiently against his hand, wanting what he offered and then teasingly withheld.

Desire coiled tight inside. She felt his hot breath against her neck as he lowered his weight on top of her, then the scrape of his teeth. She gasped. He pulled away slightly at the sound, and she gazed up into eyes as dark as the night sky.

Valdemar.

Melinda jerked awake, groggy and disoriented in the dank subterranean air. Beside her, Valdemar slept, oblivious to her dream. He was so close she could feel his feathery soft curls against her forehead and the heavy press of his arm about her waist. Panicked and embarrassed, she sprang away from him.

He came awake like a startled tiger, instinct alerting him before reason. Despite the dark she could see his lips drawn back, exposing his fangs, and his eyes were wide, in search of the danger that had roused him.

He reached out for her, claws extended, and she evaded him. "Melinda," he gasped, then sighed with relief. "You startled me."

She stared back at him, panting. "For a moment, I forgot where I was."

This seemed to satisfy him. He rubbed a hand wearily across his eyes. "Come then," he said, holding out a hand to pull her back under the covers, but she hesitated, terrified after to so intimate and disturbing a dream, to be so close to him.

Valdemar sat up, fumbling with the candle that hung on the wall beside the bed. The yellow glow gave the room a much less sinister atmosphere. He propped the pillows up behind his back and stretched out on the bed again. "You can't sit on the side of the bed forever." Melinda looked back at him mutely. "You're afraid of me," he said, misunderstanding.

Without another word, he got up and left the room. With some distance between them, Melinda felt a little better. Finally, when he didn't return, she ventured into the living room in search of him.

She found him, sprawled on the couch, a limp arm hanging over the side.

"I'll take the couch," she offered. "It's your bed, after all."

Valdemar raised his head. "I rather liked my bed with you in it."

He came to stand in front of her, slowly so as not to alarm her. "I won't hurt you, Melinda." He placed an uncertain hand on her arm. It was a gentle touch, a lover's caress, and it reawakened fragments of her dream. The sensation of his mouth against her neck sent shivers down her spine. Confused by this strange new feeling, she backed away from him.

"But you did hurt me," she whispered. "In the subway...I remember...."

"Melinda," Valdemar said gently. "There is something you must understand. That wasn't me."

She searched through her disjointed memories, feeling even more bemused. "You're lying," she insisted. "I saw you sitting in the seat across from me."

"I was."

"You grabbed me, and...."

"I'm not denying I was there," he admitted slowly, as though it was something he really didn't want to tell her. "But I wasn't the only one."

"I don't believe you."

Valdemar sighed. "Under the circumstances, I don't expect you to."

Just when she thought there were no more tears to shed, her body convulsed into sobs, and tears flooded her face. Unsure of her reaction, Valdemar moved closer and took her into his arms.

"I don't understand," she said, struggling to gain control of herself. "There were others?"

"You wandered into something beyond your ability to comprehend." His breath was warm against the top of her head. "Please believe me, it was an accident. You shouldn't have been there. I should never have been there."

"So why didn't you just kill me?"

"I couldn't. You were hurt. I wanted to help you, to save your life."

"This is some life," she said bitterly. "Insane with hunger, killing endlessly ... It hurts," she said, and winced as her voice cracked.

Despite everything the desire still burned in her veins like molten lead.

Dark eyes regarded her kindly. For some reason he was no longer angry. She couldn't fathom why that was. "You're still hungry," he said, deducing the truth.

"Please don't make me kill," she begged. "I can't do it again."

"Hush," he said. "No one's going to make you kill." Then, as though he came to a sudden decision, he swept an arm behind her knees and carried her into the bedroom. He sat at the head of the bed and settled her in his lap.

"Let's solve this problem first," he said, pulling the covers up about them.

Without thinking, she laid her face against the warm smoothness of his neck. Her body pressed against his, closer than they'd been since....

"No!" she gasped, pulling her mouth away, realizing suddenly what he meant for her to do. "I don't want your blood."

"Yes, you do." He was right. She positively ached for it.

Melinda turned her face away. "I can't."

Valdemar took her face in his hands. "Have you listened to nothing I've told you? Have you learned nothing at all? Don't you know what happens when you refuse to feed?"

She stared at him through the blurry image of her tears and the haze of her pain.

"Only blood will make it better, Melinda. Isn't it more pleasant," he asked, "to do this in some semblance of a civilized fashion?"

Before she could answer, his lips settled weightlessly against hers, setting off tinges of desire. He deepened the kiss, exploring the contours of her mouth. She'd never been kissed so passionately, or so thoroughly. He held her tightly, escape was impossible. Resisting was impossible. *Resisting* was the furthest thing from her mind, she realized with a start.

"Now what will it be?" Valdemar asked, pulling his mouth away. "Will you drink my blood Melinda? Or have you decided to hunt after all?"

Her lips hovered above his neck. "I don't want to hurt you," she said suddenly, wondering why she cared after all he'd done to her. But she did care and that shocked her.

"Don't worry about me," he said. "Once you get used to the feeling, it is quite pleasant."

"Won't it make you hungry?"

"I have hunted," he murmured, positioning her mouth against the spot.

Her lips parted, but she still couldn't stop shaking.

He stroked her back. "Easy Melinda. Let me make it better."

With keen sharpness, her teeth slid through the thin skin of his throat, opening the vein with the first prick. In spite of his reassurances, she did hurt him. She felt his arms clench around her, but he made no sound. She gulped two compulsive swallows before she found the will to suckle more tenderly.

To her horror, she found she wanted more, wanted it badly enough to kill. Warm blood rushed into her mouth and down her throat, trickling down into her stomach in a hot rush. There was something so giving, so infinitely sensuous about it, she was getting lost in need and pleasure.

Valdemar stirred, the pressure of his hands changed from holding her to him to pulling her away. He meant for her to stop, and somewhere in her consciousness she wanted to, but she couldn't summon the strength.

Strong hands gripped her shoulders, forcing her away. Reluctantly she loosened the grip of her lips on his throat. Her mouth came free with a sucking sound, and she watched, horrified, as blood pooled about the deep puncture wound. Valdemar's eyes narrowed briefly in pain, but he continued to watch her carefully.

"I wanted to stop," she said, panting. "But I couldn't."

"It's all right," he said, still holding her firmly away from him. "In time you'll gain more control."

She laid a tentative hand on his shoulder, and pulled him toward her. Surprisingly he let her, though he tensed, ready for any sudden move. Tenderly, she licked the blood from the wound and felt him shiver.

Already the flow of blood had stopped, the puncture marks had become merely red welts. The purple bruising around the wound had faded to pink skin.

"Thank you," she whispered, appalled at how right his blood felt inside her.

He hugged her closer. "You're welcome."

For awhile there was silence between them. Then he said suddenly, "I have made a complete mess of this. I should never have let you go. I thought if you had a few hours alone with your hunger, you'd realize the seriousness of the situation and be more willing to listen to me."

"You did that to teach me a lesson?"

Valdemar shot her a dismal look. "I forgot you had a pet." He toyed with a lock of her ebony hair. "There are so many things I must teach you. Please stay, Melinda. Don't be afraid of me."

It didn't make sense, this sudden kindness. "Why do you care?"

He struggled for an explanation. "We are blood kindred. I don't expect you to understand."

"Is that why are you being kind to me all of a sudden, when you've been so ... well, menacing?"

That word made him wince, but he nodded. "I was concerned for you. Not everyone survives the transformation. The first hunt is crucial, and you were determined to defy me. It's also," he confided, "been a very long time since I've done this."

His embrace was comforting, and she didn't resist when he pulled her down under the thick covers with him. They lay motionless for a long time, then he said. "Go to sleep, Melinda. Even young vampires need their rest."

She lay silently, feeling the subtle movements of his body as he breathed, afraid to stir lest she disturb him. And sometime in the afternoon, she too, fell asleep.

CHAPTER FIVE

Melinda sat on the lavishly embroidered couch in Valdemar's living room. Of Valdemar, there was no evidence. He came and went much as he pleased, without word of where he was going or when he might return. Sometimes he returned with provisions, bottles of fine wine or items for his household. Money seemed to flow through his fingers like so much water. She suspected most of it came from the pockets of his victims. Valdemar had an attitude that suggested at some time in his life he had been, and likely still was, rich.

He had taken to bringing her crystal goblets of blood, which he presented with the flourish of a waiter in a fancy restaurant and stood over her like a doting mother while she consumed them. At first, she had recoiled from his offerings, but Valdemar was insistent. She needed blood he reasoned. If she preferred to hunt for it, that was fine by him. Trapped and defeated, she accepted his gifts, never asking where they came from.

Melinda moped about his underground dwelling, examining the

countless antiques, rummaging through his possessions when he was absent. She suspected he knew what she was up to, but he said nothing. Sometimes, she took short walks down the tracks, but she avoided venturing into the world upstairs. Her disastrous venture back to normalcy had destroyed her confidence. Her biggest fear was that she might have to remain cloistered beneath the city forever, like the ghoul she was afraid she had become.

With Valdemar gone, every sound, every drip and creak took on sinister proportions. Melinda was petrified, of the rats that sometimes crawled across the bed while they were sleeping, but mostly that they would be discovered down here, and executed in the blood curdling ways that humans destroyed vampires in the movies.

"Don't be ridiculous," Valdemar had chastised her when she voiced her fears to him. "This station's been abandoned for many years, and no one's had reason to bother me yet. Besides," he said as if she were a complete idiot. "We would hear them coming from miles away. It's amazing humans ever catch anything," he added with disgust. "They make so much damn noise."

"Would you still hear them, if you were asleep?" she asked him, anxious to rule out all possibilities.

"Yes," he assured her. "Even if I was asleep."

To Valdemar, the rats were simply part of the scenery. She had screamed in complete and total terror the first time one crossed her path.

With the speed of a mongoose, Valdemar had snatched up the poor thing mid-stride.

"What is the matter with you?" he demanded angrily, the rat's helpless head protruding from his fist.

"A rat--" she had blundered in self defense.

"Yes," Valdemar said without emotion. "This is a rat, Melinda. Tell me what possible harm a rat could do you to make you scream so?"

"Please, take it away," she pleaded.

Annoyed, he had left the room, his prey still trapped within his hand. What he did with the rat, she never knew.

Bored and utterly demoralized, Melinda paced aimlessly about. She found herself in Valdemar's study, with no notion of what had brought her there.

The present edition of his multi-volumed journal lay upon the desk, a crimson ribbon marking where he had left off. Melinda eyed the leather-bound book suspiciously. With a trembling hand she reached out and flipped the book open.

It opened, revealing a page that was blank, except for two words penned in decorated ink: *Hello Melinda*..

With a gasp, she let the book fall closed. It was a cheerful warning that he knew what she was about while he was away, and while he had been tolerant so far, he wasn't about to permit any great intrusion into his privacy.

Effectively discouraged, she abandoned her plan to pry into his private thoughts. There was always his wonderful closet to explore.

He had let her hang her clothes there, being the only suitable compartment. Melinda took this as permission to investigate the contents at every opportunity.

Prowling through his closet was like visiting a museum. Century upon century blended together, colored in the various fashions. Valdemar was sentimental, Melinda theorized. Why else would he have kept these intangible remnants of days gone by? Yet, as anchored as he was to these elements of the past, he seemed to flow effortlessly into the present, dressing himself in leather and denim, looking every bit the part of a wealthy twenty-first century thirty year-old.

So taken was she with an overcoat of cisele velvet that looked to have come from the late 1700's, that she didn't hear the quiet tread of his feet until he was almost upon her. Startled, Melinda whirled to meet him, the garment still in her guilty hands.

"One day Melinda," Valdemar said, arms crossed defiantly across his chest. "Your curiosity just might kill you." He held out his hand, she handed the garment back to him.

"What was it like, back then?" she asked, encouraged at having survived the encounter.

"You wouldn't have liked it," Valdemar told her. "Not if the sight of a rat sends you into such hysteria. There were rats everywhere, in our homes, in the streets, the gutters. People poured refuse into open sewers, and the entire place stank. We powdered and perfumed ourselves because we had no running water and didn't bathe. The cities were choked with the homeless, the poor and the sick and dying. I think you would have found it entirely ghastly."

"Do you like things better now?" she asked him.

"I would say there are good things to every age," he said, turning to hang the coat once again in his closet.

"Would you put it on," she asked him then, surprising even

herself, "for me?"

An odd look crossed his face. "It isn't healthy to be too seduced by the past, Melinda," he warned her, thrusting the thing further into the closet.

"Come on," Melinda said teasingly, "I promise I won't laugh."

"Laugh," he said looking at her with threatening amusement, "my dear Melinda, had you seen me then, you would have been quite impressed."

"I'll bet you were the perfect gentleman. I imagine you had women falling all over you, until they discovered what you were really about."

"Women did not fall upon men in the eighteenth century," Valdemar told her. "The rules of courtship and marriage were strictly enforced."

He withdrew the velvet coat, looking at it wistfully as if it brought back memories both happy and sad. He pulled it on over his T-shirt and reached up on the shelf, bringing down a dusty box containing a long, black wig tied at the back with a red satin bow. He donned the wig also, to go with the jeweled velvet jacket that was the color of old blood.

Then he reached for her hand and bowing over it, said, "Madam."

In spite of her promise, Melinda broke into peals of laughter. "Valdemar, you are a vision."

"So?" he asked catching her as laughter threatened to topple her to the floor. "If you had come across me two hundred years ago, would you have, as you put it, fallen all over me?"

Melinda answered him with more laughter. But the laughter died on her lips as she became aware of the strong arms around her, and the full lips within inches of hers. Valdemar seemed to realize it too because his mouth closed over hers, hot and demanding. She returned his kiss, exploring every inch of those tempting lips.

A sudden jab of pain made her gasp.

He pulled away from her, lips still parted. In the dim light she caught the gleam of one sharp incisor. Her blood stained his mouth. Her eyes fastened on it. His tongue flicked between his lips, savoring the stolen taste of her blood. Then his gaze dropped to her neck and lingered there. For a moment he seemed to struggle with himself. Then he looked down at his eighteenth century clothes.

"The best thing about women in those days, was their low-cut dresses, and the velvet chokers they wore around their wonderful necks...."

Obviously the moment between them had passed, Melinda thought. She let the matter drop without comment, uncertain what to do about the growing intimacy between them. She drew in a deep breath and licked the blood from the inside of her lip. "So tell me," she asked daringly, "how did you manage it, Valdemar, if the social rules of courtship were so rigid?"

Valdemar scrutinized her, as if he could not decide whether to tell her. "Well," he said eventually. "I was a man of some means. Those were the days of arranged marriages and I was under constant pressure to wed. So, I became 'betrothed' a number of times." Melinda trembled, and moved a few paces away from him. "I was very unlucky in love, you see. My fiancées kept perishing of mysterious illnesses. And, as I said, there was never any lack of the homeless, or ladies of the night...." He gazed at her ruthlessly, obviously pleased with the way his words affected her. "Why do you ask me these things, Melinda, if you really don't want to know?" He was taking off the overcoat and wig, replacing them in their allotted spot in his closet.

"Do you mean to tell me you never felt anything for those poor women?"

"Did I say that?"

"So you weren't so cold and calculating after all."

"Not always," he said, rearranging his things.

Melinda ventured a guess. "You fell in love with one of your fiancées."

He turned to face her. "There was one I rather fancied."

This was dangerous territory. "What did you do?"

"I married her," he said flatly.

"Is she ... dead?"

"No, she is just fine," Valdemar assured her.

"She's a vampire," Melinda whispered, guessing.

"Obviously," Valdemar said, "And now that you know that Melinda, are you satisfied, or must you pry every bit of my life out of me in agonizing detail?"

Melinda summoned the last of her nerve. "She left you," she said softly.

"Melinda--" Valdemar warned. "I am nearing the end of my patience."

"Didn't it bother you?"

Valdemar regarded her with a dark expression. "Suffice it to say, I am content she is happy." He held up his hand, stifling her next question. "Why don't we," he said savagely, "talk about you? Do you want to tell me what you were doing alone on the subway platform at two o'clock in the morning? Or why no man lives at your address? Hmm?"

"No," she said shortly.

"Fine," he said. "Then leave me alone."

* * * *

"I'm sorry," she said when she found him sitting on the edge of the subway platform, lost in thought. "I don't have a lot to think about right now, besides you, and what a disaster my life has become."

"You are forgiven," he said quietly.

"There was a man in my life. Until ... quite recently.

He looked up, startled.

"Well, you did ask."

"I did," he said. "How long ago is recently?"

"The night we met, actually."

"Melinda, I'm sorry...."

She waved his apology from the air. "He was seeing someone else. We had a big fight about it in a restaurant, and then out on the street. He stormed off and left me standing on the corner. It was late, and all I had in my wallet were a few dollars. I decided to take my chances at catching the last subway. What I caught instead, was you."

Valdemar grimaced, silently filling in the events that followed.

She stared off into the tunnel. "It was one hell of a bad day."

From the corner of her eye she saw him turn his head toward her, poised to speak. His apologies would only make her feel worse. She took a deep breath and said resolutely, "You're going to have to tell me how to go about this, how to pick my victims, and what I'm to do with them afterward?"

"I didn't want to rush you," Valdemar said, "not after last time. It was wrong to push you into it the way I did." He searched her face. "Are you sure you're ready to know these things?"

"No," Melinda told him truthfully. "I won't ever be ready. But, as you keep telling me, I don't have a choice, do I?"

"No," he admitted. "And, you are going to be hungry, soon."

"It would be better if I did it right this time, wouldn't it?"

"It would make things easier, less chance for error and less covering up to do afterward." He patted the ledge beside him. "Well then, sit down."

She sat next to him on the edge of the dusty subway platform where the silent tracks trailed off into nothing. He looked at her, gathering his thoughts, trying to determine where to begin.

"I have to admit, things were easier in the old days before the advent of birth certificates, social insurance numbers, certificates of death," he dismissed these things with a wave of his hand. "You must be very careful, Melinda, to work cleanly. It is best to pick victims who don't have any of the things I mentioned, people who won't be missed."

"Obviously, I was not your usual choice of a victim then," she challenged him, resentment leaking into her words with more venom than she had intended.

Valdemar fixed her with a level stare. "No," he conceded. "But, that is a story for another time. Take a lesson from that Melinda, look at the situation we're in now."

"What kind of people won't be missed?" she asked him.

"Criminals, people intent on killing themselves anyway," he told her. "People who come down into the subway to sleep on cold nights. The kind of people who rave on street corners that they have seen the devil." He laughed shortly. "They probably have, and having seen what they've seen, they are best relieved of their suffering. All the better if they are both crazy and drunk. They're less trouble that way."

"And then there are the bullies, the muggers, the murderers and the drug dealers. The world is all but choked with their kind and better off without them."

He continued, "Sometimes, when I'm in the mood for a little revelry, I dress in all my finery and go sit in fancy drinking establishments. I order champagne and make a lavish show of my money. And then," he finished, "I wait to see who follows me out into the alleyway to relieve me of my wallet and my fine, leather clothes."

"And afterward?" she prompted.

"You must make certain they are completely dead. You remember how long you thrashed around feverishly? It may take them two or three days to die, if you aren't diligent. That makes them most difficult to dispose of."

"How do I make sure they're completely dead?"

"Drink until the blood stops flowing," he said bluntly.

Melinda swallowed bile, her body heaving at the very thought of it all. "And then what?"

"Then," Valdemar said, "you have to get rid of them somehow. Burial is best. That's why I prefer my little graveyard in the subway. No one has reason to come down here, and if they do some day, I will be long gone and likely no longer living on this continent." He stared off into shadows of the tunnel.

"You make it sound so easy," Melinda said then. "But tell me one thing. What do I do with my conscience afterward?"

Valdemar turned back to look at her gravely. "That Melinda," he said, "is entirely up to you."

"What do you do with yours?"

"I don't suppose I have one," he said, "any longer."

CHAPTER SIX

Valdemar was leaving in his usual manner without a good-bye or notice of when he would return. Melinda watched him depart through the living room, down the stairs by the pool and along the final corridor that led to the tracks. She watched him disappear into the shadows like part of the night itself. She waited until he was a dwindling speck in the darkness, then she followed him.

He led her down the quiet tracks to where the subway line branched off onto the main line that ran to the surface.

She followed him with all the silence she could muster, conscious of his scathing comments about the tracking skills of humans. It was difficult even to tail him as he darted in and out of shadows and down countless tunnels. She was hopelessly disoriented, she realized suddenly. If she lost him she doubted she'd be able to find her way back.

Just as that disturbing thought flitted through her mind, Valdemar disappeared into the shadows up ahead. Melinda stumbled on a few feet, trying to quench the panic inside her. Then the darkness gave way to light shining down in a single stream from above her head. He had gone up, she thought with relief, up through the slotted roof of the tunnel and out into the city.

With the cat-like reflexes that still amazed her, she scaled the wall, hoisting herself up by the arms and through the narrow holes in the roof. As she emerged into the night air, she saw Valdemar scampering along the roof of the overpass and down onto the hillside.

He stopped a moment, to dust off his pants and straighten his jacket, then he snaked out into the busy street and was lost in the crowd.

Melinda pursued in the direction he'd taken, furious at herself for nearly losing him again, when she caught a glimpse of him rounding the corner up ahead.

He was heading down towards the waterfront where there were an abundance of party-goers and no lack of trendy, noisy nightclubs. It was an area of town she would never have walked into alone. The waterfront had undergone a dramatic redevelopment. The harbor front now boasted an assortment of glitzy tourist malls and warehouses that had been converted into restaurants and nightclubs. But, the back doors of these posh new places opened into alleyways that were little changed from the old days when the waterfront was nothing more than a stretch of dingy storehouses. It was a dangerous part of town to be on foot, once the bars had closed.

Melinda watched from the sidewalk as Valdemar cut through a crowd of people lined up in front of a warehouse with a flashing neon sign. He breezed past the doorman, stopping only to hand him what must have been a reasonable tip and disappeared inside.

Melinda eyed the lineup with dismay. She didn't have a fifty or a hundred dollar bill to secure her entrance to a popular bar.

She walked around the perimeter of the building. It was a low structure, two stories at the most. The second floor was set back from the edge of the first, providing a low roof for her to climb on. The only barrier was a low fence.

Melinda scaled the fence gracefully and walked to the back of the building. A large heap of trash was conveniently piled against the wall. She scrambled up on top of it. From there it was only a short leap to the top of the first story, where a ladder led to the upper floor. With little effort, she ascended the ladder, which ended at a door on the roof. Out of habit, she tried the lock and was momentarily frustrated to find it bolted.

She leaned on the handle, falling forward when it gave under her force, splintering wood and metal alike. Melinda smiled to herself and entered.

She was on the top level beside the kitchen and bathrooms for the upper dance floor. Melinda slunk down the hall and ducked into the crowded women's washroom, elbowing her way to a glimpse in the mirror. She was still not used to the sight of her reflection, changed as it was. She glowed with an intensity that the other women tried desperately to achieve with makeup. The pale whiteness of her skin was enhanced by her raven hair, the blood-red lips and the haunted, violet eyes. With a damp paper towel, she wiped the dirt from her jeans and brushed the tangles from her hair with her hands. She was wearing a black denim jacket that sported a multitude of silver zippers. Yes, she decided she looked like she belonged here. Now to find Valdemar.

She stepped out onto the railed platform above the dance floor into the fog of cigarette smoke and the blare of loud music that people were trying to shout above. She edged her way to the railing past the colorfully dressed bodies that gyrated to the music while they gazed about to see who was watching them.

The lower floor was a sea of bobbing heads and swinging hips as the crowd moved in time with the music. She scanned the throng for a sign of Valdemar, marveling that she could see clearly without squinting.

The tightly packed crowd made her nervous. She was suddenly aware that the smell of so much sweat and the fresh blood that flowed in the veins of the gaily dancing gathering excited her. Thirst seduced her, calling out to her beyond all reason that she should end this longing and drink from the bodies around her. She could feel the sharpness of her eyeteeth pressing against the softness of her inner lips, and as she clamped her jaw tightly shut to ensure her self-control, it reminded her of the yielding give of flesh beneath her teeth. Fervently, she willed her mind to other thoughts.

Melinda forced herself to keep moving along the perimeter of the rectangular platform that was cut away in the center to expose the dance floor below. She stopped as she passed the bar in the corner, her hand going to the pocket of her jeans. The pocket revealed a forgotten ten-dollar bill. She procured a drink, mostly as a prop, but also to keep the hunger from her mind and resumed her search.

The disk-jockey was making a loud and muffled commentary, accompanied by spot light that swept across the ceiling and rounds of applause and cheers from the floor. Melinda glanced in that direction, drawn by the light. And there, sitting on a stool at the lower bar, was Valdemar.

Staking out a clear place on the railing to rest her elbows, she settled in to spy on him. He had no lack for female attention, Melinda thought with an odd stab of jealousy. He was plainly enjoying himself, as he bought rounds of drinks for his many lady admirers.

Whatever Valdemar had to say to the adoring harem, they found it fascinating. All eyes were on him, and they laughed often. That Valdemar might have a sense of humor was something she hadn't considered.

She continued to observe him from afar, long after her fruity drink had turned to syrupy mush, and the crunch of hot sweaty bodies threatened to undo her resolve. Then, just as she was about to think of waiting for him outside, he rose and headed for the door, three of the women hanging drunkenly off his arms.

Melinda pushed her way through the crush of people that lined the staircase to the lower floor. Valdemar was heading out the door with his women friends. She followed slowly. He stopped out on the sidewalk, and against their many protests, dispatched the drunken women into one of the numerous cabs waiting at the curb. He handed the driver what looked like a hundred dollar bill and disappeared into the alleyway.

Melinda was about to rush after him, when she heard the scrape of boots on the pavement behind. She flattened herself against the wall, concealing herself within the shadows. Two men were following Valdemar.

She held her breath as two skinheads in their late teens trudged past her. Their torn leather jackets were both held together and decorated with safety pins and chains. Spiked leather bracelets adorned their wrists and they wore heavy black combat boots on their feet. One was tall and thin with the wiry strength that came from living on the street. The other was shorter, stocky, and made of solid muscle. An angry scar clove his right cheek, witness to a violent lifestyle. Both wore their hair trimmed to the regulation quarter inch length.

Melinda followed them silently as they tailed Valdemar into the shadows of the alley. In the light that spilled over the roofs of the surrounding buildings, she saw the glint of a knife.

Valdemar wandered on, whistling to himself, seemingly oblivious to what was following him. The skinheads trudged after him with a jingle of chains and the crunch of heavy boots on the gravel underfoot.

They looked at each other, a silent signal passing between them. Horrified, Melinda watched as they fell upon Valdemar, pinning him to the wall. In the dim light she could see the glint of his dark eyes and the soft gleam of the knife against his throat.

"Now, aren't you a pretty one," the tall skinhead said. "And so popular with the ladies." He pressed the knife closer against Valdemar's throat. "Now, if you'd be so kind as to hand over your wallet and that nice jacket of yours, we might just let you keep your pretty face the way it is."

"I don't think I'm going to do that," Valdemar said confidently.

The tall skinhead leaned on the knife pressing it deeper into Valdemar's throat. A drop of blood ran along the blade and down onto the mugger's hand. "Can you believe this one?" he said to his buddy. "I guess we'll just have to be more convincing."

Melinda moved closer, a wraith within the shadows.

The shorter skinhead closed in, winding up his fist for a savage blow to Valdemar's stomach. He let the punch go, then uttered a cry of surprise and pain, as Valdemar's leg shot out, catching him in the chest and heaving him backward against the far wall. With an imperceptible move, Valdemar's fist closed over the hand of his captor who still held the knife at his throat. Melinda heard the dull crunch of bones breaking, saw the glint of steel as the knife fell to the ground.

"Well?" he said to his terrified assailants. "I'm waiting, convince me."

The other ruffian picked himself up. Reaching into his waistband, he drew a gun. Melinda gasped.

Before logic could dissuade her, she dived from her hiding place, crossing the distance between them in a single, fluid step. Her body moved of its own accord as she seized the gun and the hand that held it in her iron grip. The gun went off, the bullet ricocheting over their heads in the narrow space. The skinhead howled in agony and astonishment at this demon that had descended on him from out of nowhere. Melinda dealt him a ringing blow across the head, knocking him unconscious. His mate took a step toward her.

"Oh, I wouldn't mess with her," Valdemar warned him. "She can be a perfect terror."

The skin considered his friend's plight for a second, then hugged his wounded hand to himself and made to run away. Valdemar caught him by the scruff of the neck.

"Not so fast," he said, clamping a hand over the thief's mouth.

Valdemar regarded Melinda coolly, acknowledging her presence for the first time. "Did you have to make so much noise?" he asked, kicking the gun to the side. "Now we'll really have to rush." He bent his head over the neck of the skin who still struggled in his grasp, looking at Melinda, who was coming to her senses. "Well?" he asked. "What are you waiting for?"

Melinda looked in alarm at the unconscious body she still

grasped by the wrist. The night's excitement was creeping up on her, the energy expended keeping her hunger in check now cried for release. She could smell the blood that coursed through the veins below the thin skin on the youth's neck. The acrid scent of his fear was still thick in the air. Her entire body ached to be satisfied. Of its own accord her mouth moved to her victim's neck. She felt the taut resistance of the skin, then her teeth pierced the flesh and she drank from the glorious river of blood that flowed beneath.

"Melinda," Valdemar called to her an eternity later. He shook her roughly by the shoulder. "Someone's coming."

Melinda raised her head, letting the madness drift away from her. "We can't leave them like this!"

"No," Valdemar agreed.

With calm detachment, he wrapped his hand in his jacket and retrieved the knife from the ground. Then, he stooped over the still body of the short skinhead who'd pulled the gun, and slashed the corpse's throat, obliterating the teeth marks Melinda had left there. She watched in cold horror as a black stream of the blood she hadn't time to finish leaked from the wound into the ground. That grisly deed finished, Valdemar knelt beside the fiend's partner and closed the cadaver's still fingers around the knife.

Valdemar stepped back, cocking his head to admire his handiwork.

Melinda loosened her T-shirt from her jeans and thrust her hand under it to snatch up the gun. "What about this?"

Valdemar took it from her in his jacket-shrouded hand. He returned to the knife-wielding corpse who stared up at him in the vacant stare of death. He thrust the gun into the victim's neck. It fired with a dull thud, tearing through the skin in a trail of crimson. To finish the scenario, he placed the gun in the other hoodlum's hand.

Melinda surveyed the grisly scene with a calm and icy feeling in the pit of her stomach. She tried to view the evidence through the objective eyes of the police. Hopefully, they wouldn't pay too much attention to the plight of two ruffians. Perhaps, they would assume, as Valdemar had laid it out for them, that one skinhead had stabbed his companion, and wounded, the other had retaliated with a gun blast to the neck.

Valdemar smiled, obviously pleased with the way things had turned out. He listened intently into the night wind. Then, he reached for her hand and tore off down the alley, dragging her with him.

He was really moving this time, pulling her along with speed much beyond what she had thought him capable of. The scenery rushed by her in a blur as he zigzagged down alleyways and behind abandoned buildings. Melinda was hard-pressed just to keep her feet under her.

Valdemar stopped before a squat building, astounding her by climbing up on the low roof and hauling her up after him. He surveyed the city which was quiet except for the sound of sirens off in the distance.

"Over there," he pointed. Melinda followed his leather clad arm, amazed at how far they'd come. She could see the flashing lights of police cruisers lighting up the sides of the buildings. And Valdemar wasn't even out of breath.

Satisfied they weren't being followed, he leapt down from the building, waiting for her to follow him. Then, he turned and continued on at a saner pace. Melinda ran after him, up the hillside and along the top of the tunnel, where the wind tore at her hair and Valdemar laughed insanely at the night.

She jumped down onto the tracks after him, once again in the relative safety of the subway. The rails were quiet. The last subway had long since left on its final route.

Valdemar looked at her in the shadows and howled with laughter.

"Melinda," he said, lunging at her, holding her between his arms against the wall of the tunnel. "What on earth were you doing back there, attacking that poor fool with the gun?"

Melinda let him hold her there while she gasped for breath. His arms tightened around her. She leaned her head against his chest. "I don't know," she told him out of her own confusion. "I was afraid for you."

Valdemar shook his head. "And thanks to your valiant attempt to *save* me from a couple of adolescent thugs, I almost went hungry tonight."

"You knew I was there all the time," she accused him.

"Of course I did," he said, still snickering at her discomfort. "You should have seen the look on that punk's face when you came leaping out of the shadows. I have to admit, even I was impressed."

He let her go, and she walked a few paces away from him, turning her back to him.

"Tell me," he said softly. "That you don't feel sorry for that pair."

"No," she said quietly. "They had it coming."

"What is it then?" he asked, placing an inquiring hand on her shoulder.

"You keep telling me I'm no better than you," she told him. "And now I know in my heart I'm not."

He turned her to face him. His kiss stole whatever she might have said next.

"Don't be so sure of that," he whispered against her lips.

CHAPTER SEVEN

Barbed claws seized her in the darkness. Her feet felt rooted to the ground, and no amount of thrashing about would release them. She tried to scream, but the air stuck in her throat. It was coming, whatever it was, bearing down on her. Tiny, razor-sharp teeth penetrated her shoulder. She struck out and her hand collided with something furry.

Finally, her lungs liberated an ear-piercing scream. She opened her eyes to find a pair of green orbs staring back at her from a black ball of fur.

Levering herself away, she fumbled against the side of the bed, clutching at the covers to stop her fall. She landed on her back and stared up in bewilderment at the gray light of the subterranean room.

Feeling more than a little foolish, Melinda risked a glance over the side of the bed to find her *attacker* was no more than a kitten.

Her scream brought Valdemar running through the open doorway. The scene seemed to confuse him. The frightened kitten still clutched the bedspread, its back hunched, fur ruffled in its terror. Melinda lay where she had fallen, tangled in the covers.

He retrieved the frightened animal, cradling it in his arms. "You have to stop doing that," he said. "It sets my nerves on edge."

"I was dreaming," Melinda said in response to his disapproving frown. She looked at the tiny ball of fur in his arms. The kitten hissed at her. "Where did the cat come from?"

"I found him in the subway," Valdemar said, more than a little annoyed. "I thought it might comfort you. At least he'll keep the rat population under control. Ahh," he said in frustration. "I don't know what I thought."

She shook her head to clear it of the memory of her beloved Siamese's cold, still body in her hands. "I'll kill it."

"No you won't," he promised. "You've been extraordinarily hungry because your body was weakened by the virus. You will adjust, eventually, you'll only need to feed once a month. By then you'll be well used to the feeling. You'll learn how to control yourself."

"Only once a month?" Melinda repeated. "Have you ever added up how many lives you've taken in your life--"

"No." Valdemar said sharply. "I haven't." He glared at her. "These human values you cling to so tenaciously won't serve you now. You're going to have to change your thinking, or you're going to suffer for a long time." He looked down at the kitten who, once the danger had passed, had gone to sleep in his arms. "Well? What do you want me to do about this?"

Melinda looked at the sleeping animal. "He's so tiny," she said, peering at the miniature ball of fur. "He needs someone to look after him."

Valdemar walked toward his study, taking the kitten with him. He let him explore the floor under his desk. Flame ignited the shadows as he lit the lamp and sat down.

She climbed back up on the bed, retreating behind the curtains into the darkness. From the far corner she could hear the scratch of Valdemar's fountain pen against the parchment pages of his diary. She peeked through the curtains. His broad shoulders were hunched in concentration and she could see the sharp outline of his profile against the candlelight. From that angle he was a study in contrasts, the darkness of him imposed upon the white flame. That image intrigued her. She came to stand behind him, studying him as he ignored her.

Valdemar looked up at her, his mind obviously still on his work.

"I'm disturbing you," she said, hoping he would offer assurances to the contrary.

"Yes," he said.

She should have let the matter drop then, but she had to know what it was that allowed Valdemar to live so fluidly as a vampire, while she floundered. "You have to help me," she demanded. "There are so many things I need to know."

"And what," asked Valdemar with an amused grin, "is so desperate for you to know at this particular moment?"

"Well, for starters," Melinda said, and watched him wince as he realized he could be in for hours of persistent interrogation. She struggled to think of a question that wouldn't annoy him further. "Why are we sensitive to light?"

Valdemar sat back in his chair, giving up all hope of finishing his task. "Our eyes are sensitive to a different portion of the spectrum of light. We see better in the darkness than human beings. Probably, we evolved that way as a result of millennia of hunting in the darkness." He looked at her, eyebrows raised, waiting for the next onslaught of questions.

"Why are we so pale?"

"Our bodies don't produce the same amount of melanin as humans. We don't need it, being nocturnal by nature."

"Would I get burned if I went out in the sun?"

"Yes, you would."

"Would it kill me?"

"No," he said shortly. "Of course not. You'd be uncomfortable, but you would heal."

"So I could go out in the sunlight if I wanted to, if I was protected?"

"Sure you could."

"Do you miss the sun?"

"No," he said. "The night suits me just fine."

"Why do we need to drink blood?" she asked him then.

"I don't know." he replied. "The same reason cats eat mice and sheep eat grass."

Surprise betrayed her face.

"Don't look at me like that," he snapped. "I don't have all the answers."

"I just assumed you did," she said, bemused. This was the first time she'd seen him speechless. "Are there those of us who study vampirism, like scientists?"

"There are vampires who do just about everything."

"What do you do?"

"I have done many, many things in my lifetime. Too many to mention. But right now, I live in the city and do much as I please."

"I guess you have time to do just about everything you want to," she decided, a million possibilities crowding into her already over-burdened brain.

"Surely you didn't expect me to engage in a single occupation for eleven hundred years?"

Melinda looked down at him helplessly. It was too much to think about all at once. "What is it Melinda?" Valdemar asked.

"I'm just so confused." She tried to find a way to explain her conflicting feelings.

"And what can I tell you to make it better?"

"Tell me everything!" she exclaimed in exasperation. "I want to know about you, how you became a vampire, what it's like to be eleven hundred years old, what life was like in the fifteenth century--"

"I will tell you these things," he said, appraising her desperate mood, "but not this minute and not all at once. Because the one thing you have now, in abundance ... is time."

He stood and drew her into his embrace.

Melinda looked up into the fathomless eyes that swam toward her. Gripped by warring desires, she couldn't decide whether to move closer or to run from him.

Fate intervened. The kitten picked that moment to attack one of her toes. "Ouch!"

Melinda pulled her foot from his grasp. Thinking she meant to play with him, the kitten responded by diving on her other foot.

"Hey, you!" she said, laughing. She reached down and gently disengaged his little claws. Thwarted, the kitten wandered off looking for something more interesting to play with.

She straightened to find Valdemar's face mere inches from hers. She realized she barely had to move to touch him. Her gaze centered on his full lips. The memory of how soft those lips felt against hers flitted tantalizingly through her mind.

Before better sense could intervene, she closed the meager distance and kissed him.

His mouth felt warm upon hers. Interest became need. Her body responded, molding against his.

He didn't seem to mind her taking the lead, she thought pulling back slightly to gauge his reaction. Heat smoldered in those dark eyes. He tugged her hard against him and kissed her thoroughly.

She moaned at the first invasion of his tongue. She reciprocated, boldly exploring his mouth with her own. He groaned in response. His hands moved in lazy circles, kneading the tension from her shoulders. He continued the sensuous massage on her lower back and buttocks until his fingers located the hem of her shirt. She felt the warmth of his hand as it traveled upward beneath the fabric, caressing her hip before cupping her breast. His mouth smothered her gasp. Desire let loose the hunger she held in precarious control. She tensed.

Seeming to sense her growing desperation, he pulled away from her and held out his hand. She let him lead her toward the heavily draped bed.

Melinda watched him solemnly, as he settled down beside her and began taking off his shirt. Her eyes drifted from his face to his chest, which was smooth except for a dark tangle of curls in the center. He was well built, she decided as she watched him undress, made of solid muscle, much stronger than he appeared to be. The urge to touch him became overwhelming. She placed her hand against his chest.

He covered it with his own and pulled her closer. "Come here," he whispered.

His hands strayed to the buttons of her shirt, resolutely stripping away the layers of her defenses, until she sat naked before him. His hands slid from her shoulders to her breasts, then continued downward over her hips. His admiring gaze followed the path of his hands. Gently, he pushed her back into the softness of the covers.

He lowered himself over her, covering her with his body and his warmth. His mouth explored the crook of her neck. His lips lingered over her pulse point.

But instead of the pressure of his teeth, he gave her a gentle kiss that echoed down her spine. He followed up with another, this time at the hollow of her throat. Dipping lower, he traced a line of hot kisses over her stomach, inching closer to the center of her desire. Anticipation brought a surge of wetness to that spot. She groaned aloud, startling herself.

His head came up at the sound. The heat in his gaze nearly undid her. Conscious of the effect he had on her, he slowly lowered his head until she felt the first brush of his tongue.

Her entire world shrunk to that knot of desire that demanded to be appeased. And he seemed intent on doing just that. With strokes of his tongue he dragged her to the summit and then plunged her over the edge.

Her scream of release echoed through the underground chamber.

The sound didn't seem to concern Valdemar. Smiling, he raised himself on his elbows and looked down at her. Once again, he covered her with his body. With a deep, probing kiss, he stole the last of her screams.

Every inch of his muscular body pressed against her. She felt the thick length of him against her moist opening. She tipped her hips and took him inside.

At once he was within her and all around her. She felt his silky curls against her cheek and his hot breath on her face.

He was bigger and thicker than she imagined. But after a moment, her body stretched to accommodate him. He withdrew and pressed gently deeper, wrenching another moan from her. He rocked against her, going deeper still. She matched his rhythm, yearning for yet another taste of that all-consuming pleasure.

His lips moved in tingling kisses along her neck. She felt the stinging pressure as his teeth broke through the skin and into the vein beneath.

She drifted, swept along by the soft pull of his mouth at her throat, drowning in the exquisite combination of pleasure and pain.

Valdemar shuddered against her, and disengaged his mouth from her neck. He caressed the wound with his lips, then kissed her. She tasted her own blood.

He rolled over, pulling her on top of him. Her mouth was at his throat. Hunger cried out inside her, mingled with another vague feeling she couldn't quite describe. She delayed a second, wondering if he would prevent her. Then, when he made no move, her lips parted and she sunk her teeth into his neck.

This time, it was as Valdemar had tried to tell her, a beautiful experience. She could feel the subtle movements of his body as he breathed in time with her and his heart beating against her chest. His eyelashes brushed her cheek as he shut his eyes and surrendered to her. Warm nourishing blood rushed down her throat and into her body, as he had likewise drawn sustenance from her. She could have stayed, locked in that unearthly embrace forever, yet she knew she couldn't. Reluctantly, she released him and tumbled down into his arms. He brought his face down close to hers and licked her lips, stealing back a little of his blood.

"So you do care after all, Melinda," he whispered. "You had me fooled."

Comforted, her belly warm with his blood, she drifted off into the gray land between wakefulness and sleep.

Valdemar stiffened, jarring her awake.

"Get dressed," he said listening intently. "We have visitors."

"Who?"

"Friends of mine," he said, rising, pushing her in the direction of the closet.

"Friends?"

"Yes, I have friends." He buttoned his shirt. "What did you think?"

Melinda shook her head, watching him walk toward the living

room, collecting his clothes as he went. The thought of Valdemar having friends unnerved her. He was enough to deal with alone.

She could hear voices coming nearer down the tracks: two men, two women. In the parlor, Valdemar was opening a bottle of wine. Melinda rummaged through her clothes. Nothing seemed appropriate for a social gathering of vampires. Giving up she threw on what was closest at hand and ran a hand through her hair. Nervously, she approached the door. Valdemar had left it open a crack in his haste.

Through the narrow opening she could see four people. The men were tall, taller than Valdemar. One of the women was blonde, a play of nearly silver hair against pearly skin. She looked like a ghost standing there next to the fireplace.

The other woman looked like fire incarnate. A cloud of red hair fell almost to the back of her knees. She had deep, amber eyes that glowed like golden coals in the firelight.

"Well, Valdemar," she said with a husky voice. "How long must we wait for an invitation?"

"Moira," Valdemar said with amusement. "Forgive me, I've been very busy."

"Not too busy for us, surely?" said the blonde woman with a sly smile.

"I'm never too busy for you, Kirsten."

Kirsten gave him a scrutinizing glance. "We were worried."

He hugged her warmly. "Nothing to worry about."

"Adrian, Cornelius." Valdemar shook the men's hands in turn.

The vampire named Moira moved to the center of the parlor, occupying it. She looked to the sideboard where Valdemar had laid out six wine glasses.

"So you've been busy have you, Valdemar?" she said eyeing the wine glasses, suspiciously. "Who is she?"

"What makes you think it's a *she*?" Valdemar asked smiling broadly.

Moira stepped up beside Valdemar, bending back the collar of his shirt where he had left it unbuttoned. "That love bite on your neck is a dead give away."

Valdemar rubbed the side of his neck self-consciously, then buttoned his collar.

"I don't suppose it's anyone we know," Adrian surmised.

"No." Valdemar said. "No one you know."

"So who is she then?" Moira demanded. "I want to meet the lady who succeeded in putting the bite on the elusive Valdemar when so many others have failed."

"Her name is Melinda," Valdemar said, plainly growing weary of their teasing. "And I'd appreciate it if you'd be kind to her."

"Meaning the lady has not been a vampire very long," Cornelius said with a raunchy laugh. He looked at Valdemar with a bawdy grin on his face. "Your doing I suppose? That's just like you."

"Who would have thought," Adrian said, "after all this time."

"Where are you hiding this virgin?" asked Cornelius with another snicker.

Valdemar scowled. "I'll see what's keeping her."

He walked to the bedroom door and pushed it open, his face darkening to discover Melinda had been standing there for some time eavesdropping on their conversation. As he opened his mouth to say something, the kitten ran between her legs and out into the living room.

"Oh, Valdemar," Moira said in amusement. "How thoughtful--a snack."

"Moira--" Valdemar warned. He cast a pleading glance at Melinda and came to the kitten's rescue. "The cat belongs to Melinda."

He scooped the kitten into his arms, shaking his head at the whole situation.

"Now there's a brave animal," Moira observed, "to lie in the arms of Valdemar the Vampire."

The others laughed uproariously. Valdemar did not look at all amused. "Please don't use that word in conjunction with my name," he said. "I find it offensive."

"I don't know," Adrian remarked. "I rather like it."

"I would have thought you'd be used to it by now," Moira remarked.

Valdemar turned and deposited the kitten behind the closed bedroom door. He ushered Melinda into the living room. She took a tentative step toward them, feeling as if she was being offered for their collective feast.

"This is Melinda," she heard Valdemar saying behind her. He named off the guests: "Moira, Kirsten, Adrian, Cornelius."

Names from Valdemar's journal, she realized suddenly.

A loud gasp escaped Moira's lips. She covered her mouth with her hand.

If Valdemar heard the sound, he ignored it. But, as he motioned toward the vampire named Kirsten, their eyes locked and she held him in her pale, measuring gaze. Some sort of communication passed between them, and was swiftly gone.

Cornelius had turned away, chuckling to himself.

Melinda cleared her throat. "Hello."

Adrian set down his wine glass and reached for her hand. He towered over her, filling her vision. Blond, glossy hair fell past his shoulders and he absorbed her attention with huge luminous green eyes. "Enchanted," he whispered as he kissed her hand. The touch of his lips reverberated through her body. "But, I'm sure we've met."

"I don't think so," she stammered. He shrugged then, "Perhaps not."

Melinda had the strangest feeling she was missing something significant. Something they all knew that she didn't.

"Let go of Valdemar's woman," Cornelius said, elbowing Adrian out of the way. He winked at Melinda. "Ignore him, he's a lech."

She looked at Cornelius, the joker in the group. He was fairer than Valdemar with straight brown hair that he wore pulled back into a long ponytail. "I'm not Valdemar's woman."

"You will be dear," Moira drawled. "All the ladies like Valdemar. He has that desperate, brooding quality."

"It's just an act, of course," Cornelius said with a wolf-like grin. "The truth is our good friend Val is insufferably boring."

Melinda folded her arms defensively across her chest and glowered at Valdemar who looked likewise displeased with the whole exchange.

"Leave them both alone," Kirsten said. "Have none of you any manners?" She reached for Melinda's hand and shook it. "It's nice to meet you, Melinda."

Kirsten didn't look human at all. She had an ethereal kind of beauty, until she smiled revealing a row of pointed teeth.

"Oh, Valdemar," Moira was saying from the other side of the room. "I simply must tell you about the most exquisite kill I made last week."

"You really have to hear this one, Val," Adrian said. "She had it planned for months. It reminded me of your style."

"Yes, that's why we came tonight," Cornelius said. "We were lonely for you."

"Come kill with us," Moira begged him. "For old time's sake."

Valdemar looked desperately at Melinda who appeared as if she might faint. "Not tonight. I'm not in the mood."

"Since when did you wait for the hunger to kill?" Moira asked.

Valdemar shot her a murderous look which Moira chose to

ignore.

"Neil's right," she whined, "you are boring."

"Melinda," Kirsten said, taking in the horrified look on her face. "Why don't you and I go for a walk. It's a nice night, and you look like you could use some air. Let them bicker among themselves. They've been at it for hundreds of years."

She threaded her hand through Melinda's arm and drew her to the doorway, casting a backward look at Valdemar who looked truly tortured. "Don't worry, Val, I'll look after her."

CHAPTER EIGHT

"Thanks," Melinda said gratefully when they were a few feet down the tunnels.

"That bunch can be hard to take," Kirsten said. "You looked like you needed help."

They walked on in silence for a few moments.

"This must be difficult for you," Kirsten said. "I remember how hard it was for me."

"According to Valdemar," Melinda said bitterly. "I'm the only person who ever had a rough time with this."

Kirsten laughed. "Valdemar's over eleven hundred years old. I'm sure he doesn't remember what it's like."

"Did Valdemar...."

"Make me a vampire?" Kirsten finished.

"Do you mind me asking? It seems like a personal question."

Kirsten smiled. "Not at all. And yes, it was Valdemar."

"Did you want to be a vampire, I mean, when it happened?"

"Not exactly," she said with a melancholy smile. "But at the time I thought I was in love with Valdemar." She looked at Melinda's stricken face, then reached for her hand. "Come with me. I know a quiet place where we can get something to drink. Then we can talk."

"In public?" Melinda asked. After weeks in the dark, the thought of walking down a busy street terrified her.

"Yes in public," Kirsten reassured her. "Vampires are allowed to drink in cafes. As long as they're well behaved."

"Vampire," Melinda repeated. "Valdemar hates that word."

Kirsten laughed. "It's a word, the same as any other. Valdemar doesn't like to think of himself as a wraith in a black cape. He thinks it's undignified. But, I've always thought of him that way. It's more romantic."

They emerged on a hillside and looked down into the glittering lights of the city. Melinda filled her lungs with fragrant air, then stopped mid-breath. It was as if she had never truly breathed or seen before. The cityscape glowed with luminous clarity. Warm breezes stirred her hair. All of a sudden her mood lightened.

The cafe Kirsten had in mind turned out to be a tiny place. Tables spilled through French doors out onto the sidewalk. Melinda balked as Kirsten wandered up to a table and sat down, keeping a watchful eye on the busy street in front of her.

"Relax," Kirsten said, giggling at her discomfort. "Nobody's going to know. We're not supposed to exist, remember."

Kirsten ordered cappuccino and let it sit on the table, watching the whipped cream disintegrate into brown foam. Once in awhile she raised the cup, holding it in her hands, but never lifted it to her lips.

"Tell me about Valdemar," Melinda said suddenly.

"Valdemar is ... Valdemar," Kirsten said with a smile. "He is hard to categorize."

"Did he ever tell you how he became a vampire?"

"Yes, but I think that's something he should tell you himself."

"He won't tell me much about anything."

"Valdemar's always been that way," Kirsten confessed. "He's protective of his feelings. Probably it's because he still has feelings after all this time. You have to remember, Melinda, this preoccupation with feelings is a twentieth century phenomenon."

Melinda gasped and covered her mouth with her hand. "You talk about an entire century, as if it were something fleeting, insubstantial. Do you realize that's almost four times the length of my life!"

"To us a century is a brief span of time that soon blends into another age and new ideas."

"Don't you get sick of it all? Living I mean, knowing the same people for hundreds of years."

"Some of us do," Kirsten admitted.

"What do they do about it?"

"Some get a little crazy, do things that are unwise--" She paused, on the verge of saying something further before she caught herself and smothered it.

"Do you still love him?"

"Of course," Kirsten said with a smile. "Valdemar is a good friend." She looked at Melinda with pale gray eyes that were just a shade off white. "Do you want to tell me about it, Melinda?"

Tears welled up in Melinda's eyes, spilling down her face to splash on the table. "I don't know where to start...."

Kirsten patted her hand. "It's hard, I know."

Melinda wiped the tears from her eyes self-consciously. "I've been snatched from my life and everyone who loved me and turned into a monster!"

"Really," Kirsten said, "it's not as bad as all that."

"I don't understand anything, like why he did it, or how I feel about him. Sometimes I'm terrified of him and at other times I'm attracted--" She stopped abruptly, remembering she was talking to his ex-lover.

"He's a bit much. Isn't he?" Kirsten said, unperturbed.

"Yes, well...."

"I was seventeen when my father arranged my marriage to Valdemar."

"You were? That must have been weird."

"Which?" Kirsten asked. "My betrothal at seventeen? Or being married off to a vampire?"

"Both," Melinda said. "I'm nearly twice the age you were then, and I still can't imagine it."

"Seventeen was an acceptable age to marry in the late eighteenth century. I was ignorant of the ways of men. It took me awhile to figure out that Valdemar was ... different. And yes, it was all very weird."

"I can imagine."

"Becoming a vampire was a traumatic adjustment for me, although, I'm told others take to it quite easily."

"Are there many others of us?" Melinda asked, anxious to change the subject.

"No," Kirsten said. "A couple hundred, maybe. Most of us don't procreate. We're not as interested in giving life as we are in bringing death."

"Life is important to Valdemar," Melinda mused.

"Val has unorthodox views on a lot of things," Kirsten agreed.

"The other vampires," Melinda asked, "What are they like?"

"They are as varied as different people are," Kirsten told her. "But mostly, they tend to be more like Moira and Adrian than Valdemar or I. We are hunters, predators and parasites, Melinda," Kirsten told her earnestly. "I know what a difficult transition that is to make, but it will sort itself out, you'll see. In my day, it was easier. Death was a part of our lives. We didn't believe, as you do now in the twentieth century, that we ought to have the power to prolong life. We didn't dwell on the sanctity of the lives of people, animals or any of the other things people demonstrate for in front of city hall."

Melinda looked up, her eyes gravitating to the tiny, gold cross around the fair vampire's neck. She realized she was staring. Kirsten's hand closed about it self consciously.

"It surprises you that I'm religious," she said.

"It's a strange combination of dogma," Melinda said in embarrassment. "The spawn of Satan praying to God."

"True," Kirsten admitted, in a voice full of sorrow. "But, it is my strength. I can't go to hell until I die, and that is not likely to be for a long, long time."

"You believe you're damned then?"

"Surely I am," Kirsten whispered, "But then again, we could be in hell right now."

"I wish my faith were that simplistic," Melinda confessed. "It is more my own conscience that troubles me. I don't know how I'm going to live with myself."

"Killing is the easy part."

"What am I going to do, Kirsten?" she asked helplessly. "What if someone discovers what I am?"

"Don't worry about it. The one thing that works in your favor is that humans will go to great lengths to prove to themselves that there are rational explanations for everything."

"Just like that?"

"Vampires almost never get caught. We're cunning. We make an art of it."

"Does it ever get any easier?"

"Somewhat," Kirsten said and looked off into the distance. "But it's not as if you have a choice."

"No," Melinda whispered. "My options are severely limited at the moment."

"If you need to talk, you can always come to me."

"How will I find you?"

"Call me on the phone." Kirsten reached into her purse and scribbled her number on a scrap of paper.

"I want to call my family," Melinda said. "I want them to know I'm all right."

"Stay away from them," Kirsten urged. "If you think your

conscience bothers you now, think how you'd feel if you harmed someone you love. The most humane thing you can do right now is let them go."

Melinda looked up to find the waiter standing before them. Mesmerized by Kirsten's striking looks, he'd forgotten why he was there. She'd noticed they'd received many admiring glances from the men in the cafe and passers-by on the street. Melinda shifted nervously in her seat, the unexpected attention made her nervous. Kirsten hardly seemed to notice.

"Would you kindly get us our check?" she reminded the flustered waiter.

Smiling, he walked away, shaking his head to clear it.

Kirsten looked at her watch. "I'd better take you back."

"What about the others?"

"Oh, it's safe," she assured her. "They'll be gone by now."

* * * *

The living room was dark, shadowed with the kind of blackness that can only be found underground. Adrian, Cornelius and Moira were gone. Valdemar had let the fire go out. She could feel him there, in the darkness, sitting on the sofa, the kitten on his lap. They formed an odd image, the predator and the helpless kitten sitting together in the dark.

Melinda put her hand on the door frame, steadying herself in the gloom. The light from the candle she carried thrust swaying shadows into the parlor. Valdemar said nothing as she entered. His eyes followed her as she came to sit on the arm of the chair facing him and deposited the candle in a holder on the table between them.

"I thought I was going to have to come looking for you again," he said at last.

"Sorry, Kirsten and I got talking."

"Really? And what did you talk about for all this time?"

"You."

"What about me?"

"Oh Kirsten told me lots of interesting things about you."

"I can imagine."

"She was your wife, wasn't she?" Melinda said courageously, venturing a guess. "The one you told me about."

"That was a long time ago," he said. "Does it bother you?"

"No," she said. "Why did she leave you?"

"Why didn't you ask Kirsten that?"

"Because I'd rather ask you."

"She fell in love with Cornelius," he said with a sad smile. "Neil is ... more lovable than I."

"Oh, I don't know about that," Melinda said. "I think I would prefer you to Cornelius. You have a certain charm."

Valdemar dismissed that with a snort. "Do I now?"

"Is Kirsten the woman you write poems to in your diary?"

Valdemar raised his black eyes to hers, holding her in his gaze, warning her without speaking a word that it would be best to leave this topic alone. "No."

He was dangerous in this mood but also fascinating. There were countless facets to his personality, countless secrets.

"So what about Moira?" Melinda asked with a wicked smile. "Was she your lover too?"

Valdemar shuddered. "No, not Moira." He watched her face. "You don't like my friends, do you?"

"I don't like Moira," Melinda said. "She's not like you at all, an odd kind of friend for you to have."

This seemed to amuse him. "Is that so?"

"But then again," Melinda reconsidered, "I don't really know you, do I?"

"No," Valdemar said. "You don't."

"How do you go about getting to know someone who's eleven hundred years old? And how long does it take? Fifty years, two hundred?" She looked straight at him. "Or do you ever know someone, especially when that person lives by a set of values you don't even vaguely understand?"

Valdemar sighed. "I fail to see what difference knowing everything about me would make, aside from a boring tale. And, if you keep reading my journal every time my back is turned, you'll soon know it all anyway."

Melinda tried to look composed. "You never told me not to read it."

"No," he said. "I didn't."

"So you must want me to know."

"Perhaps," he said, then refused to elaborate.

Melinda changed the subject. "Can I ask you something?"

"You might as well," he said wearily.

"Did you go with them? To hunt?"

"No."

"Why not?"

"Their hunting style is very different from mine." He stared into the candle's flame as if there was a great deal more he would say but had decided against it.

"Val?" she whispered, startling herself by using the affectionate derivative of his name. "I mean Valdemar," she amended hastily.

"Val is fine," he said with a smile. The unexpected endearment seemed to please him.

"About tonight...." she began, then words eluded her.

"Tonight...." he repeated, then shook his head. "I will never understand you. You say you hate me. You run away. And yet, you touch me so ... tenderly. What am I going to do with you?"

"I don't know."

"Neither do I." He ran the back of his hand lightly down her cheek. Cupping the back of her head, he pulled her close for a kiss that reminded her of the passion they'd shared. "I promise I'll always be kind toward you, Melinda," he said, drawing away. "That is the best I can do. Come to bed with me. It's been a long night and we're both tired."

CHAPTER NINE

Melinda sprawled in the wing-back chair, staring into the empty air. She spent many days that way. Long moments dragged uniformly into others, days passed like minutes. Often she would look up to find Valdemar watching her. It was obvious her idleness bothered him, but he offered no suggestions, as if he were at a loss as to what to do with her.

Kirsten offered her home as refuge. On the many occasions Melinda arrived on her doorstep in tears, she was always willing to talk and offer advice. Her quiet confidence had a calming effect. But once the horror of her new existence had faded in normalcy, there was still the problem of time.

How often she had wished for more time. And now that she had a wealth of it, she had no philosophy for living such a life. Her old existence had been a mad rush of deadlines, scrambling to acquire the money to pay the rent and desperately hurrying to fill each fleeting minute. That time was now an infinite commodity seemed to sap her will to do much of anything.

The business of living occupied all of Valdemar's time. He seldom rushed at anything, content to do what needed to be done or simply what interested him.

But frantic activity had been an integral part of Melinda's vitality. Now that time stretched before her like a featureless black road, her motivation vanished. She lay about Valdemar's underground abode, fashioning kitten toys for Shadow out of bits of string.

Melinda knelt and pulled the twine along the floor, twisting it back and forth like a snake. Shadow pounced and hissed, impaling the hapless bundle on his tiny teeth and claws.

Someone was coming, she realized all of a sudden. They had been approaching for some time, moving silently down the tracks. Melinda had only been vigilant enough to notice as the air shifted around her and she looked beyond the couch to discover a pair of black boots.

Melinda let her eyes draw her upwards, over the shapely legs clothed in black leggings, past the gauzy shift that ended in a blaze of cinnabar hair.

"Moira!" Melinda said, tearing her gaze from the riveting amber eyes.

"Hello Melinda," Moira greeted her with syrupy kindness.

Melinda scooped Shadow into her arms and got to her feet. Moira glared at the cat with obvious displeasure.

"Valdemar isn't here," Melinda told her self-consciously.

"Oh, I know," Moira said with a disapproving glance. "Haven't you got anything better to do than play with an animal on the floor like a child?"

Melinda straightened, drawing herself up to her full height, which was still half a foot shorter than Moira. "I have an appreciation for the simple things in life."

"Really?" Moira remarked. "How dreary."

Moira was dangerous. Unlike Valdemar who was annoyingly reticent, Moira was treacherous. She reminded Melinda of a cobra, poised and ready to strike.

The red-haired vampire circled Melinda lazily, taking in the faded blue jeans and old sweatshirt with a disapproving scowl. "You aren't Valdemar's usual choice of a lover," she remarked. "He usually prefers his women more cultured."

Melinda locked eyes with Moira. The intensity of that gaze was like placing her hand in a fire. "What do you want Moira?"

"Actually," Moira said. "I came to invite you to a little get together we're having tonight."

It had the distinct ring of deception to it, but Melinda was curious. "That's very nice of you, but I find that odd, since I get the impression you don't like me at all."

"Funny," Moira said. "I got the same impression."

"It isn't up to me to pass judgment on Valdemar's friends," she answered, feeling all the while that she was sinking into quicksand with no hope of escape.

"Nor is it mine." Moira shrugged, managing to make even that ordinary gesture infinitely sensual. "But you are Valdemar's ... whatever you are, and Kirsten and Cornelius seem to like you. So why don't you join us tonight? Valdemar hoped you would."

"All right," Melinda agreed, feeling every bit like the canary about to be devoured by the cat.

"See you later then," Moira said with a smile that was not at all kind.

* * * *

Moira lived in a neighborhood whose prime landmark was a mental institution, a number of dubious drinking establishments and boarded up stores. Delirious vagrants roamed the streets, keeping an uneasy company with the abundant drunks who staggered about in the hours after the bars had closed. Moira's loft sat above a vacant store next to a run-down hotel.

Melinda followed Moira up the winding rickety staircase to the third floor. Stairs creaked precariously beneath her feet. The walls were covered with the scrawl of numerous graffiti artists, and piles of discarded syringes littered the corners. They stepped over a filthy, emaciated youth who had passed out by Moira's door and into the cavernous space beyond.

Moira's home comprised the entire upper floor of the building. Thick wooden pillars were all that marked where walls had once been, and high arched windows looked out onto the busy street. The windows were draped now, obscured by black velvet curtains, richly embroidered with gold.

She was not surprised to discover that Moira's decor was entirely black. The room was sparsely furnished. Two black leather couches occupied the center of the room with a couple of low tables on either side. There were no lamps, no electronic comforts such as stereos or television sets. In a shadowed corner of the loft, far away from the windows, lay a huge futon, surrounded by a multitude of cushions of ebony velvet. This makeshift bed chamber was divided from the rest of the room by layers of black gauzy material that hung from the ceiling like mosquito netting. It had the look of a harem to it, and the image made Melinda nervous.

Huge canvasses hung from floor to ceiling, tribute to Moira's considerable talent as an artist. These massive works were horrifically sensuous to look upon. Moira chose the most macabre ideas for her paintings, mostly gruesome scenes of death. They were executed with such skill Melinda almost swore the blood was real. She was afraid that if she reached out a hand to touch them, the subjects might suddenly come to life and start moaning in their agony. Melinda forced herself to look away, hoping they weren't scenes from a series of Moira's kills.

Illumination came from large candelabras that hung in the only bare space between the paintings. Wax dripped down the walls to form stalactites on the wooden floor.

Adrian was slumped on the low leather couch near the heavily curtained window. Kirsten and Cornelius reclined on the nearby divan. Valdemar was conspicuously absent. Empty bottles of wine were scattered about, and there was a peculiar smell in the air. To Melinda's dismay, the gathering appeared drunk, which was unnerving since Valdemar had told her alcohol had no effect on their metabolism. What did vampires drink to get drunk? She wondered briefly, then decided she didn't want to know.

"Look who I found," Moira said. The others looked up, offering bleary greetings.

"Where is Val?" Melinda asked, her stomach sinking to the region of her knees.

"Oh," said Adrian, rising precariously to his feet. "Calling him pet names are we? How endearing."

"Yes," Moira said snidely. "She seems quite smitten with our Valdemar. But that'll wear off soon, just like it did with Kirsten."

"Leave her alone," Kirsten said, coming to her aid. "You know that's not true, and none of your concern anyway."

"Come in, Melinda," Cornelius said, patting the seat beside him. "We won't hurt you."

Melinda took the offered seat, squeezing in uneasily between Kirsten and Cornelius. "Valdemar?" she asked again.

"He's on his way," Adrian said impatiently. "What's the matter? You're not afraid of us, are you?" Melinda glared at him in reply. "Moira," he called out. "You're neglecting your duties as hostess. Get the girl some wine."

Moira snarled at him and retreated to the tiny alcove that housed the kitchen. She returned with a black goblet filled with crimson wine.

Melinda took the glass reluctantly. Nervously, she sipped at it, hoping with all her heart that Valdemar wouldn't be long.

Cornelius, Moira and Adrian were having a stomach-turning conversation that revolved around recent kills and elaborate hunting schemes. Taking pity on her, Kirsten attempted to draw her out with banal talk.

She realized with sudden terror, that the wine was indeed going to her head. It was getting very warm in the room. She was having trouble concentrating on what Kirsten was saying. Tremors shuddered down her shoulders to her hands. The wine glass fell to the floor, shattering in a rain of black slivers.

Kirsten grabbed her by the arms. "Melinda," she called urgently. Melinda tried to answer her, but her tongue was a lead weight in her mouth. Her head lolled loosely backward against the arm of the divan. The blonde vampire looked to Moira. "You drugged Melinda's drink! How could you?"

"We thought we'd spice her up a little for Val," Moira said with a nasty snicker.

"Valdemar is not likely to be amused," Kirsten warned her.

Melinda groaned, trying to rouse herself. Adrian stood over her, lifting a limp arm and letting it fall like a dead weight back to her lap. "What a cheap drunk," he said in disgust. "Val has the oddest ways of getting his kicks."

Kirsten smacked him in reply. "Ouch," he said playfully.

"You could at least put her to bed," Kirsten said.

"You're getting as boring as Valdemar." Adrian stooped and flung Melinda over one shoulder. He walked to the shadowed corner of the room and deposited her, none too gently, on the futon there. Melinda collapsed into the soft darkness behind black draperies.

Sounds and sensations took on a surreal aspect. The nearby voices seemed to distort and bounce against the walls of the room, each syllable echoing and running into the next until the words ceased to make sense. Panicked, she attempted to call out to Kirsten to ask her to explain what was happening to her, but her vocal chords seemed anesthetized.

There was a light tap on the apartment door, followed by the sounds of someone moving to answer it.

"Valdemar!" she heard Moira say. Melinda let herself sink deeper into the softness of the futon, relieved that Valdemar had arrived. Her heavy eyelids threatened to close, but she managed to force them open long enough to peer through the black gauze at the scene unfolding.

What is so urgent that you had to bring me all the way across town tonight?" Valdemar asked impatiently.

"We miss you," Moira said, nuzzling against his ear. "We were feeling sorry for all the trouble we've caused you. We wanted to make it up to you."

"I very much doubt that," Valdemar said, ignoring her advances. The floor creaked as he crossed the loft and seated himself on the leather couch. "So tell me, what is it really? Perhaps you want to play with me some more? I seem to be your current source of entertainment."

"Surely there is more to interest us than your domestic problems," Adrian interjected.

"I would hope so," Valdemar agreed. "I might remind you that my current problems are your doing."

"Hardly," Adrian retorted. "You got yourself into this one."

They were talking about her, Melinda thought dully, but her drunken mind refused to concentrate on this puzzling information. She heard the clink of glasses and the rush of liquid as Moira poured Valdemar some wine.

"Oh lighten up, Val," Cornelius said, jumping into the argument. "You like her, don't you?"

"Yes," Valdemar admitted. "I like her."

"Are you in love with her?" Moira asked. A simple question, yet there was something evil in her tone.

Valdemar sipped his wine slowly, leaving them in expectant silence. "None of your business," he answered at last.

"Speaking of Melinda," Kirsten said. "Shouldn't we--"

"Hush!" Moira hissed, cutting her off. "Haven't you meddled in Valdemar's life enough for one eternity?"

Kirsten bit off a curt reply.

Valdemar was about to come to Kirsten's rescue when he stopped mid-swallow. "You spiked my wine!" He sniffed at it. "*Tetrodotoxin*! How amusing Moira, dosing my wine with a substance for enslaving the living dead."

"Oh, but it's so fitting," Moira said. "You've been so boring lately, we wanted to make sure you were still alive."

"You'll regret that in a few hours when I'm ravenous and bad tempered from the headache I'm going to have." He looked at Cornelius angrily. "I can't believe you went along with this!"

Cornelius shrugged. "Since when does Moira confide in me?"

"I'll make sure you don't go hungry," Moira told Valdemar, offering herself to him seductively.

"I'd rather starve." Valdemar thrust her away from him. "The price of your affections are too high for me." He rubbed his temples. "How much did you give me anyway?"

"Oh just a little," Moira said, a laugh betraying the lie.

"Just a little," Valdemar echoed. He sat forward to as if stand up, then collapsed back into the sofa. His limbs refused to do his bidding. He made another abortive attempt to gain his feet, then gave up. Kirsten moved to take the wine glass from him before it fell from his hand.

Cornelius glanced down at him, slumped on the couch. "You're drunk, Val."

"Yes," Valdemar said. "That was what you all wanted, wasn't it?"

"We just want you to have a good time," Adrian said. "You've been so burdened with responsibility lately. We felt bad for you."

"Sure," Valdemar said tiredly. "Why don't you just tell me what evil surprise you have waiting for me this time, while I still have some of my wits about me?"

"Relax, will you," Adrian said with a snicker. "More wine?"

"No thanks, I've had more than enough."

There was some vital clue to Valdemar's strange behavior in their twisting, sarcastic conversation. What had they forced him into? Why did the fact that Valdemar had taken a new lover amuse them so? Melinda struggled for enough awareness to process the information, but organized thought was beyond her capacity.

"Enough of this. I'm leaving," Valdemar said.

"What's the matter?" Moira asked. "Hungry?"

"Don't be stupid," Cornelius said watching Valdemar's pitiful attempts to rise from the couch. "You can't wander around like that, you can't even stand. Remember what happened last time...." He pushed him back into the sofa.

"I have to get out of here, Neil," Valdemar said desperately. He ran a hand over his face, looking at it in surprise when it came away drenched with sweat. "I have to hunt," he said in a near whisper. "Now, while I still know what I'm doing!"

"I can't believe you're enjoying this," Kirsten snarled at Moira.

"If you feel so bad for him," Moira countered savagely, "why don't you offer yourself as the sacrificial lamb?"

"Moira," Cornelius snarled. "Leave Kirsten out of this."

"I don't know why you're all so upset," Adrian said. "He's going to get one hell of a kick out of it in the end. Feeding when you're on Zombie Punch is such an intense experience."

"You didn't have to give him so much," Kirsten chided them. "Look at him!"

"You better lie down for a while," Cornelius said.

"No," Valdemar gasped. "Get me out of here!"

"And what am I supposed to do with you?" Cornelius asked.

"I can think of a few things," Moira said, moving toward the couch in a swish of black gauze.

"Leave me alone," Valdemar warned her as she leaned suggestively over him as he lay in a heap on the sofa. Teasingly, she undid the top buttons of his shirt.

"You're so hot," she said soothingly.

"Moira, I'm warning you," Valdemar gasped, as she undid the last buttons of his shirt and slid her hands across his chest.

Valdemar made another attempt to rise, Moira shoved him roughly backward. "Will you stay still? I'm just trying to make you more comfortable." Valdemar was quiet. He shut his eyes. "That's better," Moira whispered. "Don't fight it, Valdemar, it's going to feel so good," she told him, bending her head toward his neck, covering him in a blaze of her crimson hair.

Her teeth locked on his throat. Valdemar's eyes flew open. "Moira!" he roared.

"Hah," Adrian laughed. "She got him. She's been waiting hundreds of years to do that!"

"Let him go, Moira," Cornelius said, trying to restore some semblance of order.

Of that, Moira had no intention. She continued to drink, wrenching moans of agony from Valdemar.

Melinda lay in the shadows, her mind aware yet her body sluggish from the effects of the drug. This was certainly not the friendly get together Valdemar had been expecting. She couldn't count on Valdemar to help her, she realized with dread. He didn't even know she was there.

Valdemar was still wrestling with Moira on the divan. The unexpected pain seemed to rouse him out of his stupor as he thrashed about trying to pry her from his throat. His hands found her shoulders, locking onto them with a grip that doubtlessly hurt her. Moira hung on, clinging to his neck with her chisel-like teeth. Eventually his superior body strength won over and he heaved her backward, jumping to his feet as she fell away from him. Moira stumbled backward into Adrian's arms as he moved to catch her. Valdemar's blood dripped down her chin and a shred of his flesh clung to her lower lip.

Valdemar advanced on her murderously. Blood poured from the savage wound on his neck, streaming across his shoulders and down his chest.

"That was a stupid mistake! All you've done is make me ravenous! Are you going to offer me your neck in return?" he demanded with a deadly glare. "I swear, I'll suck you dry!"

"No need to get nasty, Valdemar," Adrian said.

Valdemar stepped up to him with a snarl. "I won't forget this," he told Adrian menacingly. "I'm leaving, and if I don't see the lot of you for several hundred years, that will be too soon for me!"

"Val," Cornelius said trying to be diplomatic. He made as if to place his hand on Valdemar's shoulder, then thought better of it. "You can't go out looking like that. Lie down, please. I'll keep them in line."

Valdemar looked as if he might faint. Cornelius slipped a supporting shoulder under his arm and drew him in the direction of the shrouded futon.

"No!" Kirsten shrieked suddenly. "Keep him away from Melinda!"

"Melinda?" Valdemar asked with quiet menace. He grabbed Cornelius by the shirt, leaving a bloody hand print. "What have they done to Melinda?"

Cornelius swallowed nervously. "She had a little of Moira's wine. I'm sorry, Val. I didn't know it was spiked."

Valdemar pushed Cornelius roughly away from him and staggered toward the black curtain. A thin sliver of light cut across Melinda's face as he drew back the drapery. She looked up at him all but bathed in his own blood, and an insane hunger burning in his eyes. He took a step toward her.

Her scream shattered the silent air.

CHAPTER TEN

"Melinda," Valdemar said with an anguished groan. He knelt beside her in the shadows.

Melinda blinked in the sudden glare of light. She was sobering up a little, rising out of the paralysis and delirium. She looked at Valdemar's wounds that were still dripping blood and edged away from him.

"Listen to me, Melinda," Valdemar said. "You have to get away from me. I'm not myself right now."

Melinda tore her gaze from the blood on his chest, looking past him to the others who watched like spectators at a sporting event. He was hurting, she could see the pain in his eyes.

With a sob, she hurled herself into his arms and clung to him, anxious to hold on to the only sane thing in this ludicrous situation.

"No Melinda," Valdemar said urgently. "Don't touch me, please...."

But she was sobbing violently into his shoulder, her tears mingling with the blood on his chest.

"Shh." His arms closed about her back, claws curled outward so he wouldn't harm her.

Valdemar glared at Moira. "This is unfair." His voice was like the arctic wind. "Toying with me is one thing. Hurting Melinda is quite another. She doesn't know what she's getting into."

"Don't you think it's about time she learned?"

"She could have waited longer to learn *this*," he said the last word with a snarl.

"But she'll enjoy it," Moira protested. "Just a little Zombie Punch to enhance the experience. You always liked it that way."

"She isn't enjoying this," Valdemar snarled. "And neither am I."

"Come on Val," Adrian jeered. "Be a sport, bite her. We know you want to," he added.

Melinda stirred in his arms. The room was swaying precariously to and fro each time she tried to open her eyes. The voices seemed to come from far away, as if her body were in the next apartment. She could feel Valdemar's arms about her, the acrid smell of his blood. She was hungry, she realized suddenly, ravenous.

Reality was leaking into her drunken brain. The scenario was beginning to make sense. Valdemar was drunk, like the rest of them. And, if she was ravenous, he must be nearly insane with hunger. He had been about to escape into the night, to ravage whatever helpless souls awaited him in his subterranean hunting ground. Unexpectedly, he'd been forced to restrain himself. This he did with great difficulty. It was evident from the hard set of his mouth that he was using every ounce of his energy to keep himself in check.

"It must grate on your nerves, controlling yourself like this all the time, always being kind, gentle." Adrian said with malice. "Come on Valdemar," he chided. "What you really want to do is rip her throat out. Why don't you? She'll live."

Valdemar shut his eyes, his breathing thick and heavy. His hands clenched on Melinda's back, claws cutting into her flesh through her sweatshirt. She could sense the hunger in him.

Valdemar groaned and bent his head so his lips were against her ear. "Melinda," he asked gently. "Do you want me to?"

Surely she could spare a bit of blood, she thought. Couldn't she? A sip or two to help Valdemar regain control of himself long enough to get her out of there.

He was seconds away from losing it completely. She could feel the tension in every inch of body where it pressed against her. And if Valdemar lost it, she was doomed. "Do it, she whispered.

"Yeah Val," Adrian said, mimicking her. "Do it."

Valdemar glanced down at the sweatshirt that had absorbed most of the blood from his chest. His hands strayed to the collar, ripping it gently, enough to expose her shoulders.

He pulled her more closely against him. She could feel the soft hairs of his chest against her bare skin. He was tense, every muscle poised for the ecstasy that was coming and for the tenuous control he could not lose.

"I have been a fool," he whispered to her alone. "Making you promises I can't keep."

His lips brushed her skin, lightly, on the tip of her shoulder, then closer, closer to the jugular vein. Each kiss became more indicative of what was to come. His arms tightened around hers for both their protection. Then he slid his teeth into her neck.

At first she felt only the pleasure of his lips at her neck. Then the pressure of his mouth changed, and he began to drink in deep gasps. Each draught was a pleasure that bordered on pain, every nerve was heightened from the effects of the Tetrodotoxin. He was taking too much, she thought dimly. Too much, too fast. A wall of blackness encroached on her, threatening to drag her under.

Panicked, she cried out.

Valdemar froze, his teeth still lodged in her neck like barbed spikes. He swallowed and she felt that tiny movement along her entire spine.

Then he came to his senses. His lips loosened on her neck and he withdrew his teeth. Moira and Adrian glared at him, obviously disappointed at his diffusion of their prank.

"I pity you when she comes out of it," Cornelius cautioned. "She's going to be very hungry and more than a little hung over."

"We'd better take her with us to hunt," Kirsten suggested.

"Melinda," Valdemar said, "is going to bed."

"You can't put her to bed like that," Cornelius said. "She needs blood. In a few hours she'll be going out of her mind from hunger."

"What are you going to do when you wake up at noon with her teeth in your neck? Or perhaps you like it that way," Adrian remarked.

"Bring her with us," Moira said sweetly. "We've had our fun, we'll behave now, we promise."

Valdemar threw them a caustic look. But then his expression changed and he seemed to be considering it. "I'm hardly in any condition to take her alone...."

The world was settling, drawing her back to earth. The feeling of lightness was deteriorating into a mind-rending headache, accompanied by an all consuming hunger. No mortal hangover had ever felt like this.

Valdemar drew her into the light of the living room and sat her on the sofa. He smoothed the hair back from her face, holding her head in his hands.

"Are you all right?" he asked.

"Hungry," she told him.

"I know," he said. He looked down at the sweatshirt that was torn and hopelessly smeared with his blood. He removed the tattered garment and retrieved his own shirt from where Moira had let it drop on the floor, clothing her in it, much as one would dress a child.

"We're going to hunt," he told her. "You'll have to come with us, I can't leave you like this." He wandered into Moira's kitchen, returning with a damp towel. Melinda gasped as he wiped the blood from his neck and chest. All that remained of the wounds that would have been deadly to a mortal were faint pink marks. Valdemar straightened and donned his leather jacket. "All right," he said tersely. "Let's go."

Dumbly, she let them lead her back down the stairs to the deadly-looking Cadillac waiting at the curb outside. That model of caddy hadn't been produced for over thirty years. Evidence of many collisions could be seen in the haphazardly patched, matte-black paint job. It was devoid of hub caps and chrome. The seats inside were made of worn, black leather.

Adrian swung naturally behind the wheel as Moira and Cornelius climbed in the front seat beside him. Melinda let Kirsten and Valdemar load her into the back between them. She let her head fall against Valdemar's shoulder, conscious only of the pain that stabbed through her temples and the dull hunger in her gut.

"This is some invention, huh Valdemar," Adrian said, turning the key in the ignition. "If only we'd had these in the old days. Think of the fun we could have had!"

Valdemar scowled at his reflection in the rear-view mirror. "As I recall, you managed to cause enough trouble on foot."

As if in emphasis, the automobile sprang to life with a roar of screeching tires and burning rubber. Melinda was thrust forward, then jerked as roughly backwards with its momentum. Moira laughed as Adrian jammed his foot to the floor, swerving madly about the few cars on the road ahead of them to a chorus of angrily honking horns.

"Must you do that?" Valdemar demanded. "My nerves have had enough wear for one evening."

Adrian glanced at him in the mirror but ignored him. He was tearing down the quiet streets, slicing across the southwestern part of the city in a cloud of burning motor oil.

It was just past midnight when they hit the highway. Despite the late hour the freeway was still busy. To the whine of the laboring engine, they soared from the on-ramp, barreling down the center lane at speeds that long exceeded what the speedometer could register.

Melinda looked at Adrian's reflection in the rear view mirror. His green eyes blazed with excitement, and the wind from the open window beside him tore at his blond hair, whipping it back in a golden mane behind him. Secure in the knowledge that he was immortal, that nothing as banal as a car accident could kill him, he drove with reckless abandon and total disregard for the mortal lives around him.

"Make him stop this," she implored Valdemar. She was dizzy and the shifting momentum of the car was making her nauseated. It was like standing in the center of a hurricane, she decided, with the wind roaring all around her and the vehicle plunging toward certain disaster.

"If you're trying to impress us, it isn't working, Adrian," Kirsten told him. "Anyone can be a ghoul."

"A ghoul!" Adrian laughed maniacally. "I like the sound of that." Moira echoed his insane laughter. "Is this ghoulish enough for you, Kirsten?" he asked, and with a quick and violent twist of his arm, sent the car skidding into the next lane.

They hit the guard rail in a rain of sparks and the sound of scraping metal. The cars around them scattered, desperately swerving into other lanes and other cars to evade them. Adrian slammed into an old, green Pontiac, locking bumpers. Mercilessly, he dragged the vehicle with them as they flew down the highway, swerving from side to side in an attempt to ditch the freeloader. Finally the Pontiac broke free, spinning into concrete guardrail and erupting in a huge geyser of flame.

The highway became a nightmare of black pavement, the smell of gasoline, the orange streetlights that flickered sickeningly overhead. Melinda was past feeling afraid for herself. The night's events sent a stab of dread straight to her soul. How could she count herself among these creatures who killed wantonly and then fed from one another like savage beasts?

"That was a useless display," Valdemar remarked. Melinda slid a sideways glance at him, afraid to look him full in the face. He had that look of death to him, that she had seen only once, on the night they'd met. "Are you so bored, Adrian, that you have to kill needlessly to amuse yourself?"

"Welcome to the modern world, Valdemar," Adrian hollered back. "From what I can see, it's all about power, greed, and self-indulgence. I'm going to be part of it. I'm going to have my own piece of the action. I'm sick of hiding out, on the fringe of civilization, in some dark sewer like you!"

"The world was always full of those things," Valdemar snarled. "You understand nothing!"

That brought a sudden smile to Adrian's face. "No Val. It's you who misunderstand. And now that I know that, I won't be bothered with your stupid opinions anymore." He glanced at the road in front of him. "Oh dear," he said suddenly. "We're going the wrong way!"

They reached a section of road where the highway widened drawing the collector lanes into its core. Adrian leaned on the steering wheel, arcing the car about face. A wall of headlights roared towards them, lighting up the inside of the car.

Adrian plunged into the oncoming traffic. They shot down the center lane, tearing between two eighteen-wheel trucks. Metal grated on metal as they scraped their way through. One of the trucks veered sharply away in an attempt to escape them. The momentum sent it skidding out of control. Melinda screamed as the truck teetered precariously, then fell to its side, sliding along the roadway like a huge wounded animal.

Cars scattered on all sides of them, their headlights flickering randomly like fireflies. Cornelius was yelling at Adrian, something Melinda couldn't hear over the roar of the motor and the rush of the wind.

Melinda pressed her head into Valdemar's shoulder, shielding herself from the inevitable impact.

Then there was silence. Moira laughed. Kirsten screamed. Melinda raised her head, casting a furtive glance through the windshield at a Gray Coach bus careering toward them.

"No!" Cornelius hollered. He lurched across Moira and wrenched the wheel from Adrian's hands. The steering wheel snapped under their powerful tug of war, sending the car spiraling across the highway under the wheels of the approaching Gray Coach.

Melinda felt the bone-breaking impact as the car was tossed violently in the other direction. They spilled across the highway, knocking out a streetlight that crashed to the pavement in a shower of orange. They hit something, another car perhaps. She heard the sound of metal tearing, the crash of glass shattering and a last dull crunch as they hit the guardrail. Then the world turned on its side as they slid along the pavement before finally coming to rest.

* * * *

Melinda opened her eyes, tasting blood where her teeth had cut through her lip. Valdemar lay on the bottom of the heap where she and Kirsten had fallen on top of him. There was blood on his face from the shattered glass. Kirsten moaned and tried to pick herself up. Her pale face was marbled with blue and purple bruises that were already starting to fade.

Moira and Adrian had fared the best. They climbed over Cornelius and out through the car window, like teenagers exiting from a scary roller coaster ride.

Strong hands thrust her upwards, out into the night air to be handed into another pair of hands that steadied her on her feet. She looked up at Cornelius. He looked at her then looked away. Valdemar was standing beside her dusting himself off. His face was unreadable.

Melinda ran her hands down her bruised and battered body, astounded that she was still in one piece. She looked backward, down the road the way they had come.

The highway was littered with demolished vehicles. In the distance she could see the eighteen wheeler lying forlornly on its side. Strewn between the truck and the fallen Gray Coach were at least ten cars. Most of them weren't recognizable as automobiles any longer and one was on fire.

Melinda followed the skid marks that crisscrossed the highway, mapping out the bus' path. She could see the evidence of their collision, a pile of metal and glass scattered on the road. The Gray Coach had tried to evade them in that last split second, careening off into the center median and plowing up a row of cars in its wake.

Strewn across the highway were the remains of the passengers, some still whole and thrashing about mournfully in the last moments of their lives. Moira and Adrian fell upon them with the enthusiasm of children in a candy store.

Kirsten was praying, a pale wraith kneeling in the roadway. Cornelius looked at Valdemar. "This is getting out of hand."

"This time they've gone too far," Valdemar agreed.

"I think they might actually be insane. Val, you have to stop them."

"How?" Valdemar asked him. "Trying to control them is like trying to tame the wind."

"Reason with them," Kirsten pleaded, rejoining them. "They always listened to you."

"Yes, you're the oldest," Cornelius agreed.

"They don't listen to me anymore," Valdemar said, "and they certainly aren't interested in doing things my way. I think this brutal display was meant to illustrate that point."

"Are you just going to stand here?" Melinda demanded, wrenching her eyes from the carnage that lay across the road. "There are people dying out there!"

"Yes," Valdemar said. "I know."

Cornelius uttered a sigh of resignation. "No sense in wasting fresh blood." He turned and walked off in the direction of the wounded passengers.

"You disgust me," Melinda told him, despite the mortifying realization that the thought of all that fresh blood excited her.

"Do I?" Cornelius said turning back. "They're going to die anyway. If I don't feed from them, I'll just have to kill someone else."

"Don't do it," Valdemar advised him. "That's what they want you to do. They mean to force us all into doing it their way."

"And what difference does it make anyway?" Cornelius said. "I'm hungry, I'm tired, and somebody has to die tonight to satisfy my thirst. This is as good a solution as any. I don't know what's

going on among the lot of you, but I'm not going to be a part of it."
He opened his mouth to say something further, then shut up
abruptly and walked away.

"Cornelius!" Kirsten yelled angrily and pursued him.

Melinda looked at Valdemar under the lamp light. He had that
murderous look he could get when provoked or intent on his prey.
He was a ruthless killer despite the passion they'd shared, no
matter how he clothed himself, no matter how fine his manners.
He had dragged her unwillingly into this life with him. And now,
he wanted her to love him for it.

"You make me sick," she told him. "I can't believe you call these
people your friends."

"Melinda please--" he begged.

"Or are you really just like them?" she asked cruelly. "Is this
what you do on the nights I don't go with you?"

"No," he said, "of course not."

"Really?" she asked. "Then why did Moira ask you to come kill
with them *just like old times* Valdemar? Is this what Adrian meant
by *your style*?"

"No!" Valdemar insisted. "They've never done anything like this
before. And, I have never done anything like this, ever."

"I don't believe you," Melinda snapped.

"I'm telling you the truth."

"You don't know what truth means," she snarled. "What have
you been trying to do? Convince me you were nice? You aren't
nice Valdemar. You're a cruel and vicious killer, and you have
been for eleven hundred years. Thanks to you, I get to share the
same curse!" She stepped up to him, letting the sum of her rage
spill over into her face. "But I have one thing you don't Valdemar.
I have respect for the life around me. I have some self-control."

She turned on her heel and strode away from him across the
blood streaked tarmac. The smell of blood hung in the air like a
heavy fog. Tenaciously, it seduced her, whispering loving
endearments to her blood-starved body. It called to her like a
lover, reminding her of the sweet ecstasy of drinking another's
lifeblood, the powerful sensation of fulfillment and the compelling
pleasure pure as fire.

Her body was weakening from loss of the blood Valdemar had
taken from her. She cursed him silently, forcing herself to do what
would ease her soul rather than her body.

Someone cried out in the darkness, drawing her eyes to the dark
lump in the road beyond her. Arms and legs stretched out from it

at improbable angles. A pool of blood oozed from the broken body. Melinda crouched beside it, gingerly lifting the injured head into her lap. The features were barely recognizable, from the cuts and bruises and the shattered skull, but she guessed it was a woman. Her eyes opened, glazed and unfocussed in her pain.

"It's all right," Melinda assured her, brushing the hair that was thick with blood from her face. "You're going to be all right."

There was blood leaking between her fingers onto Valdemar's shirt and down onto her blue jeans. She was nearly drenched in it. It was an agony she could hardly bear. Every vein cried out in longing for the sustaining blood that lay in such huge quantities all around her. But she couldn't give into that carnal craving. To satisfy her hunger would make her just like the rest of them.

Cars were stopping now, and a crowd was beginning to gather. Someone had gone to call an ambulance. Melinda was alone with her self-loathing and the insatiable hunger that tore at her body.

A hand touched her shoulder, compassionately.

"Leave me alone, Valdemar," she said without turning.

He squatted beside her, looking over her shoulder at the dying woman. When he raised his eyes to hers, they were pools of softness and darkness. "Melinda," he said softly. "I am not the monster you imagine me to be."

"Aren't you?" she asked him. "Tonight you've proved to me that you're more of a monster than even I imagined."

A thin peal of laughter drew her eyes upward to the scene beyond her.

"Well, look here," said Moira, appearing out of the shadows behind the fallen Gray Coach. A telltale smear of blood marked her chin. "Our Melinda's a little Florence Nightingale."

Adrian looked at the disfigured soul in her lap. "She's dying, anyway," he said with a dismissive glance. "You might as well drink. Once she's dead the blood will be cold."

"No," Melinda said in a harsh whisper. "She deserves the last seconds of her life. This is one life you aren't going to steal, Adrian. I won't let you."

"You're only prolonging her suffering," Cornelius said, coming up behind them. "Where is the mercy, the compassion in that?" He looked down at the woman she still held in her lap. Kirsten was crossing herself, praying again, quietly. "She's going to die, Melinda. There's nothing they can do to save her now. The kindest thing you could do for her is to ease her passing. Help her," he urged her. "Drink."

"I can't," she told him, even though she was trembling uncontrollably with hunger. "I won't."

"This is stupid," Adrian said in disgust. "Look at you. You can barely control yourself now. What are you going to do in a few hours when you're truly out of your mind with hunger? Murder the first person who passes you in the street?"

"Adrian," Valdemar said sharply. "I would really advise you to make yourself absent."

"What's the matter Valdemar," he asked with dripping sarcasm. "Are you about to become a vegetarian too?"

Valdemar stood up, advancing on him, lips curled back in a menacing snarl. Melinda saw the flash of his claws under the lamplight as he snatched at Adrian's shirt, yanking him close to his face. "I have had more than enough of your company," he hissed. "Forever!"

Moira made as if to strike him, but Valdemar's other arm shot out, catching her viciously by the wrist. She gasped in sudden pain.

A quiet sigh drew Melinda's eyes to the dying woman she still cradled in her arms. She felt the last of her life flow from the broken body. Gently, she lowered the still form to the pavement.

"It doesn't matter anyway." Her words sliced through their argument as they turned to look at her. "She's dead. If you could die, you might understand the significance of that. But you don't, and I am sick to death of all of you."

"Melinda!" Valdemar yelled, releasing Adrian and Moira abruptly and chasing after her as she ran off into the night.

A siren sliced through the hushed whispers of the thickening crowd. The others fled, fading into the shadows. Melinda could hear Valdemar's footsteps on the pavement behind her as he pursued her.

She stopped suddenly, whirling to face him.

Surprised, he stumbled forward, almost crashing into her. "Melinda, you don't understand. Let me explain. There are many things I have to tell you."

"Save your explanations for your next victim, Valdemar," she said in a voice that was as cold as the ice in her soul. "I never want to see you again."

CHAPTER ELEVEN

Melinda stepped into the pool of moonlight that streamed down through the window above the door. She pulled the door softly closed behind her. She stood motionless for several seconds in the quiet house, breathing in the familiar scents of her childhood.

Everything was as she remembered it. The sofa against the long wall in the living room with the picture of the sea above it, the old recliner her father was so fond of.

There was new wallpaper on the living room wall. Melinda chuckled to herself. It was typically her mother's taste, a large floral pattern in soothing blues and greens. It didn't match the sofa, she thought absently, but then, neither had its predecessor.

The television was new. So they'd finally replaced the old black and white set. Her parents must have set a record for being the last people in the civilized world to acquire color television.

Melinda sat on the couch, feeling the lumpy old thing give beneath her. It seemed such a normal thing to do in this house she'd grown up in. It had taken over a year for her to work up the strength and the courage to come here, to face the person she had been and put her finally to rest.

But, she had to look, she had to know that those she loved were safe and happy without her.

From the wall above the television, her graduation photo looked back at her. A happy, overweight twenty-one year old in maroon robes, clutching her degree in communications. She bore little resemblance to that person now. It was hard, even in such a short time, to remember how it felt.

Melinda leaned back against the old sofa, resting her feet on the coffee table. These comforts of home were alien to her now. Her new life was barren of such niceties. Vampires needed few possessions. The things she had coveted so dearly before meant little to her now.

She thought back to the night she'd left Valdemar, soaked in the blood of Moira and Adrian's victims, lost, homeless, blood-starved and afraid. Melinda smiled, letting her chiseled eye teeth rest on her bottom lip. There were few things that frightened her now.

Valdemar had done a good job of cleaning up her apartment. She sold off the contents, then wrote a hasty note to her parents, explaining that she needed to get away for awhile. At the bank machine on the corner, she'd emptied her savings account. That little amount of money had given her the first foothold on her new life.

She worked the night shift, drifting from job to job. She waitressed, bartended, did whatever was convenient. She collected tips and money from the pockets of those who harassed her. Every so often, she wrote short letters to her parents, telling them she was okay, but never leaving a return address.

Her first inclination in those first few horrid days without Valdemar had been to leave town. She was terrified of running into Moira and Adrian. She was afraid Valdemar might come hunting for her again. She longed to move far away, west perhaps, somewhere like Vancouver. Yet she stayed, anchored to the city she'd grown up in, shut out of the only life she knew.

She had her tiny room in the York Hotel, above the bar she often worked at. She had no need for food, nor fancy clothes. She had her routines, her favorite hunting grounds. Her victims were those who would have gladly slit her throat, as Valdemar's had been. She was, as he predicted, a vampire, and could barely remember being anything else.

And yet, here she was in this place so homey, so human. It was safe to be here now. She was fed and well used to the signs of the inevitable hunger. Upstairs she could hear the familiar sounds of her father snoring. She rose and put one foot on the staircase.

Melinda leaned against the bedroom doorway. Her parents were deeply asleep, snuggled against each other. She drew silently closer to the bed, watching them as they slept, wishing for all the world she could wake them, tell them she was all right and not to worry.

They were grayer and frailer than she remembered. "This is my fault," she told herself reproachfully, then added a resolute "No." It was Valdemar's fault, all of it.

There was another picture of her on the bureau against the far wall. It had been taken at a family barbecue. She was surrounded by her cousins and her aunts and uncles. There was mustard on her face from the hot dog she had been eating. And, she was laughing, good, human laughter. She gazed at the photo wistfully, remembering the day, the warmth of the sun, the smell of the grass.

Suddenly, she had an overwhelming desire to be gone from the place, to distance herself from the things that were lost to her. She turned back to her sleeping parents.

"I love you both," she whispered to the quiet air, and was gone.

Once out on the street, the night was hers.

CHAPTER TWELVE

A haze of smoke drifted across the dance floor. They had turned off the house music, the main act was about to take the stage.

Patrons were lined up three deep at the bar. Melinda was hard pressed to keep their orders straight as she stacked the bottles on the bar and twisted off their lids with a quick flick of her wrist. Two beers, a vodka and orange for the bleached blonde teen with the borrowed I.D.

The waitresses were already short-tempered, harassed by the crowds that sat ten or twelve to the tiny tables around the perimeter. They barked their orders at Melinda, who slid the bottles back down the long bar for them to stack on their round trays.

The lead singer stepped up to the mike. There was a moment of expectant silence, a round of appreciative whistles from the men in the audience, then a round of applause.

A haunting guitar melody drifted across the smoky air, followed by a gentle bass line and a light hiss from the cymbals. The lead singer started to sing.

Melinda froze, setting the bottle of whiskey down on the bar before it fell from her hands.

It was a voice as smooth as polished silver. Crystal notes hung like raindrops in the air, then fell gently to earth. That incredible voice raced to the highest notes of the scale, then plunged downward, dragging her soul with it. It was impossible to listen with anything but her complete attention.

Melinda knew that voice.

Her eyes tore her head upward, past the faces turned in rapt attention to the stage, to the pale goddess who stood in a shroud of golden hair under the amber lights.

Kirsten!

Melinda wrenched her eyes from the stage back to the waiter standing impatiently in front of her, but it was too late. Kirsten had seen her. She held Melinda in her gray stare for a fraction of a second, then smiled briefly and returned her attention to the rapt audience before her.

Melinda turned her back to the stage, concentrating on the liquor

order she was assembling from the brightly colored bottles behind
the bar. She was trapped there. It was far too busy for her to leave,
and she needed the money to pay the rent. She refused to hunt for
money alone.

But that amazing voice seduced her gaze back to the stage.
Kirsten was incredible. Not only was her voice beautiful beyond
the realms of human vocal chords, Kirsten was the consummate
performer. Playfully she teased the men, flowing down from the
stage in a flash of silver and walking among them as far as the
microphone cable would let her. She sang as if she spoke to them
alone, then turned and sang to their girlfriends like they were best
friends. It was impossible to watch Kirsten and not love her.

The other band members, three males, were like shadowy
wraiths in the background. They were accomplished musicians.
Human, Melinda realized with a start. Regardless of their
considerable talent, Kirsten overshadowed them.

It was torture to stay there calmly behind the bar, barricaded by
the press of bodies about her. Melinda put her mind to her orders.
She sighed in tremendous relief when the last notes faded into
silence.

There was a hush, then someone turned on the blasting rock
music, and the waiters hustled to get the orders for last call. The
band had disappeared into the cramped change rooms backstage.
The house lights came on in a flash of stark glaring white. The
patrons were thinning, exiting into the night beyond.

Melinda stacked the empties in the cases under the bar and
wiped down the sticky counter.

A sparkle of silver hair caught her eyes. She looked up, into that
pale gray stare she could not deny.

"Hi stranger," Kirsten said lightly. She had changed from her
glittery stage clothes into a simple pair of jeans and a black T-shirt.
Her white-blonde hair tumbled loosely about her shoulders. She
attracted the admiring gaze of every male left in the club. All of
them longed to talk to her, ask her out, but there was something
unworldly about Kirsten's beauty that kept them from
approaching. She was intimidating.

"Hi," Melinda replied, setting down the rag and resting her
elbows on the bar.

"So?" asked Kirsten, "How are you?"

"Fine," Melinda told her, spreading her hands in an empty
gesture.

Kirsten looked around at the quiet bar. "You work here?"

"Sometimes," Melinda said. "You?"

"Sometimes," Kirsten said with a smile.

"I didn't know you could sing like that," Melinda said with honest admiration. "You were amazing."

Kirsten lowered her eyes modestly. There was an uncomfortable pause while each struggled for something to say.

"You know," Kirsten said at last, "I miss you, Melinda."

"Me too," Melinda admitted.

"Is there any reason we can't be friends again?"

"I don't know, Kirsten. Is there?"

Kirsten smiled warmly. "None I can think of. I am lonely for some female company. Things have been a little strange lately."

"Strange?"

Kirsten's eyes darted to the side, suspiciously eyeing the few remaining occupants. "Is there somewhere we can go? To talk?"

"Sure." Melinda said, out of curiosity more than good sense. She grabbed a bottle of wine and two glasses from the bar, dropping part of her tip into the till to pay for it. "I have a room upstairs."

She was suddenly ashamed to bring Kirsten into her dingy room, but Kirsten seemed to take little notice of her surroundings. She sat cross-legged on the bed, making even that simple movement seem infinitely graceful.

Melinda opened the wine and poured two glasses, coming to sit beside Kirsten on the bed with her back against the wall. She gazed out the window facing her, past the faded curtains at the yellow glow of the streetlights beyond.

"Nobody ever did tell me why we can drink wine and not eat food," she mused, raising her glass in a toast.

"We can digest liquids, juices, alcohol." Kirsten said. "But that won't sustain us. Its like water, almost."

"I miss food," Melinda said wistfully. "I miss pizza on Friday evenings, greasy french fries with gravy...."

It was obvious Kirsten had no idea what she was talking about. "We didn't have those kinds of food when I was young." She frowned at Melinda. "Oh come on Mel, ask me the obvious question."

"I can't," Melinda said woefully. "I don't want to know."

Kirsten smiled, looking all the more beautiful and deadly with her gleaming white pointed teeth. "Well, I'll answer it for you anyway, since you obviously *do* want to know ... He's fine."

Thoughts of Valdemar tumbled unbidden into Melinda's mind. She smothered the memory of his muscular body pressed against her, the touch of his lips against her neck. She swirled the wine absently in her wine glass. "Good," she said. "Now let's talk about something else." Her mind was racing, imploring her not to ask the question, not to get involved again. But the words were already on her lips. "What did you mean when you said things were strange?"

Kirsten looked out into the street at the steady flow of mortals hurrying uptown to their beds, their sleep. "Things haven't been the same since you left. Valdemar isn't talking to Moira or Adrian. He and Neil argue all the time." She looked at Melinda with pain filled eyes. "Cornelius and Valdemar have been friends for five hundred years. It's awful to watch. I suspect Moira and Adrian are up to something entirely evil, but if Val knows he won't talk about it, except to fight with Cornelius."

"Didn't you ask Neil?" Melinda asked in spite of herself.

"He won't tell me."

Her mind echoed another warning. She was getting too involved. She had been talking to Kirsten no more than ten minutes and here she was entrenched in Valdemar's life once again. "Kirsten I--"

"I know, I know," Kirsten said with a dismissive wave of her hand. "I don't want to involve you in this. I just need a friend to talk to."

"If you want to be my friend," Melinda told her coldly. "You won't tell me anything about them. I can't let myself get involved. I can't let myself care, especially about Valdemar and his bizarre problems." She was quiet a moment. "Does he know where I am?"

"I am certain he does," Kirsten said. "but he says nothing. I won't tell him, unless you want me to."

"No don't," Melinda said. "Don't tell him anything about me, not even that we spoke. Like you said, he probably knows it all anyway. But I want my own life, I want it back."

"I know what you're going through," Kirsten said sadly. "I've been through it all myself." She looked around her at the shabby surroundings. The tiny room was bare of even a picture on the wall. "Are you really all right, Melinda? Aren't you lonely?"

"Sometimes I'm so lonely I swear I'll die," Melinda told her honestly. "But I'm still here, aren't I?"

"I feel that way too sometimes," Kirsten admitted. "In spite of Neil and Val."

"Did you ever," Melinda began, "consider making someone for

yourself?"

"Melinda!" Kirsten gasped in horror. "Tell me you aren't thinking of that!"

"No," Melinda said. "Of course not. Not seriously."

"It wouldn't work," Kirsten told her. "It almost never does. Look what happened with Valdemar and I. How can you even think of it, the way you feel about Valdemar and what he did to you? She let the sentence trail off into silence.

"Loneliness drives you to think crazy thoughts," Melinda said.

"Yes," Kirsten agreed. "But forget that one. No one can know what it means to be a vampire, until they are one. Even if this person was in love with you, even if he gave his consent, he'd come to hate you eventually. Once they're looking down the long, black road to eternity everything changes. No mortal could ever understand that." She paused, catching her breath. "And it gets worse as you get older. You can't relate to a twenty year-old when you're two hundred."

"You and I get along fine," Melinda said.

"That's true. But I've walked in your shoes, as they say in this century."

Melinda didn't want to think in terms of centuries. Living through the last year had been hard enough.

" ... If you're really lonesome Melinda," Kirsten was saying, "I'll try to get Shadow for you."

"Is he all right?" Melinda asked anxiously, thinking of the kitten she had foolishly left in Valdemar's care.

Kirsten nodded. "It's not like Valdemar to keep a pet. Perhaps he just got used to having him around. Maybe he got used to a home without rats."

"No." Melinda looked around at the matchbox-sized room she called home. "Shadow would be miserable here...." She changed the subject. "Where did you learn to sing like that?"

"Oh, it's nothing," Kirsten said modestly. "I've been practicing for a hundred and eighty years."

Melinda laughed. "Practice must make perfect. You had the undivided attention of every man in the house. Even the women were in love with you."

"Vampires have to be charismatic," Kirsten told her soberly. "It's part of how we lure our prey."

"You could have marched them all out the door to their doom like the Pied Piper."

That made Kirsten giggle. She rose and poured herself more

wine. "What did you do, Melinda? I mean, before."

"I was a television producer." She sighed. At the time I thought it was what I wanted to do."

"I've always wondered what it would be like to have a career," Kirsten mused. "Why didn't you go back?"

"How in hell could I?" Melinda said, then looked quickly to the small, gold cross around Kirsten's neck.

"It's all right," Kirsten told her. "Hell is a perfectly good word. It's in the bible after all."

"My life has changed. *I've* changed. All I want to do right now is find a way to pay the rent." She shook her head. "I can't believe it. Here I am, a vampire, and I'm still worried about paying the rent."

"It's not wise to hold on too tightly to your old life," Kirsten advised. "It keeps you far too anchored in the past." She looked past Melinda to the peeling paint on the wall near the ceiling. From her expression Melinda judged that this was not casual advice, but spoken from her own experience. For a few moments the only sound in the room was the traffic from the street outside and the snatches of conversation that drifted up from the sidewalk.

Then Kirsten placed a long, thin hand on Melinda's arm. "I have to go. It's getting late and I have to...." There was a self-conscious pause, "hunt tonight." She rose and moved to the door, then turned back abruptly. "Please be careful Melinda. I don't know what Adrian and Moira are up to, but take care of yourself. Watch out for anything unusual."

"Unusual?" Melinda repeated. "Like massive car pile-ups on the 401?"

"That," Kirsten said soberly. "And much, much worse."

CHAPTER THIRTEEN

Kirsten's words continued to haunt Melinda over the next few months. She developed a perverse interest in news, reading all the daily papers and listening intently to the radio downstairs in the bar. She examined the details of each reported automobile accident, every murder, then admonished herself for her interest in their sordid affairs.

Strange things were happening in the world of humans. There was upheaval all over the world, the economy was slow and there were many more homeless people on the streets. All these things were explainable human events to do with sociology and economics. But, Melinda's feeling of foreboding, that all was not well in her city refused to go away.

She began to keep a file of unusual mishaps, notable automobile accidents, unsolved murders, and other suspicious events. Melinda poured over the clippings, looking for a clue, something to link them together, to identify them as the work of Moira and Adrian. But the linking clue evaded her. She needed another opinion. Finally, she phoned Kirsten.

"I thought you didn't want to get involved," Kirsten said, sounding weirdly normal talking on an everyday human device like the telephone.

"You were right," Melinda told her. "There is something going on. I have to talk to you."

"Why don't you come over tonight," Kirsten suggested. "Cornelius is going out. He'll be gone for hours."

* * * *

Kirsten and Cornelius lived in a Victorian townhouse. It had once been part of a long row of similar dwellings that had been demolished to make way for a shopping complex. The north wall of the house ended abruptly giving it an unfinished look as if someone had built half a house. It a was a tall, narrow building, connected inside with a maze of narrow, winding staircases.

At first glance their home looked to have been decorated in the retro-Victorian style that was popular. But, on closer examination the furnishings had a frayed look to them that could only have come from a century of everyday wear.

The ornamentation was stifling. Tiny rooms were crammed with furniture. Every surface bore some sort of lacy table cloth or doily. Stacks of books and collections of silver-framed photographs and paintings cluttered the mantle piece. Everything was embellished with its own bow or ribbon. Melinda had never seen so much flowered material in such a small space.

Kirsten seemed entirely at home among the flounces and lace. She was dressed in white this evening, a long, flowing lacy dress that appeared to come from the same era. She motioned Melinda to sit on the delicate chintz sofa.

Melinda's eyes were drawn to the gallery of photographs and miniature paintings arrayed on the table beside the couch. She smothered a gasp as her eyes settled on a tiny painting of Kirsten and Valdemar. Elaborately dressed in late eighteenth century attire, they posed serenely for the artist. It had the appearance of a formal portrait, one painted to mark an important event, such as a wedding. There were photographs too, from early in the twentieth century. Valdemar, Cornelius and Kirsten wearing a loose flapper chemise. Among these were photos of Moira and Adrian from happier times. They all looked exactly the same. There was nothing, no wrinkles, no gray hairs to mark the passage of time. Except for their vintage clothing, the photos could have been taken yesterday. Melinda forced herself to look away.

"Well?" she asked as Kirsten flipped through the newspaper clippings in the manila file folder she had brought with her. "It's them, isn't it?"

Kirsten was making three piles. "These," she pointed to the first pile, "are definitely them. Car accidents, murders, bodies with their throats slashed. They like that kind of thing." She looked at the second pile. "Airplanes crashing, bombs in washrooms--" she paused, "no, I don't think so. There'd be nothing to gain from a charred airplane wreck, no feast at the end, no reward. Moira and Adrian like rewards."

"What about those?" Melinda indicated the last pile of clippings.

"These," Kirsten said, "maybe...."

Melinda could feel the cold fingers of dread creeping down her spine. The pile of clippings was full of gruesome reports. Some were of murders in which the cadavers had been horribly mutilated, others told of strange mishaps that killed large numbers of people on the freeways and on public transit. "If that's the case, they're getting much more obvious. Next they'll be depositing bodies with teeth marks in the neck on the doorstep of police headquarters."

"They mean to force Valdemar into making a stand against them. They're taunting him."

"Why would they want to do that?" Melinda asked, despite her mind's rational objections that she didn't want to know.

"Because he used to be the leader of our little group ... but, that's all changed now and they want to drive that point home."

"What changed it?"

"Oh!" Kirsten said, wringing her hands. "That's the worst part. I think it was me."

"You?"

"Yes, me." Kirsten was quiet for a very long moment. Melinda watched the play of emotions across her face, as if she was debating whether she could trust Melinda with the tale. "It's like this Mel," she said finally with a heavy sigh. "From what I can tell Valdemar, Cornelius, Moira and Adrian were a cozy little family, a coven if you will, though I don't like that word. They used to do some well ... harmlessly evil things. They'd plan elaborate hunts months in advance. I don't mean they killed needlessly, but they made sport of it." She looked absently at the miniature on the table. "But then, Valdemar and I married. There was one major problem with that ... I was mortal, human. However, I thought I was in love with Valdemar, and when I learned the truth, I was terrified of growing old and dying while Valdemar remained young and lived on without me. And I admit I wanted the power to govern my own life. To protect myself." She closed her hand over the gold cross about her neck.

"So you convinced him to make you a vampire?"

"Yes," Kirsten whispered. "It was a big mistake. Love clouds your reason, makes you do stupid things. I wasn't qualified to make that decision. I couldn't really understand what being a vampire would mean. Once I became a vampire I couldn't reconcile my faith to the fact that I was doomed to commit a sin that was completely repulsive to me over and over again for hundreds maybe thousands of years.

"Valdemar did his best to console me, but I was so distressed I couldn't stand to be near him. I don't know what I would have done if it wasn't for Cornelius....

"Cornelius befriended me. He was easy to be with. He had a smile or a joke for every occasion. He showed me the lighter side of things. And after a time, I found that I had come to love him more than I loved Val."

Melinda was fascinated. This was a much different version of the brief tale Valdemar had told her. "Why did your domestic arrangements anger the others so?"

"At first I think they objected to Valdemar bringing a stranger into their midst. But, it was more than that. Moira had always had designs on Valdemar. Even though he didn't encourage her, I think she secretly hoped to change his mind. That Valdemar loved me only served to drive the point home that she would never have him."

"That's why she was so victorious about biting him that night...." Melinda said, putting the pieces of the puzzle together. "Why do you think he remained friends with her, if she caused him so much trouble?"

"She was someone he knew from--" Kirsten stopped, apparently realizing she was on the verge of revealing something she hadn't intended to. "From his early life as a vampire," she finished. Kirsten dove back into her story, stifling the question forming on Melinda's lips. "Val began to change. All that happened between us hurt him deeply, and he started to feel differently about the impact we vampires had on the lives of humans. Up until then, he had lived among humans in their society. He began to believe that it was wrong to cause suffering, even to mortals. After we parted, he dropped out of sight and contented himself with living on the fringes of civilization instead."

"Which, of course, angered Moira and Adrian who liked things just fine the way they were before."

"Right," Kirsten said. "Valdemar wasn't quiet about his new ideas. You know what he's like when he's in the mood to lecture."

"Yes," Melinda agreed. "He can be quite impossible."

"And there was still the problem of Cornelius and I ... Valdemar was resentful that Cornelius had meddled in our affairs. They fought over me. Valdemar accused Cornelius of terrible things. I could hear them yelling at each other all over the house. Then Neil left and the house was very quiet. I was awfully frightened."

"Valdemar came upstairs then. I expected him to be angry with me, but he was kind, as if he'd come to a painful decision and was now at peace with himself. He told me that he didn't want me to be unhappy anymore and that if I loved Cornelius I should go to him. So I did."

"Just like that?"

"Yes," Kirsten said in a low voice. "Just like that. Afterward, things settled down a bit. Moira and Adrian were more accepting of me. Things were never quite the same, though. To my knowledge Neil and Val have never discussed the issue again. I suppose they spoke their minds to each other and there was nothing more to say."

It was all starting to make a dreadful kind of sense. Melinda shuddered remembering the scathing comments Moira and Adrian had made when they discovered her existence. "And things were quiet until I came along," she blurted out. "What do you think it was that caused Valdemar to go after me--and then change his mind about killing me?"

"I don't know," Kirsten said hastily and looked away.

Melinda studied her intently. "You *do* know Kirsten," she said. "You just won't tell *me*."

"No," Kirsten insisted. "I know nothing."

"Damn it, Kirsten--"

"Only Valdemar knows what goes on in his head," Kirsten said in a feeble defense. "If you want to know, you'll have to ask *him*."

"You know I won't do that," Melinda said, making a final plea. "Even if I did, he probably wouldn't tell me."

Kirsten's gray eyes were unyielding. "We have more pressing matters to discuss, Melinda."

"What do you intend to do, Kirsten?" Melinda asked, surrendering to the notion that it was hopeless to question Kirsten further. Valdemar's ex-wife could be as maddeningly closed-mouthed as he when she chose. "What if Moira and Adrian really are doing all these terrible things and have no intention of stopping?"

"I plan to make them stop," Kirsten said simply.

"Kirsten you can't," Melinda said horrified that Kirsten would even consider taking them on herself. "You're no match for them."

"I'm not as innocent as I look," Kirsten warned her.

"I don't suppose you are," Melinda said. "But they're truly evil. Moira and Adrian don't care about anything or anybody, not even their own lives. Who knows what lengths they'd go to prove a point."

"Maybe so," Kirsten admitted. "But I know one thing, Valdemar *will* do something about this. He won't say so, but I know him well enough to know that he's only biding his time. I can't let him do this alone. It wouldn't be right."

Melinda stared into the piles of newsprint, wondering how she came to find herself wrapped up in this mess once again. No one had forced her to come here tonight, she told herself furiously.

"I really don't want you to get involved Melinda," Kirsten said, as if she'd read her mind. "But I need your help. I need you to watch and listen for me in places I can't. You have a shrewd mind, which is more than I can say for Cornelius. Cornelius is a lover of fun and good times, he has no conception that the rest of the world doesn't live by his rules. And, as much as he loves me, he doesn't believe either of us."

"Sure," Melinda said, and wanted to slap herself for agreeing to such a preposterous thing. "I sincerely hope we're wrong about this."

"Me too," Kirsten agreed too readily to disguise that despite her brave talk, she was desperately frightened.

* * * *

The bar in the York Hotel became the headquarters for their

clandestine meetings. Kirsten found excuses to sing there often, and Melinda offered to lock up most nights. The two lingered long after hours, pouring over their collection of newspaper clippings.

"They did this. I'm sure," Kirsten said gravely, looking at one of the ragged pieces of newspaper Melinda laid on the table.

"It definitely has their mark," Melinda agreed. It was a grisly account of a high speed car chase that ended up with the pursuing police car smashing into the side of a movie theater during the busy Friday night horror feature. Part of the wall had caved in, and it had taken police and firefighters most of the evening to rescue those trapped inside. The casualties were numerous.

A sinister element overshadowed the newspaper report, noticeable to those wily enough to read between the lines. Mutilated bodies had been found in the outer foyer. Police were still trying to unravel the mystery as to how they had been killed so far from the site of the crash. Had they fled wounded into the foyer? Or were Moira and Adrian waiting for them outside? To Melinda's way of thinking it was more likely the latter.

Melinda closed her mind to the memories of Moira and Adrian's harrowing car race down the 401. She refused to think about how she and Valdemar had foolishly accompanied them, drunk on Moira's *Zombie Punch*. She could still smell the burning rubber and hear the crunch of tearing metal. It was as fresh in her mind as if it had happened yesterday, instead of almost two years ago.

That rage and disgust was still bottled up inside her. She was repulsed at what Moira and Adrian considered an evening's pleasure. That such events were allowed to happen in an otherwise civilized world was repugnant.

"There's only one person to talk to about this," Kirsten said, gripping the table and standing up.

"Who?"

"I'm going to talk to Valdemar," she said, as if she'd been making up her mind about it and the matter was now settled.

"Kirsten ... you can't!" Melinda protested. Valdemar was the last person she wanted to bring into this.

"Don't worry," Kirsten reassured her. "I won't mention your name."

* * * *

Melinda stared into the starlit sky. It was far past closing time and the streets had long since emptied of people. She was sitting on the roof of the hotel, where she and Kirsten sometimes went for privacy on warm nights. From Kirsten there had been no word for two days, the silence was beginning to trouble her.

At last she saw the slight, pale, form making its way across the parking lot behind the building. Melinda rose and went downstairs.

"Well?" she asked, accosting Kirsten in the shadows before she even reached the building. "What did he say?"

"Oh, he said many things," Kirsten told her. "None I'd care to repeat."

"He didn't believe you," Melinda said, feeling her stomach tighten in fear. She couldn't decide if she felt better or worse that Valdemar had refused to become involved.

"Didn't believe me!" Kirsten said with frustration. "He was furious! Which of course means he believes me only too well. I think he only means to protect me, which is foolish since I'm already involved."

"I think Valdemar has an inflated view of his ability to fix this," Melinda said, more unkindly than she meant to.

"Perhaps," Kirsten acknowledged. "Either way, he took the liberty of informing Cornelius what I was up to."

"He didn't!"

"He did," Kirsten said. "And as you can well imagine, Neil was not pleased. Most of the time Cornelius is easy going, but when he gets angry he makes up for it with interest. That's why it took me so long to get back to you. Neil has been keeping a very close watch on me, but I knew he had to sleep sometime," Kirsten said with an evil wink. "So here I am."

"Now what?" Melinda asked, wondering if it wouldn't be easier on both body and soul to move to Australia and forget the entire matter.

"My conscience won't let me ignore this," Kirsten told her. "Vampires don't have to behave like monsters simply because they can."

"We can't let them get away with this. We're the only ones who can stop them," Melinda agreed.

"I can't believe you're getting yourself into this," Kirsten said, "knowing how you feel about all that's happened."

"Nor can I," Melinda whispered. "But my soul is tarnished enough. I can't look the other way and allow this to continue. I can't forget what I already know." She looked beyond Kirsten at the sky that was already beginning to show the first amber rays of the approaching morning. "No, it's more than that ... Valdemar did this to me. He destroyed my life ... for a reason he refuses to share with me. There is no way I can make you understand the suffering this has caused me, Kirsten. The circumstances under which we became vampires are too different. But now I have the power to correct some of what is wrong in the world. I have the means to stand between those who would cause misery and prevent it. I must do this!" She watched Kirsten's expression change from outrage to calm acceptance as she held her in her boiling violet stare. "I won't be able to live with myself if I don't."

"Melinda," Kirsten said so quietly she was forced to listen to her. "There are many things you don't know about Valdemar and what happened between you."

"Tell me, then," Melinda said, gripping her by the arms for emphasis. "I have to know."

"I can't," Kirsten whispered. Pain filled her gray eyes.

"Why?"

"The tale is not mine to tell."

"If you won't tell me, I may never find out." Melinda swallowed hard. She released Kirsten and walked a few steps away. "And I will hurt forever," she finished.

Kirsten glanced nervously from Melinda to the lightening sky. "I better get back."

"Sure," Melinda said, watching her flee into the dawn.

CHAPTER FOURTEEN

"Here," Kirsten said, thrusting a book into her hands.

Melinda looked down at the leather-bound volume. Valdemar's journal, she realized with a start. "I don't understand."

Kirsten shifted uneasily. "I kept thinking about what you said, about hurting forever. I couldn't get it out of my mind...." She fingered the lace on her cuffs. "You're not going to ask him, and he probably wouldn't tell you. I figured the only way you'd ever know the truth was from his diary. So ... I took it when he wasn't looking," she finished quickly.

"You stole Valdemar's journal?" Melinda asked, incredulously. "He'll be furious!"

"He isn't going to find out," Kirsten said. "That particular volume was well hidden. Probably because it's all about you." She paced back and forth in the narrow confines of the room. "Hurry up and read it Melinda, so I can take it back."

Melinda sat down heavily on the bed. "I've never seen this one."

"Like I said, it wasn't easy to find."

"I'm almost afraid to read it."

Kirsten sat on the other end of the bed and folded her knees up against her chest. "It's up to you. I just thought you should have the chance."

Slowly, Melinda opened the journal. She shut her eyes, took a deep breath, then looked down at the words before her.

There are still times when she looks at me with the same fear in her eyes; even now that we are lovers and she knows there is nothing to fear from my touch. It's as if nothing can erase the memory of that first night.

I can still remember the first, exquisite taste of her, the way she smelled vaguely of perfume and sweat ... the feel of her limp body in my arms

It was then that I came to my senses and could finally think beyond the raging hunger, that I realized what they had done. I often wonder how much she remembers ... but I'm afraid to ask. I don't want to remind her of it now that she has come back to me again. My hold on her is so tenuous and I need her so much ...

She re-read the page, stopping when she came to the word "they".

"They," she said aloud, and looked at Kirsten. "Oh, My God!" she whispered. "You were all there, weren't you?"

Kirsten nodded slowly.

"Even you, Kirsten?"

She looked away. "I'm afraid so, Melinda."

"Did you...." She lost her voice and had to repeat herself. "I mean, did you," she motioned to her neck.

Kirsten bit her lip and nodded.

... I looked down at the woman in my arms and wondered how she could possibly be alive after what they'd done to her. I was thinking only of the taste of her blood--that with a few mouthfuls it would be all over. And that disgusted me.

I lashed out at Moira who offered to finish the task for me. They tired of the game when I wouldn't do as they wished. Kirsten was trying to reason with me, pointing out that it was kinder to finish the victim off swiftly and spare her a lingering death. I knew she was right. The virus was already in her bloodstream, and it would kill her slowly without another dose to act as an antidote. But the look on my face made Kirsten turn away and leave with the rest of them.

I couldn't kill her--I still don't know why. Perhaps I was angry with Moira for manipulating me. Or maybe Melinda's courage impressed me. The red tracks of her nails were still visible on Adrian's cheek as he left. "Good for you," I thought, because I wanted to hit him myself.

So I took her home, wondering as I crawled down the pitch black tunnels, what I was going to tell her, how I would explain it. I wasn't thinking coherently. I was still drunk and in scant control of my hunger. Somewhere in the back of my mind was the thought that eternity was a long time to regret what I was getting both of us into ...

"You were all drunk. Just like that night at Moira's." She stopped and stared at the other vampire in horror. "I was supposed to be dinner, wasn't I."

"Yes," Kirsten said, examining the faded bedspread.

"It wasn't Valdemar who attacked me," she whispered.

Kirsten looked up, meeting her eyes. "Moira thought if Val got a taste of the hunt, he'd go back to being the way he was. I didn't realize what she was up to. I was drunk and hungry." The gray eyes never left hers.

"No wonder Moira hated me. It must have been quite a shock to find dinner reincarnated as Valdemar's new lover."

"Moira was livid."

"Why didn't someone tell me what I was involved in?"

"We were trying to protect you, Melinda," said Kirsten. "I'm sorry, we didn't do a very good job."

Melinda looked miserably at the text before her and forced herself to read on.

... I sat at the foot of the bed, hungry and ill-tempered, and I watched her sleep. Every anguished moan caused me to agonize over my dilemma: kill her swiftly or make her one of us.

Hours later, she regained consciousness. She took one look at me and screamed.

I'll never forget the look of consummate terror in her eyes, nor the sound of her scream echoing off the cement walls.

It's always a shock when they find out we're real. I tried to make her understand, but everything I said came out wrong. To taste of her was so tempting, but it had to be her choice.

When I couldn't stand to watch her suffer any longer, I locked the bedroom door and went to sit on the subway platform and contemplated ugly thoughts. Only a few more hours, I kept thinking. Then I could appease my hunger and it would all be over, one way or another.

I had her in my arms, my mouth against her throat, and the hunger screaming at me through every sense. I tried not to frighten her further, but she thought I was going to kill her and she screamed again, this time right beside my ear. It will echo in my mind forever ...

Melinda grimaced, remembering the sensation of his teeth penetrating her throat.

... It was unbearable, to watch her writhing in the agony of the metamorphosis. I tried to remember what it felt like, but over eleven hundred years the memory dims and I couldn't conjure it with any clarity.

Not all survive the metamorphosis. Some die, from the rapid loss of blood, or from the stress of the physical and chemical changes. Many can't complete the first kill and starve to death. I couldn't let her die. We were bound by blood. She was my offspring, my kin.

So I forced her to kill, to complete the final stage of the transformation. Perhaps if I had eased her into it more gently, things would have been different. I should have enlisted Kirsten's help, but I was afraid of Kirsten's scorn. Especially for making the same mistake twice.

It was heartbreaking to fall in love with her a little more each day, while each day she grew to hate me more.

"He tried to tell me," she said sadly. "He kept saying it was all a big mistake. But I saw him when I got on the subway. It was the last thing I remembered before ... well, you know." Melinda rubbed her neck. "He promised me together we'd somehow make it all better, but I didn't believe him."

"You might have," Kirsten said. "If it wasn't for Moira."

"She was trying to make Valdemar hurt me," Melinda said, thinking back to the night of the party.

"Valdemar would never have hurt you."

"When that didn't work, she settled for trying to make me despise him even more."

"Moira wanted you out of the picture."

"Well," Melinda said, miserably. "It worked."

"She accomplished nothing. Valdemar hates her for it."

"And now she wants to destroy him?"

"You have to remember," Kirsten said gravely. "Moira is not entirely sane."

Melinda shut the journal and handed it back. "Here, take it away.

I've read enough."

For a few, long moments they eyed each other warily.

"So, what's it like," Melinda asked bitterly, "making friends with dinner?"

"Please don't say that," Kirsten begged. "You don't know how many times I've wished I'd stayed home that night. I'm so sorry Melinda. Please forgive me." She glanced reluctantly at the look of anguish on the other vampire's face. "Perhaps I should go."

She gathered up the stolen journal and reached for her shawl.

"Don't go," Melinda said as she put her hand on the door knob.

Kirsten turned back expectantly.

"It's not you," she said. "I'm angry because one night my life was snatched away from me. And now here I am, living like a fugitive. I want somebody to pay for my pain."

"If you want to punish somebody," Kirsten said. "Make it the one responsible. Make it Moira."

"You're right," Melinda said. "We have to do something about Moira. No one else should have to suffer this way."

CHAPTER FIFTEEN

Someone was pounding tenaciously at the door. The sound jarred Melinda unwillingly from the depths of sleep. She turned over, burying her head in the darkness under her pillow.

But the persistent hammering refused to go away. She sat up, squinting in the narrow shaft of light that escaped from around the edges of the blanket that covered the window.

"It's me Kirsten," came a muffled voice from the other side of the door.

Melinda leapt to the door, stumbling among the covers that clung to her legs. She pulled the door open, yanking Kirsten inside and shutting it with her body by falling against it. "Are you crazy Kirsten? It's high noon on a sunny day. What are you doing up at such an hour?" She rubbed her stinging eyes and looked at the shrouded form in front of her.

Had she not heard the muted cry, she wouldn't have recognized Kirsten. The slight vampire was covered from head to foot in layers of black cloth. She wore a wide brimmed felt hat, covered by a gauzy black scarf that served as a veil and her eyes were obscured by a huge pair of sunglasses. Another scarf was wrapped around her neck and a flowing, ebony dress reached almost to the ground. Sable cowboy boots peeked out from under it as she moved, and on her hands were black gloves.

Melinda stared at her feeling her heart freeze in her chest. "What's wrong?"

Kirsten was taking off her hat and gloves, removing the layers of gauze from around her head. "Did you know they were putting in a new subway line?"

"I don't ride the subway," Melinda told her. "I'm afraid of running into Valdemar. Why?"

"Well, Cornelius and I went to visit Valdemar," she held up a hand, motioning Melinda to be patient and not cut her off at the first mention of his name. "Val was in a good mood for a change. Anyway, he got this crazy idea that we should take his subway car and go cruising down the new subway line, to see where it went...."

"And...." Melinda prompted.

"It's really futuristic looking, all fancy tile and gleaming silver--"

"Get to the point, Kirsten. You're interrupting my sleep."

"You won't believe who painted the murals in those new stations," Kirsten said with raised eyebrows.

"Who?" Melinda asked impatiently.

"Moira," she whispered looking about, as if the walls were listening.

The significance still eluded Melinda. "Moira? So?"

"I know this is crazy, Melinda, but when I saw them, my heart just stopped. I had this awful feeling that Moira's planning something big. She works that way. First she'll scout out her territory, get to know it from the inside. And how better to get to know a new subway line than to paint the murals inside before its finished. She probably has every square foot memorized and catalogued in that sinister mind of hers."

"Kirsten this is ludicrous," Melinda said, stifling a yawn. "Taking on a whole subway line is too ambitious, even for the likes of Moira and Adrian."

"How can you say that?" Kirsten countered. "You've been reading all those clippings. Their schemes have been getting more and more obvious, bigger and bigger with each stunt. You said so yourself."

"That's true," Melinda agreed reluctantly. "But those are still isolated pranks, not anything like what you're suggesting."

"Neil and Val didn't believe me either," Kirsten said, hugging her arms and shivering despite the warmth in the room.

"If it will make you feel better," Melinda said, "I'll keep an eye on this subway stuff--"

"It's too late for that," Kirsten said urgently. "They're opening the line tomorrow at noon. The mayor and a whole array of dignitaries will be riding the first car. And after that they're opening the line for free rides. Do you realize how many people will travel that subway tomorrow? Melinda, we have to be on that first train!"

* * * *

Melinda stepped from the glaring white light of the platform into the lavishly decorated subway car that looked more like a set from the Orient Express than a commuter train. It had been difficult to sneak into the subway system in the daytime with the security cameras rolling and the transit police prowling the route. But, once in the relative safety of the shadowed tunnels, luck had been with them. Invitations were being collected at the entrance to the station above, no one had expected interlopers to crash the Mayor's party from the murky tunnels.

"So this is where our tax dollars go," Kirsten whispered, sounding like any other outraged citizen. She looked around in disgust at the black lace curtains that hung in the windows and the red velvet cushions that covered the functional seating.

"It looks like a funeral parlor."

"And a fitting metaphor that is," Melinda replied. Despite the upbeat mood of the party and the men and women in formal day dress, the gathering had a sinister overtone. It had the imprint of something that was indelibly engraved on Melinda's mind, but she couldn't place it.

Men in dark gray suits obscured the bar at the far end of the car. They queued up like church goers for communion, or more likely sheep being orderly herded to slaughter. Instead of being butchered however, they returned with civilized smiles and drinks for their female escorts.

"What do you see?" Kirsten asked anxiously from beside her.

"I don't know," Melinda whispered. "It reminds me of something, somewhere I've been...." She stopped then, clutching Kirsten's arm to steady her. "It reminds me of Moira's apartment!" she said victoriously, glad to have placed the oppressive feeling. "You were right Kirsten. This whole place has Moira's finger prints all over it. She might as well have signed her name in blood above the doorway."

"Oh, it's hers, all right," Kirsten said in obvious distaste.

"You ladies look as though you could use some company," a friendly voice said from behind them.

Melinda looked up into a young handsome face, willing the intruder gone. Her mind was more than occupied with other thoughts without having to be polite.

Kirsten, on the other hand, seemed quite pleased to have his attention, and the visitor seemed more than taken with Kirsten. She was trapped there, racking her brain to think of appropriate small talk.

"Why don't I get you a drink," their guest offered.

"That would be very nice of you," Kirsten said demurely, watching him squeeze his way through the crowd to the black, lace-draped bar in the corner. "He's cute, isn't he?" Kirsten said. "He's one of the aldermen."

"Really Kirsten," Melinda said crossly. "Don't you think we have better things to do than pick up men?"

"Relax," Kirsten said. "How better to hide than in a crowd of people. Besides, we're on the second car. I'm sure our good friend Moira has commandeered herself a place of honor on the first car. I'll keep our handsome alderman friend occupied, you watch for Moira."

The train lurched into motion, whisking them off as if on a pillar of air down the tunnels. A tour guide's voice echoed through the overhead speakers, outlining their itinerary and spewing ridership statistics. They were coming up on the first station. Melinda peered between the heads that blocked her view for a peek at the tiled mural that had so worried Kirsten.

To the ordinary eye, the mural would have been a common place thing. It was a futuristic representation of the subway train, painted in the wide, aggressive brush strokes that were Moira's trademark. The subway appeared to race through the tunnel at high speeds, leaving a streak of smoke and sparks in its wake. It could easily have been interpreted as a promise from the transit authority that the new subway would get one faster to one's destination. But, like the black draped windows, the smoke and the fire spoke to Melinda as the forerunners of disaster. Knowing Moira, that was exactly what she had intended.

A sensuously husky female voice took the microphone. Melinda loosened her grip on the glass of champagne in her hand, realizing with a start that she had been squeezing the glass with almost enough force to shatter it. She forced herself to smile politely during Moira's commentary on the artwork they were passing.

Kirsten and the alderman were still chatting away as if this were truly a social function, obviously pleased with each other's company. Melinda peered between their shoulders through the door that led to the car in front, her eyes locking on the black and crimson form that stood out as if the crowd had parted to give her a better view. She tore her eyes away, and turned her body slightly in profile not wanting to alert Moira's acute vampire vision to her whereabouts.

Another round of champagne was served, this time by roaming waiters who clung precariously to the center poles that ran down the middle of the car, as the subway rattled off again down the tunnels.

The noise level in the car rose noticeably as the party goers indulged in the abundant alcoholic beverages. They were picking up speed. Lights that marked the sides of the tunnels flashed by in bolts of lightning as they barreled down the tunnels. Kirsten shot Melinda a gray warning glance, but no one else seemed alarmed by the change in velocity. They expected such things from the city's expensive new subway line and fancy new subway cars.

A sudden change in direction sent them staggering sideways in a wave of spilled champagne and yelps of surprise. They crossed a junction in the tracks and headed off in another heading.

"Would you excuse me?" Kirsten asked their guest politely. "I need to get a napkin from the bar to wipe off my dress," she gestured in embarrassment to the spilled champagne on her powder pink gown and dragged Melinda with her.

Smiling, they moved among the other passengers, elbowing their way to the door that separated the two cars. Moira still stood at the microphone, extolling the virtues of the new subway and its artwork in a voice of molten copper. Melinda's eyes dove to the booth that housed the driver. Doubtless there was a corpse slumped over the throttle in that tiny booth, a cadaver the city would discover tomorrow with two crimson teeth marks in its neck. It didn't take a lot to imagine that the driver of the train was without question, Moira's blond consort, Adrian.

They hit a section of rough track and the train began to screech as it tore along the rails that were rusty with disuse. Terror knifed through Melinda's mind at the sound. It was a memory she would never forget, a nightmare from two years previous, when she had stepped onto a train out of the depths of hell that she had mistaken for the last subway.

"Oh no!" she gasped, clutching Kirsten's arm. "Moira's taking us to Valdemar's!"

CHAPTER SIXTEEN

"She wouldn't!" Melinda exclaimed, even as the tightening vice of dread locked on to her soul, "would she?"

"She would," Kirsten said with certain grimness.

"Then we have to stop her," Melinda said, wrenching open the narrow door that ran between the train cars. She looked down at the fragile-looking chains that linked the cars together. The two sides rattled back and forth, tossing her from side to side on the narrow platform.

"Hey! Miss!" someone yelled behind her, but she had hauled open the door to the next car and staggered inside, dragging Kirsten after her.

The door slammed shut with a whoosh and a bang, causing heads to turn briefly in their direction, then back to the seductively smooth voice that addressed them from the front of the car.

"What now?" Melinda asked.

"We have to confront her," Kirsten said. "What can she do to us in front of all these people?"

"I hardly think an audience of mortals would keep Moira from her prey," Melinda cautioned.

"We can't let this go on any longer," Kirsten hissed back. "We're getting too close...."

They squeezed their way through the press of smartly clad bodies, past the smiling Mayor and another group of grinning aldermen. It was like trying to run through honey, Melinda thought, casting a desperate glance out the window. They were getting dangerously close. She had come to know these tunnels like her own neighborhood.

Only a handful of people stood between them and Moira now. To all appearances, the fiery haired vampire hadn't noticed them yet. Melinda was just about to reach through the last three or four bodies who would stood in rapt attention and grasp the microphone, when an arm from out from the crowd reach out and seized Kirsten, yanking her back with angry force.

Melinda whirled to defend her friend, looking up into the face of the tall male in the tuxedo who wore his hair tied back in a long ponytail.

"Cornelius!" Kirsten attempted to snatch back her arm, but Cornelius hung on with force that was visibly hurting her.

"What are you doing here?" Cornelius asked. He glanced at Melinda, recognizing her suddenly. "You!"

"I'm trying to stop a disaster," Kirsten told him defiantly. "What are you doing here in the middle of the day, Neil?"

"I was invited," Cornelius said. "I figured I ought to check out this insane idea of yours, after all the fuss you made. Imagine my surprise Kirsten, when I woke up this morning and found you gone from our bed."

"Well?" Melinda asked , not caring whether she incurred Cornelius' wrath. "What are you going to do about this, Cornelius? Surely you've noticed where we're going?"

"Yes," he answered, a hint of worry showing in his face, then swiftly camouflaged with anger.

"Neil, you can't let her do this," Kirsten said desperately. "Val has been your friend for five hundred years."

"Valdemar is perfectly capable of defending himself," Cornelius snapped.

"Not against a mob of one hundred and fifty mortals and two insane vampires!" Melinda grabbed his shoulder. "Don't you think he's just a little out numbered?"

Cornelius looked down at the hand that gripped him and shook it off roughly. "And what do you care anyway? Last I heard you never wanted to see him again."

"I've changed my mind," Melinda growled back.

Kirsten looked up at Cornelius, heedless of his fury and unapologetic for her deceit. "Since you're here Neil, what *do* you intend to do about this?"

"I intend to wait and see what happens."

"Wait and see!" Melinda nearly shouted. "In a matter of minutes, we'll be on Valdemar's doorstep! This is dangerous to us all, Cornelius!"

He gave that thought serious consideration. "It's possible," he said after a second, "that Moira merely means to frighten us, to impress upon Valdemar what she could do."

"I doubt it," Kirsten said. "This time I'm certain she's out to destroy him."

"Whatever she's up to," Cornelius snapped. "You're to stay out of it Kirsten. Do you understand? You are the one person besides Valdemar that Moira truly has reason to hate, you and your fledgling friend." He snorted in Melinda's direction.

"This concerns all of us," Melinda argued. "We can't allow any of our kind to behave this way."

"How they behave is no concern of mine," Cornelius snarled.

"Then why are you here?" Kirsten asked him.

"To ensure you don't get yourself killed."

"We're running out of time," Melinda warned them. "And if you're too squeamish to dirty your hands in this, I'll damned well do it. I have nothing to lose."

She spun on her heel, falling into the party goers in front of her. From behind she heard Kirsten call her name and echoed by a muffled curse from Cornelius.

She dove through the remaining passengers, lunging at Moira and snatching the microphone from her hand in mid leap. A sea of astonished faces looked back at her. Kirsten had wrestled free of Cornelius and come to her aid.

"Well, who do we have here?" Moira cackled. "Batgirl?" She swiped at Melinda with her long red talons.

Melinda ducked the blow and tossed the microphone to Kirsten.

"That's enough Moira," she heard Cornelius saying, as she hauled open the door to the engineer's compartment.

There was indeed a corpse at the throttle. A huge gash of crimson cut across his neck and soaked into the brown uniform in a dark stain. Dying, he had fought against Adrian, as evidenced by the numerous gashes in his clothing. Angered, Adrian had been none too fastidious in his feeding, ravaging his neck with ferocious savagery. Horror-stricken eyes stared blankly at the ceiling.

"Well, if it isn't Melinda, the world's only vegetarian vampire." Adrian lifted the corpse by the hair. Its vacant eyes leered helplessly back at her. "I don't suppose you'd care for a bite?"

Something out the window tore his glance from her. Melinda followed his gaze, staring out the window in mute terror at the otherworldly gray station they were approaching.

Over fifty years ago, the station had been constructed as part of an ambitious transit expansion that was later abandoned. They had laid the utilitarian gray tile and started on the electrical wiring, then boarded the place up and forgot about it. It was the end of the line, where the tracks trailed off into oblivion. Oblivion and Valdemar's graveyard.

It was two in the afternoon. Melinda could picture Valdemar sitting bolt-upright in his bed, then dressing furiously to meet the intruders. He would be ready for them by now. But there was no way he would be prepared or able to defend himself against the menace Moira had in store for him this time.

In a maneuver of sheer desperation, Melinda flung herself at Adrian, knocking him off balance. She seized the throttle and threw the train into reverse.

A chorus of surprised yelps issued from the crowd outside. She could hear Kirsten and Cornelius furiously engaged in an argument with Moira. Chaos was descending on the party. The Mayor was asking questions.

Adrian bounced off the window of the tiny cabin, recovering himself with fluid grace. With lightning speed, his arm flashed out of nowhere, catching Melinda in a ringing blow across the head. She felt the sting of his claws scraping across her cheek, then the wet flow of blood down her chin. Adrian's eyes lit up in excitement.

She fell, twisting to keep herself from tumbling into Adrian in the narrow space. She was terribly outmatched in the height, weight and experience. She drew back her elbow and slammed it up between Adrian's ribs with all the force she could muster.

The blond vampire swore, doubling up in spite of himself. His hand hit the throttle. The train lurched to a standstill.

The door flew open in a flurry of grappling hands. A cloud of fiery hair streaked towards her as Moira charged through the cabin door. Kirsten and Cornelius toppled in on top of her. The gathering outside craned their necks to get a better view of the curious events in the engineer's compartment.

There was a scuffle between Adrian and Cornelius, a flurry of harsh curses and the dull thud of punches being thrown in close quarters. Melinda looked up into Moira's burning amber eyes.

"I should have known I'd see you again, little trouble maker," she sneered, her fangs gleaming white in the low light. She snapped her teeth at Melinda, who turned her face away, realizing too late that was exactly what Moira wanted.

Moira's teeth sliced into her neck, ripping flesh and material as she chewed through Melinda's collar. Melinda shrieked in pain, feeling her life force rushing from her body in a hot wave under the powerful suction of Moira's mouth. She jerked her knee up between them, dislodging Moira in a ferocious kick.

From the corner of her eye, she saw Cornelius fall, victim to one of Adrian's savage punches. Kirsten moved to tackle Moira. Cornelius recovered and came to Kirsten's rescue.

Freed of his assailant, Adrian thrust the train back into motion, coming to a screeching halt in front of Valdemar's station.

Melinda scrambled up onto the console in a shower of her own dripping blood. She lunged at Adrian, too late.

Adrian hit the door release. The outer doors hissed open, discharging the passengers onto the dusty gray platform. Moira licked her lips hastily, then leapt through the cabin door, retrieving the fallen microphone.

"As you can see ladies and gentlemen," she said between ragged breaths. "This station isn't finished yet. But if you'll just go up the stairs on your left, I'm sure you'll be quite impressed with the interior...."

Adrian grinned like a wolverine.

* * * *

Melinda dashed through the doors in pursuit of Moira and Adrian who were disembarking with the rest of the throng.

Cornelius caught up with Moira as she was heading through the door, yanking her back by the shoulder. "You can't do this, Moira," he growled.

"Tell them it's a mistake," Kirsten urged her. "Turn this train around and get out of here."

Moira laughed, a sound like nails grating on slate. "Of that I have no intention." She looked dejectedly at Cornelius. "Really Neil, I'm disappointed in you. Surely you can see the humor in this."

"I see nothing funny in any of this," Cornelius said. "What could you possibly find amusing about hurting someone who is supposed to be your friend?"

A storm cloud descended on Moira's face. "You are mistaken. Valdemar and I have never been friends."

"Maybe not," Kirsten argued, "but doing this accomplishes nothing!"

"On the contrary," Moira countered. "This will suit my purposes splendidly. Now if you'll excuse me, I must see to my guests." She hurried off with the satisfaction of a hostess at a party that was going well.

"What now?" Melinda asked. "We can't let her take a tour of humans into Valdemar's home."

Cornelius frowned watching the retreating Moira with a dark expression. "I'd say the matter is beyond our control."

"Not entirely," Melinda said, squaring her shoulders and

marching after Moira.

Kirsten made as if to follow her, but Cornelius yanked her roughly backward. "Where are you going?" he demanded angrily.

"I'm going to help Melinda," she said. "So let me go Cornelius, because I *will* do this, whether you approve or not!"

Cornelius shook his head. "I don't know what Valdemar does to earn such loyalty from his women. Even the ones who'd rather see him dead than alive come running to his rescue." He looked up to find Kirsten several paces beyond him, then swore under his breath and followed her.

* * * *

Melinda raced up the cement stairs, ignoring the people who jumped back in fear of the bleeding banshee that pursued them. Tufts of hair escaped from the French braid she had spent so long on that morning, and the sequined jacket was torn beyond repair. Her collar was dyed red with her own blood and was now congealing into a thick and uncomfortable mess.

She rounded the corner into the soft candlelight of Valdemar's bathing chamber. The crowd had gathered there, in awe of the superb craftsmanship and the abundant marble work.

Tiny gold crested waves rippled across the surface of the pool. People milled about aimlessly, reclining on the low marble wall that flanked the huge bath and leaning against the smooth pillars. Melinda looked up through the hanging chandeliers with their multitude of white candles to the winding marble staircase.

And, leaning against the marble banister with his arms crossed defiantly over his chest, was Valdemar.

He was dressed as if he had known they were coming, in a black tuxedo and a paisley cummerbund. Dark woolen pants with satin seams and black patent shoes completed the outfit. If he was handsome before, Melinda thought, now he was stunning. Exquisite and deadly.

There was no way to tell if he was shocked to find this horde in his home in the middle of the day, as he stared out passively over the gathering with eyes as black as a moonless night.

Melinda backed up hastily, crashing into Kirsten and Cornelius as they rounded the corner behind her. That movement drew Valdemar's attention. His eyes flitted from Moira, whom he had caught in his murderous gaze, to Melinda. He blinked, the only evidence of his surprise, taking in the blood on her face and neck in that fraction of a second. His eyes slid to Kirsten and Cornelius in their tattered formal dress, then back to Melinda. He gave her an odd, questioning look, then his attention was stolen by the dilemma before him.

CHAPTER SEVENTEEN

Melinda held her breath. Moira was moving up the stairs toward Valdemar.

He watched her approach, following each step with his black eyes. She stopped on the step below him and looked fearlessly into the gaze that would have caused anyone else to flinch and turn away. Melinda listened acutely, straining to hear their conversation above the murmur of the crowd.

"Moira," she heard Valdemar say, "why am I am not surprised to find you here?"

"No tour of the subway would be complete without a trip to your station," Moira said in a voice of saccharine sweetness. "I thought the Mayor might be interested to see how comfortably you live below his fair city. The subway project is dear to his heart."

Valdemar gave her a look that could have been boredom, but Melinda knew it was not. She had seen that expression once and hoped never to experience it again. "I promise," he said holding his temper in perilous restraint, "you will regret this...."

"Oh no," Kirsten whispered to Cornelius. "I've heard that tone before. "This is going to be bad. Very bad."

"What's the matter, Valdemar?" Adrian asked, coming up the stairs to stand behind Moira. "Doesn't your hospitality extend to mortals?"

"You've had your afternoon's amusement," Valdemar said in a voice that demanded action. "Now get them out of here!"

"Or you'll what?" Moira asked, donning her most charming smile. "What exactly will you do to me Valdemar?"

Valdemar stepped down, forcing her to back up a step into Adrian. "I will make you so sorry," he promised, "you will rue the day you met me."

Moira laughed, a sound that was not at all pleasant. She motioned to the delegation below her. "If you'll just follow me...."

"This is awful," Kirsten said, looking earnestly at Cornelius. "There's no way he can live here now. He's going to have to get out of here, tonight!"

"The city will look into this for certain," Melinda agreed. Cornelius glared at her in answer.

"And now they all know what he looks like," Kirsten whispered. "Neil do something!"

"What do you want me to do, Kirsten?" Cornelius demanded angrily, "Devour one hundred and fifty mortals to keep them from running back to city hall to find out why there's a vampire living in one of their abandoned subway stations?"

"No, of course not," Kirsten snapped.

"And thanks to you and your *friend*," Cornelius shot a scathing look at Melinda, "we're all in this together. They know what we all look like."

"Then we have nothing to lose," Melinda said with determination. She walked a few paces across the marble bathing chamber, turning to look back at Cornelius pointedly. "I stood by once and watched her maim and kill fifty people. I don't intend to do that again."

"She's right," Kirsten said, following her. "If we let her get away with this, none of us will ever be safe."

" ... aren't you going to offer our guests some refreshments?" Moira was asking Valdemar maliciously as she marched the delegation by him into his refuge.

Valdemar opened his mouth for a curt reply, then stopped to glare at Adrian as he brushed roughly past him.

Cornelius pursued Melinda and Kirsten who were most of the way up the stairs, cursing under his breath. Valdemar held his ground, blocking their way.

"Moira's feud is with me," he said tersely to Cornelius. "I would advise you to stay out of it." He looked urgently at Kirsten, his eyes lingering in inquiry as they swept by Melinda. "Get them out of here. I have enough problems to deal with already."

"I'm not a child, Valdemar," Kirsten said, addressing him directly. "And I'm not leaving."

"Nor am I," said Melinda staunchly. "This concerns us all."

There was a crash from inside, someone knocking something over in the crowded space.

Valdemar shot Melinda an undecipherable look. "I'll talk to you later," he said, then fled inside to defend his turf.

Moira had invaded Valdemar's wine rack and was serving drinks in his best crystal. There were people slouched on the delicate antique sofa and leaning against the fragile end tables. Someone had knocked over a vase, the pieces were scattered across the

Persian carpet and crunched under the feet of the throng that crammed into the tiny parlor.

The party had spilled over into the bedroom. At least twenty people reclined on Valdemar's imposing bed. Someone was using his desk as a coffee table. Wet rings of spilled wine marked the priceless wooden surface where people had set down their glasses. Another reveler was reading Valdemar's journal, yelling choice phrases across the room to his buddies.

Some of the more intoxicated guests had even stripped down for a dip in the large marble bath below. Melinda shot a smoking gaze at Moira who presided over the chaos with unconcealed glee.

"This is wonderful," she heard one of the guests exclaim to Moira. "Where did you find all the marvelous antiques? It must have taken weeks to set this up."

"Oh, it was nothing at all...." Moira purred.

"I have a space you simply must look at," another implored her. "I had something very much like this in mind...."

"Valdemar," Moira called out as he walked by her to rescue on of his treasured possessions from the grasp of a curious guest. "The Mayor wants to meet you."

" ... Valdemar," the Mayor was saying, "is that a European name?"

"It is," Valdemar said curtly, having no choice but to shake the Mayor's hand.

"Valdemar's been such a great help with the decorating," Moira was telling the Mayor.

"You're to be commended for the work you've done down here, and stayed within our budget as well." The Mayor beamed at Moira. "You've outdone yourself this time."

"She has indeed," Valdemar agreed dryly, putting a buddy like arm around Moira. "If I could have a word with you, in private...."

"I'm afraid there's something else that requires my immediate attention," Moira said anxiously.

"I insist," Valdemar said with a savage smile in the Mayor's direction. His arm tightened on Moira's shoulder. She smiled up at him politely despite the stinging grip of his long nails on her arm. Valdemar nodded in the Mayor's direction. "If you'll excuse us...."

"Of course," the Mayor answered, flowing into another group of admirers.

"What should we do?" Melinda asked Kirsten as they hovered in the doorway to the living room. They were certainly no longer attired for a formal gathering in their tattered and blood spattered clothes.

"If we could just get Moira away from the rest of the guests...." Kirsten said, watching Valdemar and Moira walk toward them. "And this looks like the perfect opportunity."

"Yes," Melinda agreed. "Once we have Moira, it'll be easier for Valdemar to get rid of the rest of them."

"Once we have Moira, I want to wring her neck personally," Kirsten said.

"All right," Cornelius said crossly. "Let's just do it. I've had it with this whole scene. I just want to get out of here." He looked at Kirsten. "And you're coming with me."

Valdemar and Moira had reached the staircase and were engaged in a furiously whispered argument.

" ... I don't know why you're so upset Valdemar," Moira was saying. She gestured to the marble bath full of drunken revelers. "Especially when I was considerate enough to bring you lunch!"

"Listen to me...." Valdemar hissed at her. He had her by both arms, his claws making bloody indentations in her flesh.

"Leave Moira to us," Kirsten said as the trio surrounded them. "We'll look after her while you deal with the others inside."

"Yes," Cornelius offered. "As you said, you have enough problems. Let us take this one off your hands."

That distraction was all Moira needed. She squirmed from Valdemar's clutches, grasping the thick, black electrical cable that ran down the side of the wall above the pool. It gave under her weight, coming loose from the wall.

Valdemar leapt to catch her. Cornelius reached out with a swipe of his own, but she evaded them, swinging out over the pool on the sagging cable.

"No!" Melinda screamed, leaping from the staircase in pursuit of Moira. A fraction of a second lay between her and Moira, but it was as if time had stopped. Her augmented strength and speed were not enough.

Melinda crashed to the wet marble floor and flailed about trying to gain her balance on the wet surface. Helplessly, she watched as Moira yanked the cable apart and dropped the longer end into the pool.

There was a terrific flash of light that seared her sensitive eyesight. Screams hung in the air, then died into silence. A loud crackle issued from the pool. The air was choked with the acrid smell of burning flesh.

"Moira!" Valdemar yelled, bolting from the staircase. Kirsten was already running, hot in pursuit of Moira who had landed on the far side of the bath.

"What's the matter Valdemar?" Moira called over her shoulder. "Don't you like soup?"

Melinda raced off to assist Kirsten, joined by Cornelius who had finally torn his eyes away from the catastrophe before him.

Still laughing, Moira had made it down to the platform level, heading for the waiting subway train.

Valdemar closed the distance between them, lunging at Moira and snagging her about the knees, toppling her face down on the platform. The others skidded to a stop, nearly falling on top of them.

He turned her over roughly. "What gives you the right," he asked her, panting in his fury, "to squander life this way?"

"It is my legacy to take lives as I please," Moira spat back at him. "Have you forgotten you're a vampire, Valdemar? Oh, I'm sorry, you don't like that word."

Valdemar's hands gripped her throat, slamming her head backward against the concrete floor. Moira looked up at him, the first vestiges of fear flickering in her eyes.

"I had to do something to get your attention," she whispered.

"Well, you have my undivided attention now," Valdemar snarled, his hands clenching about her neck, making her gasp for breath. "And I am so completely disgusted with you I wish you were dead!"

"So kill me Valdemar," Moira said defiantly. "Prove to everyone that you're no better than I am."

He recoiled from her words as if she had struck him, his hands fell from her neck. He stood up, yanking her roughly with him. "Prove to *me*," he said, "that your pathetic life is worth living. Go back upstairs and convince the Mayor there's been a terrible accident. Then get those people out of my home!"

Moira answered him with a bloody swipe across the face and tore off along the platform in the direction of the tracks.

Kirsten dashed off after Moira, cornering her before she reached the tunnels. They wrestled with each other on the narrow ledge.

"I am not as easily manipulated as Valdemar, Moira," Kirsten hissed, her gray eyes blazing like two swords.

Valdemar said something blasphemous. "Let her go, Kirsten!" he yelled. "She's mine."

Moira looked up as Valdemar moved towards them. Her leg shot out, catching Kirsten in the torso with every once of her strength. Valdemar reached to catch Kirsten as she fell away from Moira, but she was inches beyond his grasp.

Kirsten teetered on the edge of the platform, then fell to the tracks below, landing in a shower of blue sparks on the third rail.

CHAPTER EIGHTEEN

"Kirsten!" Cornelius screamed. He vaulted from the staircase to where Kirsten lay like a crumpled puppet on the rails.

Sparks still hung in the air like raindrops. There was a loud sizzle, the power going out. Melinda watched the row of bulbs hanging from the ceiling fade to orange, then die.

Cornelius knelt beside Kirsten, lifting her still form into his arms. He cradled her gently, smoothing the hair from her soot-covered face. He called her name.

Kirsten was dead, Melinda realized with calm logic that was more likely shock. The kind of voltage running through the third rail would be enough to stop even a vampire's heart.

Tears splashed from Cornelius' face onto Kirsten's closed eyelids. He was still talking to her quietly, reminding her that he had thought this whole thing a bad idea.

Drawn by Cornelius' cry, Valdemar scrambled down to the tracks, forgetting Moira who dashed off down the platform.

"Not so fast," Melinda snarled, lunging out and pinning her against the tiled wall. She wrenched Moira's arm sharply up behind her back, holding her there with all the force she could summon.

Valdemar crouched beside Cornelius, shutting his eyes tightly, as if by not looking he could somehow change the course of events.

"I tried to stop her," Cornelius said, to no one in particular.

"I know," Valdemar said softly. "I tried to stop her too."

Valdemar straightened, taking a purposeful step toward Moira who looked at him with undisguised fear. She struggled in Melinda's grasp, in a last effort to free herself. Melinda wrenched her arm harder.

"Let her go," yelled a voice from above.

Melinda looked up to where Adrian stood on the stone stairs above them. Defiantly she pushed Moira harder against the tiled wall.

"I said, let her go." Adrian held up two articles, a crude torch made out material torn from Valdemar's drapery and a can of gasoline.

Valdemar froze. His eyes widened as he realized what Adrian held.

Adrian turned his attention to Valdemar. "Tell her to let Moira go, or I swear, I'll torch the place."

"Adrian," Valdemar said, "don't be stupid....''

Adrian smiled. He unscrewed the metal cap on the old gasoline can and dumped a liberal amount over the torch. He held up a match. "I think it's you who's being stupid, Valdemar." He glanced at Melinda who still held Moira firmly pressed against the wall. "I'm not bluffing." He motioned to the doorway to Valdemar's living room with a flourish. "I've already spread the gasoline."

Valdemar was very still, only his eyes betrayed the fact that he took Adrian's threat very seriously indeed.

"That would be suicide, Adrian," he said calmly. "There's a gas main running through that pipe right above your head."

Adrian grinned. "You play a lousy game of poker, Val," he said. And dropped the torch.

Moira shrieked. "Adrian, No!"

There was a flash. Melinda blinked to clear the image that lingered on her retina. Through tears, she looked up to find a wall of flame where Adrian had been standing.

A loud hissing noise tore through the cavern, the flames rushing up to meet the gas main above. There was a blinding flare, then a colossal explosion. She opened her mouth to shout a warning, but the air was knocked from her lungs. She felt the impact, the shaking of the concrete foundation and realized in astonishment that she was lying on the ground, Moira beneath her. Melinda squinted through the searing glare. Where Adrian had been standing there was only roaring flame.

A blazing pathway ran through the open doorway to Valdemar's home. Part of the wall had collapsed giving an unrestricted view of the inferno inside.

Valdemar's face was pale with horror as he surveyed the flames shooting out from the floor above. Remembering suddenly that there was a group of more than one hundred and fifty mortals up there, he hurled himself in the direction of the staircase.

"Val no!" Melinda screamed, releasing Moira. She seized Valdemar's arm as he tore past her, but he threw her off.

"Let me go, Melinda," he said fiercely. "There are people dying up there!

He bolted off, then turned back. "Don't let Moira get away," he said, then disappeared into the flames.

Suddenly unrestrained, Moira cast a anguished glance at the spot where Adrian had been standing, then fled into the tunnels.

There was another explosion, then an ear-splitting crack. Melinda looked around wildly in search of the danger, then screamed, as the roof rushed down to meet the floor.

She dived into the tunnel as the upper floor collapsed in a shower of cement boulders. A thick screen of cement dust hung in the air, making it impossible to assess the damage.

"Valdemar!" she shouted with every ounce of air left in her lungs. There was only the roar of the blaze and the sound of cement falling in a rain of dust to the platform.

Flames leapt from the ragged hole where the floor had fallen away, their hot tongues flicking out greedily in search of more to consume. She called Valdemar's name again, chasing back the almost certain knowledge that Valdemar was dead. What silver bullets, wooden stakes and crosses couldn't do, a torrent of flame and several tons of falling concrete likely could.

Vampires never fought among themselves, Valdemar had told her proudly. That those who stole their lifeblood from others would squander it so recklessly filled her with fury.

With speed fueled by rage, Melinda raced down the tracks, kicking up gravel in her wake. In seconds she had reached the junction where the tracks met the main line. She could see Moira up in the distance, a crimson wraith fleeing into the darkness. She forced her legs to carry her faster, to cover more ground in her desperate strides.

Moira turned, risking a glance over her shoulder at the maniac who pursued her. Melinda heard her laughter as it ricocheted off the circular walls of the tunnel. The gap between them was closing.

She threw herself forward, snagging a handful of scarlet hair. They tumbled to the ground as one, each scrambling to gain the advantage.

Moira twisted to the top, straddling Melinda and pinning her arms against the ground. Melinda looked up into eyes of searing amber fire. "So you want to fight, do you Melinda?" she asked, curling her lips back to expose her chiseled fangs. "You could have just said so."

She was deceptively strong, a seasoned warrior and several hundred years her senior. Melinda had only her anger as battle armor. Moira licked her lips. "Your blood is so sweet," she said in remembrance of the vicious bite she'd dealt Melinda in the subway car. "I will savor every drop."

Melinda watched the gleaming fangs brush past her eyes as Moira lowered her head. She waited until Moira was almost certain of her victory, that fraction of a second just before her teeth hit the vein. Anticipating the ecstasy, Moira lowered her guard.

Melinda heaved herself upward, dislodging Moira and twisting free of her grasp. She scrambled upright, waiting for the next assault.

Moira rolled gracefully to her feet, appraising Melinda with a new respect. "Not bad fledgling," she hissed, then her foot shot out, snagging Melinda's legs and knocking her once again to the ground.

She dived onto Melinda, slamming her head against the metal rail with a resounding smack. Melinda felt the pain knife through her mind. Desperately, she freed a fist, catching Moira across the cheek. Pain reverberated up her arm. She heard a bone crack and couldn't tell if it was her hand or Moira's jaw that had broken.

They were both bleeding now, rolling in their own blood on the ground. Moira fought with every weapon she possessed, a tornado of teeth, nails, elbows and knees. Melinda returned the blows, revenge charging her assault more than skill.

"You have made a grave mistake," Moira snarled, "tangling with me." She issued a vehement blow that grazed Melinda's cheek like a handful of razor blades.

Melinda caught her arm, hauling it backward with a cruel twist. "No," she gasped, staggering to her feet. She twisted Moira's wrist further. Moira hissed in pain. "It's you who's made a mistake."

Moira stumbled backward, pulling Melinda with her in a deadly dance. Melinda fell, tumbling onto Moira in the gravel between the tracks. Moira hit the ground, sprawled beneath her. Melinda's head slammed against her shoulder, jolting her to awareness.

With a violent twist, she maneuvered her head toward Moira's neck, baring her teeth and driving them deeply into the jugular vein.

Moira's blood was scalding hot. It burned its way down her throat like acid. She howled in agony, vainly trying to free herself from the deadly fangs locked into her neck. Melinda held on with savage vengeance.

Moira thrashed violently against her, tearing at Melinda with her talons, ripping thick strips of skin from the side of her face. But she was beyond feeling anything except the rage inside her.

She drove her teeth further into Moira's neck, opening her throat to the rush of steaming liquid. She gulped the blood into her system, feeling Moira become weaker with each convulsive swallow.

Finally, Moira ceased to make any noise at all, but Melinda would not be done with her. Only when the flow of blood trickled into nothing and the silence stretched into long minutes, did Melinda pull her teeth from the still body.

She lay atop Moira, locked in that deadly embrace like a lover. The rage and the vengeance were gone. There was only sickness and repulsion at the ugly deed she had committed.

Finally, Melinda raised her head from the corpse's neck. Moira's arms fell limply to the ground. She stood uncertainly. Accusing eyes stared up at her, witness to the grisly thing she had done. Melinda looked down into the sightless amber eyes, then stooped and turned the body onto its face and walked off down the tunnel.

* * * *

The station was in darkness when she returned, the only light came from the fires that still burned in the station above, fueled by the thick carpets and tapestries of Valdemar's home.

Cornelius was gone, he had taken Kirsten's body with him, anxious to be alone with his grief.

Most of the ceiling was missing. Dust hung in the air, suspended by the dense smoke. It stung her eyes and ripped the breath from her throat, but Melinda continued to stand there. She had to go upstairs. She had to look.

Half of the staircase was missing. It fell sharply away on one side, giving an unrestrained view of the rubble on the floor below. Melinda put a hesitant foot forward and looked down, gasping when she caught a glimpse of paisley among the debris beneath her.

She jumped from the staircase, scraping her hands on the sharp bits of cement. She hauled on the fabric, it gave, revealing a foot of cloth from Valdemar's jacket.

Breath caught in her throat she looked at the mountain of wreckage that covered him. He must have been upstairs when the ceiling and floor collapsed about him. Melinda began to scrape frantically away at the jagged rocks of cement, knowing that by now the city would be searching frantically for the whereabouts of the missing train. It was only a matter of time before they located it and the bodies of its one hundred and fifty passengers buried under a mountain of smoldering ruin.

Her hands were bloody from the sharp edges of the cement and the splinters of marble when she finally liberated one of his arms. She felt his hand. It was cold, charred black with soot and blistered. She guessed there wasn't a bone in it that wasn't broken.

Frantically, she renewed her efforts, heedless of her bleeding hands, uncovering his legs, his torso and finally his face. He was too still to be conscious.

Melinda placed her legs against the final slab of marble that kept him pinned to the floor, levering herself between him and the monolith that held him. She put her entire soul into the task, using strength much beyond what a human could possibly wield. He came free suddenly, falling against her, as she staggered backwards.

Melinda looked down at the still form she held. His face was blistered almost beyond recognition, his clothes mostly burned away, showing black, blistered skin underneath. From the odd angle he was lying she could tell he had numerous broken bones. She looked at the dark stain on the ground where he had been trapped. He had lost a lot of blood. Melinda felt his scorched cheek, it was colder than his hand.

Just as she was convinced he was dead, the dark eyes flickered open. Valdemar looked up into her face with uncomprehending pain, then his eyes fell slowly closed. "Melinda," he whispered. "Please, leave me alone...."

"No!" She barely recognized her voice, tinged as it was from anguish and hoarse from all the smoke. She shook him gently, trying to rouse him again. She called his name, but he remained silent.

Life was quickly slipping away from him. Even a vampire's borrowed life could be extinguished. Until Kirsten died, she hadn't really understood that.

She looked down into Valdemar's charred face, remembering the passion they'd shared, the heat in his dark eyes when they made love. A multitude of conflicting feelings overlapped. But from out of her confusion came one over-riding thought: she loved Valdemar. He'd given her his blood. He'd given her back her life. She was hurt and she was angry. But no matter what else had happened between them, she simply couldn't let him die.

Blood, her sluggish brain told her. Only one thing could resurrect a vampire. Valdemar needed blood, warm nourishing blood from a living being.

There was nowhere she could go. He would never survive the journey out of the tunnels. And there was something very fitting about using the blood she had stolen from Moira to save his life.

Hesitantly, she raised her wrist to her mouth, resigning herself to what she was about to do. She shut her eyes, tasting the saltiness of her own skin, then the distinctive taste of her own blood. She bit deeper, choking from the pain and from the blood that ran down over her chin and onto Valdemar's face.

His blistered lips parted and he drew in a rasping breath. "No," he breathed. "Melinda no!"

She covered his mouth with her wrist, ending his protests, giving him no choice but to swallow the blood that was already rushing down his throat.

His tongue caressed her wrist. She shuddered at the touch remembering how his lips felt against her neck. But then instinct took over and he began to suck at the wound with increasing strength. It hurt, a terrible wrenching agony that tore back through her veins to her heart. She forced herself to hold her wrist at his mouth, in spite of the pain and the black haze of unconsciousness that loomed before her. She willed the curtain backward, forcing herself to remain conscious.

Finally, when there was no more she could safely give, she pulled her wrist from his mouth. Valdemar sighed deeply, but his eyes remained closed. She felt his cheek. His skin was warmer to the touch. The mangled hand was solid, whole.

Standing was a precarious accomplishment. Her system was still struggling to adjust to the sudden infusion, then equally sudden loss of blood. She teetered on her feet a few moments, then when the world stopped spinning, she bent and lifted Valdemar into her arms.

He moaned as she hauled him over her shoulder and started down the tracks. Something sparkled on the edge of the shadows. Melinda reached down and snagged the glittery thing. Kirsten's cross. She tucked it into the pocket of her ruined pant suit and continued on.

Progress was slow in her weakened condition and burdened by Valdemar's weight. She had to stop many times in the labyrinth of the tunnels before she saw the pale glow of dawn.

It was dark in the house Cornelius had shared with Kirsten, and for a heart stopping moment, Melinda feared he wasn't home. But he answered the door after several minutes of her persistent pounding.

Cornelius looked down at the burden she carried. Obviously he hadn't expected to find Valdemar alive. Now that Kirsten was dead the entire world seemed lost to him. But, he reached out his arms to relieve her of her burden.

Melinda fell against him, staggering at the sudden relief of weight. Surprise crossed Cornelius' face as he caught a glimpse of her blood-smeared wrist, the telltale evidence of how she had saved Valdemar's life, but he held his tongue.

He looked at the fading darkness. "You better come in, Melinda. It's nearly dawn."

She followed him upstairs to the bedroom he had shared with Kirsten. He laid Valdemar on their bed, heedless of the blood that soaked into the white lace bedspread. It was as if it was all ruined for him now, this Victorian home with all of its memorabilia.

Valdemar's eyes opened briefly, staring up at Cornelius, as if he couldn't understand how he'd come to be there.

"Sleep Val," Cornelius said. "You're safe now."

"Kirsten?" Valdemar asked, his voice nothing more than a whisper.

Cornelius started to answer him, but the words caught in his throat. He choked back the tears and swallowed hard. "Kirsten's gone," he told him finally.

But Valdemar had already sunk back into unconsciousness.

"Leave him to sleep," Cornelius said. He was looking at her again with a strange expression that might have been respect. "That was a dangerous thing to do," he said, catching her when she would have fallen to the floor under the weight of her own exhaustion. "You could have killed yourself. Little good that would have done."

"It's all right," she said in grim remembrance of what she had done to Moira. "I've drunk my fill tonight."

"Moira?" Cornelius asked incredulously. Obviously everything he'd ever thought about Melinda had just been proven untrue.

Melinda nodded. " I didn't even know vampires could die."

"Of course vampires die," Cornelius said gently. "We have remarkably long life spans, but we do not live forever."

"Oh," Melinda said, then her eyelids closed of their own accord.

They were in the living room. She didn't remember Cornelius taking her downstairs, but he was bending over her now, setting her down on the chintz sofa. "Go to sleep," he told her kindly. "I'll see to Valdemar."

* * * *

She awoke to the long shadows of late afternoon. Cornelius had thrown a blanket over her. He was sprawled in the chair across from her, still clad in the tattered tuxedo he'd been wearing yesterday. He hadn't even thought to find a blanket for himself, she thought with guilt. Sleep had helped to regulate her body. She felt stronger, more in control.

Melinda sat up, looking in disgust at the ruined black sequined jacket and white silk shirt that were coated with dried blood. She rose and donated the blanket to Cornelius and crept upstairs in search of the bathtub.

She peeked silently into the bedroom. Valdemar was still deeply asleep, but there was color in his lips and his breathing was strong and steady. She turned and closed the door to the bathroom, running a scalding hot bath and gratefully climbing into it.

There was a bathrobe hanging on the back of the door. She wrapped herself in it, the suit was beyond repair.

Something fell to the floor in a flash of gold as she bundled the ruined suit into a ball. Melinda reached down, finding the cross that had belonged to Kirsten. Cornelius was waiting for her in the hallway when she emerged. He had changed his clothes and tied his hair back in the usual ponytail.

"Valdemar is asking for you," he said quietly. "He won't believe me you are all right."

"Will he be okay?" she asked suddenly shy, and wanting only to be gone now, to be alone.

"I suspect he will be," Cornelius said, then he was quiet. "I think, Valdemar had resigned himself to his death," he said after some thought. "The pain of being betrayed by his friends, and ... seeing Kirsten die...." Cornelius said the last word with conviction, as if he had to say it to convince himself the nightmare was true, " ... destroyed his will to live. He's had a very long life after all. I don't think he had the stomach to continue. Please talk to him, Melinda," he begged her quietly. "He was less than happy to find himself alive, and more than a little confused to discover the one person he was sure hated him had come to his rescue."

"Perhaps it is best I don't see him," she told him. "I promised myself that we would never cross paths again."

"You owe him some sort of explanation," Cornelius insisted. "I know things have been ... difficult between you, but you must talk to him, Melinda. He's getting sick of talking to me."

"All right," Melinda reluctantly agreed. She reached within the pocket of the bathrobe and retrieved the slender gold cross. "Here," she said offering it to him. "I found it in the tunnel."

Cornelius folded it tightly into his fist and held it against his heart. He closed his eyes as if in prayer, a gesture he had no doubt absorbed after long years living with Kirsten. "No," he whispered, handing it back to her. "Give it to Val, he gave it to her."

CHAPTER NINETEEN

Melinda stood in the bedroom doorway, willing her feet to cross the narrow space between the hallway and the bed, to talk to Valdemar as she had promised Cornelius.

Valdemar's eyes were closed, his lashes long and dark against his inhumanly pale skin. Her blood had healed him. His skin was once again smooth and flawless. He looked deceptively peaceful, harmless even. It was easy to forget that behind that innocent and handsome face was the soul of killer.

Reflectively, she sat on the bed. Cornelius had gone back downstairs, leaving her alone with him. Valdemar's eyelids flickered, then opened into pools of ebony.

He looked at her for a long moment as though he didn't believe she was actually there beside him when everyone else was dead. Then he laughed weakly. "If it isn't Melinda, the woman who says she never wants to see me again and then appears out of nowhere and risks her life to save mine." He scanned her face, but when she offered him no answers he said, with the dry humor that was so like him, "I must know why Melinda, the curiosity is killing me."

Melinda shrugged. There were so many things she wanted to say to him, a multitude of questions to ask. To say anything would be to start an avalanche of emotion. "I don't know why," she whispered and looked away.

"You could have left me to die," Valdemar said gently, drawing her attention back to him. "After all, I've had an extraordinarily long life."

"Are you so unhappy to be alive?" she asked him then.

"Surprised," he told her, " ... especially to find you here."

"You know I couldn't have left you to die," she said. "My feelings for you are ... complicated."

"This I know," he acknowledged with a smile. "My feelings for you are also ... complicated." He thought on this for a moment. "Are we even then?" he asked her. "Now that we are both alive, though we would choose not to be?"

"Yes," Melinda said. "I suppose we are." She looked at him angrily. "You misled me about many things Valdemar. You told me vampires couldn't die."

"I told you it was impossible for vampires to commit suicide," he corrected.

"Whatever," she countered. "And I found out that is not entirely true."

"I am finding out that a lot of things I believed are no longer true," Valdemar bitterly. "Do you?" he asked her softly, "still wish I had killed you?"

"Sometimes," she told him with the bluntness of total honesty. "You have shown me a very loathsome part of my soul."

He accepted that with a nod.

Melinda reached into her pocket and withdrew the cross. It dangled from her fingers in a sparkle of gold as it reflected the candlelight. "Cornelius told me to give this to you."

Valdemar reached for the tiny cross on its gold chain, draping it across his palm.

"Kirsten thoroughly believed she was going to hell," Melinda said. "Do you think she did, go to hell I mean?"

"I don't believe in hell," Valdemar said, still gazing at the delicate gold thing in his hand. "Nor heaven for that matter." His fist closed upon the cross, tightly, as if it might suddenly evaporate.

"So, what will you do?" she asked him, anxious to talk about something else besides death. "Now that...."

"All my possessions have been reduced to ashes?" Valdemar finished. "They were only things," he said soberly. "I can always get more things."

"But your journal. You wrote that journal over hundreds of years."

"I have a good memory.". He looked beyond her, lost in his thoughts. "Everything I touch turns to ashes, sooner or later."

"Are you going to stay in Toronto?"

"No, I think I would like to live in Europe again. Somewhere," he said with amusement, "impervious to fire and out in the open so it won't collapse. It might be nice to live in a castle again, and I've been growing tired of North America. It's time I went home."

Melinda smiled. The thought of Valdemar living in a castle

suited him perfectly. "And how exactly, do you intend to acquire a castle?" she asked him in spite of herself.

"I intend to purchase one, of course," Valdemar said. "Even the most modest of investments yield considerable returns over eleven hundred years."

"I'll keep that in mind," she said, laughing at the simplicity of it all.

"What about you?" he asked. "Are you going back to your cramped quarters above the York Hotel?"

"You knew where I was," she said, outraged. "Don't you have anything better to do than spy on me?"

"On the contrary," Valdemar said. "I wasn't spying on you at all. I was walking by on the street one evening, and I heard Kirsten singing. So, I stopped in the doorway to listen to her and found you working behind the bar."

"I need to get away," she said after a moment. "I need some time alone to think, and the world is a big place. I'd like to see some of it."

They were quiet for a moment, having run out of safe things to say.

"Promise me something," Valdemar said suddenly. "Promise me sometime you'll forgive me for all of this."

That simple entreaty released the tears that were soon running down her cheeks and spilling over onto the blankets. Valdemar reached forward and wiped them away. She looked up, into those black eyes she could never forget. "I don't know if I can do that, Val."

"Perhaps not." He let his hand fall from her cheek. "Have a good life, Melinda."

Melinda stood up, anxious to be beyond the range of his touch. She moved to the door, then looked back suddenly, but he had already turned his face away from her.

CHAPTER TWENTY

Melinda flipped through the map of Canada, forcing herself to look beyond the familiar cities scattered along the American border. She was searching for a destination unlike any place she had ever been, a place that offered peace and quiet and long periods of darkness. She scanned the exotic sounding names of the far north: Inuvik, Aklavik, Tuktoyaktuk.

Summer was fading fast in the south. The first few nights of killing frost were already creeping across the land. It was the season of death, when the ground grew cold and the leaves withered and fell from the trees.

Almost before the idea had finished taking shape in her mind, Melinda was on a plane, heading for the purifying cold of the far north.

She roamed the permafrost for months, drifting from one tiny, secluded settlement to another, staying only a few weeks in each. Sometimes she found a place that could support her for a few months and set up a nomadic sort of housekeeping. The long periods of unbroken darkness eased her mind and settled her soul.

* * * *

It was dark in this daytime that was so like the night. Melinda walked across the glistening landscape that reminded her of the sugar icing her mother used to put on birthday cakes.

She was wearing a fur coat that was white like the scenery, gloves of snow rabbit fur and pale boots. Only her hair flew loose about her shoulders beneath her hood, blending in with the dark sky as her clothes became an indistinguishable part of the countryside.

Her vampire metabolism still amazed her. She could feel the cold that surrounded and caressed her yet didn't bite at her fingers. It was as though she sat beside a glass window, looking out into the cold but feeling only a fraction of it.

A polar bear lumbered out onto the ice a hundred yards from her. She had felt him moving toward her off in the distance long before her keen eyesight had picked him out from the background. He stopped to sniff the air, scenting her in the icy breeze that blew unhindered past them. Melinda was still, entrapping him in her stare. *Come nearer*, she willed him, and cautiously he came.

He was strong smelling on the clean air, an exquisite and imposing creature weighing easily eighteen hundred pounds. He reared up on his hind legs in challenge, towering over her, issuing an echoing growl into the darkened sky.

Melinda looked up into the black eyes set like ebony jewels in the white fur. His jaw dropped open, exposing rows of ivory teeth set against his crimson tongue. He could devour her easily, and knowing that excited her. She met his threatening gaze, following it down as he dropped back to all fours and crept toward her.

His breath was visible in the frigid air. Melinda removed a glove and reached out to touch the coarse white fur. He tipped his nose up to catch her scent again and in doing that he looked into her eyes.

In that moment he was hers completely. Melinda sunk her teeth into the thin fur on the underside of his neck.

Scalding droplets of blood fell to the ground beneath, freezing into garnet icicles against the virgin snow. The bear rumbled, his teeth snapped the air beside her face, then he was still. His warm blood rushed into her core, warming her from the inside, insulating her against the hostile environment. His life-force was as potent as he, and Melinda realized suddenly that she could drink her fill and not harm him.

She dug her fingers deeply into the thick fur, kneading the solid muscle beneath her hands. He growled softly, she felt the vibration flow from his throat into hers.

It was an insubstantial sort of feeding that would sustain her only a few short days, yet it reduced her need for human victims. It was a wholesome act, as if they were both creatures feeding from the goodness of this icy land, rather than the leavings of human urban society.

The polar bear sunk to his side, Melinda felt his strong legs weaken beneath him. She knelt with him on the ice, bending above his head, drinking until she was sated.

She straightened eventually, opening her eyes, drifting back into the present. She stroked the white muzzle gently, then wandered a few steps away from him. A rough snort broke the silence, she turned to look back at him, but the polar bear was already loping away from her, disappearing back into the frigid scenery around them.

* * * *

Rumors followed Melinda like shadows. Dogs howled at nothing in the quiet, sunless days. Parents resurrected grisly folk tales to threaten their children into good behavior. Yet, in the silent hours just after midnight, they too felt the icy grip of dread and they performed rituals to ward off demons.

Melinda paid these stories little heed. Sometimes in the first weak, sunny days of spring, she longed to roam southward to the familiarity of the crowded cities. She thought of the darkness that could only be found in the narrow streets between buildings, the vast underground walkways and the smell of many human bodies in close contact. And once in a while, walking under the featureless sky, she thought of Valdemar. But the fragile summers were as brief as dreams and the days grew swiftly shorter until darkness claimed the season.

CHAPTER TWENTY-ONE

Melinda awoke one evening, as the bleeding sun died on the horizon. A feeling of expectation hung in the air as the day lingered between the last evening and the perpetual night. She poured herself a glass of blood-red wine, then went to sit by the window. A shadow crossed the walkway. She went to the door.

It opened, letting in a blast of sub-zero air, and she looked into those black eyes that opened into eternity.

"Valdemar," she said, standing in the open doorway, despite the considerable cold. "It's been awhile," she murmured at last, having nothing more appropriate to say.

"Three thousand, seven hundred days and ten hours," Valdemar said dryly. He looked around him at the stark white landscape and the black sky that was featureless except for a scattering of diamond stars. "Surely you didn't have to move to the arctic to get away from me, Melinda."

Melinda smiled. "The arctic has many things to offer, peace, quiet, and long, dark winters."

"I prefer a warmer climate," Valdemar said shivering. He looked longingly at the fire in the living room beyond. "Are you going to ask me in Melinda? Legend has it you must invite a vampire into your home, otherwise he is powerless to cross the threshold."

Melinda laughed. "So they say. Very well, Valdemar the Vampire, come in. I wouldn't leave you to freeze on my doorstep, although I admit there was a time when I might have."

"You realize," Valdemar said teasingly, "if you do let this vampire into your home, he may bite you."

"I think you should tell this vampire," she said with mock seriousness. It had a strange sense of rightness to it. Somehow she'd always known he'd come looking for her, "he may have underestimated his hostess."

"I'll remind him to be on his best behavior," he promised, letting the door swing closed behind him. He was dressed in black, in a long coat of lightweight thermal material that covered him from the tips of his ears to the tops of his boots. He was waiting, despite his self-assured manner, for her to make the next move.

She drew him into her living room to the raging fire and the open bottle of wine. He looked exactly as she remembered him, a study in contrasts: ivory skin, raven hair, and those ebony eyes she didn't want to look too closely into, at least not yet.

He let her seat him on the couch and sat still while she looked down at him. "So," she asked finally. "What brings you to the cold north?"

He frowned, looking down at his hands, his boots, anywhere but into her eyes. "I came to tell you a story."

"What kind of story?"

"A story about us," he said. "Cornelius is insisting on it."

"And how is Cornelius?"

"Fine," Valdemar said with a mischievous grin. "He has a new lover, and he's tired of watching me pine for you." He was quiet for a few moments, then he said, "I wanted to let you go, Melinda. It seemed to be the kindest thing to do. But I couldn't. You made me think differently. You made me think about things I didn't want to think about, things I had forgotten. You gave me a little of my humanity back."

Melinda turned away from him, retrieving the bottle of wine and another glass. It was an old human sort of habit, she thought ironically, drinking to relieve her distress. "This story," she said. "I think I already know how it goes."

Valdemar took the offered glass of wine. "Do you?"

She nodded. "I know it wasn't you who attacked me." She watched as the expression on his face slowly turned from polite curiosity to wonder.

"How," he asked incredulously, "do you know this?"

Could she tell him? "I read it in your journal," she said, leaving out Kirsten's part in it. She let that thought sink in for a moment. "You tried to tell me, but I wouldn't believe you. After all, you were sitting there when I got on the subway."

"Go on." He waited for her to continue.

"Moira and Adrian got you drunk and took you hunting," she said, daring to say it aloud for the first time. "They made a feast of me, and they saved the choice bit for you."

Valdemar winced.

"But you couldn't do it, could you Val?"

"No," he whispered. "Tempting as you were."

"So you took me home, and you kept me for yourself. And that made your friends angry with you."

"Only Kirsten understood."

"Because she'd been in my place most recently," Melinda supplied. "And because she felt responsible."

He sighed. "Moira was already upset with me for bringing Kirsten into our group. I didn't realize how much her wrath had grown over the years. She was determined to get even with me for abandoning her, as she saw it. She was sure if she could give me a big enough shock I would revert back to my old ways and all would be as it was before. It was all a grand game to her, a form of entertainment. And I was arrogant enough to believe there was nothing she could do to hurt me." He looked to her for sympathy. "They were my friends, Melinda. I trusted them."

"Those we trust have the power to betray us more than anyone else," Melinda said.

"Yes," Valdemar agreed. "I should have seen it coming, but I wanted to believe they had accepted you. I never thought Moira would be jealous enough to try to poison you."

"Why didn't you tell me the truth?"

"I was afraid if you knew how we'd been thrust together you'd never believe me that I loved you. I thought I could protect you."

"You never told me you loved me, Valdemar," Melinda said. "It might have made a difference."

"You are a child of my blood," Valdemar said earnestly. "How could I not love you?" He searched for the right words to explain himself. "I offered you what was most sacred to me, life. But, I expected too much. I expected you to understand things beyond your experience to comprehend."

He stood and paced a few steps away from her, then turned back. "I hoped it would prove to Moira and Adrian that they couldn't bend me to their whim, but it only made them more determined. They still weren't satisfied, even after you left me. They wanted to ruin me, to impress upon me that my position as leader of our group was finished and hence forward things would be done their way."

"It turned out very badly indeed," Melinda said, staring at the red shadows the fire cast on the coffee table. "On top of everything else, I hated you. I abhorred what you were, what I was. I hated you for destroying my life."

"I guess that was to be expected," Valdemar said. "Kirsten hated me also at first, despite my best intentions."

"And on top of that, I drove you crazy."

"Yes," Valdemar said with harsh laughter. "You had the most disarming way of looking into my soul and ferreting out the most painful moments of my life."

"I don't know what you mean," Melinda insisted.

"Yes you do," Valdemar said, mimicking her. "*That dress in your closet, Valdemar. Those poems in your diary, Valdemar, who are they for? Tell me your pain Valdemar.* And what would you have done with that information, Melinda? Hmm?"

"It was coin to bargain with," Melinda said, as if explaining it to herself. "Insurance against you hurting me again. But you were the one person I didn't need to protect myself from."

"Loving you," Valdemar said, "was like preparing for battle."

"Well," she said. "We aren't at war anymore, Valdemar."

"I don't have much of a stomach for war," he said. "I'm getting too old to fight."

"I miss you," Melinda admitted. "On clear nights I sit by the window and look at the stars. All my life, I have wondered what was up there, and it occurred to me suddenly that if I live long enough, I just might find out."

"I wouldn't be at all surprised if you were the first vampire in space," Valdemar said and then he laughed.

"Lately, I've started to think about time differently. All of a sudden, I have time on my hands. Time to just live, time to enjoy the beauty around me." She reached out a hand to touch his cheek.

"Then you forgive me?" he asked solemnly.

She nodded. "I'm supposed to be dead, Valdemar. One day everything and everyone I ever loved will be dead, and time slips through my fingers faster than I ever thought it could pass by."

Valdemar looked at her with those black eyes that could never be called human. Eyes that looked out on eternity, as if it were his to take, and yet spoke of such pain, such tenderness ... "I'm not supposed to be here either," he said. "I have cheated time twice, and whether you count that as right or wrong, it is also a wonderful gift."

"You always did see it that way," Melinda said. "But you couldn't make me understand." She held him in her gaze. "Are you going to tell me?"

"Tell you what?"

"Tell me about you. Who you are, who you *were*. About the lady who belonged to the dress in your closet?"

"I suppose I might as well," Valdemar said. "You'll pry the information out of me eventually won't you?"

Melinda smiled wickedly. "I would make it my life's work."

Valdemar looked beyond her, into the flames of the fire. "I was," he said slowly, as if it were a struggle to remember, "dying. It's odd, I can remember the sickness, the pain, the fear, and yet I can't remember. It's almost as if I heard the story second hand." He furrowed his brows in concentration. "In my twenty-ninth year a plague swept through our village, and when it was gone there weren't many of us left. My wife and children were among the first to succumb. My land and my livestock were failing from neglect. I was dying, and one night when I was all alone sweating out the last of my life, I opened my eyes to see a beautiful woman standing over me. I kept seeing her in my fevered sleep. And then, I got better. But of course, I wasn't better ...

"I thought of my transformation quite differently than you," he said after a time. "To me it was a small price to pay for the privilege of knowing the future. That's why I could never understand Kirsten's insistence that she was irrevocably damned, nor your anger over your tarnished soul and lost life. To me, eternity was a gift. I had been saved from my pathetic existence and my meaningless death by a beautiful angel. I loved her with all my being. And as you have so perceptively guessed, Melinda, she broke my heart."

"Did she have a name?" Melinda asked.

"Yes," Valdemar said and smiled to himself. "Her name was Rowena. I suppose she pitied me. She came back for me, took me with her, kept me much the way you'd keep a pet. I was a diversion, entertainment when she was bored. Until she got bored with me for good." He walked to the window, his back to her, looking out into the darkness. Melinda watched his reflection in the glass.

There was one more nagging mystery to solve. Melinda had a sneaking suspicion the two were somehow connected. "What about Moira? Why did she want to be your lover so badly when she had Adrian and it was clear you didn't want her?"

"Because she was created to be my lover," Valdemar said, turning and coming back to stand before her.

"You made her?" Melinda asked. It didn't seem like the kind of thing Valdemar would have done.

"No," Valdemar said. "Rowena made her. Perhaps she felt guilty abandoning me. Whatever her reason, she made Moira to keep me company. But, Moira was never the woman for me. It was an unfortunate situation. There was really no reason for her to exist.

We made a tragic pair, me longing for Rowena and Moira pining for me. Our common pain was the only basis of our friendship. Moira made Adrian to take my place. Or maybe it was to make me jealous. Either way it didn't work."

Valdemar sat down beside her again, pulling her into his arms. "Come back to me, Melinda. I can't live without you and I can't die. Please don't leave me to suffer so."

She tore herself from his gaze, the look that compelled her to do things against her better judgment. "Leave you? You don't seem to want to go away."

"No," Valdemar said, "But, you must do this willingly this time. My conscience can't handle any more guilt."

"You told me once you didn't have a conscience," Melinda said.

"I seem to have found it again, and since then it has done nothing but torment me. So you must think about this Melinda, eternity is a long time to be stuck with me."

"You have it wrong, Valdemar," Melinda said. "Eternity is a long time to be stuck with *me*."

He smiled then, and pulled her into his arms. She looked up into his eyes.

Melinda snuggled deeper into his embrace. His body was still cool from the air outside. But the heat in his eyes betrayed the fire between them. His teeth scraped her earlobe, then meandered down her neck. She sucked in a breath as hunger so briefly appeased by the polar bear's blood flared back to life.

His fingers bunched in the hem of her sweatshirt. He tugged it up over her head and tossed it on the arm of the couch. She stripped off his coat and dropped it on top of her sweatshirt. Tugging the hem of his shirt free from his jeans, she slid her hands across the hard muscles of his back. But eventually that felt too restricting. She undid the buttons of his shirt. Grasping the sides, she pulled it down over his biceps and added it to the steadily growing pile of their clothes. He kicked off his boots and gazed at her, dark curls still tousled from the wind and eyes wild with hunger.

Outside the wind picked up, scudding dark clouds across the horizon. The fire dimmed, briefly losing to the wind before gathering its strength again. Melinda uttered her own groan of frustration as she worked on the button of Valdemar's jeans. He raised his head and smiled at her efforts. But instead of helping her, he lowered his head and took the tip of one breast into his mouth. Offering a dual onslaught, his cool hands strayed to the zipper of her jeans. Razor-sharp nails grazed her buttocks as he pushed her jeans over her hips and down into a puddle of denim on the floor. Finally she worked the button of his jeans free and drew them down over his thighs, taking the silk of his briefs with them. He responded by skimming off her lacy underwear. Then he sank to his knees before her.

She moaned as his mouth found the tender place between her thighs. His hands cupped her buttocks, taking more of her into his mouth. She felt the keen edge of his teeth, then the rough caress of his tongue. Desire surged, sexual arousal tinged with bloodlust. Her head rolled backward, shaking loose a cascade of dark curls. Her hands gripped his shoulders as his tongue stroked her to the peak of her desire. As if from far away, she heard her own hoarse cries as her tension broke. Her head rolled forward, blinding her behind a curtain of her own hair. Blinding her to all but a surge of hunger and the pulse that beat in Valdemar's neck.

He released her, letting her slide through his arms until she rested on her knees. Her mouth found the vein. He tensed as skin parted beneath the sharp points of her teeth. Blood, hot and salty, poured down her throat.

Valdemar lifted her, pressing his arousal deep inside her. Her body closed around him, taking him deeper as his teeth claimed her throat.

The wind rose to a vicious roar. Oblivious, Melinda clung to him as he urged her toward the fulfillment of their mutual desire. Valdemar's harsh cry of release mingled with hers as she rode the last waves of pleasure. He pulled his mouth from her neck. She looked up eyes glazed with passion. Her blood stained his lips. A trickle of his own blood flowed in a crimson trickle down the center of his chest. He pulled her hard against him, smearing them both with his blood.

In the fireplace, a powerful gust flattened the last of the flames. The fire gave up the fight and died out.

And then there was only silence and the howling of the wind outside.

CHAPTER TWENTY-TWO

"Must you drive so fast?"

Melinda dug her nails into the leather upholstery as the Porsche slid sideways, wheels spinning on the wet pavement.

"One hundred kilometers is hardly fast," Valdemar replied righting the car with a quick twist of his arm.

She peered into the shifting fog. "You can't see a damned thing!"

Despite her keen eyesight, she found it hard to catch more than nebulous glimpses of the landscape. It took a great amount of will to believe there was still solid ground beneath them, that the road had not been swallowed up by the all-consuming mist.

"I know where I'm going, Melinda," Valdemar said, turning off Airport Road and heading north. "I live here, remember? And besides, in ninety years, I've never received so much as a speeding ticket." The low sports car hit a pothole hard, the sudden impact throwing her against the door. She cringed at the sound of the exhaust system grating against asphalt.

"Cops always miss drivers like you," she said sullenly, out of frustration that had to do with something else entirely.

At first returning to urban life seemed like a wonderful adventure, but now that the adventure was unfolding into reality it seemed like a bad idea, becoming worse with each passing minute. In the hour since her plane had touched down at Pearson International, she'd been herded through the baggage claim, jostled, elbowed. Even though Valdemar had been there to meet her as promised, the walk from the arrivals level to the nearby parking garage had set her nerves on edge. She'd jumped at the sound of every car motor starting and flinched at the multitude of headlights flying toward her down the parking ramp. Coming home to Toronto from the quiet Canadian North was going to be a much bigger adjustment than she'd expected.

"If you'd stop trying to drive from the passenger seat, you might feel better," Valdemar snapped, then added more compassionately, "We're almost there."

Relieved, she looked at the scenery before her, familiar routes nearly unrecognizable in the heavy fog. They left the highway and turned into a narrow lane where the streetlights resembled antique lamp posts.

The street wound its way up a low hill, ending at last in a wide crescent. Gravel crunched beneath the Porsche's wheels as they turned into a wide driveway and came at last to a stop.

Melinda peered through the car window at the large gray structure that lurked behind a curtain of fog. They were greeted by the barking of several vicious-sounding dogs, which ceased their alarm abruptly when Valdemar stepped from the car.

A gentle wind parted the fog like drapery and Melinda gazed at last at her new home.

A laugh escaped her lips, echoing off the nearby walls. She backed up a few paces for a better view while Valdemar waited patiently, arms crossed, for her pronouncement.

Rising out of the fog, complete with turrets, draw bridge and moat, was a medieval-looking castle.

"You're kidding ... right?"

"Now Melinda," Valdemar said, with mirth of his own, "you have to admit, the place has atmosphere."

Melinda stepped back from the fence, the only barrier between her and the glinting eyes of a large Doberman. "Tell me you didn't have this monstrosity built especially for you."

"The previous owner left town," Valdemar offered cheerfully. "I got it for a steal."

"I thought you were going back to Germany."

"I was," Valdemar said, a little wistfully. "But then I found this place and I thought you'd be more comfortable in your native country. After all this time, I have grown fond of Canada."

"You bought this place for me?" she asked incredulously. "An ordinary house would have sufficed."

"It appealed to my ... sense of humor," Valdemar said.

Melinda stared down the fog shrouded street where drifting mist offered glimpses of several other mammoth estates. One was built in Spanish architecture and several others imitated English country estates. "But you have neighbors!" she stammered.

"And how better to hide than in a crowd."

"How very quaint. Do you trade gardening secrets over the back fence?"

Valdemar ignored the jibe. "So far, my neighbors have been most hospitable."

"Sure, until they find out what you really are."

"And how will that happen, Melinda? I'm not likely to make a meal out of one of my neighbors. And neither are you," he warned.

"Don't they ask you questions? Like what you do for a living and why you're never about in the daytime?"

"Of course they do."

"What do you tell them?"

"I tell them the truth, Melinda."

"Which is?"

"That I'm a well-known artist, who's just a little eccentric and prefers to paint at night."

"You paint?" she said, amazed. "Are you any good?"

"The people who buy my paintings seem to think so."

Laughter began deep in the pit of her stomach, bubbling up over her lips, reducing her to helpless hilarity.

Valdemar smiled, the smile that could make her believe he really was a wealthy twenty-nine year-old. "Shall we go inside?"

"Oh absolutely, I can hardly wait to see the interior of this place."

Hollow footsteps echoed across the wooden drawbridge. Underneath, Melinda could hear the trickle of water. The bridge ended at an arched doorway, through which the rich glow of a fire could be seen.

The door opened abruptly, startling Melinda, and revealing an impeccably dressed, silver-haired man.

He gave Melinda only the briefest glance and bowed slightly to Valdemar. Valdemar said something in German that sounded like a greeting and an order. The man nodded once and turned toward Melinda.

Valdemar motioned to the elderly gentleman. "Melinda, this is Hilliard Greif."

Hilliard inclined his head. "Welcome."

"Mr. Greif is my ... assistant. Should you need anything, do not hesitate to ask him. Come," he said, handing over the car keys so Hilliard could see to the details of parking and unloading the luggage.

Melinda studied Hilliard as he walked away. He had a gentleman's manners, but the measuring look he'd given her as they'd been introduced made her skin crawl.

"Does Hilliard live here too?" she asked as they crossed the threshold.

"He does."

"All the time?"

Valdemar regarded her curiously. "Yes, Melinda. Why?"

"Nothing," she said with a shrug, trying to appear more relaxed than she felt.

Compared to the size of the impressive estate, the entrance hall was small. An imposing chandelier, ablaze in a multitude of low watt light bulbs and a Persian carpet were the only decorations in the foyer. A two way fireplace beckoned to the sitting room beyond.

She wandered into the antechamber and gazed through the full length window. "Are you crazy Valdemar?" she asked suddenly, face pressed against the glass. "There's a golf course out there."

"Yes," Valdemar said. "Do you golf Melinda? I'll give you a game sometime, after dark of course...."

He's lost his mind, she assured herself with a shake of her head. Either that, or after fifty years of living like a recluse, Valdemar had become a responsible member of society. *This isn't fair. All the rules have changed.*

"Let's go upstairs." Valdemar drew her away from the window and the lilac leather couch that seemed so inviting.

She followed him back into the foyer and up the spiral staircase to the second floor, where the white plastered walls were nearly obscured by paintings hung in neat rows. Additional chandeliers hung a regular intervals, illuminating the hall in their dull orange glow. Plush carpets crushed beneath their feet.

One of the paintings demanded her attention and Melinda lagged behind for a closer look. Up close, the picture deteriorated into a maze of rough brush strokes, yet from a few feet away, the effect was striking. It was a painting of a beautiful blonde woman, sitting before her dressing table brushing her knee length hair. Her gray eyes looked out of the painting with mischief, as if she had been captured in that moment by a lover. Melinda recognized both the woman and the look. *Kirsten!* The gold framed painting was signed simply V.B.

"You are good," she said, realizing suddenly the "V" stood for Valdemar. "What does the "B" stand for?"

"Berthold," he said impatiently, waiting.

"Valdemar Berthold? Now, I could be wrong, but don't both those names mean "great ruler", or something like that?"

"They do in fact."

"Someone had big plans for you."

"Yes," he said, annoyingly not revealing whether this was his original name or something he'd invented for himself. "Someone did."

"Aren't they both first names?"

"They are," he wrapped an arm around her waist to draw her away, "my first two names."

"How many do you have?" she asked, unnerved that he had more than the usual one or two.

"A few," he said tersely and pulled her with him.

It was oddly out of character for him to accumulate names from his former existences, when he was so ruthlessly practical in the rest of his life. But Valdemar was prone to odd moments of sentimentality. Melinda thought of the closet in his last home full of eighteenth century clothes and shrugged.

Valdemar led her up a spiral staircase, housed in one of the six turrets, to the third and upper floor of the castle. He looked tense, she thought, as if he was anxious to be somewhere else.

Melinda followed him silently, still trying to work her mind around this unfamiliar Valdemar who lived in a bedroom community north of Toronto, whose speech had suddenly become full of modern mannerisms. There had been so many other things to discuss when he'd come to visit her, she hadn't thought to ask him what he'd been doing for the past ten years. Stupidly, she'd assumed he existed much as he had before, on the fringes of society, living in some rat infested crypt.

Or has he finally realized that can be dangerous?

He rushed her along the labyrinthine hallway. Through open doorways, she caught glimpses of libraries, ballrooms, sitting rooms, all furnished in the overly-decorated style Valdemar favored.

Melinda craned her neck for another peek into those rooms, bumping into Valdemar who had stopped without warning before a door of darkly stained wood. The gleaming brass handle turned beneath his hand, opening into a series of rooms as richly embellished as the rest of the place.

"These are your rooms."

Melinda looked around in delight and astonishment at the suite before her. To be so lavishly accommodated in such spacious surroundings made her feel both lonely and claustrophobic.

Valdemar gestured toward the seemingly endless hall. "My rooms are in the next wing."

She nodded absently, still trying to take it all in.

"I'm afraid I must leave you now," Valdemar said, confirming her earlier suspicion. "I have business to attend to in the city."

"Take me with you." Suddenly she didn't want to be alone.

"That isn't possible."

"Why?"

"I really don't have time to explain," he said, trying to extract himself from the argument he knew was coming.

"I can't believe you planned to be elsewhere on the night I return to you after ten years."

Valdemar's expression was as dark as his coloring. "Something came up unexpectedly. Unfortunately, it can't wait until tomorrow."

Melinda regarded him skeptically.

"Please don't argue Melinda. We do have forever...."

She sighed deeply, hating him for reasoning with her. "Go then, if you must."

"Hilliard will see to anything you need."

"Sure," she said curtly, wishing he'd just go if he was going and leave her to panic in private. "Fine."

"I will see you later then?" he said uncertainly, walking in the direction of the door.

"Right," she said, then, "Val?"

He stopped, turning back.

"Who is Hilliard?"

"He is, as I said Melinda, my assistant."

"Is he ... human?"

"No. He is not."

A multitude of questions sprang to her lips.

"We will have to talk tomorrow," Valdemar said. "I must go."

"Bye," she said with an exasperated wave. One of Valdemar's most infuriating traits was that he kept to his own timetable and would be forthcoming with information when it suited him.

He looked at her briefly, torn between his obligation to her and his impending appointment, then he was gone.

Melinda sank down onto a nearby couch, watching him depart through the mahogany door.

Damn! she cursed in silent outrage. *How could he leave me like this?*

A disturbing notion wrenched her from her annoyance. Valdemar's affairs were dangerous business under the best of circumstances. *What on earth is he into this time? More accurately, what have I gotten myself into?*

Melinda yanked her thoughts from the path they wandered. *Ten years of living alone is making you paranoid. He could have gone to see his real estate agent. There's no sense worrying about nothing."*

Deep in thought, she traced the embroidered lines of vines up the arm of the divan she was sitting on to where they blossomed in a floral pattern on the seat and back. She snorted softly. Definitely Valdemar's taste. It would never have occurred to her to embroider a couch. Looking about, she counted six couches in her sitting room alone. People who lived in castles seemed to thrive among clutter she decided.

God, I'm going to smother to death among all this stuff! she thought, then immediately felt guilty. It was that kind of thoughtfulness that softened her heart ... and ultimately drove her crazy.

Melinda rested her feet against the coffee table, and considered the huge fireplace on the far wall. *Big enough to park a car in. I wonder how many trees you'd have to kill to get a fire going in that ...*

Beyond the sitting room was a spacious bedroom and she rose and wandered through the arched doorway to investigate.

She gravitated to the four-poster bed that was draped with thick tapestries, a defense against the blinding light of day. With the drapes closed, it would be dark as a tomb inside. Valdemar had a bed much like it in his last residence, but that was his bed, not hers and she could no more imagine sleeping in it than living in this absurd representation of a castle.

Another doorway revealed a bathroom with a pool-sized bathtub, a pedestal sink of white marble with a round gilded mirror above it, and a wooden cabinet containing an assortment of freshly starched, white linens. Overwhelmed, she circled back to the bedroom and sat forlornly on the massive bed.

There was a light knock at the outer door; Hilliard with her luggage. He bowed stiffly in greeting.

Melinda studied him, searching for the telltale signs: the pointed eyeteeth, the claw-like fingernails. But Hilliard didn't smile and his nails were neatly manicured.

"Will you require anything else this evening, Madam?" he asked politely when she merely stared at him.

"No-no, I'm fine ... thank you," she told him, heaving a sigh of relief when he left.

Staring out the bedroom window, she strained her eyes to pierce the thick curtain of fog. *Valdemar has to come back sometime. It's his castle, after all.* She might as well unpack. She might be here for a long, *long* time.

* * * *

Melinda awoke in the utter dark before dawn, disoriented by her unfamiliar surroundings. A symphony of strange sounds assaulted her acute hearing. Moisture dripped between crevices in the stone exterior. She swore she could even hear the scamper of tiny feet on the smooth rock.

Now that's silly. A new building like this couldn't possibly have rats!

Attempts to will herself back to slumber only made her feel even more lonely and displaced. Eventually, she heard a soft tread on the stairway below, followed by a door opening quietly down the hall. Footsteps trailed off inside into silence.

Go back to sleep! she ordered her weary mind and body, but sleep was maddeningly elusive. Finally her annoyance at being abandoned overcame her and she went in search of Valdemar.

She wandered the shadowed halls until she came to a door so decorated with brass fixtures it could only be his.

His door was not locked. She prowled through the outer rooms until she came at last to his spacious bedroom. Pale as a ghost, she stood in the doorway, gazing in awe at a bed large enough to sleep half a dozen people. Silently, she crossed the threshold.

Black eyes flashed open, glinting like dark jewels in the faint light. "It used to be considered improper for a lady to wander into a man's bedroom, Melinda."

"I couldn't sleep," she said, sitting on the side of his bed without invitation. "Being in such large rooms alone makes me feel ... lonely."

Valdemar surveyed her with an expression of annoyance tinged with amusement and waited for her to continue.

"Coming here seemed like such a good idea when we were sitting in the living room of my house up north. But, now that I'm here the reality of it all is ... more than a little overwhelming." She gestured to the empty air. "I'm not used to city living anymore, and we never did discuss how things were going to be between us after all that's happened...."

Valdemar held up the heavy blanket, making a space for her underneath. She crawled in beside him, next to his warm, naked body.

"Stop worrying. You'll get used to civilization again, and we have the rest of eternity to talk about us." He opened his mouth to say something further, but she held up a hand to silence him.

"Please don't start right now."

He laughed softly, pulling her against him.

"My uh, boldness offends you, doesn't it?" she said, hinting at an apology for invading his territory and robbing him of sleep.

He drew the covers up about their necks and snuggled down underneath. "No, I think I'm finally getting used to you."

"Used to me? Since when has it been proper for lovers to have separate bedrooms?"

"Until very recently."

"How many centuries ago is recently?" One had to be specific when talking to Valdemar.

"It is still common practice among the wealthy."

"And I suppose a true lady would wait for her lover to come to her, which of course he wouldn't do until they'd been lawfully wed, or something charmingly archaic like that."

"Yes," Valdemar said with a gentle kiss on her forehead. "Something charmingly archaic like that."

"And then I suppose she would coyly pretend she wasn't interested in his attentions. Do I have it right?"

"More or less."

"What a waste of time."

"It was called courtship, Melinda."

"I wouldn't have the patience."

"Patience is not one of your strengths."

"No," she agreed, nuzzling into the warm hairs on his chest. "It's been a long time...."

"It's only been a few months since I saw you last...."

"That's still a long time to me."

Valdemar traced the outline of her lips with his finger. "I suppose to you it is. Sometimes I forget how young you are."

His lips settled against hers, warm and feather soft. He nibbled on her bottom lip, teasing her with one razor sharp incisor.

His kiss grew more purposeful. Refusing to be distracted, she pulled away, resisting the urge to look in those dark eyes that could only mean trouble. "So where were you? What could possibly be more important than our long awaited reunion?"

"Must we talk about it now?"

"Can't imagine anything I'd like better."

"Really? Knowing you as I do, I doubt that." Determined to prove his theory, his mouth closed over one nipple. With his tongue, he teased it to a taut peak. Even through the silk it felt delightful and she moaned out loud. His mouth quirked into a smile at the sound. Encouraged, his hands followed the contours of her body until his fingers located the hem of her nightgown where it lay gathered against her thigh. Warm hands traveled upwards under the gauzy fabric until he found the place that ached with desire. With deft fingers he stroked her, until she writhed helplessly beneath his sensual onslaught. Deciding the material of her nightgown had become too confining, he pulled it over her head and tossed it aside. "You were right," he said then, "it has been a long time."

The months that they'd been separated suddenly seemed like years. Once he'd reawakened the desire between them it felt like forever.

Damn it he was smooth. *And so he should be, after that many years of practice. And he knows how to push all my buttons.*

She pondered that, torn between wanting to know and wanting him. He was so maddeningly attractive, so infuriatingly good at what he was doing.

Oh what the hell, she thought, surrendering to the inevitable.

She ran the tip of a two-inch nail down his spine and looked finally into his fathomless eyes. The passion she saw there stole her breath.

Valdemar hissed, gathering her under him. "Come here, little devil."

Long nails caught in her hair as he slid an arm behind her neck, tilting her chin upward, exposing her throat. Hot lips caressed her skin, moving expertly to that tender spot between neck and shoulder, teasing her with little nibbles.

Melinda dug her nails into the hard muscles of his shoulders. The smell of fresh blood filled her nostrils, setting her hunger free. She thrust her hips against him as he entered her and they began to move together in a common rhythm.

She clutched a handful of his dark curls, pushing his mouth harder against her neck. Dimly, her body registered his hot breath on her throat, the brief pain as his teeth pierced her flesh. Tension shattered into hot waves of pleasure.

Sensation dissolved into the gentle pull of his lips against her throat, the tiny movements as he swallowed, then moaned deep inside and collapsed against her.

"Melinda...." he murmured into her shoulder. With deft strokes, he licked the last drops of blood from the puncture wound on her neck.

The smell of her blood lingered on his breath. Flakes of drying blood crumbled from her fingertips. She felt him stretch against her, warm and satiated while hunger surged through her like electricity.

"Valdemar ... I'm starving!"

He laughed, pulling her with him as he rolled onto his side. "I thought you wanted to talk."

"It can wait," she said, her lips against his jugular vein, her self control rapidly disintegrating.

"Can it?" he asked and laughed again. But he pressed his palm between her shoulder blades to urge her closer.

She breathed deeply, savoring the familiar smell of his skin and hair. Her teeth pierced his throat.

Then there was only blood.

Senses returned one by one. First the warm sensation of her mouth against his throat, then his unmistakable musky scent. Opening her eyes, she looked beyond his shoulder at the unfamiliar room, dropping suddenly into the present.

Tenderly she withdrew her teeth and released him. They lay together, limbs still loosely intertwined.

"There was a time," she said after a moment, "when I was sure I would never see you again."

His dark eyes opened. "I never doubted we would be together."

She settled against his shoulder, his blood warm in her stomach. "What made you so sure?"

Taloned fingertips caressed her cheek. "You are a part of me Melinda, regardless of how that came to pass. I knew eventually you'd come to realize that's what matters. All I needed was the patience to wait for you to come back to me."

"But you gave up and came looking for me. You weren't so patient after all, were you Valdemar?"

She felt his lips curving into a smile against her ear. "Cornelius seemed to think it was a good idea."

"Since when do you take Cornelius' advice in matters of the heart?"

"Since he ran off with my last wife," Valdemar said without humor.

There was a long silence. The arm about her shoulders became increasingly heavy. Long black lashes brushed against her cheek as he drowsed off.

It all felt very familiar, including the way he'd skillfully evaded all her questions.

"Valdemar?"

"Later," he murmured. Then he was asleep.

CHAPTER TWENTY-THREE

Screeching tires and grating metal reverberated through her dreams.

Clutching the covers, Melinda bolted upright, a scream dying on her lips. From the open window, she could hear the roar of evening traffic. The aromas of at least a dozen dinners cooking, drifted up the hill.

Valdemar's bed. Absently, she patted the cold space beside her. Valdemar's house north of Toronto, she thought, orienting herself. The noise that jarred her awake must have been an accident on the nearby highway.

She looked around, scarcely surprised to find Valdemar had already vanished, leaving only a discarded shirt on a nearby chair as evidence he'd been there recently.

When I find you Valdemar, I will be tempted to put you on a leash.

Her bare feet sunk into soft carpet as she padded to the chair and borrowed his shirt to cover herself. Unobserved and unchecked, she wandered through his cavernous rooms.

His private wing of the castle was as cluttered and over-decorated as her own. Valdemar seemed obliged to fill every inch of space to the density of downtown real estate. *How on earth did he acquire all this stuff in ten years?* Each piece had its own place, planned with the exactness of putting together a jigsaw puzzle. He would notice instantly if she so much as misplaced a spec of dust.

His ballroom-sized bedroom was dominated by the huge bed, and bordered by a bathroom more befitting a roman emperor. Thoughts of an hour-long hot bath tempted her, but there was exploring--and downright snooping to be accomplished first.

The right wall of the bedroom branched off into an office on one side and a studio on the other. Melinda flipped on the light switch and was relieved when the room bloomed into light--albeit low watt light. *Electricity. That's a good sign. Candles are such a pain.*

Plastic crunched under her bare feet. Globs of oil paint splattered the covered floor and walls. Valdemar, although annoyingly fastidious in his other habits, it seemed was a messy painter.

Half a dozen easels were scattered throughout the room, their paintings in different stages of completion. His work had a vividness that human artists only hinted at. Valdemar wasted few brush strokes. He planned his paintings with the precision of a paint by number, each fleck of oil paint having its own purpose.

His style commanded attention. It was difficult to look away from one of his paintings. *No wonder people buy the things.* She tried to imagine one of Valdemar's vivid medieval market scenes over the couch in someone's living room and shook her head.

She glanced over her shoulder into the study on the far side of the corridor, then moved to investigate. Orderly rows of books lined the walls from floor to ceiling, leaving space only for a high-tech compact stereo. The electronics looked out of place among the titles in Latin, French, German, English and a language full of peculiar combinations of *dd's* and *wy's* she guessed was Welsh.

It was oddly reassuring to see the CD player among Valdemar's possessions, a dramatic contrast to the way he'd lived before, shunning most of the technology the twentieth century had to offer.

An intricately carved desk took up the center of the room faced by two comfortably upholstered chairs. Melinda sat down running her fingers appreciatively over the rich wood finish. Valdemar's absence provided the rare opportunity to unabashedly explore the personal space he guarded like gold.

Serves him right for running off on me again. Her hand strayed to the drawer with its shiny brass handles. Predictably, it was locked. But a cloth-bound book and silver fountain pen lay enticingly atop the impressive piece of furniture. She gazed at them dubiously. So Valdemar had begun a new journal. She fingered the soft cover nervously. *Dare she?*

Mischievously, she flipped it open, laughing when she realized all the entries were written in German.

"If you want to spy on my private thoughts this time, Melinda, you'll have to learn German," said an amused voice from behind her.

Melinda spun about, the evidence in her guilty hands, to find Valdemar reclining against the door frame. "How very unkind of you," she countered.

He sauntered up behind her and rested his hands lightly on her shoulders. "Consider it an incentive to learn a new language."

She tipped her head back and looked into his face. "And what language will you write it in once I learn German?" she asked wickedly.

"Welsh."

"You would...." she began, then remembered that it was *his* home, *his* diary.

Valdemar shook his head. "The things a man has to do to get some privacy."

Melinda gazed into his onyx eyes. "Aren't you glad to have me back?"

"There is something to be said for peace and quiet," Valdemar said. He ran a teasing finger over her collar bone. That brief touch brought memories of the night before rushing back into her mind. "So, mischief-maker, it is seven o'clock in the evening. Are you going to get dressed tonight or do you intend to sleep all night as well as all day?"

"I better make myself presentable," she said, reluctantly escaping from his embrace and heading for the door.

"You can't wander the halls like that," Valdemar said, catching her. His eyes swept disapprovingly downward. He disappeared into his bedroom. A moment later he returned with his own robe and wrapped it snugly about her.

"Will you be here when I return?" she asked before he complain further about her immodesty. "Or are you going to disappear on me again?"

"I assure you I will be here."

"Good," she said with a grin, "I have questions, many questions."

Valdemar winced theatrically. "I can hardly wait."

"Just see that you do wait," she said, and hurried off to her own rooms.

* * * *

She found him downstairs in the drawing room, engaged in a serious conversation with Hilliard spoken entirely in German. *Well at least he didn't fly the coop entirely,* she thought, annoyed at having to search for him. Valdemar was accustomed to doing as he pleased, whether it inconvenienced her or not.

Hilliard bowed formally as she entered. "Good Evening."

Gray eyes lingered on her as he straightened from the bow.

"Evening," she repeated, meeting those probing eyes.

Hilliard looked quickly from Valdemar back to Melinda, then excused himself and left the room.

Valdemar busied poured the wine that was sitting in a crystal decanter on the sideboard. It splashed into the heavily carved goblet in a bright crimson swirl that reminded her of fresh blood. Melinda looked hastily away. Tonight she was mildly hungry, in a few days that hunger would become an all-consuming terror. There was no denying it. Hunger took care of itself, as she had so tragically found out. And hunting in the country's largest city was infinitely more complicated than hunting in the arctic.

"So ... " she murmured. "Do you own any drinking vessels that aren't crystal, any shirts that aren't silk? Is there anything that covers your walls or your floors that isn't sewn with gold thread?"

"And what is wrong with crystal, silk and gold?" Valdemar asked, politely handing her the goblet.

"I'm not used to so much wealth, at least not in my immediate surroundings. It makes me uncomfortable."

"Most people wouldn't feel that way."

"I'm not most people."

"No," he said taking the wine glass from her hand and pulling her against him. "You certainly are not."

There was a soft clink as he set the glass down on the table behind them, then she was lost in the feathery soft caress of his lips against her neck. He had barely touched her and already her body was aching for his. But there were so many questions...."Oh no you don't, Valdemar," she said, attempting to pry herself away from him. "I know what you're trying to do."

He held on to her a moment longer with arms as strong as steel. "And what is it I am trying to do?" he asked, his lips moving softly against her throat.

She suppressed a moan. "You're trying to distract me so I won't ask you what you know I'm going to ask you."

"And isn't this more pleasant than hours of your ardent cross examination?"

She dug her palms into his chest and raised her head, forcing him to look at her. "Valdemar ... "

With a sigh of resignation, he let her go. "Very well, Melinda, what is it that you must know?"

She reached behind him, retrieving her glass of wine. "Who--no let me rephrase that--what is Hilliard?"

He stared at her mutely, offering no answer.

"He is not human," she prompted, "and yet, I sense he is not one of us. So what is he Val? What other kind of ghoul is there?"

"I resent being called a ghoul," Valdemar said sharply.

"You don't appreciate being called a Vampire, either."

"No, I do not."

"Perhaps there is a nicer German--no Welsh word for it then," she said lips quirking into a facetious smile. He was leading her off-topic in one of his meandering arguments. Damned if she'd let him get away with it.

"The Welsh word is *Sugnwr Gwaed*. Blood Sucker."

"Well it's to the point, at least," she conceded. "Are you going to tell me? Or do I have to ask him myself?"

Valdemar frowned. "That would be most impolite. Would you

like it if Hilliard asked you what manner of ghoul *you* were?"

"Hilliard knows damned well what I am. I saw the way he looked at me."

"You are imagining things. Hilliard has no interest in your affairs."

"What makes you so sure?"

"He has worked for me before."

"He makes me nervous."

"And why is that?"

"He stares at me strangely." She shuddered. "He makes the little hairs on the back of my neck stand up." Valdemar was arguing in circles again. Melinda crossed her arms defiantly. "You haven't answered my question."

He mirrored her posture. She read the warning in that pose and chose to ignore it.

"There are some things you are not yet ready to know, Melinda," he said when it was clear she would not relent.

"And you will decide what I'm ready to know?"

"I will decide what I am ready to tell you."

She pursed her lips and glared back at him, violet eyes locking with his black stare. "How am I supposed to learn about my world if you won't tell me anything about it?" she asked softly. "I resent being kept like your treasured pet."

Instantly, she wished the words unsaid. Too late, she recalled the tale of the lover who treated *him* that way.

Visibly hurt, he turned away from her. "That was unkind Melinda. I have never treated you as a *pet*."

"I am certainly not your equal," she said angrily.

"Yet you are determined to be, aren't you?"

"Yes," she said, circling him and staring up at him from under her brows.

Valdemar threw up his hands in frustration. "And Cornelius thought women were headstrong in the eighteenth century!" He studied her thoughtfully. "What will you do with this information? Assuming I decide to tell you?"

To that she had no good answer. "What I didn't know almost got me killed once," she said, staring out the window into the threatening sky. "Contrary to the popular saying, ignorance is not bliss, it's downright dangerous."

Valdemar leaned against the window frame, wearing that dour expression he bore when he knew he was about to lose an argument.

"Besides," she added. "What do you think I'm going to do? Maraud across the countryside creating ghouls to amuse myself?"

"I would hope not."

"We are going to have to trust each other some time ... "

He considered that carefully, giving her a very straight, measuring look. "It is possible," he said at last in a low voice, "to drink a small amount of blood from a human being and not kill him, but to drink from him repeatedly over a period of time and thus bind him to your service."

"Oh, my God," she breathed. "I thought that was nonsense out of horror books and old movies like the rest of vampire lore."

"Some of the things written about vampires are true."

"And is it like the legends say, that he will live as long as you continue to drink from him?"

"Fundamentally, yes. But the actual process is not quite that simple. It is something that must be done correctly or the person dies."

"Why would anyone willingly enslave themselves to a vampire?" she asked in horrified fascination.

"I have no idea. I have never asked him."

"Did you ... make Hilliard?"

"Not I, no."

"But he is in your service now."

"He was looking for employment, and I have engaged him before. It was a convenient arrangement.

"Do you know who made him?"

"Yes."

"Who?"

"Someone you have not yet met."

"Another friend of yours?" Valdemar's *friends* were a dangerous lot.

"Not a friend exactly; someone I know."

"And he doesn't mind you using his servant?"

"I suppose *she* has no use for him at the moment."

"And is it you who now drinks from Hilliard and keeps him enslaved?"

"What do you think, Melinda?"

She covered her mouth with her hand. "I think it's sick."

"You insisted I tell you this."

"I did," she admitted, looking at the floor.

"And is there anything else you *must* know this evening?"

Melinda traced the pattern on the carpet with her toe. "Where is

Cornelius?"

Valdemar cocked his head to look into her eyes. "I don't know. When I returned from the arctic I found he had sold his house in Toronto."

"Is that why you decided to buy this ... castle?"

"I had to live somewhere ... "

"You changed your mind about going back to Germany, or was it Wales. Why? Did it remind you of Rowena?" Now she was venturing into dangerous territory. Rowena was one topic that was definitely off limits.

"Yes," he said, surprising her by answering the question. "I lived there with her for ... a long time."

"Is Rowena," she began, encouraged by this rare moment of openness, "still alive?"

"I really don't know," Valdemar said quietly. "We haven't spoken for many, many years."

Best to leave that topic alone, Melinda thought and changed the subject. "Aren't you worried about Cornelius?"

Valdemar looked genuinely surprised. "Why on earth should I worry about Cornelius?"

"He's supposed to be your friend and you don't even know where he is. What if something has happened to him? Aren't you concerned he might be lonely now that Kirsten is dead?"

"Neil makes friends easily enough," Valdemar said. "And if he has need of me, he will find me."

"But you didn't get a chance to tell him where you were, or that we are together again."

Valdemar gestured to the huge drawing room about him. "If Cornelius is searching for me, he will find me. Have no fear of that."

"Does he blame you?" Melinda asked. "For what happened to Kirsten?

"We stopped blaming each other over Kirsten long ago," he said absently. He reached for her, taking her into his arms. "Tell me something, Melinda. When you rescued me, what made you think of taking me to Cornelius?"

She shut her eyes against the memories, the explosion that still echoed in her nightmares, the rain of falling concrete, Valdemar lying burned and close to death beneath the ruin of his home. She could feel her throat closing up on her, the tears that even ten years later were precariously close to the surface. "I didn't know what else to do. I knew Cornelius wouldn't let you die."

The dark eyes before her were filled with sadness of their own. "I have to admit, we weren't the best of company for each other just then."

"I should have stayed ... "

"I wish you had, but you were determined to get away from me."

"It was myself I was running from," she whispered.

"And you've stopped running now, from both of us?"

"I had to come back sometime," she told him, realizing with a start it was the truth.

Valdemar smiled, hugging her closer as if she might vanish again. "Now that sounds more like the Melinda Barnes I used to know."

Melinda leaned her head against his chest and listened to the quiet sounds of his breathing.

"Come," he said, suddenly offering his hand. "Such serious talk, and we've only been together a few hours. Let me give you a tour of your new home."

* * * *

The ground floor housed the formal rooms: the foyer, an extensive library, an official-looking study, and a stately ballroom for entertaining. A narrow hallway led to a utilitarian kitchen that gleamed with infrequent use.

Upstairs, on the second level was Valdemar's own living room and several guest rooms. The third floor contained their private suites, and the deck was home to a rambling roof garden.

It was a world of difference from her pre-fab house, where a single room had been living room, bedroom and study. The only other room had been the tiny, cubicle bathroom.

There wasn't much to unpack. Melinda eyed the four crates that had been delivered during the day. She no longer needed the heavy parkas and moccasins. Her meager possessions wouldn't even make a dent among Valdemar's closely-packed decor.

She glanced down at the neatly manicured gardens that were still in bloom, despite the lateness of the season. Only a week ago, she'd almost missed her midnight shift at the radio station due to an early snowstorm.

It took only an hour to stack her belongings in the closets and arrange a few treasured books on the shelves. Valdemar had taken refuge in his studio. He was rushing to finish several paintings for a showing next week, he explained.

Melinda sighed and tried to ignore the uneasy feeling that accompanied the first few days in a strange place. A refrain from

one of Kirsten's songs echoed through her memory.
In your eyes, I see the threatening sky
And the clouds that promise rain ...

CHAPTER TWENTY-FOUR

Glittering snow stretched forever into the horizon, rising now and then into sculpted peaks. The black sky was dotted with stars, even in the daytime, as day and night ran together in the arctic winter.

Melinda glided across the frosted landscape, snow crunching beneath her moccasins. She was dressed like the scenery in her coat of white fur and her black hair blowing free against the sky.

She sensed the polar bear long before he came into sight. Already she could feel the thick, white fur beneath her fingers, the hot blood rushing into her mouth.

He wandered out onto the ice before her, and sniffed the air to catch the scent of this tiny creature in white fur that promised him no harm.

Come to me, she willed him, and he came close enough for her to feel his warm breath upon her face and smell the thick, hot blood beneath the fur. In a matter of seconds he would be hers. She would drink deeply of his lifeblood, then set him free unharmed ...

Melinda moaned and rolled over, her hand plunging unexpectedly into feather pillows instead of soft fur. Momentarily confused, she hovered on the edge of consciousness, becoming aware of the agony that yanked her from her dreams. Hunger burned in her veins like molten lead. Denying that lust was impossible.

Ashamed, she pressed her face into the pillow. She'd wanted to show Valdemar she had her own way of being a vampire, that she'd matured in the past ten years. But there she was, writhing in the throes of hunger like a fledgling.

Opening one eye, she peered about the heavily curtained room. Judging from the shadows, it was still several hours before sunset. She pulled the covers over her head and curled into the fetal position. It helped to ease the pain in her gut. Though her skin felt like it was on fire, she was shivering violently, and she wedged her tongue between her teeth to keep them from chattering.

Convulsions forced the pointed tips into the softness of her tongue, drawing blood. She swallowed it eagerly. Even that brief taste of her own blood sent shock waves of pleasure pulsating through her body. She groaned in spite of herself and thrust her fist between her jaws so she wouldn't scream.

Bewildered at this sudden and vicious onslaught of hunger, she forced her mind to count the days since she'd last fed. It was much too soon for her to be in the grips of such voracious hunger. Only yesterday she'd been mildly hungry at most.

Desperation led to carelessness. Caution was imperative now that she was back within close reach of television reports, police and forensics experts. She must be prudent for her own sake as well as Valdemar's.

The prospect of stalking and draining the life from a human being without leaving evidence of the crime was unlikely in her present state. She wondered if she could even stand up.

Valdemar would help her, whether for his own safety or hers. But that she had allowed hunger to strip her so effectively of reason was something she didn't even want to admit to herself.

She shuddered as another wave of pain-tinged desire washed over her, threatening to drag her under into the murky depths of unconsciousness. Blacking out would be disastrous. If she didn't get herself far from the castle grounds before Valdemar awakened, she'd never hear the end of it.

Grasping at the bed's wooden columns, she thrust her unsteady feet on the floor, heedless of the red sparks that shot through her vision. *So far, so good.* She took a few steps in the direction of the bathroom. *Even better. Okay, now what? Have a shower, then a little wine. Hopefully, the sun will be low enough on the horizon so I can get out of here. Then what? Just get yourself into the shower. Think about one thing at a time. And think clearly, for God's Sake!*

Warm water soothed her shivering body. Melinda thrust her hands against the smooth tile, forcing herself to stand under the gentle spray. With abstract fascination, she concentrated on watching the water swirling into the brass drain. It kept thoughts of hunger from her mind. But coldness was creeping outward from her heart, turning her limbs to lead. And all of a sudden she was being sucked down into the whirlpool of silver water.

Help me Valdemar! she thought desperately, as her head hit the side of the marble tub ...

Another second of unbearable agony, then warmth all around

and inside her, warm salty liquid rushing into her mouth and down her throat. She lay still, luxuriating in this miracle that had chased away the pain.

But only one thing could appease the hunger!

Melinda choked on the blood she was drawing into her mouth with powerful sucking movements. Her eyes snapped open, and she attempted to wrestle free of whomever was providing her with this heaven-sent nourishment.

Powerful hands held her to the vein that was the source of that sustenance.

"Drink a little more," Valdemar said. The words echoed beside her ear and resonated through his chest. She tried to object, but her mouth was full of blood and it came out as a wet gurgle. "It's all right," he said, but his voice was strained and she knew she'd hurt him.

Vague images of their struggle flitted through her mind. Somewhere in her subconscious, she recalled him wrestling to subdue her. If she looked, she knew she'd find deep claw marks on his bare arms and chest. Had she been that out of her mind with hunger? Despite his considerable strength, Valdemar had been hard pressed to control her. She took a couple more mouthfuls, gently this time. Then she loosened her lips and pulled her teeth from his neck. He hissed softly.

The next thing she knew, she was sitting next to him on the bed, naked and soaking wet. Melinda burrowed back into his shoulder, afraid to face him.

"Perhaps you'd like to tell me about this," he suggested in a tone full of restrained anger.

She wanted to cry. She wanted someone to explain to her why after twelve years she'd suddenly found herself like an unprepared fledgling in the clutches of such a ravenous hunger. Drawing blood from another vampire was reserved for love, procreation and at worst, acts of outright desperation.

Valdemar gripped her shoulders and held her away from him. She looked down at the two angry, red teeth marks on his throat, and held back the urge to lick the final drop of blood from the wound. She swallowed the last of his blood.

His hands tightened on her shoulders, and she felt the pinch of his claws against her flesh. "Melinda, look at me!"

She raised her head, slowly bringing her eyes in line with his. "I'm sorry," she whispered, running a finger over the welts on his neck that were fading to pink prick marks. Valdemar winced as her fingers brushed the spot.

"I certainly hope you are. That was a rather rude awakening. You were none too gentle."

"But it's not time yet," she said, genuinely confused. "It shouldn't have happened so soon."

Valdemar sighed. "Any drastic change in your surroundings can throw your system out of its natural rhythm. Have you learned nothing at all in the last twelve years?"

"That can't be it," she protested. "I mean I took precautions, I--"

"Partook of some polar bear?"

Damn him! How did he know?

There was wisdom in his words. Human blood had vastly superior sustaining powers. The blood of animals was like trying to exist on a diet of bread and water. Possibly, she was malnourished. And she knew from unfortunate experience what happened when vampires starved themselves.

"Thanks to you, I need to hunt tonight. Besides being inconvenient, it is also dangerous. This is the city, Melinda."

"I don't know what's the matter with me," she insisted. "This snuck up on me out of nowhere. I wasn't even hungry yesterday." She paused, trying to order her thoughts. "Maybe I'm sick."

"Vampires don't get sick," he said. The loss of blood was starting to make him ill tempered.

"Never? You mean you've never been ill in eleven hundred years?"

"I have been injured," Valdemar said. "But I've never been ill, no."

"Are you all right?" she asked, pressing her lips to his throat.

Her touch made him flinch, but he closed his arms around her. "I'll live."

"Something's wrong with me. And I don't know what it is."

"Maybe this has all been too much for you," he suggested. "It must have been quite a shock, me appearing out of the blue."

"Not really," she said, her lips moving against his chest. "You always came looking for me when I ran away before. No Valdemar, this is something else." She stopped talking suddenly trying to grasp the elusive memory that lingered just beyond conscious thought. "It felt like…" She drew her breath in sharply and choked back the memory of red wine spiked with something acrid. Hot bodies pressed against her like it was yesterday, bodies dripping enticingly with fresh blood.

"Like what?" Valdemar asked. "Melinda, answer me."

Melinda shuddered. "The night at Moira's; the same relentless hunger ... " She pushed herself away from him and searched his face. "You didn't!"

Valdemar eyed her cautiously. "Didn't what?"

"Spike my wine."

"Of course not! The party at Moira's put me off Tetrodotoxin forever." He tipped her head back and examined her closely. "Hunger can sometimes feel--"

"I'm not a child, Valdemar," she snapped, wiggling out of his grasp.

"That is exactly what you are."

"I'm thirty-eight years old!"

He gazed at her with that pained expression which meant he was biting his tongue, and she remembered he was at last count, eleven hundred and twenty-two.

"Look Val," she said in breathless frustration. "Assuming I'm a bloody infant compared to you, I still know what I felt."

"It's impossible, Melinda. I don't have any Tetrodotoxin in the house. And I would never dope you up without your knowledge."

He pushed her back against the pillows and covered her with the heavy quilt. "Get some rest," he said. "I'm going out."

"Valdemar?" she asked as he went to get up.

"What now?"

"Thank you."

He patted her shoulder. "You're welcome," he said. And left.

CHAPTER TWENTY-FIVE

The swollen, setting sun drenched the walls in crimson. Melinda stood at the bay window and gazed out at the countryside. Stretching muscles cramped from sleep, she forced her groggy mind to wakefulness and longed for coffee.

Caffeine was the last food craving to die. In the outpost radio news room she'd worked in up north, the aroma of coffee had permeated everything. A phantom yearning, one taste was enough to send her stomach into threatening, twisting knots. Wine would have to do. At least it looked like blood.

Days fell upon days like identical dominoes. There was a timelessness to Valdemar's well-run household.

Some days it seemed incredible that two vampires could live undetected on the outskirts of Toronto, companioned only by a ghoul of a servant. On other days, the situation seemed laughable, and unbearably sad.

She missed the solitude of the northern winters. She missed her independence. Most of all she missed Kirsten.

Having Melinda as a constant companion was a difficult adjustment for Valdemar. She noted his attempts to make room for her in his life, the many times he bit back a cynical remark in an effort to be patient and kind.

One day very soon, she would have to go back to work. Valdemar cared for all her needs. But his generosity only hurt her pride, and she was going stir-crazy from inactivity.

Frustrated, she gulped a generous mouthful of Merlot and let the ruby liquid trickle down her throat. A long yawn escaped her lips. She opened her mouth for another, then stopped to wonder at this strange lethargy.

Dumbly she wondered at the drowsiness that crept outward from her heart, deadening each limb in turn. The wine glass fell from her hand, crashing to the floor in a splash of crimson and crystal.

Through the cottony insulation in her brain, Melinda watched it fall. A red haze crept inward from the periphery of her vision, dissolving into blazing hunger that hijacked both will and conscience.

She raided her closet for hunting clothes. Randomly, she tossed the items onto the bed, a black bustier, a pair of skin-tight jeans, ebony suede boots and her leather motorcycle jacket. In a compartment of her mind, her conscience cried for reason. She shouldn't need blood yet, something was desperately wrong. But she had ceased to be Melinda. She had become only need ...

Blood, her body demanded as she fled into the sheltering trees that bordered the golf course. Once she got to the city limits, she'd hitch a ride downtown.

* * * *

The double-decker commuter train cruised into the station. Last train east to Pickering. Doors whooshed open invitingly on the green and white train. Melinda scanned the brightly-lit interior through slitted eyes. In the third car, a lone youth slouched nonchalantly in his seat, Nike shod feet slung up on the seat opposite him.

Knee length suede boots made scarcely a sound on the carpeted floor as she gripped the metal pole and swung up into the train.

The bottom level was deserted, not even a conductor in the booth. Melinda loped up the spiral staircase to the upper level.

She sank into a seat at the far end of the train. Panting with anticipation, she tried to gain control of herself. Already, she could feel her two-inch nails sinking into yielding flesh, feel skin parting beneath the pressure of her teeth, and taste that first ecstatic mouthful of blood.

"I can't do this," she whispered to herself. It was all a great mistake. She had to get herself off the train and far away. Uncertainly, she gained her feet, but the train cruised out of the station.

Drunkenly, she fell back against the plastic seat, promising herself she'd get off at the next stop. She looked up to find the sole passenger sauntering toward her.

Smells overwhelmed her senses. The scent of her victim's skin, the smell of the sweat that dripped down his back from the warm sweatshirt he wore under his leather jacket.

"Hey foxy," he said, staring at her bosom.

"I'd appreciate it if you'd leave me alone," she said, shocking herself as the words slurred into each other.

"Rough night?" he asked, still gawking at the white swell of her breasts beneath her open jacket.

"You could say that," she mumbled.

Her drunkenness and implied helplessness seemed to entice him. He looked around the car, pleased to find it deserted. Standing between the facing seats, he blocked her escape. His hand strayed to his fly. "Want some of what I've got here Baby?"

"Please," she whispered, a plea to herself as much as him, "go away."

"Now Babe, didn't your mother ever tell you a girl who goes around dressed like that is just asking for it?"

Above his labored breathing, she heard the hiss of his zipper. Clammy fingers closed upon her breast.

Melinda sprang.

Sounds of tearing cloth and her own wet swallows filled her ears. He uttered an aborted shout of surprise, then whimpered weakly and fell silent.

Torrents of hot blood poured down her throat, a rush of purest pleasure that soon dissipated into cold reason.

Slowly, Melinda opened her eyes to face the awful truth. The dismal memory of his heart faltering lingered in her mind.

Sickened, she turned away and glanced out the window. In a few seconds the last westbound train would fly past them in a clatter of tall swaying cars.

Self preservation was crucial now. She checked her refection in the darkened glass. Anguished, violet eyes stared back at her. She licked a crimson drop from the corner of her mouth.

The train slowed, entering the station. She scanned the platform. Only two passengers who were already moving toward cars in the front of the train. She slipped an arm under the victim's shoulders and twisted his limp right arm about her own.

In spite of her burden, she had scaled the staircase in seconds and hovered in the doorway. The passengers had boarded; the platform was empty. Chimes signaled the train's imminent departure.

Melinda stepped from the train into the darkness between the tracks. She could see the dim glow of the approaching westbound train.

She leapt for the far tracks, letting her burden slide to the metal rails. With a swift backward glance, she checked that he was well positioned and dove for the nearby bushes.

The train roared into the station with speed inspired by the late hour and customarily empty tracks. Too late, the engineer spied the figure sprawled upon the tracks. Steel screeched against steel as the train lurched to a stop.

Repulsed, she looked away from the shreds of flesh that spattered the platform. They'd have enough pieces to collect without debating how much blood had been left in the body.

His blood was an appallingly warm and comfortable weight in her stomach. Her body pulsed with vitality as the first of that blood was absorbed into her veins.

In the distance, she heard the wail of sirens.

Melinda faded into the shadows. A light breeze stirred the foliage around her. Cautiously, she sniffed the wind, scenting something familiar ... almost. Valdemar? No, not Valdemar. Something lurked in the darkness, and it was watching her.

Like a child awaking suddenly in a dark room, she imagined eyes staring out at her from every bush and shadow. The wind grew stronger, stirring tendrils of her hair. Leaves rustled with a low hiss. Behind her, she heard a twig snap.

Forgetting stealth, she blundered into the trees, stumbling over roots in her haste. She threw the sum of her vampiric powers into her stride, pushing aside branches and brush as easily as air.

Even though she matched the speed of the cars on the nearby

road, whatever was coming behind her was faster still. Waving brush marked its passage. The wind whistled her name.

She plunged through a thicket of thorns, scarcely feeling their barbs clutch at her thighs. A shadow reared up in front of her. She collided with a tree. Gasping, she hugged its solid trunk in relief and sought another route of escape.

Melinda bolted for the open road. Its black ribbon of asphalt wound up the hill. There were no trees to hinder her progress now. She scanned the horizon. No headlights lit the sky above the crest of the hill. She concentrated on channeling speed and strength into her pumping thighs.

It was several miles later before she realized she was no longer being followed.

* * * *

She strode into Valdemar's chambers, past the intricately carved desk where he sat in the middle of some complicated calculation regarding the estate's ledgers. If her presence had attracted his attention, she didn't notice, but went instead to sit on the floor before the fire like a child. Motionless, she sat there, staring into the flames, feeling the heat upon her face and the sinister warmth within her.

Every sense, every nerve was alive, nourished by her feeding. She was more aware, more vibrant than she had felt in a decade. A cacophony of early morning sounds assaulted her through the open window, the morning rush hour that almost obliterated the songs of the birds.

From behind her she heard a rustle of papers followed by the soft tread of footsteps coming towards her. He stood, looking down at her, arms crossed in concentration, but when she took no notice of him, he crouched down beside her.

"Did it ever occur to you to knock?" he asked, annoyance biting into the tone of his voice.

Violet eyes snapped upward, locking with his. "Sorry," she said coming to her senses. "I was preoccupied."

"So I noticed."

"I'm disturbing you, aren't I?"

Valdemar threw her an intense look, biting back a caustic remark. "Something is bothering you?"

She nodded mutely.

"Well? What is it?"

"I'm not sure."

Valdemar drew in his breath, summoning his patience and

stretched out beside her on the rug, taking her chin in his taloned hand. "You went hunting tonight ... " he prompted, looking into her eyes from under dark brows.

"You followed me!"

"I did."

"So it was you!"

"I suspected you knew I was there ... "

She frowned, an angry retort dying on her lips, and thought of that eerie sense of surveillance. "I felt you ... " Her eyes flitted from side to side in concentration. "But there was something else ... no, somebody else. It felt like you, yet I knew it wasn't you." She turned her head and looked full into his face, waiting for the explanation she hoped he'd have.

"You're imagining things, Melinda," Valdemar said, waving her suggestion from the air. "I followed you, and you felt my presence, that is all."

"No," she insisted. "There was something there. It chased me half the way home!"

Valdemar studied the scrapes on her leather jacket and the burrs that clung to her jeans. "Melinda that is nonsense. I would have noticed if we were being trailed by another of our kind."

It made such logical sense, and she wanted desperately to believe him. "So why did you follow me then?"

He shrugged. "I was worried about you. You haven't hunted in the city for ... some time."

"Why didn't you just say you wanted to come with me?"

"I wanted you to do it yourself--to prove to yourself you still could."

"And instead you've proven you don't trust me!"

That comment wounded him. Hurt flickered briefly in his eyes before it was quickly extinguished, replaced by his iron control. "That is untrue, Melinda," he said, staring into the fire. "I was concerned for your welfare, nothing more."

Melinda leaned her head against his shoulder, wary of the eyes he purposely averted from her. "Forgive me," she whispered. "I didn't mean that. I'm not myself tonight."

"I'd say you're more yourself than you've been for ten years." He waited for her to absorb that comment, to confront him with her denial. "Tonight," he said softly, "you had your first human victim in over a decade, and you had forgotten how good it feels."

Melinda swallowed, the taste of blood still fresh in her mouth. What he said was true. "My body feels good," she admitted. "My conscience isn't speaking to me."

"The truth is," Valdemar said, "You feel wonderful, and you can't believe you've denied yourself this for so long. Is that not so, Melinda?"

"Yes," she murmured and looked at him helplessly. "How can it feel so good and so terrible at the same time?"

His arm closed about her shoulders. "This is how you are supposed to feel, Melinda. You have never learned what it means to be a vampire. You have never allowed yourself to be what you are."

"Murder is wrong, Valdemar."

"There isn't an animal on the face of this earth that doesn't kill and eat another living thing, be it animal or vegetable, in order to survive. Such is the nature of our world, Melinda. We are as much a part of nature as any other creature. There is a reason for us to exist, though I don't pretend to know what it is."

She struggled out of his embrace. "But killing human beings Val.... For God's sake, I pounced on a guy, drained him of blood and chucked his body under a train." She paused, trying to organize her argument. "I don't even know what made me do it. One moment I was standing at the window drinking wine, the next thing I knew I was bending over that poor fool's body, drinking his blood. It was like someone else was doing it. I wasn't at all in control of myself. I don't even remember how I got downtown."

"Obviously," Valdemar said, "you were hungry."

Melinda looked away from him, disgusted. "No kidding."

Valdemar sighed. "Because you are so young, you can still remember your human feelings. The fear of death and suffering is still fresh in your mind. But, if you look deep into your heart, Melinda, you will realize you no longer feel those things, do you? If you did, you would never have run back into that smoldering station to save my life."

"That was different," she insisted. But was it really?

"You are still struggling with this after all this time," he said with an astonished shake of his head. "You must remember that you ate other creatures as a human being, and you enjoyed it."

"I didn't have to go out and kill them myself! They came wrapped in plastic and styrofoam from the supermarket."

"And is it so different?"

"Yes!" she hissed in horror. "I sucked the life out of some poor fool! And you're right, Valdemar, it felt so good. It felt so damned good. And now I can hardly wait to do it again."

"That is how it feels, Melinda."

"Didn't it bother you at first?' she asked hesitantly, knowing his early days as a vampire was a topic he almost never discussed.

He glowered at her a moment, searching for a way to escape the topic and finding none, he swallowed resolutely and continued. "Morals were a lot different then," he said slowly. "We didn't think about human rights the way you do today. I was, after all, born before the Magna Carta."

Melinda felt her eyes widening. Sometimes the reality of who Valdemar truly was frightened her. But she was determined to hear him out this time, so she returned his level gaze and refused to be intimidated. "Do you mean to tell me you felt no remorse at all in the taking of a human life?"

"I didn't say that," Valdemar insisted in his defense. "In truth, I don't remember how I felt about it. I didn't know what it was I had become. We had no horror movies or books to enrich the legends, and I lived in a tiny, isolated village. Death was a part of our lives. At twenty-nine years old, I was already nearing the end of my life. And if I had managed to escape disease and old age much longer, I would have likely perished defending my land against another raiding clan."

He was watching her intently, trying to determine the effect of his words. They stared at each other silently for a few moments.

"Let yourself feel these things, Melinda. Allow yourself to be who you are. It is much too late to go back to being who you were."

"But that's just it," Valdemar," she said at last. "I don't know who I am. Especially now that I'm here in the midst of your life once again, and I have none of my own.

Valdemar took her head gently in his hands, hands that were strong enough to crush a man's skull if he chose. "You are my lover," he said softly, "And anything else you choose to be."

With one taloned finger, he traced the outline of her lips. She let her eyes fall shut, savoring the warmth of his touch and the hot lick of the flames at her back. Her lips parted in invitation. She felt the slow slide of his tongue between them. He deepened the kiss. She uttered a soft murmur of pleasure. With gentle pressure, he eased her head back against his shoulder, exposing her throat.

His mouth left hers to explore the tender skin between her neck and shoulder. The touch of his lips made her shiver.

"Since you have fed tonight," he whispered his meaning plain, "and I have not…"

She drew in a deep breath and let it out slowly. His teeth pierced her neck. She shuddered against him at the first pull of his mouth against her throat. Warm blood rushed from the vein, drawing with it a keen rush of pleasure. She moaned, collapsing against his reassuring weight, allowing him to share in the blood she'd stolen from another.

He took only a couple mouthfuls, then raised his head. She looked up into dark eyes that reflected the red glow of the flames. Cupping the back of her head, he kissed her again. She tasted blood.

For a long time they sat quietly, arms wrapped around each other, warmed by the blood inside them and the heat of the fire.

And in that moment it all felt so very right.

CHAPTER TWENTY-SIX

The door opened with a quiet click and soft footsteps padded across the carpeted floor. Melinda felt the air move as someone brushed against the closed draperies of the bed. A clink as the metal of the silver tray met the wood of the table, another stirring in the air as they passed.

Melinda waited until the outer door closed and Hilliard's polished shoes echoed off down the hall. When she was satisfied she was alone, she held open the curtain and looked out.

On her bedside table was a silver tray bearing a crystal decanter and a matching goblet. She glanced at the clock. *Right on time, Hilliard.*

Each evening he brought the same arrangement, setting it silently by the bed before she awakened. He did the same for Valdemar, probably thought he should for her, yet she had never requested it.

Hilliard was a source of discontentment between them. Valdemar refused to employ any more servants, other than the weekly cleaning company. He didn't want people prying into his life, he said. Melinda resented Hilliard's constant presence.

His eyes followed her everywhere. He managed to overhear each conversation, every argument she had with Valdemar. He was always under foot, politely offering his assistance when none was needed.

Frowning, she crept to the low table and scrutinized the decanter in the bright light of afternoon It hurt her eyes to do so, and she had to shade them with her hands. Under Valdemar's careful tutelage, Melinda was developing a taste for wines. "I don't care about things like that," she'd insisted the first time he'd offered her a glass from his extensive cellar, along with the obligatory lecture on its properties. To her dismay, and Valdemar's intense satisfaction, she was growing knowledgeable of red wines, the more expensive, the better. It became a game between them to see if she could guess the vintage. Wine it seemed, was one of the few things they could agree on.

She removed the crystal stopper and sniffed at it. It smelled like wine. But then, she didn't really know what Tetrodotoxin smelled like in its natural state. No signs of sediment.

Though Valdemar dismissed it as a foolish notion, Melinda was sure her wine had been spiked. It was the only thing other than blood she'd consumed since she arrived.

The sensation of being drugged was unmistakable. Tetrodotoxin was the only poison powerful enough to affect the vampiric metabolism. Quite simply, it made them drunk, and afterwards ravenously hungry. She found it most unpleasant. More like paralysis than inebriation, it induced a feeling of being disconnected from one's body. In small doses, Valdemar insisted, the drug could be quite pleasurable. It heightened the experience of feeding. But that one incident at Moira's had cured Melinda of the urge to experiment.

To humans the drug could be deadly. Victims were often mistaken for dead, frequently buried. Trapped underground, paralyzed while their sanity disintegrated, they were later dug up and used as slaves in voodoo rituals. So the legends said.

Something was behind the mysterious hunger that haunted her. Melinda poured an ounce of wine into the glass and swirled it against the light. Nothing that she could see or smell.

Pursing her lips in concentration, she picked up the decanter and strode into the bathroom. Usually, she drank two or three glasses of wine in the early evening. She measured that amount, then dumped the glasses one after another carefully down the drain, taking care not to leave any evidence on the white marble.

That done, she returned the decanter and glass with the ring of red wine drying at the bottom of the glass to the tray. She discarded her nightgown and entered the bathroom, locking the door behind her. Once he heard the water running, Hilliard usually came to retrieve the tray.

Sure enough, when she exited the shower, the tray was gone.

She found Hilliard in the kitchen, washing the wine goblets. Valdemar, presumably, had left. She couldn't sense him anywhere nearby.

With the water running, Hilliard hadn't heard her approach. Melinda concentrated on moving as stealthily as Valdemar as she crept closer.

She pulled her mouth into her most disarming smile, gleaming incisors resting against her full lips, and tapped Hilliard on the shoulder. "Boo!"

He jumped, losing his grip on the crystal. The fragile goblet shattered, scattering clear shards into the stream of silver water. He turned off the tap, buying himself time to regain his composure before turning to face her. Melinda noted the crimson splash in the bottom of the sink and caught her breath. Hilliard had cut himself.

He spun to face her. "Good evening," he said, and colored nearly as red as the blood that dripped from his finger. "I'm sorry, Madam. You startled me."

"Sorry," Melinda replied coolly, her violet eyes never leaving his face. She reached for the paper towel dispenser above the sink. "Hilliard, you cut yourself."

He became aware suddenly that he was in the presence of a supposedly ravenous vampire and in the process of bleeding on the floor. Fear blanched his face from scarlet to gray. Politely, Melinda handed him the paper towel. She smiled wider, exposing her chiseled eyeteeth. "Better put a Band-Aid on that."

Hilliard looked down at her two inch nails and gingerly reached for the towel. Melinda released it, allowing her nails to glide smoothly over the back of his hand as their fingers met. She looked into his eyes. Hilliard was terrified.

"Something wrong?" Melinda asked with aggressive politeness, as he bandaged himself.

Hilliard cleared his throat and composed himself. "Not at all. I didn't hear you enter."

"Really?" Melinda asked. "Perhaps you weren't expecting me."

"You are up earlier than usual."

"Am I?" Melinda stepped closer, and then froze. The smell of blood overwhelmed her senses.

Why did Hilliard smell like blood? The cut on his finger was bandaged and too small to account for the thick odor.

He backed up into the sink. No easy way for him to retreat now. He watched her face, sensing her hunger.

"I got up early," she said with quiet menace, "to see what it is you've been putting in my wine."

Hilliard swallowed, but to his credit, that was the only movement that betrayed his panic. Melinda moved close enough for him to feel her breath on his face. Though he was a good head taller, it seemed as if she towered over him. Vampiric intimidation she called it when Valdemar used that tactic against her. She traced the blue line of his jugular vein down the side of his neck. "Maybe you'd like to tell me why you've been spiking my wine with Tetrodotoxin." She threw a buddy-like arm around his shoulders. "I'd hate to have to get ... unpleasant about this."

To illustrate what unpleasant might mean, she tightened her grip on him, planning to draw him away from the sink. But when her arm touched his back, Hilliard gasped deeply. Melinda stopped. She was using only a small fraction of her considerable strength, certainly not enough to cause pain.

"Hilliard, what is it?"

He stiffened, torn between her accusation and the new thing she'd discovered. His lips closed in a tight line and he stared into space beyond her shoulder.

Gently, Melinda gripped him by the arms. He resisted at first, using all his strength. She threw more strength into the tug and found she could move him easily, much to Hilliard's obvious dismay.

She held him firmly still with one hand and lifted the wool fabric of his black suit with the other. The smell of fresh blood sent her hunger soaring. The back of his starched, white shirt was covered with blood.

In one fluid motion, she yanked the shirt from his pants and tore the back in two. Hilliard bit his lip to keep from crying out as strips of rended flesh came away with the shirt material. Melinda gasped at the ruin of his back. The raw traces of claw marks were easily recognizable. But, the precision with which they had been executed appalled her. Nothing random about it, they were not the result of a fight. The wounds had been made slowly and carefully to inflict as much pain and suffering as possible.

"Hilliard who did this to you?"

Obviously used to interrogation and torture, he looked mutely away.

Melinda reached up and gently turned his face toward hers.

"Surely," she asked in a whisper, "not Valdemar."

That comment surprised him. "It is not Herr Berthold's way to be cruel," he said after a moment.

Melinda donned her most intimidating glare. "Who then?"

Hilliard merely closed his eyes.

"I asked you a question." The timbre of her voice hinted at the unspoken threat. "In fact, I believe asked more than one."

Hilliard offered no clue as to his tormentor.

Melinda frowned. She wanted to strangle him, to beat a confession out of him. But judging from his injuries, he had a high tolerance for pain and intimidation. He wouldn't tell, even if she killed him. She couldn't kill him. He had the answers she needed. She decided to try a new tactic.

Grabbing his hand, she propelled him across the kitchen. The sudden movement knocked him off balance, and he was forced to follow her. She led him down the grand hallway, past the gallery of Valdemar's paintings to the servant's quarters at the side of the building.

She gripped the handle and felt the frustrating resistance of the lock. Melinda hissed in annoyance and put her weight into the twist. The lock gave way with the sound of splintering wood. Hilliard shuddered.

The door flew inward with a bang. Melinda snarled as she looked around. His quarters were as obsessively neat as Valdemar's. She dragged the reluctant Hilliard to the bed.

"Take off your jacket and sit down."

Silently, he obeyed, and eyed her warily as she rummaged in his medicine cabinet. Her search turned up a roll of gauze in a faded box and an equally ancient bottle of Detol.

Hilliard was still sitting as she left him when she returned. Gingerly, Melinda ripped the shirt up through the collar and reached around to pull the two halves off his arms.

Hilliard tensed, eyes screwed tightly shut, waiting for what was to come. He moaned softly as the first bit of antiseptic hit the skin. "I can take care of this myself," he said through clenched teeth. "It is nothing."

"Right," Melinda snapped as she wound the gauze around him like a mummy.

Nursing duty finished, she sat on the bed beside him.

"Answers now, Hilliard."

The plea was in his eyes if not on his lips. She noticed the pallor of his skin, the bruised lines beneath his eyes. He was weak, whether from pain or fear, she couldn't tell.

Melinda sighed. "Perhaps I should discuss this with Valdemar."

"No!" Hilliard said suddenly.

Violet eyes regarded him with keen interest. "Why shouldn't I Hilliard? What are you afraid Valdemar might find out?"

Again that laconic stare.

She drummed her nails on his knee. Hilliard, resolutely kept himself from looking down at the deadly claws. "I am sorely tempted to beat the information out of you." She scowled at his dispassionate gaze. "But I doubt it would do any good, even if I was to reduce to you a bloody pulp. Don't underestimate me Herr Greif. I would do it."

"I have no doubt of your ability Miss Barnes," he said feebly. He paused, fighting with the urge to tell her more. "There are things said about you."

"What exactly," Melinda asked, cold eyes boring into his skull, "is said about me?"

With an impressive amount of will, he pulled his eyes from hers. "That you killed ... another of your kind," he said, staring intently at his shoes.

Only one person besides Valdemar would know about that, Melinda thought with freezing dread. Vampires were fiercely protective of their brood. "Who told you that?" she asked more calmly than she felt. "Cornelius?"

Hilliard started. "You are acquainted with Herr Romulus?"

"You could say that."

Hilliard took a deep breath, glanced at Melinda, then looked quickly away. "It was not Herr Romulus."

"Who then?"

"I can't tell you," Hilliard said, wearily. "Kill me then, if you must."

Melinda swore, long and fluently, making him blush and look away.

"Hilliard, I have no intention of killing you." He didn't look greatly relieved. "Now whether or not you choose to admit it, I know what you put in my wine. What I want to know is why?"

The same mute testimony.

"Let's try yes or no," she suggested when he insisted on staring straight ahead. "You were trying to kill me?"

Not even a blink. She thought for a second. "Someone made you do it."

He blinked. His eyes slid sideways, then he gained control of himself and focused his eyes ahead.

"Someone tortured you into doing it," Melinda said, taking a guess. Hilliard sucked in his breath, but remained silent.

"Who?" she asked. "Why? Why would someone want me ravenous?" She didn't like where that train of thought was leading her. "To induce me to do something reckless." She remembered that eerie feeling of surveillance. "To flush me out," she murmured, fitting the pieces of the puzzle together in her mind.

From the corner of her eye, Hilliard moved. She whirled toward him, just in time to catch him as he slumped forward. His eyes were open slightly, showing slivers of white. Mouth slack, his breath came in labored gasps.

Blood loss? The shock of his injuries. He was cold to the touch, but not shivering.

She shook him. He moaned softly

"Hilliard?" Another rough shake.

"Too long," he whispered, and was gone again.

"What's too long? Hilliard answer me."

He gestured aimlessly toward his neck, then collapsed into a spineless mass in her arms.

It took a moment for the significance to sink in. Since Valdemar last drank from him, she extrapolated. Hadn't Valdemar said it needed to be done properly. Not like Valdemar to forget such a thing. Perhaps it was because Hilliard was hurt.

She studied her silent prisoner. He was close to death. It didn't take a genius to figure that out.

"Hilliard," she said urgently. "What do I do?"

Another directionless wave.

"How much?" she asked, and shook him hard. "I don't know Hilliard. You have to tell me."

"A little," he whispered, weakly, and then fell silent.

Melinda regarded him nervously. How it worked, she really didn't understand. *Just like Valdemar not to tell me any of the useful details.* But it made sense that whatever vampiric enzyme was responsible for changing body chemistry could be used to preserve and heal a human being, cum ghoul.

With long nails gripping his shoulders, she bent her head and hesitantly brought her lips to his neck. His skin was surprisingly smooth and supple, considering he had to have been at least sixty when he was transformed.

Skin parted under the pressure of her teeth. Hilliard whimpered. Melinda took a couple of tentative mouthfuls. His blood had a stale taste, as if it had been thinned and preserved over the years. She swallowed again. A little, he'd said. How much was a little?

She drank a little more, realizing what a dangerous proposition it was. Vampires drank to kill. Only with each other, with a partner of equal strength was it safe to sample another's blood.

But strangely, at the point when the victim usually began to weaken, Hilliard's heartbeat grew stronger. She felt his body heave as he took a deep breath. His eyes flickered open. She pressed her lips against his skin, levering her teeth from his neck.

Melinda laid him back into pillows on the bed. He sighed and closed his eyes, as if the whole experience had exhausted him.

"Thank you," he said whispered.

"How do you feel?"

Hilliard smiled weakly. "Much bet--"

The door slammed inward, hitting the wall and bouncing halfway back. Valdemar caught the door on the rebound and strode across the threshold.

He looked from Hilliard to Melinda, his face darkening like the sky before a summer storm. In one glance he noted the teeth marks on Hilliard's neck, the telltale drop of blood in the corner of her mouth.

"Explain this to me, Melinda," he said. Then before she could open her mouth to obey him, he gripped her chin in his taloned hand, yanking her face up close to his. "Is this what you do with what I tell you in confidence?"

"Do you want to know?" she snapped, knowing that to show fear would only make her look all the more guilty. "Or are you content to presume and listen to yourself rant?"

He impaled her with a murderous look.

"It's a long story," she said, momentarily losing her self-assurance.

"I have time," Valdemar said. His claws left angry punctures on her chin when he took his hand away. Grabbing her by the wrist, he hauled her from the bed. "You," he snarled at Hilliard. "Stay right where you are. I'll talk to you later."

Hilliard blanched, but said nothing. Melinda turned to look at him apologetically, but Valdemar thrust her through the door and out into the hallway. The door closed with a booming echo of finality, leaving her alone with Valdemar.

"Your explanation," he demanded.

In a shaking whisper she told him of her suspicions, of her encounter with Hilliard and his precarious condition.

To her amazement, he listened carefully, taking her comments very seriously. She hadn't expected him to believe her. That she had finally convinced him there was something amiss made her very nervous indeed.

"Wait for me in your rooms," he said when she finished, and disappeared back through the door to Hilliard's room.

Melinda crept closer and pressed her ear against the wall. Leather soled shoes crossed the carpeted floor. The bed gave beneath his weight. Briefly, she considered eavesdropping, then remembered the dangerous look in Valdemar's eyes and fled upstairs.

Even in the relative safety of her rooms, she was still trembling. The wooden staircase creaked, and she cringed, anticipating the verbal assault that was coming.

He approached quietly behind her, and she remained where she was, staring at his ghostly reflection in the dark window. He studied her face in the glass, then circled her with his arms. She waited, sure of his anger, but he brushed the hair from her neck and kissed her softly.

"Melinda, there is something I must tell you about Hilliard."

"What?" she asked, turning in his arms.

"Hilliard," he said tiredly, "is the property of another. Your interference in this could be taken as an act of aggression."

"Aggression?" she demanded. "Someone tortures him into spiking my wine. I interrogate him, you scare him half to death ..."

"Hilliard had information I wanted," Valdemar said without apology.

"He's just a pawn in this, a slave. It's cruel."

He dismissed her argument with a snort. "The world is full of oppressors. I am not forcing Hilliard to be my servant. He is here by a matter of contract." He searched for the right words. "When I drink from him, I do so by agreement. By drinking from him, you've damaged that bond, stolen him in fact."

"I was only trying to help him," she insisted, appalled. "What should I have done instead?"

"You should have waited. I was home soon enough. Hilliard would have lasted that long."

"I didn't know that. He was suffering. I was afraid he was going to die. And," her voice broke, "it reminded me of my own suffering," she finished quickly.

Valdemar's eyes softened, as did the hard line of his mouth. He cupped the back of her head in his palm and pressed it against his shoulder. "Hilliard is grateful for your kindness. But you must be more careful, Melinda. This whole affair disturbs me greatly."

"So you believe me?" she asked, all the more nervous because Valdemar was suddenly acting reasonable. "That I wasn't just suddenly hungry for no reason. It's been twelve years after all, Valdemar. And no matter how young and inexperienced you think I am, I'm not stupid."

Whatever Hilliard told him obviously upset him. She had no doubt he'd wrung the truth out from his taciturn assistant. Melinda stopped herself from wondering how.

"Hilliard may be indebted to you," Valdemar was saying. "But he can still be used by others against you."

"Who would do such a thing?"

"I can think of one person in particular," Valdemar said quietly, "who would be very interested in knowing about you."

"Who?"

"Oh no, Melinda," he said, holding up a hand to stop the string of questions coming. "I have seen what you do with what I confide in you. Leave this to me. I will deal with it." He looked intently into her eyes. "Though you refuse to believe it, after 1122 years, I do know better than you."

CHAPTER TWENTY-SEVEN

A furious blast from an automobile horn, a rush of air, as the Honda's bumper grazed her thigh. Melinda vaulted for the sidewalk as the driver flashed her an obscene gesture and screeched off.

The streets of downtown Toronto were busier than she remembered, the sidewalks only marginally safer.

The bar district had extended beyond its former borders in her ten year absence. The old poultry slaughter house was now a trendy market. Black clad youth packed the sidewalk. Nose rings had gained popularity.

Fragments of conversation assaulted her senses. She forced her mind to sort through the cacophony and stopped herself from jumping at every siren or loud noise.

Lately every shadow seemed to conceal something sinister.

Several times she'd imagined faces outside her third floor bedroom window. She'd stopped telling Valdemar about the phantom eyes that followed her everywhere. She'd stopped trusting her instincts.

Melinda looked around nervously. No one paid her any heed, except the panhandlers on each corner. Perhaps it had been a mistake to come downtown on a busy Saturday night, but she had to see how ten years had changed the few blocks that had once been home turf.

Heading east, she crossed the street. Best to leave the trendy, desperately-trying-not-to-be bunch at the popular bars alone. Up ahead the York Hotel beckoned.

The old brick building had a fresh coat of white paint and a patio around the side, a big improvement over its former state. A folding, chalkboard sign on the street ironically advertised the night's act as, *The Vampire's Kitchen*. Melinda smirked at the name. Too bad she didn't have time to catch their act.

On the far side of the building, the street was quiet. She braced her foot against the drainpipe, and with a couple of easy hand over hand movements, poked her head over the sill of one of the second floor windows. Inside, the matchbox-sized room was as scantily decorated as she remembered. The same dresser under the window, a similar bed with a yellowing bedspread against the wall.

Poverty, she understood. The suffocating wealth of Valdemar's estate made her feel like the proverbial bull in a china shop. Even in her own rooms she was afraid to make any sudden moves in case she broke one of the priceless antiques. Caught in the nostalgia of the moment, she dropped lightly to the ground and circled around the building to the main entrance.

Wooden doors opened into a room hazy with smoke. She passed the crowds that huddled around the glass video tables and ignored the crack of snooker balls. A vacant drum kit and a couple of mikes waited on the riser in the corner.

The bartender wasn't anyone she recognized. Melinda leaned against the bar. "I'll have a 'Sidecar'."

"Don't know that one," the bartender replied lazily, overtly hoping she'd settle for a beer instead.

"No?" she asked, circling the wooden counter. "Let me show you." She smiled, showing a devastating row of gleaming teeth. He moved aside to let her in.

"Come here often?"

Melinda reached for the bottle of Cointreau. "Used to."

"Why'd you stop?" He was getting buddy-like now, forgetting only seconds before he'd been shown a rare glimpse of the soul of a predator.

"I moved," she said and offered him a cold smile. He busied himself with another customer.

She slapped the money on the counter and toasted him with her glass. "Thanks."

Again, she surveyed the room, noting three already drunk rednecks playing pool. They looked as if they could drink a gallon each and still be lively.

Over the lip of her glass something moved. Melinda blinked. The shadows were full of vampires. Scanning the darkness, she noted there were two of them, moving rapidly toward her.

Panic startled her to hyper-awareness. Only the most ancient vampires could move with such stealth.

Coolly, she managed to set her drink back onto the counter, nod to the bartender and start backing toward the staircase. She divided her attention between calculating the distance to the stairs and keeping tabs on them.

Closer now. It didn't look good.

At that moment, the band claimed the stage in a rainbow of lights. Caught in the glare, momentarily blinded, her attackers froze. Flame-haired and blond, they sparkled like jewels.

Melinda flattened herself against the wall, confronted by the memory of a streak of scarlet leaping at her from the darkness. Chiseled eyeteeth, dripping with her own blood had grazed the air beside her face. She wrestled the recollection back into a dark compartment of her mind. Moira was dead. Melinda, of all people knew that for sure.

On closer inspection, the beautiful woman didn't look so much like Moira, but the cinnamon hair and amber eyes were the same.

She stole a glimpse at the woman's male companion. Illuminated by the spot lights, his blond hair glistened. Melinda looked into luminous green eyes, set in a face as scarred as the surface of the moon. But there was no mistaking the familiar madness in those eyes.

Adrian! And he was with a woman who looked hauntingly like Moira.

Having seen enough, she launched herself onto the staircase and hit the second floor running. Ground swayed beneath her as she dove through the open door and dangled by one hand from the fire escape. Then it was off down the alley.

It can't be, she told herself, as her feet pounded the pavement. Adrian was dead. She'd watched him burn. First she had to lose them. Then she had to find Valdemar.

As one they vaulted the fire escape. Melinda heard their feet hit the ground almost silently.

She streaked across the parking lot, ducked between buildings. Enough of trying to keep to the shadows, she concentrated on running. Northward now and east. A desperate glance behind her showed they were still gaining.

Behind City Hall she raced. Clipping the northeast end of Chinatown, she headed for Yonge Street and then dipped south, hoping to lose them in the crowds on the busy street. Like a hurricane, she whipped through pedestrians, stepping into the road when the crowds were too thick, nearly colliding with an unsuspecting rickshaw driver.

The evening show at the Canon Theater was just letting out. Playgoers flooded the street in a stream of bright colors. Melinda plunged through the crowd, daring a glimpse behind her to find her pursuers considerably slowed by the task of elbowing patrons out of the way. Snatching the opportunity, she darted into the concealing shadows of an alley and fled.

* * * *

"Ridiculous," Valdemar said, shaking her off roughly. "Adrian is dead. You know that as well as I."

"I'm sure it's him," she insisted. "He's badly scarred, but I'll never forget those eyes. You have to believe me."

"I was willing to believe you about the wine, about Hilliard. But this is impossible Melinda." He looked her up and down, noting the hair that hung from her braid in loose tendrils, the wild look in her eyes.

"I know this sounds weird," she said, raising a hand to cut off his curt retort. "He was with this woman who looked just like Moira."

Valdemar's eyes narrowed.

"Do you know who she is?"

"Get some rest," he said in the school teacher voice, reserved for occasions when he felt she was being particularly unreasonable. "It's late."

CHAPTER TWENTY-EIGHT

Tepid water splashed against her face, rinsing away the soapy foam. Melinda groped for the towel and stopped mid-reach.

She stared into the mirror, beads of water dripping from her face. So rarely she bothered with mirrors these days. Makeup was no longer needed. Vampires had a luminescent quality that drew the eye more readily than the most vibrant lipstick.

Perhaps that was where the legend about vampires shunning mirrors came from. Maybe it wasn't so much that they avoided them, as that after hundreds of years they were bored with the sight of their own faces. More likely it was painful to look at one's face so perfectly preserved when those you loved had long since passed into memory.

"When do we stop comparing?" she asked the twenty-six year old face that held her thirty-eight year old mind. "At eighty? Ninety? When does it cease to matter?"

She should ask Valdemar, but so many of her concerns seemed trivial to him. Kirsten had never laughed away her worries. But Kirsten was dead.

"I should consider myself lucky," she said, frowning at her reflection. "All my old friends are probably dyeing their hair and investigating plastic surgery." She glanced again at her flawless, unchanging reflection. "So why don't I feel lucky?"

Melinda turned away from the mirror. What she needed was a walk in the fresh, evening air. Outside, the leaves were turning from green to crimson. The change of season reassured her time did march forward.

"Where do you think you're going?" Valdemar asked, as her fingers closed on the handle of the front door.

"I'm going for a walk," she said, defiantly.

He leaned against the door, cutting off her route to freedom. "For the past two weeks, you've been trying to convince me that someone's been following you. I don't think an evening stroll is wise, Melinda."

"Valdemar ... " She drawled his name in frustration. "I've rearranged the furniture in my rooms three times, I've read ten books and five magazines. I can't stand being cooped up in here."

"It isn't safe."

She hauled on the door. With superior strength he held it shut. If she applied any more force she might splinter the wood. "I thought you didn't believe me."

"I'm reserving judgment."

"And I'm going out."

"You," he said with finality, "are not."

Melinda sprang across the lobby, heading for the hallway that led to the back door. Guessing her destination, Valdemar swore and bounded after her. She darted around Hilliard who was coming down the hall with Valdemar's customary tray of red wine. In seconds she was through the door and across the golf course beyond. Behind her, she heard the silver tray crash to the floor as Valdemar and Hilliard collided.

The sky was fading from cyan to indigo, and the night air was crisp with frost. From where she stood on the crest of one of the rolling hills, the turrets of the castle were barely visible. Hills dwindled into open farmland that stretched for miles in all directions.

There was no one in sight; the highway traffic was only a distant rumble. Her body ached from days of inactivity. Melinda leapt the short fence beside the road and began to run across the open field.

She flew by the dark sentries of trees and vaulted another decrepit rail fence, plunging into the ghostly stalks of a cornfield. She pushed her body to its limits, testing how high she could jump, how fast she could run. A car drove by on the dirt road beside the field. She paced it easily, before it geared up and sped away.

Cautiously, she looked back over her shoulder, realizing she'd come further than she intended. It was time to turn back. Valdemar would be angry enough as it was.

Something shifted in shadows. She feinted left, darting away from the sudden presence. Blond hair and gleaming teeth flashed in the moonlight. Melinda sprang to the right. Claws clove the air behind her, snatching at a handful of her hair.

Behind her someone swore. A male voice. Adrian. She didn't need another glimpse of those fangs to know it was him for sure. He was right behind her, anticipating her every move.

Running now, faster than she would have thought possible. Out on the open road, only a narrow strip of dirt stood between her and the concealing crops.

Adrian's footsteps drummed a rapid fire beat on the dirt road behind her. He'd given up all pretense of stealth, wanting only to catch her now. And he was furious she'd eluded him this far.

Crossroads beckoned up ahead; the promise of freedom.

Something suddenly came between her and the sky. They collided in a blender of earth and stars, teeth and claws.

Her arms wrenched behind her. A knee pressed at the back of her neck, holding her against the road. She tasted dirt in her mouth. Black boots approached from the corner of her sight.

"We meet again, vegetarian," he said. Adrian without a doubt. She'd never forget that mocking voice, but his words were oddly slurred.

He squatted beside her, his face menacingly illuminated by the moonlight. And suddenly she knew why his speech was so strangely distorted.

Adrian had no lips.

Where his mouth had been was only a thin, brittle ridge of skin that barely covered his jagged teeth. It gave him a perpetual rictus grin. Lidless eyes examined her with a corrosive stare. His cheeks were tattered patches of skin that stretched across the sharp bones of his face. It was the countenance of a man who'd been burned alive and somehow lived to tell the tale.

"What's the matter?" he asked. "Disappointed I'm not as dead as you thought?"

She answered him by throwing the sum of her strength into wrenching herself from the powerful arms that held her.

Hands like iron vices thrust her face harder against the dirt. She aborted her attempts to free herself. Whomever held her was stronger than Valdemar. And vampires, unlike other species, improved with age.

"This?" said a honey-smooth, female voice above her. "This is the vampire killer? It doesn't seem possible."

"Don't be fooled," Adrian warned with a grudging morsel of respect. "She is more than she appears."

"Not Valdemar's usual fare ... "

"Perhaps his preferences have changed in his old age," Adrian said, yanking her head up by the hair. He studied her, tilting his head to make sure she got a good look at him. "She is comely enough."

A disdainful snort from above. "Aren't they all," the voice said, plainly bored.

"I didn't come to discuss your progeny," Adrian said, impatiently. "We have a score to settle."

Progeny? Melinda thought, a horrifying scenario starting to take shape. *Vampire Killer? A score to settle*?

Claws like needles impaled her skin. She tired to wrestle free, but Adrian seized her wrists and with a deft twist, turned her over. She snarled up at his face upside down against the sky.

"Well?" said the other voice. "Let's have a look at you, vampire killer."

Slowly she brought her eyes downward to meet that voice.

Amber eyes seized her. Helpless as a deer mesmerized by the headlights of an oncoming truck, she stared into that commanding face.

"I seem to be at a disadvantage," Melinda said, marveling at how steady her voice sounded against the pounding of her heart. "Since you already know me, and yet we haven't been introduced."

A feline smile. A laugh that was not at all pleasant. "I'm your grandmother."

"Her name is Rowena," Adrian said, annoyed at the pace of the interrogation. "She made Valdemar."

Melinda swallowed, the pieces of the puzzle snapped suddenly together. This was the legendary Rowena, the woman who made Valdemar a vampire over eleven hundred years ago. The woman who also made Moira to be Valdemar's lover. "Yes, I know," she whispered with the sinking feeling this was going to be very bad.

"Splendid," Rowena said. "Then we can dispense with the introductions."

"What do you want?" If Rowena was about to murder her, she wanted to know up front.

"I came," Rowena said, "to find the truth about an event that leaves me greatly saddened."

"As did I," Adrian interjected. With twisted talons he grabbed Melinda by the chin, tearing her gaze from Rowena and forcing her to look at him. "Imagine my agony, awakening in this condition, to find my lover murdered and you mysteriously at large."

"I don't suppose you gave any thought to Kirsten's death," Melinda growled back. "Or that you nearly killed Valdemar."

"Valdemar seems to have survived the ordeal without any lasting scars," Adrian said. "I was not as fortunate."

"You don't deserve my pity, Adrian. You did it to yourself. Valdemar warned you--"

"Enough," Rowena snapped. "Moira was of my lineage. I came to find out how she died and to see that those responsible are justly punished. So, mewling spawn of Valdemar, what do you have to say for yourself?"

"I--" Melinda stammered, aware that even the most well

intentioned statement could prove fatal.

"Tell us how you sucked the life from Moira," Adrian growled. "I want to hear it."

His twisted claws dug into her shoulders as he hauled her from Rowena's grasp. Her feet flailed in mid air as he yanked her neck to his mouth.

Melinda retaliated with a swift kick to the groin. Adrian hissed, spattering her with warm saliva.

Stupid to attempt to use force against him, Melinda rebuked herself. Pain was obviously what was keeping him going. She looked into his eyes, appalled to see her own fear staring back at her.

Adrian reciprocated by snatching her closer. Striking with the speed of a rattlesnake, his teeth tore into her throat.

Melinda struggled against him, shredding the fabric of his jacket with her nails. But her struggles only fueled his anger.

Viciously, he yanked his fangs from her neck and closed the crust-like remnants of his lips about the seeping wound. But his mutilated mouth was too inflexible to contain the flow of liquid. Blood ran in ruby rivulets into her collar.

She abandoned herself to panic, using her teeth, claws and feet against him.

"Enough!" Rowena said sharply. She grabbed a handful of Adrian's white-blond hair and yanked his head backward. "What good will it do," she asked in response to his hungry stare, "to kill her and go ignorant?" She turned venomous eyes on Melinda. "There are so many more effective ways to acquire information."

Rowena placed the tip of a serrated nail against Melinda's cheek. Slowly, with surgical precision, she dragged the nail from eyebrow to jaw.

Involuntarily Melinda moaned as skin parted and sticky blood oozed from the ragged wound. She fought to think beyond the searing pain and the urge to scream.

The thick smell of blood filled the air. Rowena's eyes glittered with the wonder of a child in a candy store. "See," she admonished Adrian. "The results are far better my way."

"She hasn't told us a thing," Adrian sulked, tightening his grip on Melinda.

"She will," Rowena said with chilling confidence.

"This isn't necessary," Melinda gasped and licked at the blood running down the corner of her mouth. She was appalled at how painful the encounter had been, terrorized by the realization that she was in very serious trouble with no hope of escape. Moira had nearly killed her. And Moira was Rowena's child. "I would have told you what you wanted to know."

"Really?" Rowena asked, her face centimeters from Melinda's. "And did you show poor Moira the same mercy, little killer?"

"Moira was trying to kill me!" Melinda blurted back, horrified when her voice broke.

"Is that so?" Rowena asked maliciously. "And what exactly did poor Moira do to you?

"Moira hated me," Melinda said urgently. "I don't know why. She thought I stood between her and Valdemar. She could have had him for all I cared then. I hated him for making me a vampire."

"You didn't want to be a vampire?" Rowena repeated. "Now that is ironic," she said in a voice that was anything but sympathetic.

"Moira terrorized me," Melinda said, the feigned interest making her nervous. "From the moment she knew I existed.

Rowena's laugh shattered the pre-dawn silence. "Moira hated you because she thought you ruined her chances of having Valdemar. And all the time you didn't even want him. Do you expect me to believe this?"

"It's true," Melinda insisted. "Ask Adrian."

"Is it true?" Rowena asked him.

Adrian shrugged. "You know what Moira was like when she had her heart set on something. But she didn't deserve to die for her shortcomings."

Rowena regarded her suspiciously. "But you stayed with him, even though you hated him."

"We met by accident ... " Melinda said, parceling out the pieces of information.

"This," Adrian snapped impatiently, "is ancient history. Hurry up and find out what you want to know. You promised her to me." He glanced nervously at the sky. "And it is almost dawn." He nuzzled Melinda's throat with his misshapen mouth. "One, long, exquisite drink of her young blood to heal my wounds." He looked pleadingly at Rowena. "Free me. I have done everything you asked. I found the child-killer for you. It isn't fair to keep me this way, wounded and half-starved from existing on the thin blood of animals." And when his appeal seemed to fall on deaf ears, he added, "It's fitting that she should cure me after she so brutally murdered Moira."

"You're right, it's almost day," Rowena said, completely

unaffected by his entreaty. "There is much more I need to know. We'll have to take her with us."

"Valdemar will come looking for her," Adrian said anxiously. "Get it over with now, then it'll be too late for him to do anything. I've been waiting ten long years for this."

"And you would have waited longer if I hadn't run into Cornelius. We would never have thought of looking for Valdemar so close to Toronto. Wales, Germany maybe. How long would it have taken us to search Europe? It was just coincidence we found out about Valdemar's supposed painting trips to the far north. You can be patient a little longer."

Melinda opened her mouth. Adrian clamped a leather-like hand firmly over her parted lips. "Not a good idea," he cautioned, before she could scream. Yanking her up by the wrists, he hauled her off with them.

Bushes whipped her face and tore at her hair. Scenery rushed by at a dizzying pace. Melinda shut her eyes and steeled herself for the inevitable.

* * * *

Her cheek collided with the damp earth.

"We should leave her out in the sun," Adrian grumbled from nearby. "That would make her talk fast enough." He laughed maniacally to himself. "Then she'd look more like me. A fitting companion. Perhaps I won't kill her after all."

Melinda stifled the urge to spit dirt from her mouth. Better not to draw attention to herself. She concentrated on figuring out where she was. Somewhere not far away from the castle, she deduced. The smell of the vegetation outside was familiar. Off in the distance she could hear the unmistakable din of morning traffic. She sampled the air again. No blood-smell of livestock; not a barn then. A root cellar more likely.

On the other side of the stone wall, another conversation was in progress.

" ... I want you to distract him, lead him astray."

"What should I tell him?" a familiar voice asked, plainly afraid.

Hilliard. Melinda's heart sank. Together they were helpless, both at Rowena's mercy.

"Tell him anything," Rowena snapped. "You're a resourceful man, Hilliard. Tell him she ran away."

"But I--"

His protest ended abruptly. Melinda winced at the sound of flesh tearing.

"Tell him whatever you choose," Rowena hissed. "Just see that Valdemar is occupied until I am finished with this ... business."

Adrian shook Melinda roughly. "Don't go to sleep on us now."

She glared back at him. "I see your suffering hasn't taught you any humility."

Adrian opened his mouth for a harsh reply, then scowled at her darkly as Rowena approached.

"Now, let me see if I have this straight," Rowena prompted. "Valdemar confused dinner with love. Moira took exception to this and tried to turn love back into dinner. You took exception to that and killed Moira."

"I left Valdemar," Melinda said with as much authority as she could muster. "I just wanted out of it all."

Rowena turned her intense gaze on Adrian. "Well?" she asked, eyebrows raised.

"She ran off," he conceded. "Valdemar was angry with us for upsetting his precious offspring. He went soft over her."

"I fail to see how this concerned Moira," Rowena said, scowling.

"Horrible things started happening," Melinda stepped up the pace of her story. "Strange catastrophes where large numbers of mortals were killed. Kirsten was sure--"

"Kirsten?" Rowena sniped. "I wouldn't have thought the merry ex-wives of Valdemar would be so friendly."

"Kirsten," Melinda repeated, ignoring the jibe, "was sure Moira was behind all those terrible events. We were afraid she was angry enough with Valdemar to do him harm ... "

"I heard about the party in the subway," Rowena said impatiently.

Melinda didn't want to remember, but the movie screen in her inner mind was already replaying the blinding flash and zooming in on the bodies floating in the pool.

"Kirsten and Moira got into a fight," Melinda struggled to force the memory back into the past. "Moira pushed Kirsten onto the tracks. She hit the third rail as she fell and was electrocuted. I thought for sure Valdemar was going to kill her, but Adrian--"

"Adrian what?" Rowena asked with a side-long glance at the scarred vampire.

"Adrian thought he could call Valdemar's bluff. He threatened to set a trail of gasoline on fire if Valdemar wouldn't let her go." She looked at Adrian. "Damn it Adrian. It was your own fault. Valdemar warned you about the gas main."

"And who has suffered more than I for my foolishness?" Adrian asked caustically.

"Don't talk to me about your suffering," Melinda snarled. "What about Valdemar? What about the mortals you killed?"

Adrian shrugged. "Is it my fault Valdemar couldn't bear the thought of mortals suffering? I didn't make him run back in there."

They were waiting for her to continue, to pick up the thread of Adrian's story.

"Valdemar told me to catch Moira. It was the last thing he said to me. But then the whole place exploded. I was racing down the tracks after Moira. I only meant to detain her," she explained, helpless to stop the words tumbling from her mouth. "But she sunk her teeth into my neck, and in my struggling, I got the better of her ... " Her voice cracked, dying into silence. "And then I came back for Valdemar," she whispered.

"Ah," Rowena said sarcastically. She got to her feet and cast a disdainful eyes back at Melinda. "True love triumphs after all." She sauntered up to Adrian. "She's yours. I have all the information I need."

CHAPTER TWENTY-NINE

The door swung shut, cutting off a blinding flash of daylight. Melinda looked nervously at Adrian who, it seemed now that the moment had arrived, was content to take his time. He squatted before her, resting patchwork hands against his knees. With a twisted claw, he traced the outline of her face. She tensed, gathering her strength.

"So vegetarian," he said quietly. "It's just you and me now."

Melinda glared at him, putting all the malice she could summon into that one black stare. "Over my corpse."

Adrian laughed gleefully. "Only too happy to oblige." He placed an arm around her shoulders and lowered himself to the floor beside her. "Melinda," he said with a shake of his head. "If only things had been different, perhaps you would have been mine."

It took only one close-up look at his unblinking eyes, the blistered and peeling skin, the black and crusty remains of his lips. "I would never have been yours," she snapped and dealt him a spiked cuff across the cheek. "And a little humility is good for the soul."

Stoically, he endured the injury, offering not even the satisfaction of a blink as blood beaded from the puckered skin.

His twisted nails grazed the spot where she'd been sitting. Melinda was already up and running, putting all her strength into one reckless dash for the door.

Adrian lurched after her. She reached the door and hauled it from its hinges, prepared to brave even the burning sunlight.

He snatched the door from her grasp and slammed it shut. It hung there, drunkenly suspended by one hinge. Even the light that leaked in around the frame made her eyes tear.

Blindly, she flailed against him, her fists useless against a wall of solid muscle. He seized her, heedless of her blows. She jerked her knee up, and was satisfied to hear a painful grunt as her boot collided with his stomach.

Limbs entwined, they tumbled. The wood door sent a shower of splinters into Melinda's back as she slid to the floor under Adrian's weight.

With superior strength he pinned her spread-eagled to the dirt floor. With his rough, bony chin, he burrowed into the crook of her neck. She felt the prick of his teeth, the warm wetness of her own blood leaking into the dirt beneath.

Melinda heaved against him in one last attempt to dislodge him. Adrian growled deep in his throat and dug his teeth deeper.

There was a lightness in her limbs, a dreamy floating sensation that made it hard to concentrate. Like freezing to death, the end was deceptively blissful. The tips of her fingers and toes prickled, then grew cold.

Valdemar, she thought distantly. *After all that's happened, it shouldn't end like this ...*

* * * *

A motorcycle engine roared. Wood splintered, then there was light, inconceivably bright.

Through heavy eyelids, she watched as two dark figures leapt from the bike. The motorcycle careened past them, smashing into the far wall before its motor finally stalled.

Black leather covered them head to toe, down to the thick gloves and heavy boots. High necked jackets reached far up under the black helmets with heavily tinted visors.

"Adrian," one said and swore viciously. "I wouldn't have believed it."

Adrian wrenched his teeth from her neck, discarding her like a broken toy. He hurled himself at the intruders.

As one they leapt toward him and circled him like hungry wolves. He lashed out with teeth and claws, catching one across the chest in a slash of crimson blood and torn leather.

With lightning speed, the other snaked a foot between his legs. The unexpected movement toppled Adrian to the floor. Like vultures, they were on him. Helmets discarded, they dove for jugular vein and wrist. Melinda caught a glimpse of black hair and blacker eyes.

Valdemar.

But who told him?

Another darkness in the doorway. A flash of a tailored sleeve and gray-blond hair.

Hilliard, she thought. Her last thought for a long time.

CHAPTER THIRTY

Anxious voices called her from the darkness. Melinda wanted to answer, but it was so desperately hard to think. She floated in a sphere of velvet darkness, devoid of sensation. For a long time, she was content to stay that way.

Vaguely, from that outside world, she felt herself handled. Where was she now? Still in the root cellar? No, there had been motion. Valdemar had come. Home then? Home. Yes. She tried to fasten on where exactly home was, but the thoughts twisted from her grasp. Visions of a cramped downtown apartment drifted through her mind. No, that was long ago. Images of frozen landscape flitted into memory, but that too was gone now.

Easy to sink into comforting oblivion where there was nothing to regret and no one to answer to.

I'm dying, she thought, then wondered why the idea didn't frighten her. Valdemar would be upset.

Valdemar. That notion roused her to semi-awareness. However, where there was consciousness, there was also excruciating pain. And she didn't want to go there.

Someone called her, urgent and insistent. She was touched again.

Blood dribbled across her closed mouth. Pooling against her upper lip, the overflow ran into her nose and trickled down her throat. She tried to cough, but flesh covered her mouth, forcing her to swallow instead.

She choked down another mouthful of blood. Warmth flowed down into her stomach and out into her own veins, leaving needles of agony in its path. Hunger seized her, and instinctively her lips sealed about the wound as she succumbed to the primal urge to feed.

Pain, her first thought as mind and body flowed back into one. Pain, then blood that would take away the pain, then only blood.

"Melinda?"

Somewhere in the depths of her memory she recognized Valdemar's voice, his scent, the taste of his blood. Comforted, she let him care for her. But when the blood had chased back the torment enough to think, she came to her senses with alarm.

Too much, she was taking far too much blood. Not even Valdemar had that much to spare. Already she could feel him weakening, yet she couldn't bear to separate herself from the flow of sustenance her body demanded.

"She's taking too much, Val," said a voice full of concern. The speech was familiar, ever so faintly accented. "You can't give her anymore. It could kill you."

"I won't let her die," Valdemar snarled.

Warm breath caressed her cheek as the speaker peeled back an eyelid to examine her. Annoyed she moaned and flicked her head from his grasp. "She's badly hurt. Even if you gave her every drop in your body, it wouldn't be enough." And when there was no coherent answer to that threat, he said, "You'll be no help to Melinda dead."

"I said leave it!" Valdemar hissed, pulling her protectively closer.

A sigh and a moment of hesitation. Then there was the wet sound of teeth piercing flesh, the smell of new blood. A drop splashed onto her face. "Will you waste it?" the voice asked.

Unfamiliar arms about her, pulling her away. She held on to Valdemar with savage need, but she was easily torn away. Melinda whimpered for the nearby nourishment being denied her.

"Easy," someone said, positioning her head in the crook of their elbow.

Unfamiliar-tasting blood rushed into her mouth. Thick, vampire blood. She knew this presence, had been near it many times. Melinda tried to assemble the puzzle, but the consuming hunger would not let her think.

Strength was returning, rended flesh knitting painfully back together. Familiar smells surrounded her: the perfume of roses from the garden outside, the linen sheets fresh from the laundry. Home. Valdemar's castle. Her own room.

Slowly, Melinda opened her eyes, and tipped her head backward to look up into the face above her. Tired hazel eyes looked back at her. It took a moment to place the face. Long brown hair tumbled about his shoulders. He was still dressed in black leather, only the helmet was missing. She choked on a mouthful of blood, and pushed his wrist away.

"Cornelius!" Vocal chords refused to obey her, the sound came out as a rasp.

Cornelius leaned back against the headboard. "Hi Melinda," he said, wearily. Dark circles ringed his eyes and his face was drawn and haggard.

"Hi," she returned grimly. "You look awful."

"So do you."

She tried to smile, then gave up. It required too much effort. Instead, she reached for his wrist and turned it over, gasping when she saw the purple bruises. "Thanks," she whispered, pressing her lips against the tender skin. "Are you all right?"

"I've been better," Cornelius said.

Questions tumbled from her mouth as fast as she could form the words. "What are you doing here? How did you know?"

"Hilliard," he said, patting her shoulder to stem the flow.

"But Rowena tortured him. She warned him not to tell ... "

"Valdemar," he finished quietly. "Apparently, she didn't include me in her orders."

"I thought you sold your house and left the country."

"I did. I went home to Italy, where I ran into Rowena. Her visit seemed innocent enough at first, but the more I thought about her sudden interest in Val after five hundred years, the more it worried me. So I came to see what was really going on."

"Valdemar!" Remembering suddenly, Melinda vaulted from his arms. Unable to find her equilibrium, she swayed precariously while multi-colored points of light shot through her vision. Valdemar was nowhere in sight, and the abrupt movement cost her the sum of her negligible strength. "I took too much from him," she said anxiously. "I didn't mean to, but--"

"Valdemar's all right," Cornelius said, catching her and lowering her to the pillows. He reached for the comforter that was scrunched up at the end of the bed. "He's resting," he said soothingly, but his eyes betrayed the lie. "Now rest Melinda, or you'll undo all Valdemar sacrificed to save you," he warned. He stood up uncertainly. "I have to hunt as soon as it's dark.

Except for the rustle of leather upon leather, Cornelius moved silently from the room. Through the fringe of her eyelashes, Melinda watched him leave, listening for the sound of the heavy oak door softly closing and his noiseless footsteps trailing off down the carpeted stairs.

Ignoring the sweaty feeling of blood rushing from her head, she crawled from the bed and staggered to the door.

Walls caught her fall several times, and the floor tossed perilously beneath her feet. The door to Valdemar's rooms seemed to rear up at her suddenly. Misjudging the distance, she hit it with a dull thud and tumbled across the threshold.

He had been resting, as Cornelius said, at least recently. The bedclothes lay in a heap as if he'd abandoned them suddenly.

At first he was nowhere to be seen, until she looked beyond the huge bed to the Persian carpet in front of the cold fireplace. There, hunched over, feeding with the intensity of a kill, was Valdemar. Unbelieving, Melinda gaped at the flame-haired form in his arms.

CHAPTER THIRTY-ONE

They sprang apart like startled cats, Rowena looking disdainfully annoyed, Valdemar rushing toward Melinda. She turned back through the doorway to run away, but her strength evaporated, and the floor reached up to smack her across the face.

"Melinda!" Valdemar groaned as he gathered her crumpled form into his arms. Blood scented his breath. He swallowed, then sat back against the wall and sighed. "Melinda what are you doing here?"

"I was worried about you," she murmured, feeling only sick and dizzy and earnestly wishing she hadn't seen what she'd just witnessed.

"Don't," Valdemar ordered, "worry about me. I can take care of myself."

"I was afraid I'd killed you," she whispered.

He pushed the sweaty mat of hair from her forehead. "No, I'm fine," he said, more gently.

Rowena sauntered toward them daintily dabbing at the blood on her neck with Valdemar's handkerchief. With a shrug of her shoulders, she rearranged her blouse, then looked down at Melinda and snorted. "Next time Valdemar, lock the door."

The sight of Rowena's face so close to her own horrified Melinda and she tried to wrestle out of Valdemar's arms, but he held her still. "Shh Melinda, it's not what you think."

"Do you answer to the child?" Rowena asked, voice full of menace.

"Shut up for God's sake," Valdemar hissed back at her. And when Melinda squirmed again in his arms, he ordered in a harsh whisper. "Will you go somewhere else Rowena, you're frightening her."

When Rowena showed no sign of removing herself, he carried Melinda to a nearby chair. She would gladly have bolted from the room if she'd had the strength, and if Rowena was not blocking her path to the door.

From her seat in the wing-back chair it was impossible to see Valdemar's expression as he faced Rowena. But from the set of his shoulders she could tell he was prepared to do battle.

Rowena regarded the ceiling, as if praying for patience. "See if I offer you my help ever again." She turned to leave, then stalked back toward him. "I don't know what it is with you Valdemar," she said with an exasperated sigh. "I did so much to make you happy. I made you a lover." She gazed down at Melinda, plainly puzzled. "And this is what you choose over Moira."

"Moira was nothing to you but a convenient way out of your commitment to me," Valdemar thundered. "Don't insult me by pretending you cared about her."

"Obligation?" Rowena spat back. "I gave you life. What more did you want?"

"You," Valdemar said plaintively. "I wanted you."

"What was so wrong with Moira? The two of you had so much in common: art, music, literature. Why wouldn't you have her?"

They faced each other like onyx and amber chess pieces, each holding back what was too painful to say.

"She wasn't you," Valdemar said. "I am also your child, *Rhonwen*." He spoke the Welsh version of her name softly, almost like a prayer. "Have you forgotten?"

"I forget nothing." The air bristled with the energy between them. "Especially that you vowed never to create another."

"It was an accident," Valdemar said flatly, his face purposely averted from Melinda, "The result of one of Moira's pranks."

"Easy enough to blame the deceased," Rowena snarled. "The

offspring is the result of your cowardice, nothing else."

"That is Adrian's opinion," Valdemar growled. "Will you take his word over mine?"

Rowena drew her mouth into a theatrical pout. "Oh, do tell me yourself Valdemar. Break my heart with the story of how losing Kirsten threw you into a depression that lasted nearly two hundred years. Explain how you came to Canada just to be close to her and tried to win her back with pity by throwing yourself from society and living in an abandoned sewer ... "

Valdemar glared at her. "Adrian has obviously missed his calling. He should write fiction."

"Even Cornelius admits that Moira tried to bring you around, but you refused all her efforts to make you feel better."

"Cornelius should declare his mouth as a weapon next time he crosses the border," Valdemar remarked caustically. "I'd hardly call getting me drunk and setting me loose on an unsuspecting mortal nurturing me back to health!"

Rowena patted Melinda's forearm. "I presume this is our unsuspecting mortal. But you aren't as helpless as you appear," she asked, peering into Melinda's reluctant eyes, "are you little vampire killer?"

Melinda froze, afraid even to cringe, lest she incur any more of her wrath.

Valdemar brushed her hand off roughly. Threads of Melinda's shirt material came away with her nails.

"That's enough, Rowena," Valdemar hissed. "If you have something to say. Say it to me."

"What was so different about this particular mortal that the killing bothered you?" Rowena asked, pretending to be rebuffed.

"It was a sordid affair," Valdemar said, disgust evident in his tone. "Not at all honorable."

Rowena laughed. "Honorable? How like you to say such a thing. But that isn't the truth, is it Valdemar? You wanted to punish Moira."

"When and who I kill is my concern," Valdemar said acidly, the corners of his mouth tightening in anger. "Not yours, and never Moira's."

"And was it an *honorable* option?" she asked Melinda, staring down at her as one would question a child.

Melinda swallowed nervously. "Valdemar and I disagree about a good many things."

This seemed to amuse Rowena and she laughed huskily, turning back to Valdemar with vicious merriment in her eyes. "And I suppose you're hopelessly in love with this one, like the others?"

"My feelings for Melinda are my own business," Valdemar snapped. "And where have you been for the past five hundred years, Mistress Rowena, that you couldn't drop in to say hello?"

"We were talking about Moira," Rowena pointed out coldly.

"Yes," Valdemar snarled, "we were."

They confronted each other, panting with anger. Melinda had the impression of flowing, molten copper, offset by Valdemar's calm darkness.

"She hated both of us. You, for creating her, and me for refusing her. Between us, we made her completely miserable."

Rowena glared at him, eyes turning from amber fire to golden ice. She paced a few steps away, pretending to examine an oriental vase on one of the small side tables.

"You talk as if you're the first person ever to experience the death of a relative." He snatched the vase from her hands and set it down gently. "What about Kirsten? What about my loss? She was dear to me. Moira knew that, but that didn't stop her from killing her in cold-hearted spite. And now you come to murder another of my children."

"You're exaggerating Valdemar. I didn't cause your precious offspring any undue harm."

He indicated Melinda with a swipe of his arm. "Look at her!"

Rowena shrugged. "Adrian's handiwork, not mine. What did you do with him anyway?"

"He is ... restrained. After what he did, he's lucky he isn't dead."

"You," Rowena snapped, "are the one who's lucky. You could have easily killed yourself giving the child that much blood."

"My concern, not yours."

"You were content for me to be concerned when you were about to perish from loss of blood. You could say thank you."

Valdemar scowled, then sighed. Hesitantly, he placed his hands on her shoulders and looked deeply into her eyes. "Thank you *Rhonwen*. Under the circumstances it was ... kind of you."

"You are the most disagreeable of all my brood, Valdemar," she said, breaking out of his hold and throwing herself petulantly into the chair opposite Melinda's. "I don't know why I have such feelings for you."

"How far are you going to carry this feud?" Valdemar asked, looking down at her. "Melinda's life is not going to buy back Moira's. You don't even know for a fact that Melinda killed her."

Rowena's head jerked up like a cobra striking for the kill. "The child confessed to it." Confused, she searched Valdemar's eyes, but he kept his gaze carefully neutral.

"She was frightened."

"Adrian said--"

"Adrian is insane."

"If she didn't do it, then who did?"

Valdemar crossed his arms over his chest. "I did."

Without thinking, Melinda was on her feet. "Val no!"

He turned on her, eyes black with anger and seized her by the shoulders. "Melinda, for once you will do as I tell you and be quiet, or I will rip out your tongue."

"No," she whispered, blasting him with a scathing look of her own. "I can't let you do this."

He set her down hard on her feet and held her in his corrosive stare.

"It happened the way I told you," she told Rowena, realizing with a sickening feeling she had just destroyed Valdemar's attempt to protect her.

"This one is just like you, *Cariad*," Rowena muttered. "You deserve each other." With that comment she left the room, slamming the door hard enough to knock the paintings askew. Melinda studied the carpet, conscious of Valdemar's claws still imbedded in her shoulders. Motionless, she waited for the tirade that was coming, but he was alarmingly silent.

Forced to deal with too many stresses, her body finally gave in to the tremors that resonated down her spine. She risked a glance at Valdemar and swiftly looked away.

Eventually, it occurred to him she was suffering and he loosened his grip on her and led her toward the bed. Wordlessly he covered her with the heavy, gold quilt, and turned away.

She wanted to call him back, to say anything that would make the situation right again, but he was gone before she could think of something appropriate. Exhausted, she turned her face into the pillow and slept.

CHAPTER THIRTY-TWO

Melinda came to her senses with the feeling time had passed.

Eyes closed, she listened into the still of the room, becoming aware of soft breathing; Valdemar asleep beside her. His eyes opened.

"You came back," she said groggily.

"Someone has to keep an eye on you," he said. "To make sure you don't get yourself killed."

"If you're going to yell at me," she suggested, "why don't you just do it. Suspense is beyond me right now."

He regarded her coolly, looking every bit as fierce as he had when he'd left. For a few more moments he kept up the pretense of anger, then sighed and pulled her against him. "I'm not going to shout at you Melinda."

"You're still mad at me," she said warily.

"I am not angry," he said exasperated. "This time I thought I'd lost you for certain."

"I'm sorry," she whispered, not knowing what else to say.

"I know," he said, lips against her temple.

She pushed herself up on one elbow, noting with relief that her arms had some strength in them. "Do you love her, Valdemar?"

A pause, a hesitation, but he didn't evade the question by asking who. "Yes Melinda, I do."

"Do you want her back?"

"Rowena is not offering to take me back."

"If she was?"

Another pause, longer this time. "It wouldn't be the same. We have grown apart over the centuries." He looked down at her, probing her face. "But that isn't really what you want to know, is it?"

Was she really so transparent, she wondered.

"It is possible," Valdemar said, "to love many people in different ways. It didn't bother you that I still loved Kirsten."

"Kirsten was my friend."

"Kirsten was safely married to Cornelius," he corrected.

"Perhaps Rowena will marry Cornelius too," she said, a pitiful attempt at a joke.

Valdemar smiled. "I shudder to think ... yet there have been stranger matches."

"Like you and me."

He folded her protectively back into his arms. "Quite honestly, you are not the kind of lover I envisioned."

"Yeah? Well I would never have imagined you in a million years."

Laughter rumbled through his chest beneath her ear. She should have the good sense to be quiet, but there was one thing she had to ask. "Valdemar?"

"Lord, Melinda what now?"

"Where is Adrian?"

"Adrian can do you no harm at the moment," he said, sidestepping the question.

"Don't tell me this place has a dungeon to go with the moat," she said sarcastically. But by the look on Valdemar's face, she realized she'd hit closer to the mark than she intended.

"Melinda don't start. You needn't concern yourself with Adrian."

"Adrian has a few liters of my precious blood in his stomach," she pointed out.

"And you have absconded with more than your share of mine," he said. "Shall I take it back?"

Melinda frowned, risking the chance that he had no intention of making good on his threat. "What are you going to do with him?"

"I haven't decided."

"You can't leave him locked up forever. It's not like you to make someone suffer."

"You assume a great deal about what I would and wouldn't do."

"He isn't dead," she ventured, preparing for an onslaught of his wrath. "I heard what you told Rowena."

"Were you smart, you would concern yourself more with Rowena than Adrian. That was a foolish stunt you pulled, interfering when I was trying my best to protect you. She could well have killed you," Valdemar continued, sitting up. "I would have been powerless to prevent it. There are others stronger than I. Think about that, Melinda."

Think about it? She'd done nothing but think about it. First Moira, now Adrian and Rowena, there seemed no end to the line of people who wanted her dead.

"Do you think she'll come after me again?"

"She gave me her word that she wouldn't. Likely she has realized you are useful in keeping me at bay."

"She seems terribly disdainful for someone who's supposed to love you. I can't imagine what you ever saw in her?"

"I couldn't begin to explain it to you." He gave her a stern look. "It's none of your business."

A knock on the door brought a merciful end to the conversation.

"Come," Valdemar called, rising. He looked curiously at Hilliard who stood awkwardly in the doorway. "What is it Hilliard?"

"I came to see about Miss Barnes," he said, taking a few stiff steps in the direction of the bed.

"Melinda is feeling much better," Valdemar said, eyeing him warily, as if even Hilliard might still be a threat to her.

Melinda squeezed his hand. "I'm fine, really."

Hilliard cleared his throat nervously. "I feared the worst when we arrived at the farmhouse."

"If it wasn't for you, I would probably be dead--" She patted his shoulder, then stopped abruptly when the light touch caused his eyes to narrow with pain.

Valdemar paced the distance between them cautiously. "Hilliard?" A cuff link fell to the carpeted floor as he rolled back his servant's sleeve. Disgusted he looked away. Melinda didn't need to look.

"I'm sorry," Valdemar said, softly.

"There was nothing you could have done to prevent it." His voice was tight with pain. "Rowena does what she likes."

"Rowena always has," Valdemar agreed, conscious of Melinda's eyes on him.

"Sit down," she said, moving over to give him space on the bed. "You look worse than me at the moment."

He eyed her nervously, deducing he would have to endure more of her nursing care. "Madam, you needn't--"

"Oh, let Melinda mother you if she must," Valdemar said with a smirk. "She means only to be kind. Perhaps it will keep her mind off other things that are none of her concern."

"What ever possessed you to enslave yourself to a demon like Rowena?" she asked, carefully helping him from his jacket and shirt that were getting soggy with his blood.

Hilliard turned his head, wincing as the movement sent shocks of pain through his tortured body.

"Never mind," she said, heeding Valdemar's threatening look. "It's none of my business."

It took her a moment to recognize the welts that crisscrossed his back and upper arms. Like fat, fluid-filled worms, they wove an intricate pattern in his pale flesh.

"Whip marks?" she asked Valdemar. He nodded mutely.

"I can't believe you let this go on under your own roof?" she said incredulously.

"Hilliard has not asked for my assistance," Valdemar pointed out.

"I don't believe you," she told him, rising to her feet in

indignation. "You could prevent this!"

"Really Melinda? And what would you have me do?"

"Tell Rowena to stop!" She enunciated the words as if speaking to a two year old, a sentiment not lost on Valdemar.

"Rowena is not obligated to do as *I* say."

Melinda shot a last angry glance in his direction and fastened her attention on Hilliard. "Do you intend to endure this sort of abuse in silence forever?"

Instantly, she was sorry she'd said it. His pride was bruised enough without adding insult to his injuries.

"How can I defend myself against her?"

Melinda sighed. "Will you just get me some disinfectant and gauze?" she snapped at Valdemar. He glared at her in reply, but nevertheless did as she asked, returning a short time later with first aid supplies.

Silently, -he watched her clumsy attempts at first aid. At first his lack of action angered her, until she surmised that after eleven hundred years he'd likely forgotten what to do for human injuries. Finally, looking as useless as he no doubt felt, he turned to leave.

"Help me," Hilliard blurted. And when Valdemar kept walking, he blurted, "Give me the ability to defend myself against her. It is within your power to bestow."

Valdemar froze, one hand poised against the door frame. Slowly, he turned back and focused his black stare on Hilliard. His face was absolutely impassive, a look that made Melinda shudder.

"What exactly," he asked, "is in my power to bestow?"

Hilliard, having ventured so far, would not tarnish his pride by begging.

"I will not," Valdemar said, coming to stand at the bedside, staring down at him, "make you a vampire. If that is what you're asking. I will *never* do that again. I have enough *children*." His eyes darted to Melinda. "And enough of their woes."

"I am not asking you to fight my battles for me," Hilliard protested. Valdemar fixed him with a freezing glare. "Ask Melinda," he snapped. And left the room.

CHAPTER THIRTY-THREE

Melinda watched Valdemar leave in startled disbelief. "I can't believe he said that!" she blurted to the space where Valdemar had been standing. "He can't be serious."

Hilliard regarded her like a doomed man watching the executioner sharpen his ax.

Bemused, she sat back down on the side of the bed. The movement made him crinkle his eyes in pain. "I sympathize with your suffering, Hilliard. But, what you're asking ... "

"You cannot know what it's been like to be at her mercy for hundreds of years," he said in a hushed voice, as if Rowena might suddenly materialize out of the woodwork. "The subject of her whims and her cruelties ... "

"This existence is a curse of its own," she said, curling deadly nails into her palms. "You would only be a different type of slave, imprisoned by your hunger, cut off from humanity. There is very little joy in this life."

"In my life there is no happiness," Hilliard said. "I exist from moment to moment in utter terror of her. To think of spending eternity this way is unbearable. Usually, if I was living under Herr Berthold's roof, she left me in peace. But now, not even Valdemar can protect me."

Melinda thought of the scars on his back and grimaced.

"Rowena has lived too long," Hilliard said. "She has forgotten the pleasures of life. Her only enjoyment comes from the pain of others." He reached for her hand and holding on to it, begged her earnestly, "Please don't abandon me."

"Don't look at me like that. I don't even *know* how to do it," she confessed. "And I'm in no condition ... "

"Will you think about it?"

"I'll think about it," she promised, regretting it instantly.

* * * *

"Are you crazy!" she sputtered when she found Valdemar in his studio.

"If I am it is because you have driven me to it," he answered, never taking his attention away from the thick strokes of blood-red paint he was applying to the canvas.

"I can't believe you're actually suggesting I make Hilliard into a vampire."

"It was Hilliard's suggestion, not mine."

"You told him to ask me!" she nearly shouted. "Do you really want me to do that?"

"You do as you please regardless of what I tell you," Valdemar said. "You are the one who interfered in this."

Tired of arguing and ordering, he was abandoning her to her own judgment. She didn't like this new tactic.

Pondering what that might mean, she looked over his shoulder at the work in progress. The foreground was dominated by the black silhouette of a mountain with the sun setting behind it in every shade of crimson imaginable. "Who taught you to paint?" she asked, daring him to ignore her. "Moira?"

"I taught Moira," he said, putting his palette down on a nearby stool. "Were we not just discussing Hilliard?"

"If I make him a vampire," she said, speaking her thoughts aloud. "He would be my offspring, my responsibility ... "

"Exactly."

"Do you think I should?"

"Oh no, Melinda," Valdemar said. "I am past dispensing advice. You want so badly to be my equal, you think you know better than I, you decide. But, weigh the consequences carefully. I am tired of cleaning up after you."

"I don't know if I'm ready to start making other vampires."

"It is not something to be entered into lightly," Valdemar said, turning back to his painting.

"It's a hard decision."

"It is."

She circled his easel, poking her head around the side, so he'd have to look at her. "Do you regret making me?"

Valdemar laid his brush on the easel ledge, giving up on painting entirely. He reached for her and she let him pull her from behind the easel. There was a splash of red on his nose that smeared against her cheek as their faces met. "Never," he said holding her tightly.

"We haven't always been friends," she said, breathing in the smell of linseed oil and turpentine.

"No we haven't," he agreed, stepping back from her and looking earnestly into her face with soft, dark eyes. "Melinda, it isn't easy for me to let you go this way."

"You let me go twice before."

"That was different. I believed I could shield you, even from afar. It's much harder now knowing I can no longer protect you. It makes me feel, well ... old."

"Val, you are old."

"Older than I ever thought I'd live to be," he said, sounding infinitely weary.

"I should do it then?"

He kissed her eyelids, first one, then the other. A custom from another century. "It's your decision."

* * * *

"You're sure about this?" she asked Hilliard two weeks later. They were sitting in his private quarters, Melinda cross-legged in the middle of his bed and he in the stiff-backed wooden chair in front of the fireplace.

He turned, eyes glowing, the firelight putting flaxen highlights back into hair long ago turned gray. "I'm sure."

Though she had recovered fully, the thought of what she was about to do made her feel weak. Valdemar's careful instructions were a jumble of meaningless words in her head. Hunger was making her irritable, and Hilliard showed no signs of backing out at the last minute.

"Not everyone survives this," she said tracing the pattern stitched in the quilted bedspread.

"I know," he said softly.

"And you're willing to risk it anyway." Melinda searched his face, her heart sinking at the determination she saw there. "It hurts," she said, remembering.

Hilliard looked back into the fire. "So does being whipped."

She frowned, having nothing relevant to say to that. "Come on then."

"Now?" he asked, showing the first signs of reservation.

"Now," she repeated, "before I change my mind."

To his credit, he didn't flinch as she undid the collar of his shirt and pulled him hard against her.

"Last chance," she whispered, her lips against his throat, doubting even that it was possible to stop now with his blood so close. "Once I start, it's go through with it or die."

Hilliard drew in a shaking breath. "Do it."

She set the hunger free, plunging her teeth into his throat. From a distance she heard him gasp and moan at the first pull of her mouth. She drank deeper, taking as much blood as possible, trying to push him under into unconsciousness. Finally, the survival instinct took over and he struggled against her, but she held him fast, glorying in the taking of blood in such abundance.

Only when he was a limp and heavy weight in her arms, did rational thoughts start to sift back into her mind. *Stop drinking just before the heart ceases beating*, Valdemar had told her. But did that mean one heartbeat before the end or two? She pulled her mouth away. Hilliard was barely breathing, his complexion an unhealthy gray.

Melinda laid him back against the pillows and covered him with the quilt. *What now*? she thought, wiping blood from the corner of her mouth with the back of her hand.

Behind her the door opened quietly.

"Come on Melinda," Valdemar said, his eyes flickering over the deathly still form in the bed. "There's nothing more you can do for Hilliard right now. He'll either survive or he won't, you can only wait."

"How will I know when to do it again?"

"Trust me," he said, taking her by the arm. "You'll know."

* * * *

Brutal screams brought her running to his room.

Hilliard lay in a quivering lump in the middle of the bed. His eyes didn't register any recognition of her when she turned him over. His skin was ice-cold to the touch, but her hand came away damp with sweat. Down the hall, she could hear Valdemar's footsteps coming towards them.

"What's wrong?" she asked, as he approached the bed in a more sanely pace, hands in his pockets.

Valdemar regarded the shivering form coolly. "Nothing. The change has started." He sat on the bed beside her. "You don't remember?"

"All I remember is being terrified and in incredible pain." His calmness infuriated her. "What do I do now?"

"Drink from him again."

"But he looks like he's dying!" she said, trying not to shout in her panic.

"It's entirely possible," he said, taking Hilliard's chin in his hand to examine him more closely. "But I think old Hilliard is made of stronger stuff."

"Did I look this bad?" she asked, trying to shake the memory of excruciating pain and terror from her mind.

Valdemar nodded. "Worse." He pressed his lips against the top of her head. "Don't delay Melinda. He is suffering."

She bent her head towards his neck. "Forgive me Hilliard."

* * * *

When she raised her head Valdemar was sitting in Hilliard's chair, pouring wine from a crystal decanter.

"You're taking this awfully calmly," she said, flopping down beside him.

"I fail to see any reason to panic," he said, handing her the glass.

Anger sharpened her words. "You're enjoying this, aren't you."

"Not at all," he said, looking genuinely surprised.

"You're glad I'm going through all of this, so I'll know how it was for you."

"I cannot deny I am hoping you will understand more fully." And when she looked truly desperate he said, "Melinda, it's almost over."

"What happens next?"

"After the chemical changes, he'll develop new teeth and nails."

That part she did remember: the impossible pressure in her jaw, the wet sound of her gums tearing, nearly choking on blood and her own teeth as a new pair of razor-sharp incisors cut through her flesh.

Leaning over Hilliard, she examined him closely. A thin line of blood ran from his mouth, giving him a sick-looking grin. A sliver of white showed from his half open eyes. Carefully, she pried his upper lip back, noting that his eyeteeth hung precariously by threads of flesh.

"Do we have any ice?" she asked Valdemar.

"I don't know," he said, momentarily confused. "In the kitchen maybe." And then realizing his only servant was in the process of turning into a vampire, he said, "I'll check."

Melinda pressed the makeshift ice pack against Hilliard's cheek and watched in horror as a virgin pair of gleaming white incisors poked through the bloody remnants of his gums. His mouth was half open, his breath coming in ragged gasps. If he knew she was near, or cared, he gave no sign.

"He isn't fully conscious," Valdemar said reassuringly. Indeed, there were gaps in her own memory of her change. The process took a lot longer than she remembered.

His hands twitched and flailed about, as if he could shake away the agony. Cracked and flaking fragments of his nails lay like dripping wax at the base of his fingertips. The tips of thick, claw-like nails began to sprout from his hands.

Hilliard's eyes opened. He looked at her, lucid and in agony. She didn't need Valdemar to explain what that crazed look meant.

"No!" he croaked, trying to scramble away from her. But she caught him and hauled him close.

"It's all right," she said, trying to sound rational when she was as frightened as he. "You're just hungry."

"It's overpowering ," he gasped, eyes wide in ravenous terror.

With trembling hands, he traced the altered outline of his teeth, stopping in horror when the saw the talons on the ends of his fingers.

"It doesn't always feel this bad," Melinda said, trying to reassure him. "The first time is the worst."

He stared at her numbly, realizing what he was going to have to do. She held out her wrist.

Hilliard shut his eyes. "I can't," he said, shaking.

"If you don't feed," she told him calmly. "You'll die."

He looked down at her wrist, then at Valdemar who looked back at him impassively.

"It would be a shame to have come this far and suffered this much," Melinda said, gently placing a hand behind his head, pushing his face closer to her exposed veins. She could feel his breath on her skin. *No*! her mind cried. *I don't think I want to do this!* Too late. Hilliard gripped her wrist in his hands and sank his teeth into her flesh.

It hurt. A lot. She moaned in spite of herself as he missed the vein and tried again. Clumsily he pressed his lips against her wrist and sucked hard. She leaned against him, feeling the blood flowing from her body into his, completing the transformation.

"That's enough," she heard Valdemar say an eternity later. "Melinda, make him stop."

Frightened, she grasped him by the back of the head and pried his teeth from her arm. He glared at her, insane with hunger and gnashed his teeth in the direction of her wrist. Carefully, she held him away until the hunger faded from his eyes and was slowly replaced by reason.

Then it all caught up with her, the worry, the loss of blood. Feeling weak and sick, she fell back against the pillows, wanting only to crawl into the blankets and go to sleep.

Hilliard was sitting at the end of the bed, his hand pressed against his mouth. With vacant dread he stared into space as if he couldn't believe what he had just done. Her blood was smeared across his cheek and down his chin.

"It's awful," he whispered when she crawled down to sit beside him.

"Not like you thought it would be?"

"No." He gathered her wrist between his hands. "I couldn't stop myself. I wanted it so badly. I'm sorry if I hurt you."

"It's better now." She turning her wrist to show him the new skin.

"I can't bear the thought of doing it again," he confided and looked sideways at Valdemar, who offered no words of comfort.

"Trust me, when the time comes you won't be thinking much about it at all." She let her head slide to his shoulder and shut her eyes.

"Did I take too much?" he asked as she grew heavy against him.

"No," Melinda assured him. "I need to rest, and then to hunt." She looked up at him with a sick smile. "And so do you Hilliard."

CHAPTER THIRTY-FOUR

"I'm coming with you," Valdemar said firmly.

"It isn't necessary," Melinda insisted. She hated when he hunted with her. It made her feel like a child.

"I'll decide what is necessary." The set of his mouth told her that no amount of arguing would change his mind. "This is Hilliard's first hunt. Who knows how he'll react."

"He wanted this," she said angrily. It reminded her of the beginning of a sick joke Cornelius was fond of telling. *How many vampires does it take to make a sandwich?* "Hilliard has lived among vampires long enough to know what to expect."

"Fledglings," Valdemar said with a pointed look in her direction, "are not always discreet. Caution is most important in the city."

He stopped talking abruptly, realizing they were discussing Hilliard as though he had neither eyes nor ears. But the subject of their argument was oblivious to their conversation. Shivering, he cowered in Valdemar's big leather chair, staring into space with pale and haunted eyes. Hunger, she thought with pity, remembering what those first unexpected throes felt like.

Someone knocked at the front door, loud enough to send a resounding echo through the cavernous hallway. Still expecting Hilliard to answer, they ignored it. As one they realized the irony of the situation.

"I'll get it," Melinda said tersely. She strode across the foyer and hauled open the heavy door, to find Cornelius on the threshold. "Evening Neil," she snapped and turned back toward the study, leaving him to see himself in.

"Evening," he repeated, clearly wondering at her ill humor and why she'd taken on the butler's duties. He opened his mouth for a greeting in Valdemar's direction as he entered the den and nearly tripped over the chair in which Hilliard was sitting.

Incredulously, he took a second, longer look at the chair's occupant.

"Whoa, Hilliard, what's new?" He glanced at Valdemar, eyebrows raised. "This is a surprise."

"It wasn't me," Valdemar snapped, to which Cornelius' eyes widened further. Astounded, he glanced at Melinda, then started to laugh.

"Well Melinda, you seem to have recovered."

"I'm fine," she said, clipping off the ends of the words in annoyance. She sighed. "Sorry, Cornelius, Valdemar and I were in the middle of a *discussion*."

Cornelius shrugged. "Things are back to normal in the Berthold household I see." He inclined his head in Hilliard's direction. "More or less."

Valdemar regarded him darkly, refusing to participate in the humor of it all.

"Perhaps I should pick another time to visit ... "

"Actually, Melinda *and I* were just about to take Hilliard hunting," Valdemar said. "I would appreciate it if you'd see to our other problem."

"What other problem?" she asked, but Valdemar grasped her firmly by the arm. "Come Melinda, it's time to see to the care and feeding of your offspring."

* * * *

A crisp breeze stirred her hair as they stepped from the warmth of the castle into the autumn night.

"I don't know if I can do this," Hilliard said, his first words in a long time.

"You don't have a choice," Valdemar said, taking him by the shoulder and pushing him forward.

"I wish you'd let me handle it," Melinda said, yanking Hilliard from Valdemar's grasp. "I'm quite capable of teaching him how to hunt."

"It isn't your ability that concerns me," Valdemar said, shutting the car door on any further questions. Open mouthed, she watched as he climbed arrogantly into the driver's seat, then decided it wasn't worth arguing about.

"You're going to be fine," she reassured her apprehensive offspring and gave up on Valdemar.

They parked on the fringes of the downtown. Clinging to the darkness, they crept down into the tunnels south of Davisville

Station. Valdemar led them down the tracks that ran in labyrinthine routes all the way to the waterfront.

We must be close to Queen Street, Melinda thought, as the ground sloped downward. When it came to the subway system, Valdemar knew the tunnels like hometown streets. They'd been just that for nearly thirty years.

Shortly after one a.m., the trio emerged south of Union Station where the streetcars disappeared into the underground network of the rapid transit tunnels. From there, they headed north through the row of insurance companies and hotels to Queen Street.

In spite of the cool weather, the streets were still packed with noisy crowds. Melinda scanned the passersby. None seemed appropriate. But there was one element that attracted the rowdy, the downtrodden, and the insane--the Queen Streetcar.

She grasped Hilliard by the elbow and followed the press of bodies that surged to board the streetcar. Valdemar followed with silent approval.

"Hey, d'you got the time," a female voice slurred in her ear. Melinda turned, looking into a pasty white face. A wide band of dark roots contrasted sharply against white-blonde ends of her hair, and a black leather jacket hung loosely on her thin frame. With buddy-like drunkenness, she repeated the question.

"One thirty," Melinda said, trying to shake this unwanted friend. To her dismay, the blonde parked herself in the seat next to her.

"Been waiting twenty-five minutes for this damned car," she said, putting her wallet back into her battered vinyl purse.

Across the aisle Valdemar shook his head in warning. Melinda sighed and settled back, waiting for the earliest opportunity to extract herself.

"You're a quiet one tonight," her companion said in a voice loud enough to make Melinda cringe. "Didn't you have a good night?" She elbowed the dark vampire with a "just between us girls" wink and smiled, showing a row of brown, rotting teeth.

"Tired," Melinda said, trying her best to look that way.

"Oh," said the blonde and wandered off down the car in search of more interesting fare. The group of equally intoxicated men at the back made a better audience for her spirited banter.

Good, Melinda thought, relieved. Then her eyes narrowed with interest. One among the group didn't seem to be enjoying the young lady's company at all.

A wiry man with pock-marked skin, black hair and an equally black disposition was taking obvious exception to her attention.

"Let me know if she comes on to you, and I'll fix her," he said to the fellow next to him, who turned away from his whiskey-laden breath.

"Now, why you'd have to go and be like that," the blonde asked, her voice rising an octave in offense.

"I'll tell you why," he hollered, drawing the attention of the entire streetcar. Steadying himself on the back of another seat, he lurched drunkenly towards her. "Sluts like you spread disease--"

"Now that's enough," said a chivalrous bystander.

Melinda shot Valdemar a *he's mine* look.

"Yeah? Tell me that when you're dying of AIDS."

Still ranting obscenities, he staggered towards the door as the streetcar coasted to a red light and stopped.

"Can you believe that guy?" the blonde asked her audience.

Melinda watched as he marched around the streetcar and slammed his fist against the back window. "Whore!"

Mouth open, the blonde whirled to see him standing in the street, hollering obscenities as the trolley car pulled away. Shaken, she straightened her purse on her shoulder, patted her hair smooth and rang the buzzer for the next stop.

"Stay back," Melinda whispered as she passed Valdemar and followed her.

Spike heeled boots clicked off down the sidewalk as the wraith-like form disappeared between two buildings. Hugging the shadows, Melinda waited. From behind she heard the footsteps of a man driven by drunken rage. The guy with the bad skin was hot in pursuit.

Up ahead, the streetcar reached its next stop. Valdemar and Hilliard got off and melded into the darkness.

"You!" the blonde exclaimed when she saw who was following her. Then thinking better of it, she turned to run.

Hampered by her high heels, she was easy prey. He caught her by the hair and threw her to the pavement. Twisting, she jerked one of those spike heels in the direction of his groin, but he pinned her legs beneath him with his weight. His hands closed around her neck. "Harlot!" There was a dull crack as her head hit the asphalt. "The world don't need no more of yer kind!"

Melinda sprang. Uttering a wet grunt of surprise, the drunk released his quarry. Without looking back to see what miracle had liberated her, the woman sprinted off down the alley.

Cupping her hand firmly over his mouth, Melinda hauled him back into the shadows. From out of the darkness, Valdemar approached, Hilliard firmly in tow. With a look of horror he regarded his intended kill, who gazed back equally terrified.

"Well Hilliard?" Valdemar asked quietly. "This is what you wanted."

She could see the raw hunger in his eyes. *Better feed him soon before he blacks out and gives us a really hard time.* "Go on Hilliard. You know how it's done."

"Here?" he asked, trying to keep his teeth from chattering.

"Food doesn't come from the supermarket anymore," Valdemar said, watching the victim squirm in her arms.

"Think about it," she said, as Hilliard stepped tentatively closer, "fresh, warm blood ... "

Hilliard's self-control evaporated. She held on, long enough to make sure he didn't chicken out, until she could sense that the victim was weakening. Then she bit deeply into the other side of his throat, sandwiching the kill between them, and together they drank.

* * * *

Much later, she found Hilliard sitting in the glass living room, gazing out at the first pink tinges of dawn.

"You ought to get some sleep."

He looked at her sickly. "I can't believe what I did."

"I think that every time," she said, sitting on the couch beside him.

"You never did get over it, then?"

"No." The word hung in the air between them.

"It is...immensely ... pleasurable," he said, licking his lips thoughtfully in memory.

"It is," she said. "That's the cruelest part of it."

Hilliard flexed his arms. "I feel ... strong, whole."

Melinda patted his shoulder. "That's good."

"You've healed me, given me back my life." Puzzled, he studied her. "You had no reason to, really."

"Your suffering touched me," she said. "You reminded me of someone."

"Who?"

"Me," Melinda said, staring out the window.

"Thank you," he whispered.

"You're welcome," she said, standing. "Good night, Hilliard."

"Good night," he said, hesitating, "Melinda."

CHAPTER THIRTY-FIVE

The cellar was more indicative of a fifteen century dungeon than a modern basement. Mold grew in black patches scattered across the cement walls and the sound of moisture dripping was ever present.

Melinda had almost missed the sub-basement as she prowled through the castle's subterranean rooms. In fact, the door was camouflaged well enough to mislead even the most vigilant.

In the creepy underground, it was hard to keep her mind from wandering through dismal scenarios. Valdemar had been talking about installing a new wine cellar. Recently, she suspected, he'd found another use for the space.

She took another step down the winding cement staircase. It was dark enough to challenge even her sensitive eyesight. Not even a sliver of light showed beneath the door above. Feeling a little like Alice in Wonderland, she flicked on the flashlight and continued down.

The steep staircase descended far beyond what she considered a reasonable distance, possibly two stories. Eventually the stairs ended and her feet touched the smooth concrete floor. In the darkness up ahead she heard a soft hiss. Using the wall as a guide, she crept forward.

Cement walls ended in a row of iron bars crudely sunk in cement. *Aha!* she thought in triumph. The dungeon at last. She scanned the dark cell for signs of Adrian.

He was there beyond the bars, she could see his pale form in the darkness.

"Well vegetarian," he sneered. "I was wondering if you'd pay me a visit."

"Adrian," she said, putting as much scorn as possible into her voice. His proximity made her nervous, even with the bars between them. "You look like shit."

The flashlight's beam caught him, drenching him in a splash of yellow light. Snarling at the unexpected onslaught, he buried his head in his arms.

She stared at the form crouched in the corner, knees drawn up against his chest and his arms wrapped protectively about his head. His blond hair was matted and dirty and his clothes hung in shreds. Yet there was something ... Melinda moved closer, training the flashlight on his long, thin hands. She gasped quietly. The skin was smooth, healed.

Adrian raised his head, his eyes reflected the golden light. "Will you put that thing away," he asked in a more civil tone. "It hurts my eyes."

Blinking, Melinda regarded him in rapt fascination. Though he still lacked lips and eyelids, the skin on his cheeks was nearly flawless.

"Valdemar has taught you well," Adrian said. "You're nearly as cruel as he."

It occurred to her suddenly that without eyelids he couldn't close his eyes. With a flick of her thumb, she plunged them into darkness.

Squatting on the floor, she peered at him through the bars, a shadowy figure in the gloom. "And you're lucky to be alive."

Adrian laughed harshly. "Am I?"

She shrugged. "It looks like my blood did you some good after all."

"A little more would have solved most of my problems." She heard the rustle of his clothes as he turned toward her. "So what extravagant demise does Valdemar have in store for me?"

"I don't know," Melinda said. "He won't tell me."

"This is a social call, then? I'm sorry I have no tea to offer."

"You seem awfully glib about your impending doom."

Adrian sighed. "Why are you here Melinda?"

"I came to see how you were. I have no idea why."

"How do you think I am?" he asked angrily, then answered his own question. "I'm wounded and hungry. So hungry that I ache. Valdemar feeds me only what it takes to keep me alive, and leaves me alone in the dark with my pain. He is cruel, Melinda, far more cruel than you can imagine. Remember that."

"And you were stupid Adrian," she retorted, trying not to think about it. "You could have come to us. We might have helped you."

"I very much doubt that," he said coldly.

Rather than react, she posed another question. "Adrian, did you want to be a vampire?"

"What?" he asked, at once annoyed and intrigued. "Don't you have anything better to do Melinda?"

She stared at him, waiting. "I was wondering ... "

"You were wondering what exactly?"

"If your nasty nature is a result of unhappiness, or whether you were just born a son-of-a-bitch."

Adrian laughed, a sound like metal scraping against metal. He came to stand beside her, hands gripping the bars between them. "I was born a son-of-a-bitch," he said and laughed some more. "And no I didn't plan on becoming a vampire." He leered at her through the bars with lid-less eyes. "But I came to like it a lot."

Melinda rose to leave, then turned back. "Adrian?"

A long silence, then, "What?"

"How much blood would it take. To make you well, I mean?"

"What kind of masochist are you?" he demanded, then hastily considered it. "Quite a bit."

* * * *

Restlessly, Melinda punched the pillow and sat up.

What do vampires take for sleeping pills? Deciding she really didn't want to know, she yanked the curtains about the bed open and emerged into the gray light. She sat in the daintily embroidered chair beside the bed and picked up the book on the table beside it. But fantasy failed to hold her interest, and she tossed the book aside.

The vision of Adrian crouched in the corner of the dungeon refused to leave her mind's eye. With lurid clarity, she conjured the ache of his hunger, the futility of a life he hadn't asked for in which everyone close to him had hurt him.

You treat everyone's pain as if it were your own, Valdemar had said once.

Adrian's right, I am a masochist.

* * * *

The cellar door was easier to find the second time.

Her footsteps sounded impossibly loud in the silent house. Hilliard slept in the daytime now too. Melinda smiled. He was adjusting to his new life as if he was born to it. Soon they would need to find (or make) a new servant, but in the meantime Hilliard was in no great rush to relinquish his position. Praying the two vampires would stay asleep, Melinda slipped down the winding staircase to the dungeon.

By the circular beam of the flashlight, she could see his vague outline, crouched as she had left him in the corner. His arms were wrapped around his shoulders as he shivered violently.

Famine was a sensation no vampire ever forgot. First, the sweats, then the tremors that shook the entire body. After that came the sensation of acid coursing through the veins, then finally the blackouts and the raging insanity. Adrian would have no humans nor animals to ravage for their blood. Down in the dungeon it was unlikely anyone would even hear his screams on the floors far above.

Emerald eyes glistened in the shadows. "Back for another gawk at the freak?" he asked between shudders. "Or do you like to watch?"

With theatrical slowness he took his wrist between the gleaming points of his teeth and bit down. Drops of ruby blood splashed onto the cement floor.

"No!" Melinda gasped, horrified. So that was how he kept the madness at bay, recycling his own blood while his body slowly starved. "Adrian, don't do that!"

"What are you going to do about it?" he asked, drops of his own blood dripping from his teeth. "Offer me more of yours?"

Shutting his eyes, he slid his teeth back into the oozing wound in his wrist.

It was more than she could stand. Slowly, Melinda slipped her wrist through the bars.

Adrian froze. For several moments he stared at her bare wrist. Afraid it was all a cruel joke, he approached cautiously. Their eyes met. Tentatively, he took her wrist in his hands.

Melinda thrust her other hand through the bars and gripped him by the hair for insurance. "Be gentle about it this time," she warned.

To her immense surprise she barely felt his bite. His body heaved with relief, and he massaged her palm gently with his thumb as he drank.

Just as she felt herself weakening he stopped and looked up at her with luminous eyes. "I don't understand," he said, licking the blood from his mangled mouth.

"Neither do I," she whispered.

Adrian slumped against the bars, breathing heavily. Sweat dripped from his forehead, down his face, gathering in a spreading wet patch at the neck of his shirt.

"Hurts," he moaned when she shook him, then was silent.

He was changing. Healing. Melinda could see smooth skin emerging from the crusty remnants of his lips. On his brows, a shadow of blond stubble was growing. She noticed suddenly his eyes were hooded by a thin membrane.

Fascinated and horrified, she inched back along the corridor. Adrian groaned and called her name, but she sped up the stairs, not daring to risk being caught there by Valdemar.

* * * *

"Valdemar wants to see you in his chambers," Hilliard said, standing awkwardly in her doorway. He looked like he wanted to tell her a great deal more, then stood at attention waiting to be dismissed.

Melinda met his gaze. "You better take cover Hilliard. This could be ugly."

* * * *

Long legs stretched out from Valdemar's favorite chair, ending in a pair of ebony cowboy boots. She hesitated in the doorway, trying to peer around the side of the chair, but Valdemar saw her first.

"Come in Melinda," he said quietly. His voice was devoid of anger, but when she looked up into his eyes they were harsh and unyielding. Never had she seen him in a mood of such calm fury.

She looked at Cornelius who reclined languidly against the window frame, a snifter of brandy dangling from one hand. There was an uncharacteristic frown on his face.

Melinda circled the chair, her heart sinking to find it occupied by Adrian. One glance brought her back to the night she met him. Tall and lean, he had towered over her and pierced her with his deep, green eyes. His smile could be both sensuous and cruel, she remembered and braced herself. Freshly bathed and dressed as he was now, he looked both handsome and lethal.

From beneath a fringe of blond lashes he gazed up at her. "Ah," he intoned, "my savior."

"Perhaps," Valdemar said behind them, "you'd care to explain."

Adrian grinned, full lips drawing back to reveal teeth as white as his skin. "Yes, enlighten us, Melinda."

"You have no cause to complain," she snapped.

"I'm not complaining," Adrian corrected, "only wondering how you came to be my guardian angel."

"I believe *I* asked you a question, Melinda," Valdemar said impatiently, standing between them. "Adrian nearly killed you ... "

She looked from Valdemar to Cornelius then back to Adrian. "I couldn't stand to watch him suffer," she said meekly.

"No one asked you to watch."

"No." There wasn't much she could say to that.

Valdemar glared in Adrian's direction. "If you only knew how much suffering Adrian has caused over the centuries. A good deal of it mine. And yours."

"Damned if it makes any sense to me," Adrian muttered.

"You told me to start making my own decisions," she said, a pathetic attempt at her own defense.

"I did not tell you to meddle in mine," Valdemar snarled, each word dripping menace. He scowled down at Adrian. "But what's done is done. Get out of my house Adrian. And if I so much as catch you within miles of me or any of my kin, I will kill you. Do you understand?"

Adrian grinned. "See you Val," he said, standing up to leave. "Bye Neil." He stopped before Melinda and bowed with a great flourish. "My lady."

"Adrian," she said, "Go to hell."

"Aren't you a pair," he remarked, looking back at them. Then he was gone, laughing, into the night.

Silence stretched from seconds to minutes as Cornelius fidgeted uncomfortably and Melinda and Valdemar eyed each other warily. There was a new element to his measuring gaze, the grudging respect one gave an equal.

"I trust things are as you wanted," he said finally, "and that you are finished rearranging my life."

"Your life!" she snarled back. "What about the way you rearranged mine?"

"So, it comes back to that," he said, too quietly, and she wished she could swallow those words. "Damn it Melinda!" Valdemar slammed his hand against the marble mantle. The impact rocked the room and she watched in horrified fascination as a crack spread from under his closed fist. Oblivious to the damage, he whirled on her in fury. "I tried to make you a new life. I gave you my blood, my love. I have nothing more to give you."

"I'm trapped," she whispered. "Between who I was and who you want me to be."

"I can't live with your constant interference."

"Are you asking me to leave?"

He glared at her like white fire. "Make your own decision."

She glowered at him through the tears that sprang from the corners of her eyes, then rushed from the room.

"I was just leaving," Cornelius said into the hush that followed. "In fact, I think I'll go back to Venice."

* * * *

Melinda heard Cornelius' booted feet behind her as she bolted through the main door and out across the drawbridge. Desperate to be alone, she ignored him and put a little more speed into her step.

Superior strength and speed won out and he grasped her by the elbow.

Whirling, she nearly struck him. With a fencer's reflexes, he deftly ducked the blow and continued on as if nothing had happened.

Melinda regarded him darkly. "You have incredibly bad timing Neil."

"Don't do this," he said in earnest. "The last time you left him he sulked around my house for ten years."

"He wants me to leave," she said, trying to keep the tears from her voice.

Cornelius looked up at the yellow glow of Valdemar's window. "He'll come around."

She shook her head. "I don't think so. This time Val is seriously annoyed."

"Even Valdemar can't stay mad forever."

"What makes you so sure?"

"He eventually forgave me for running away with Kirsten," he said, very softly. She noticed suddenly that his eyes changed color with the light. In the dimness they seemed a light brown, but inside she would have sworn they were hazel. He wasn't handsome like Valdemar and Adrian, but he had a kind face and a pleasant smile. She had to remind herself that in the beginning Cornelius had thought she was a very bad idea indeed.

"How long did it take?"

"Only about twenty years."

"Twenty years," she repeated sorrowfully.

"There is one thing you don't know about good old Val," Cornelius was saying. He slipped his arm around her waist and they walked a few steps down the drawbridge. "He has a fascination with what he can't have."

"What's that supposed to mean?"

"Come home with me," he said, and smiled.

"To Italy?" she asked, wondering what it was he was really up to.

"Italy? Are you kidding, with all this going on?"

"Where then?"

"My apartment," he said. "Unless you fancy a crypt in St. James Cemetery."

"I don't know Neil."

"Don't you want him back?"

"I want him," she said, too quickly, then added, "We make each other crazy."

"That's it exactly."

"What?"

"What Valdemar sees in you. You intrigue him because you're a creature of this century and because you're willful and unpredictable."

"He tolerates me because he feels obligated," she said miserably.

"Were that the case," he said. "If he had only wanted to save your life, he could have made you like Hilliard. You would have been his servant."

That was a possibility she hadn't considered.

"Trust me in this," Cornelius said. "Stay at my place. Give Val a few days to cool off."

"Why do you want to help me?" she asked suspiciously, then before he could answer, she said, "You just want your part in the mischief."

"That," he agreed with his ready smile. "And the fact that after five hundred years, I'm sick of listening to Valdemar's romantic woes."

CHAPTER THIRTY-SIX

"What do you mean you don't know where she is?" Valdemar paced back and forth across his study, stopping before Cornelius, hands on his hips.

"I am not her keeper."

"She left with you the other night and I haven't heard a word from her since."

Neil helped himself to a generous glass of cognac and tasted it thoughtfully while Valdemar stewed. "You told her to leave."

"I told her no such thing!" He poured himself a hefty drink, then added a pinch of white powder from a decorated snuff box.

"Sounded to me like you wanted her to leave," Cornelius said with a shrug.

"I wanted to teach her a lesson." He swirled the liquor in the glass. "I was angry about Adrian."

"Melinda has a mind of her own," Cornelius said. "Although the incident with Adrian was ... most unexpected."

"Tell me about it," Valdemar snapped.

"Look on the bright side. It's not the solution you or I would have chosen, but it got Adrian off of our hands." He chuckled to himself. "Poor old Adrian looked genuinely perplexed. I think he's finally met his match." Another thought occurred to him and he laughed out loud. "Maybe Melinda's run off with him."

"Cornelius, I'm not in the mood."

"You're in a mood, all right." He looked pointedly at the glass in Valdemar's hand and the white film floating on the top. "And getting drunk is not likely to improve it."

Valdemar scowled at him, then turned to stare out the window.

"Oh come on Valdemar," Cornelius, exploded. "Haven't you learned anything about women in eleven hundred years?" And when he got only a cold glare in reply he said, "Look Val, if you love her, go find her."

"I'm tired of fetching her," Valdemar said moodily.

"Maybe you wouldn't have to if you didn't work so hard at chasing her away."

"Meaning what?"

"You figure it out." Cornelius said, rising. "But since the lovely Miss Barnes is now without a suitor ... "

"Don't even think of it Neil. She is mine."

Cornelius grinned. "Is she now?" He gave Valdemar a sporting slap on the back. "Don't worry, I'll give you a head start."

* * * *

Melinda awoke in the pink shadows of dusk. Uncurling, she sat up on the couch and looked around at her strange surroundings. The living room was sparsely decorated. Black curtains covered the floor to ceiling windows. An overstuffed leather couch, matching chair and a scattering of chrome end tables were the only pieces of furniture. Cornelius' apartment in Harbourfront, she thought, fitting the pieces of the previous night's events together in her mind. From the docks below, the Island Ferry blew a departing whistle.

She realized suddenly the pounding that had awakened her was not a headache, but someone hammering persistently on the front door. Foul tempered already, she staggered to the door and hauled it open without bothering to look through the peephole.

"Adrian," she droned at the sight of the blond leaning casually against the door frame. "Why do I always find you at the end of a very bad day?"

"I was looking for Neil," he said, plainly shocked to find her there.

"He went ... somewhere."

Adrian contemplated her rumpled clothing and tousled hair. "Lover boy has thrown you out again I see."

"Excuse me," she said, starting to shut the door, "but I'd rather die than talk to you right now ... "

His foot shot out, propping the door open. "Not so fast. I came for a reason."

She shot him an expression of theatrical boredom.

"I would have told Valdemar," he said leering at her, "but I've been banished."

"Join the club," she snapped, then said, "Hurry up Adrian, I'm severely lacking in patience this evening."

"Hilliard's, shall we say, rather dramatic transformation has been discovered," he said, lowering his voice to a serious whisper. "And Rowena is royally pissed." He sauntered off down the hall, then turned back. "You ought to be careful Melinda."

* * * *

Midnight passed without any sign of Cornelius. At two a.m. the bars closed and by two-thirty the waterfront was quiet. From beyond the panoramic window, Lake Ontario tossed violently in the October winds.

"Wait for me," Cornelius had said. "You'll see Melinda. A few well-placed words and Valdemar'll be down here as soon as I leave."

"Wait," Melinda muttered to the empty room. "You didn't say wait all night Cornelius. What if Valdemar tells you to damned well keep me? What will you do then?" With a smirk, she pictured his face. "No Neil, charming as you can be, I don't think we'd get along at all."

By three a.m. the spacious apartment had become a confining, albeit tastefully decorated, glass box. A walk would help lift her dark mood, she reasoned as she strode down the hall toward the elevators.

The chill air was a welcome diversion. She breathed deeply, savoring the damp smell of the lake. At its customary dock, The Island Lady bobbed in rhythm with the waves. Judging by the tiny flakes of confetti still blowing in the wind, the harbor cruise ship had hosted a wedding that evening.

The Island Lady looked like a giant, triple-tiered wedding cake. Railings on each deck were gaily painted red like icing. The Lady made no pretenses of ever having sailed the Mississippi. Her paddlewheel was no more than a series of neon spokes on each side that flashed off and on to give the impression of motion.

As the party boat rocked eerily against the quiet dock, Melinda could almost hear the echoes of the night's party carried aloft on the wind. She'd always wondered what it looked like inside. With one hand on the cement post, she vaulted the narrow distance between the dock and the boat and landed on the bottom deck.

She pressed her face against the glass window. Inside, the tables had been stripped of their party fare, and the chairs stacked neatly against the wall. Moodily, she strolled along the deserted deck, kicking at the pieces of confetti that lingered between the cracks in the wood. Once she had wanted to be married. But that now seemed a lifetime away. *Til death do us part* took on an entirely different meaning for vampires.

An interior staircase led to the second deck, which was also enclosed for dining. Outside, red wooden ladders linked the levels. Melinda ignored both conveniences. With an effortless leap, she grasped the railing of the second deck and swung up. It didn't contain much to hold her interest, so she climbed again, emerging on the third and upper level. The deck was covered only by a canvas canopy. A small stage at one end was reserved for the band. The rest of the dance floor was open for dancing under the stars.

Like a mate on the poop deck, she surveyed land and water. A car went by on the Gardiner Expressway, its lights a beacon and its motor loud in the silence. A newspaper blew along the dock.

In the shadows of the Terminal Building there was movement. Something hit the deck below her.

The Island Lady roared to life. Motor laboring, she struggled to turn her nose from the dock to the open water.

Melinda peered over the railing to find the side of the ship infested with black-clad figures. They crawled out of lifeboats, emerged from under tarps, and swarmed the ladders. She readied herself to leap for the pier below and was startled to find that the gap between the boat and the dock had suddenly grown to more than thirty feet.

Something grabbed her foot. She wrenched it away, only to be seized and her arms yanked sharply backward. From the corner of her eye she saw several black-clad figures drop to the deck around her, and there were more coming.

Slaves, she realized suddenly. Like Hilliard had been. Drained almost to the point of death, their vacant eyes were no more than black holes in pallid faces. Drained of will as well as blood, they had been stripped of even their own survival instincts. Their will belonged entirely to the master. Hilliard had once explained it to her, but even his cursory description had made her uneasy.

Beneath her, The Island Lady rumbled, heading out onto the lake. Melinda liberated a booted foot and launched a kick into the stomach of the closest. He grunted and stumbled backward and finally plunged into the lake. The resulting splash stole their attention for a second, long enough for her to send a taloned hand slicing across the throat of another of her assailants.

The smell of his blood invigorated her. She let go of all inhibitions and set the predator within her free. With a violent lunge, she sent the others tumbling away and fell upon the hapless slave.

His blood was weak, but she drank eagerly as his failing heart pumped it into her mouth. Straightening, she wiped the blood from her face with the back of her sleeve and surveyed the now distant shore. Warm blood trickled down into her stomach. She was going to need the strength for the long, cold swim back to the city.

Devoid of new orders, the ghouls huddled at the far end of the deck, shuffling about uncertainly. On some unseen signal, they surged forward.

Melinda sprang for the gangplank, choosing the cold water instead of their company. But she was knocked flat mid-leap. She struggled to recapture the breath the fall had knocked out of her.

Vice-like hands turned her to face the sky. She spat crimson hairs from her mouth and looked up into Rowena's blazing eyes.

"Hold her," Rowena barked.

Melinda was seized by hands, feet and shoulders.

"You've been busy, haven't you," Rowena said, staring disdainfully down at her. "First you kill my child, then you steal my servant, and now Adrian is walking around fresh as the day he was born. Do you like playing God, Melinda?"

"You had no right to torture him," Melinda grunted, trying to wrestle a limb free.

"Hilliard was mine," Rowena said. "To do as I pleased with. As for torture," she laughed huskily. "When I am finished with you, you will be begging me for the quiet sleep of death. What I did to Hilliard was only a small agony compared to what I have in store for you."

"Take off her boots and her pants," she ordered her slaves and grinned like a wolverine. "I will start with your little pink toes and work my way up." She leered at Melinda, eyes flashing like amber coals in the darkness. "I do hope I enjoy your blood as much as Adrian did."

Denim tore as her jeans were ripped from her body and tossed aside leaving her pale flesh bare and vulnerable in the moonlight. In the tip of her big toe she felt the piercing intrusion of one incisor.

She screamed, imagining all kinds of horrors to come. Rowena raised her head.

"Really Melinda," she said, bored. "And I thought you were made of stronger stuff."

"What are you going to tell Valdemar?" she shrieked back at her. "You're supposed to love him."

"Valdemar won't be thinking of you at all," Rowena said. "Once he has me back."

She bit into the bridge of Melinda's foot, sucking from the multitude of blue veins that branched out into her calf. Hot blood gushed over her ankle and onto the deck.

With tortuous bites, Rowena traced an intricate design from ankle to knee. Her body became increasingly heavy, as strength seeped away from her along with her blood. Frantically, Melinda channeled her remaining stamina into levering her torso from the deck, only to be unceremoniously slammed back against the wooden planks.

The smell of her blood hung like fog in the air. Her body, robbed of its most precious fluid, responded with insistent hunger. She fought the dual agonies of pain and desire, as Rowena worked her way up the inside of her thighs.

Soon her legs were slick with blood. Rowena rubbed her body against her suggestively and trailed her razor-sharp nails up Melinda's rib cage under her shirt.

"I can't decide." She propped herself up on an elbow that dug into her chest. "Whether I'm in the mood for forearms or breasts."

With a desperate tug, Melinda freed one hand and raked her nails across Rowena's face. Her head jerked backward from the force of the blow, but when she turned back to Melinda her eyes were shining with amusement.

"That settles it. Arms it is."

Teeth like needles perforated her wrist. Like a knife, they tore upwards, slicing open the inside of her arm like the white belly of a fish. Weakened, her screams degenerated into whimpers.

Off to starboard a motor sputtered and shallow waves from its wake slapped the side of the boat. Footsteps scrambled across the lower deck.

Someone hollered "Stop!"

Rowena straightened, annoyed at the intrusion. "Will wonders never cease," she said dryly.

Melinda cracked open an eye to see Adrian towering above her, haloed by the moonlight. In the darkness below she could see the flat form of a water taxi bobbing in the waves.

"Let her go Rowena."

Momentarily abandoning her prey to the hands of her ghouls, Rowena whirled on him. "Excuse me, but for a moment I thought you were giving me an order."

"I was," he said, rearing up to his full height. He gestured to the figure stepping off the ladder behind him. "Were you vigilant my lady, you'd notice that not even Hilliard takes orders from you lately."

Hilliard, always the consummate gentleman, merely inclined his head in greeting. Steel gray eyes regarded her fearlessly.

In a desperate attempt to protect her offspring, Melinda found the breath to scream. "Hilliard! Get out of here!"

Dismissing Hilliard with a snort, Rowena lunged at Adrian. Seeing her momentarily occupied, Hilliard dove into the mass that held Melinda. Confused, with no new orders forthcoming, some struggled to retain their grip on her, while others sought to topple Hilliard.

Thrust up against the railing in the scuffle, Melinda caught a quick glimpse over the side. Numerous bodies littered the bottom deck, evidence of Adrian and Hilliard's arrival. But The Island Lady was still chugging contentedly out into the open lake, past the dark shadow of the Toronto Islands. At least one ghoul was still at the helm.

Adrian was busy swatting away a fistful of claws meant for his throat. "You'll notice I'm somewhat recovered," he snarled, deflecting the deadly blow.

"Last I heard you wanted her dead," Rowena growled back, and threw another punch.

"I've changed my mind."

"Is your memory so short that you give no thought to Moira?"

"I have been thinking of Moira," he said, grunting with exertion. "And I've been wondering why I endured the unpleasantness of her company for hundreds of years." He dodged another strike. "I've decided I like being treated with kindness."

"You were always weak."

"No Rowena," he said, countering the insult with politeness, "it is you who are weak."

The storm started in her eyes then continued down her rigid posture and ending with the brilliant flare of her hair, until it seemed as if her entire body boiled with hatred.

"Seize him!" she screamed, frustrated by her failure to subdue him. Finally given clear orders, her minions released Melinda and hurried to obey.

Suddenly unhanded, Melinda struggled to her feet. The effort required more strength than she had, and she collapsed against the railing. "Rowena will kill you in a second, Hilliard," she said, gasping for breath. "You aren't experienced enough to tangle with the likes of her."

"I'm not leaving without you," he said, nervously watching the struggle before them.

Adrian floundered in a sea of hands, as Rowena's lackeys tried to get a handle on him. Blood spattered the wooden deck as he gutted the nearest.

Blood, Melinda thought, *what I need is some of that blood.* But before she could launch her sluggish body in that direction, Adrian slipped on the slick deck and went down.

Rowena smiled, the annoyance finally subdued. "When I finish with our little martyr here," she promised Adrian. "I will have you for dessert."

Melinda grasped Hilliard's hand. "Do as I say," she ordered, trying to urge him over the side. But just as she was about to dive head first from the deck, Hilliard turned, putting his body between her and the approaching Rowena.

"You were always a nuisance, Hilliard," Rowena snarled, trying to remove him from her path. "Did you think becoming a vampire would improve your miserable lot in life? Well, you are mistaken. I can dispatch you just as easily."

"No Hilliard!" Melinda screamed, trying to pull him from Rowena's path, but he held his ground.

Realizing she wasn't going to get a clear shot at Melinda without first eliminating Hilliard, Rowena sighed. "You are as stupid as your predecessor," she muttered and charged at him.

Hilliard dodged her, but superior strength won out and she caught him easily. Coming to the defense of her offspring, Melinda hurled herself at Rowena. With one hand, she was seized, tossed aside like a rag doll.

Skidding to a stop many feet down the deck, Melinda watched

in horror as Rowena clamped her hands around Hilliard's throat and twisted. Skin and muscle tore. Desperately his fingers clawed at the powerful hands that held him. A torrent of his blood flooded the wooden planks as arteries were severed. A resounding snap brought his struggles to an abrupt end. Hilliard's eyes glazed over. With a wet, sucking sound, Rowena tore his head from his body.

In disgust, she dropped the pieces of the corpse to the deck. Wiping her hands on her pants, she turned to Melinda.

Melinda took one last look at remained of Hilliard's body. Retching, she scrambled for the ladder. But Rowena seized her by the scruff of the neck.

A motor flared and something heavy bumped against the side of the riverboat. On the bottom deck, there was a scuffle of footsteps and a sharp grunt. The Island Lady drifted to a stop. The footsteps moved to the ladder. Rowena turned, hauling Melinda with her.

Valdemar vaulted the railing and crossed the deck with a single stride, followed closely by Cornelius.

With one, sweeping glance Valdemar summed up the night's events. His eyes flickered from Hilliard's crumpled form to Adrian who still struggled in the hands of Rowena's slaves. Finally, they settled on Melinda. "Rowena," he said sorrowfully, "you gave me your word."

"Adrian's craftsmanship," Rowena said levelly. "Think what would have happened if I hadn't shown up."

Valdemar regarded Adrian who was all but bathed in the blood from the deck and the ghoul he'd disemboweled.

"Don't believe her Valdemar."

"Do you honestly expect me to believe *you*, Adrian?" He stalked toward Adrian like black fury. "After what you did last time. And after she *helped* you." He looked down at the blond vampire. "I told her yours was a useless life and not worth saving. But no matter it will be soon over."

"For God's sake Valdemar, for once I'm telling you the truth!"

Melinda opened her mouth in Adrian's defense. Rowena clamped an immovable hand across her face.

Valdemar advanced on Adrian.

"Offer him his throat," Rowena ordered her ghouls, who hauled Adrian's head backwards, exposing his neck.

Melinda drew back her lips, forcing an incisor into the fleshy part of Rowena's palm and sucked for dear life. Rowena shrieked in pain, momentarily releasing her grip.

"Damn it, Val, he's telling the truth!" Melinda hollered.

Valdemar froze. Very slowly he turned back to Melinda. "Who did this to you?"

"Rowena," she told him gasping for breath. She motioned to the lump on the deck. "She ... " her voice cracked and tears welled up in her eyes. "Hilliard's dead."

The spell broken, Cornelius sprang to Adrian's aid.

"I am sick of your cruelty," Valdemar hissed, ignoring the tumult around him and advancing on Rowena. "For six hundred years I loved you with my *soul*, while you taunted me with other lovers. You kept me hoping."

Trapped between Valdemar and the railing, Rowena eyed her routes of escape. He moved first, pinning her against the wooden rails. "Admit it, you enjoyed my pain." He bared his fangs; his eyes were hard as onyx. The pointed tips of his nails drew rivulets of blood from her arms. "And now," he whispered, "you would destroy the happiness I have waited eleven hundred years for. I won't let you do it Rowena."

Rowena gave Valdemar a fearful estimation. "*Cariad*," she purred seductively, "you misunderstand. I have missed you. I wanted you back." She pouted, lowering her eyelids and peeking out from under the crimson fringe of her eyelashes. "But you had ... replaced me. Take me back. Let me live in your castle." She released Melinda. "I will let the child go."

Valdemar's hands tightened; his nails dug into her flesh up to the cuticles. "How stupid do you think I am, *Rhonwen*?"

Rowena's eyes hardened to flaming amber. "You are stupid enough to forget that I made you Valdemar. And I can just as easily destroy you."

"You won't find it that easy," Valdemar growled, eyes narrowing.

"Val no!" Melinda croaked, placing a restraining hand on his arm. "Let's just get out of here."

He shrugged her hand away easily without relaxing his grip on Rowena.

Cornelius and Adrian floundered on the deck in a flurry of hands and feet, as they wrestled with Rowena's ghouls. A well-aimed blow took out the throat of one of the wraiths and sent it skidding down the wooden planks.

Melinda looked at the bubbling body of the slave that landed at her feet and crept forward. Blood spurted from the severed jugular vein. He was dying rapidly. There was no way he would survive. Sighing, she pressed her mouth into the warm, ragged flesh and drank.

A small measure of strength flowed back into her battered body. She straightened, relieved that darkness no longer threatened to overwhelm her with every step.

Across the deck, Valdemar and Rowena circled each other warily.

"Is this the life you want Valdemar?" Rowena asked. "Always being second guessed by your headstrong offspring, and a group of fools for friends?"

"Valdemar," Melinda said, creeping closer. "Don't do it. Let her go."

His arm shot out, grabbing her by the shirt. Effortlessly he hauled her from the deck. "Melinda," he snarled, never taking his eyes from Rowena. "I told you to stay out of this."

With a flick of his arm he sent her flying across the deck. Her head hit the railing with a crack and she lay there reeling.

Laughing, Rowena sprang. Melinda watched in horror as Valdemar went down. She could expect no assistance from Cornelius and Adrian, who were still doing battle with the last of Rowena's disciples.

Elongated incisors tore through cloth and skin, leaving two scarlet slashes in Valdemar's chest. He moaned and flailed against her, but she held him tight. Grinning, she worked her way upward through the torn cloth, biting through one flat nipple on her way to his throat.

With one mighty heave, Valdemar gained the upper hand and he rolled on top of her. "Now," he said panting, "you show how you truly feel for me, Rowena. Did you think I didn't know?" With a look of hatred and sorrow, he sank his teeth deeply into the milky white skin of her throat.

Rowena howled with rage and twisted her head so her teeth met Valdemar's throat. Ripping skin and muscle aside, she attempted to chew her way to his jugular vein.

Cornelius ripped another ghoul from Adrian's back. With loathing he looked at the pale wraith who floundered in his grip. Deciding finally to preserve his strength, he caught the hand that shot out to punch him and bit into the wrist. Within seconds, there was another lifeless body on the deck.

Adrian looked at the rapidly dwindling army and decided time was of utmost importance. "Just get rid of them," he hollered at Cornelius. "Killing them takes too long." He grabbed the two bearing down on him, and with a powerful flick of each wrist, sent them flailing over the side and into the water below. Cornelius followed suit.

When they had finally cleared the deck, Valdemar and Rowena were still locked in a fatal embrace.

"Do something!" Melinda shrieked as Cornelius and Adrian rushed toward them. "She's going to kill him!"

Adrian looked down at the pair as if deciding between two evils. Choosing Rowena, he grabbed a handful of her scarlet hair and hauled her head backward.

She roared with fury as her teeth came free with a mouthful of flesh from Valdemar's neck. Razor-sharp canines snapped at Adrian's wrist, but he continued to restrain her while her howls turned to whimpers and then to silence.

Finally Valdemar stilled. For a long time he lay with his head against her breast while the sky brightened from navy blue to mauve. The air was quiet except for the gentle slap of the waves against the hull.

He straightened suddenly, and without looking at any of them, put one foot on the ladder and disappeared over the side.

Melinda watched as he strode across the bottom deck to the row boat he'd moored to the side. As he reached the boat, a ghoul leapt out at him from the shadows. His arm shot out, sending it stumbling backwards into the water.

With one tug, he snapped the rope that secured the boat in two, and cast off.

"Come on!" Cornelius looked urgently at the few ghouls who were climbing like drowned cats out of the lake. "We have to get out of here."

Melinda surveyed the blood-soaked deck. Overhead a streamer fluttered in the wind. Between the bodies strewn across the sparkle of confetti could still be seen. She looked from Rowena's pale corpse to Hilliard's broken body and burst into tears.

Cornelius took her by the arm and led her toward the stolen water taxi, leaving Adrian to stare out across the lake at the approaching morning.

"You said this was all going to work out," she said miserably, as Cornelius busied himself hot-wiring the engine. The vacant, sorrowful look on Valdemar's face refused to leave her mind. It persisted even when she closed her eyes like it was burned in her retina.

"I was wrong," Cornelius said, and he looked nearly as bad as Valdemar.

"What about Adrian?" she asked as they tore off across the quiet lake.

"Adrian can take care of himself," Cornelius said, staring at the shoreline.

CHAPTER THIRTY-SEVEN

For hours Melinda lay in the center of Cornelius' round bed with the dark curtains closed tightly on the day outside. In the living room she could hear him moving about. Cornelius, it seemed, wasn't resting any easier.

The bedroom door opened. "Hey, look who's here," Neil said with forced cheerfulness. Melinda raised her head to find Valdemar standing beside him, carrying a canvas bag. "See, I told you he'd come," he said, then left them alone.

Melinda watched as Valdemar drew a chair up to the bedside. "Hi," she said finally.

"Hi," he repeated, straddling the chair and resting his forearms on the back. He set the bag on the floor beside him. "I brought you some clothes."

"Thanks," she said. And for a few moments they regarded each other miserably.

"I'm sorry about Hilliard," Valdemar said, eventually.

The mention of his name was enough to make her start crying all over again. Melinda bit her lip in an attempt to keep the tears at bay. "He's gone," she said. "He was only my child for a little while, and now he's gone forever."

"It's hard to suffer through the loss of an offspring," Valdemar said. "But Hilliard had a long life, and at least the last few weeks were pleasant, thanks to you."

"I'm sorry about Rowena." She didn't know what else to say.

He didn't reply, and she blundered on.

"Feels terrible, doesn't it?" she said, remembering how it felt to have killed Moira. "Especially because you loved her once ... "

"There are no words for how I feel."

"So," Melinda said, changing the subject. "Why are you here?"

"Cornelius said I should fetch you."

"He's afraid you're going to leave me here."

"He didn't sound worried to me," Valdemar said irritably.

"Oh come on, Val. Did you really believe I was going to run off to Italy with Cornelius?"

He almost smiled. "No, you're too much for him."

Melinda rolled to her side and propped herself up on one elbow. "There's something I have to tell you."

His eyes narrowed warily. "What is it?"

She looked down at the black and white paisley pattern on the sheets. "I've been a fool," she said, noting his raised eyebrow surprise. Before he could readily agree, she continued, "I've been trying to right every wrong I come across, as if it could somehow change what happened to me."

Whatever he'd been expecting, this wasn't it. He rubbed his hands wearily over his eyes. "Now you tell me this, just when I'm coming around to your way of thinking."

She stared at him dumbly. "You were?"

Valdemar rested his chin on the back of the chair and stared at her. "I plucked you out of your life and thrust you into this mess. I was so sure of my righteousness, when all the time it might have been kinder to let you die. I thought I knew what I was doing. Recently I've come to the conclusion that when it comes to you I know nothing at all."

"And I interfered in things I couldn't possibly understand and I nearly got us both killed. I'm sorry. I felt ... smothered by your life. I so desperately wanted you to love me and respect me."

"I do love you, Melinda," he said. "I've loved you since the moment I first saw you."

"I love you, too. But I'm afraid to be with you," she admitted, watching his face. "And I'm terrified of being alone in all eternity without you."

He came to sit on the side of the bed and pulled her up into his arms. "Don't be afraid Melinda," he whispered into her hair. "As long as I am alive you will never be alone. I'll always be there when you need me. Even," he added softly, "after you've grown bored with me and moved on to other lovers. We'll always be blood kindred, and a small part of us will always belong to each other."

She looked up into his soft dark eyes. "I can't imagine wanting another lover. The one I have is more than enough trouble."

"So is mine," he said laughing, then was suddenly serious. "Once more I will ask you to come home with me."

"But," she stammered. "I make you crazy."

"Yes," he said with a sad smile. "You do."

"You still want me?"

He nodded. "Someone has to. I can't loose you on the world. So decide Melinda."

Before she could answer, there was a light tap on the door. The scowl on Valdemar's face told her it could only be Adrian.

"I wanted to talk to Melinda," he said, peering into the darkness inside.

Valdemar indicated the bed with a sweep of his arm. "Ask her then, not me."

"Come sit Adrian," Melinda offered, patting the empty space on the bed beside her. Hesitantly, he sat beside her while Valdemar glared at him from the corner.

"How'd you get back?"

Adrian grinned. "I decided it was a nice morning for a swim."

"What about the boat?" she asked, thinking of the grisly scene they'd left there.

"Well ... " Adrian seemed a little embarrassed. "There was this extra gallon of fuel on board, and ... well there was a terrible fire. I'm sure it'll be on tonight's news." He shrugged. "It seemed, fitting somehow."

"Regular phoenix, aren't you," Valdemar said sarcastically. "Have you considered a career in pyrotechnics?"

"Come now Val," Adrian said, the smile fading. "Aren't we going to be friends, after all we've been through together?"

"Maybe," Valdemar said, "in a few centuries."

Adrian sighed and looked at Melinda. "My sweet angel," he said, reaching out to touch the soft skin on her face. A glance at Valdemar made him suddenly drop his hand. "I realized when I was in the process of nearly meeting my maker that I never thanked you properly." He studied the smooth skin on the back of his hands in wonder. "You've changed me Melinda. I shall never be the same again." He kissed her on the forehead, daring Valdemar to step between them.

Valdemar snorted. "Things are definitely not going to be the same."

"What are you going to do now?" she asked, glancing away from those mesmerizing green eyes.

"For starters," Adrian said and looked at Valdemar, "I'm getting the hell out of here. And when I find a place that suits me, I'm going to settle down and make myself a proper lover."

"Don't let us keep you," Valdemar said.

Adrian took the hint gracefully. "Good-bye Melinda. I hope our paths cross again." And to Valdemar's freezing glare, he winked and left the room.

"So," she said when he had gone. "What about us?"

"What about us?" he repeated.

"Are we…" she started to say as he walked toward her. He turned the chair around and sat down facing her. There were so many things she still needed to know. So many things they had yet to work out between them. She got up off the bed and went to stand before him, intending to settle it all right there and then. But he grasped her hand and pulled her down into his lap.

She straddled his legs, linking her feet around the bottom of the chair. That movement put her face very close to his. He moved his head a fraction of an inch, capturing her lips. Giving up on interrogating him, she followed his lead and explored his mouth with her tongue.

His lips were warm, meaning he'd fed recently. She pressed against him, desperately wanting a taste of that blood. Every inch of his muscular body pressed against hers. She could feel the evidence of his desire for her through the thin material of the T-shirt she'd borrowed from Cornelius.

The thought of the other vampire in such close proximity stopped her cold. She pulled her mouth away. "We're in Neil's bedroom."

Valdemar chuckled. He dipped his head to explore the sensitive skin at the base of her neck. "He wouldn't dare come in while we're alone together in here."

"I'm sure he can hear us," she objected. Concentrating, she located Cornelius moving from the living room to the kitchen. As a vampire he likely had no reason to be in that particular room of the apartment. He was probably trying to get as far away from the bedroom as possible. "I can hear him!"

Valdemar didn't seem at all concerned that his friend might be privy to a very private moment. "I'm sure he'll take the hint and go out."

As if in emphasis, she heard the balcony door open and the soft tread of Cornelius' feet against the cement outside.

"See?" With little bites, Valdemar teased the tender skin between shoulder and neck. Every touch of his lips, every scrape of his teeth rippled down her spine in tiny waves of desire. She moved against him impatiently.

While his mouth worked its magic on her, his fingers tugged at the bottom of the T-shirt, pulling it up over her hips. He hooked his thumbs into the elastic of her underwear, and she stood up long enough from him to pull them down and toss them away.

As she settled back against him the friction of his jeans against her bare skin nearly undid her. Enough teasing, she thought as she undid his belt. He levered himself off the chair so she could undo his zipper and slide his jeans and briefs down. She looked down between their bodies, seeing the extent of his arousal, realizing that he wanted her every bit as badly as she desired him.

Cupping her bottom, he raised her and ever so slowly lowered her upon him. She closed her eyes at the intrusion of his flesh into hers, allowing the sensation to wash over her. Still holding her, he rocked her gently against him.

Hunger soared. She gave up on gentle, taking him at a faster pace. She heard his rich laughter as he matched her rhythm and together they raced toward the fulfillment of their desire.

Her teeth found his neck as she convulsed around him. She felt his answering bite as she broke through the thin skin and into the hot river of blood beneath. He bucked against her as he found his own release.

She came back to her senses slowly. Raising her head from Valdemar's shoulder, she looked down into his face. He smiled up at her drowsily.

The balcony door opened and she heard Cornelius padding back into the living room. Time to leave, she thought. They'd outstayed their welcome.

Valdemar obviously had the same thought, because he raised her up and set her on her feet. His blood thrummed through her veins, energizing her. Pulling the T-shirt down far enough to cover her, she searched in the bag for a pair of jeans and a clean pair of panties. Finding them, she sat down on the side of the bed to put them on. Valdemar busied himself rearranging his own clothes.

"Well?" she asked. Are we going home?"

Valdemar offered his hand and gallantly helped her to her feet.

"My Lady, I thought you'd never ask."

THE END

Printed in the United States
39939LVS00003BB/127-570

9 781586 087333